# FATAL CROSSROADS

*A Novel of Vietnam, 1945*

## Also by Seymour Topping

*Journey Between Two Chinas*

*Peking Letter, A Novel of the Chinese Civil War*

# FATAL CROSSROADS

*A Novel of Vietnam, 1945*

## SEYMOUR TOPPING

EastBridge

Norwalk

Signature Books

Chartered in the State of Connecticut, EastBridge
is a nonprofit publishing corporation under
section 501(c)(3) of the United States tax code.


EastBridge has received a multiyear
grant from the Henry Luce Foundation.


*Library Of Congress Cataloging-In-Publication Data*

Topping, Seymour, 1921-
  Fatal Crossroads : a novel of Vietnam 1945 / Seymour Topping.
    p. cm.
  ISBN 1-891936-69-7 (hardcover : alk. paper)
1. Vietnam--Fiction. 2. World War, 1939-1945--Vietnam--Fiction.
3. Americans--Vietnam--Fiction. 4. French--Vietnam--Fiction.
5. Colonies--Fiction. I. Title.

PS3570.O663F38 2004
  813'.54--dc22

                                                    2004022170

Printed in the United States of America

This novel is dedicated to the American agents of
the Office of Strategic Services who served in Vietnam during 1945,
most notably to Lieutenant Colonel Peter A. Dewey, who was
killed near Saigon on September 26, 1945, the first American
fatal casualty of the Vietnam War, and the late
Lieutenant Colonel Archimedes L. A. Patti,
chief of OSS operations in Indochina.

Maps

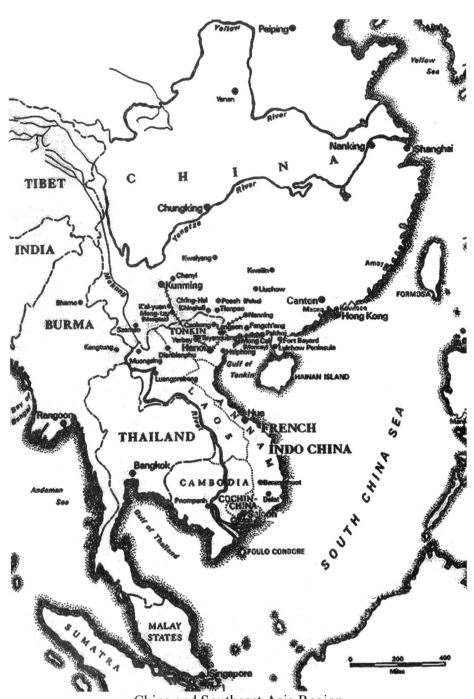

China and Southeast Asia Region

China placenames are in the official Wade-Giles style of 1945

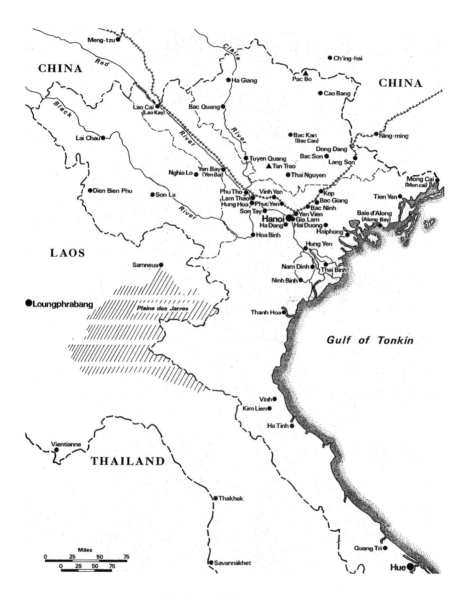

Northern Vietnam 1945

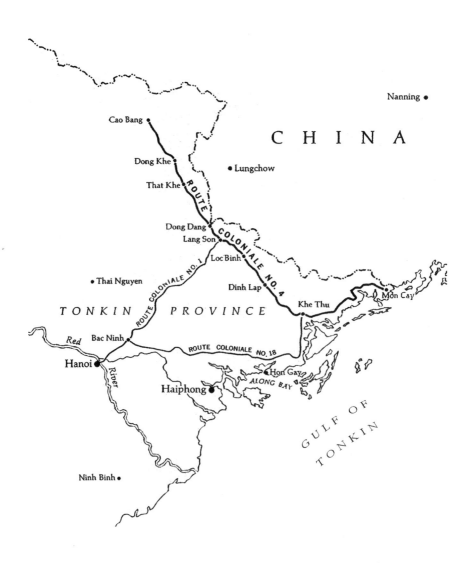

Tonkin Province in Northern Vietnam 1945

# Prologue

HO CHI MINH *was not always an enemy of the United States. There was a time in the last months of the war against Japan when American agents lived with him and trained and armed his guerrilla cadres. One of them, a medic, saved his life. This novel portrays that haunting episode virtually ignored in the official American military annals of the Vietnam War. It tells of an opportunity lost in dealing with Ho Chi Minh, which might have spared us the agony of our Vietnam War.*

*Most of what has been written about American involvement in Vietnam dates from February 1950, when President Truman recognized the puppet regime of Emperor Bao Dai and pledged military aid to the French colonial army. I arrived in Saigon, days before the Truman declaration, on assignment for The Associated Press after covering the Chinese Civil War for three years. Only about a dozen Americans were then resident in Saigon, most of them staff of the American consulate. Soon after, I saw a reenactment of what I had witnessed in China: the assembling of large American diplomatic and information staffs, military and economic aid missions.*

*During the next two years, while reporting the failing French struggle with Ho Chi Minh's Vietminh, I learned of a hidden episode in American involvement in Vietnam. It centered on a small band of agents of "Wild Bill" Donovan's Office of Strategic Services, known as the OSS, the forerunner of the Central Intelligence Agency, who in 1945 had been ordered to enlist Ho Chi Minh in combating the Japanese army in Indochina. These agents operated across China and Vietnam as the United States stood at a fatal crossroads. Truman was deciding whether to pursue President Roosevelt's aim of rescuing Indochina from colonialism through the establishment of a trusteeship leading to independence or yield to Charles De Gaulle, who was insisting on restoration of French suzerainty as a precondition for his cooperation in Europe against Stalinist expansionism.*

*Former agents of the OSS and historians, as cited in my Acknowledgments, have written in past years of the OSS engagement* with Ho Chi Minh. *My own memoir,* Journey Between Two Chinas, *published in 1972, told of French resentment of the covert OSS operations. I have chosen to encapsulate the episode in novel form so as to narrate in human terms my perceptions of the encounters of the OSS agents with the Vietnamese, the conflicting roles of the French, Chinese, British and Japanese, and the events that put the United States on the road to its Vietnam War. The reader will recognize the historical figures. The other characters in this novel are based on real individuals or are fictional. They serve to recall a turning point in history and bitter lessons that should not be forgotten.*

*Scarsdale, New York*
*July 2004*

# FATAL CROSSROADS

*A Novel of Vietnam, 1945*

# -1-

**Chungking, China**
**March 7, 1945**

DUNCAN SQUINTED THROUGH the misted window at the dense morning fog wondering if he'd make it out of the wartime Chinese capital by nightfall. Standing in bare feet, his white silk shirt open, he folded his arms and shook his head, jaw clenched. His features relaxed into a gentle smile when Suzanne emerged from the pantry singing out: "Coffee!" and as he watched her walk across the living room, limping slightly, to place the silver tray on the chow table before the couch. She was wrapped in a black dressing gown, jet-black hair cascading over her shoulders. He thought of the time he remarked on her youthful loveliness, and how she reminded him with an amused smile she was thirty-five, two years older than he.

"*Bon matin*," Duncan exclaimed, kissing her, savoring the Arpege perfume lingering from the evening.

"*Désolé, Chéri, pas de croissants*," Suzanne said. "Ah! My love! If only we were in Paris. Still there's good coffee ... strong coffee, French style, not your weak American brew. I bought Tonkin beans yesterday from a Kwangsi peddler in the Tung Ssu Pailou."

"You should know by now," Duncan said, as he sank into the couch beside her, "I'm not chauvinistic about coffee, wine or women."

"Quite sensible," Suzanne said, the dark eyes smiling. She crossed her legs and balanced her cup on her knee, "So you're leaving tonight?"

"Yes, if this bloody fog clears, for Kunming on an Air Force C-46. We take off just before dark—less chance of running into Jap fighter patrols. Then over The Hump in an Air Transport Command plane to a base in India and on to Washington."

"You haven't said, Travis, why you're being recalled so suddenly."

Duncan shrugged. "I'm not sure," and then, chuckling, "Perhaps they've discovered I'm sleeping with a French spy."

"Entirely possible," Suzanne said. "Come now."

Duncan sipped his coffee. "Consultation at the State Department. Proceed to Washington without delay. Nothing more. My guess? The ambassador wants someone else—and pronto—to run his Political Section. No doubt he'd prefer some type less critical of Chiang Kai-shek. I haven't disguised my feelings about how the Generalissimo is screwing up our war effort." He shrugged. "Also, I suppose, foolishly, I've irritated him. Briefing him a couple of weeks ago on those dead-end talks between Chiang and Mao Tse-tung on a common front against the Japs, His Excellency suddenly asked why I'm at the Chinese Communist mission on Tseng Chia Ai more often than the Gimo's Foreign Office. I told him I found talks with Chou En-lai more informative. But then I got smart-ass. Besides, I said, the food at the Communist Mission is better. The ambassador walked out of the room."

"Hardly diplomatic," Suzanne ventured with a mocking smile.

Duncan nodded, a brooding expression replacing the wry smile. He put down his cup, lay back in the corner of the couch, and stared up at the gecko lizard crawling along one of the loft's bamboo rafters. "Yes," he said. "But after reporting to the Department on this miserable war for four years, I find it hard to kowtow before some blowhard fresh out of Washington."

Suzanne filled Duncan's cup and looked at him caressingly, the shock of black hair, now tousled, the deep-set blue eyes, the firm angular jaw—gift of his Scottish forbearers—and the scar on his lean body, never explained, visible through the dark tuft of hair on his chest. But she was scarcely listening to his familiar outpouring about the fumbling conduct of the war. She was anguishing over whether to reveal to him what she would be doing three days hence.

Softly, Suzanne said: "Travis, even if Washington okays your return you may not be able to get back to Chungking. With the

Japanese pushing west, closing on Kunming … who knows … they may turn north toward Chungking. You've heard the rumors. Chiang is debating moving the capital further inland—perhaps to Sinkiang. If he does, I'm not sure where I'd land, Travis …"

Duncan nodded: "There's no telling how things will play out in the next weeks. The Jap offensive might peter out. Could be their last gasp. The Navy and MacArthur are beating the hell out of them all across the Pacific. But, for sure, this war is not for long." He grasped Suzanne's hand, smiling reassuringly. "Never give up on me. Whatever happens, I'll find you, my love, somewhere … wherever somewhere is."

On the previous day, Duncan had come to say goodbye, not expecting to spend the night with Suzanne. They lunched in a restaurant on the Street of the Fairy Grotto just opposite the building where Suzanne lived. She was staying in a small loft apartment in a two-story stucco building, above the shop of a tobacco dealer. As the correspondent of the *London Observer*, Suzanne Dumont could have chosen to remain in the Press Hostel, maintained by Hollington Tong, the government information minister. Although a good place for news tips, she'd declined to stay on there, discomforted by the nightly passage of prostitutes through the boisterous hostel.

At lunch they feasted on spicy Szechuan dishes, and when the bottle of French wine brought by Suzanne was emptied, they downed small cups of yellow rice wine. With each cup, the conversation became more lively as Suzanne derided Duncan's contention that French Impressionists had borrowed from the Taoist landscape painters. Chinese diners at nearby tables slyly glanced and giggled in cupped hands at the tall foreigner, his seersucker jacket draped over the back of his chair, and the slim Western woman in the Chinese silk *cheongsam*, tossing back cups of *shaohsin* wine.

As Duncan was paying the bill the air raid sirens sounded. He and Suzanne looked at each other, surprised. Japanese air raids were infrequent during March, when Chungking was still wrapped in its near-perpetual fog. But the fog had dispersed that morning, and the

Nationalist capital, atop a rocky promontory wedged between the Yangtze and Chialing rivers, lay exposed.

Chungking sprawled over a succession of steep cliffs ascending to a cluster of peaks. Half a million inhabitants, most of them refugees, lived in congested alleys, gaps between squalid mud-brick houses. Other than government buildings, there were few targets of military significance for the Japanese bombers. The raids by some fifty to two-hundred planes at a time were intended mainly to inspire terror. Stubbornly, for seven years the Nationalists had been holding out in Chungking while the Japanese limited themselves to sorties from bases in East China.

When Duncan and Suzanne emerged from the restaurant, the red balls were atop the iron pyramids on the hillsides, the initial warning signal that Japanese bombers were approaching. The narrow cobbled street already was nearly deserted. People were packing into the myriad dugouts, which had been hollowed out of the cliffsides during the years of bombing.

"Let's go to the Canadian Embassy shelter," Duncan said as the sirens sounded, the signal that bombers soon would be overhead. He took Suzanne's arm. "It's just down the street."

Suzanne sighed and glanced up at Duncan. "My apartment is much more comfortable, *Cheri*," she said.

Duncan smiled, hesitated, and then put his arm around her. They crossed the street and entered the shop, which was stacked with dried tobacco leaves, just as the proprietor was hastily locking up, and then walked up the garbage-strewn back stair to Suzanne's apartment.

The elegant furnishings of the apartment, comprising one large room and a pantry, contrasted strangely with the shabbiness of the building. When Suzanne moved from the Press Hostel, Duncan led her to his favorite antique shops where he helped her select rare pieces sold at bargain prices by impoverished refugee families. The loft's splintered floor was covered with rich Sinkiang carpets. An eighth-century T'ang horse stood on the Ming chow table before the couch and a golden Tibetan Buddha presided on the mantelpiece. The dirty white plaster walls, cracked in places, exposing the lath, were hung with scrolls, and as Duncan entered he glanced, as he always did, at the precious Ch'i Pai-shih scroll, a gift from his own collection, of delicate shrimps mingling on a sea bottom.

When the thud of Chinese antiaircraft fire sounded Duncan and Suzanne were lying propped up against the red lacquer bedstead sipping cognac, listening to the bomb explosions stitching across the city. Soft, silken pillows lay beside them. If a bomb struck the building directly they knew they would be buried in the debris, but if one just landed nearby they would cover their faces with the pillows to guard against the glass and other shards which the concussion would send flying. During the years of incessant bombing, Duncan had learned the wisdom of this precaution.

When the all clear signal sounded, Suzanne rolled over onto Duncan with a yelp and he yielded without resistance to her invitation to stay the night. The need to clear his desk at the embassy chancery, he felt, had suddenly become less pressing.

After breakfast with Suzanne, Duncan went out on the street and signaled for a sedan chair. The fog had dissipated. Instantly, the tall foreigner in the seersucker suit and the white Panama hat was surrounded by sedan chairs and rickshaws, their coolies shouting and jostling for his fare. Duncan mounted a sedan chair suspended on a hammock of bamboo slats slung between shoulder poles. The two bearers, front and rear, hoisted it and trotted down the street with the lead coolie chanting: "*aiya szela, aiya szela*," and the other replying with the same traditional cry.

The city was throbbing with life once again. Duncan's sedan bearers darted through the throngs of pedestrians, rickshaws and bicycles. They cursed as army trucks and old wheezing cars nosed through with horns blaring. A pair of farmers in patched blue tunics and conical straw hats trotted alongside Duncan's sedan chair on the way to the market, carrying a squealing pig trussed to a pole. The street was lined with bustling shops housed in mud-plastered bamboo frames whose owners were loudly hawking native tobacco, rice, crude shoes and candy. Duncan caught the smell of roasting chestnuts and the sweet aroma of opium. The flower stalls were festooned with early plum blossoms.

Duncan relished life in Chungking. The city lacked the imperial splendor of Peking or the Eurasian sophistication of Shanghai, both of which he knew well, but it had the earthy quality of peasant China. He never tired over the years of exploring its byways: taking in the pungent smells and clatter of the open markets, the Buddhist temples resplendent with their golden-tiled roofs, the finger counting games played amid shouts in the wine shops, and buying a plump persimmon or pork dumplings from a street vendor.

It was also possible—usually in a wine shop—to meet with Vietnamese exiles to hear news of their underground struggle for independence. He gathered intelligence for the embassy—but also, always—after listening sympathetically to impassioned speeches, Duncan in Vietnamese would ask quietly of the exiles: "Mai Khang … do you know of her?"

On rare occasions, when he was feeling low, yearning to dream, Duncan would visit Liao's opium divan. Not so strange a diversion for seasoned China hands. Although opium was banned by government edict, both foreigners and high Nationalist officials patronized Liao's. They reclined on damask couches on the lower floor of the old stone mansion, once a mandarin's palace, in cubicles with beaded curtains. Liao, flattered by the patronage of an American diplomat, would escort Duncan to a curtained alcove on the upper floor. One of the slim girls in a clinging *cheongsam* would kneel beside his couch preparing the pipe and tending to the opium over the flame of the lamp. After seven or so pipes there might be dreams of Vietnam, of *her*, amber eyes in golden countenance gazing at him as they danced, her body supple in the silken *ao dai*. In the morning the girl of the lamp would bring jasmine tea and soon after he would return reluctantly to the business of the embassy.

Duncan was jostled about in the sedan chair as the bearers descended the last of steep sandstone steps to the foot of the mountain. Seeing and smelling the sweat pouring down the neck of the front bearer, Duncan recalled his first ride in a sedan chair years ago, how revolted he was at being borne by men. But then, gradually, he came to accept it, if for no other reason than that he should not deny the coolies their livelihood.

Duncan was deposited at the ferry landing beside the gray, silt-filled Yangtze. The crowded ferry would take him across the river to the landing on the south bank, where Duncan parked his jeep. The American embassy compound in which he lived was situated on a fairly distant hillside overlooking the Chialing River.

As the ferry moved slowly in the eddies of the river, Duncan thought of Suzanne—of their love affair and of their first meeting at the British embassy party soon after she arrived in Chungking only two months ago. Entering the embassy reception hall, Duncan's gaze turned at once to Suzanne, splendid in a fuchsia brocade dress and bold sparkling earrings, in animated conversation with Zinovi Pechkov, the head of the French Military Mission. Their eyes met for a moment. Duncan shook hands with the British ambassador, and bowed as he walked past the Chinese envoy, Chou En-lai, and the Australian ambassador. He was chatting with a group of foreign correspondents when Suzanne, limping a bit, joined them. There was a magnificence about her, Duncan thought as he smiled at her, the strong handsome features, full lips painted bright red, searching dark eyes under thick eyebrows and the shining black hair, tied back.

Jeb Davis, the Reuters correspondent, jovially greeted Suzanne. "That was a good story on the Japs reinforcing their occupation force in Indochina. I got a call-back on it."

Suzanne bestowed a rewarding smile on Davis and turned to Duncan. "So you're Travis Duncan. General Pechkov has told me about you. Expert on Indochina. All that. You learned to speak Annamese at the Sorbonne. Could we talk one day?"

Duncan, beguiled by her directness, said: "Of course," just as Suzanne turned to the British ambassador who had approached, calling out to her: "There you are!"

"She's always working," the Reuters man said. "Tough lady. I knew her in London. She's the daughter of a French university professor ... English mother. Her husband was a French army officer ... killed early in the war." He flicked the ash from his cigarette and shook his head. "She was working in Paris for *Le Monde* when the Germans occupied the city. She joined the resistance. Caught a bullet in the leg in a firefight. That's the limp. Smuggled out in a fishing boat to England. In London, she joined the *Observer*. Damn good reporter."

Watching Suzanne being escorted off, Duncan wondered just what Pechkov had said to her about him. He and Pechkov had sparred often over Indochina policy; the Frenchman knew him as a fierce opponent of the restoration of French colonial rule. Nevertheless, his exchanges with Pechkov had always been good-natured. A much decorated hero of the French Foreign Legion, who lost his right arm in World War I, Pechkov was De Gaulle's personal emissary and a formidable figure in the Chungking diplomatic community. Duncan had paid a formal call on him not long ago and written a dispatch for the State Department on the Frenchman's views. Pechkov was frank about his persistent efforts to persuade Chiang Kai-shek to concur in the restoration of French rule of Indochina and in his demands that the Generalissimo ban the revolutionary activities of Vietnamese nationalists in South China.

Suzanne was in Duncan's office two days later. Sitting across from him at his desk, wearing a khaki bush jacket, Suzanne talked about Japanese moves in Indochina. Duncan was intrigued. This woman seemed better informed than his embassy's Political Section. Two days later, he telephoned her and the following day, escaping Chungking's clammy fog, they drove out to the hills on the South Bank and parked in Southern Mountain Gardens. They spread a blanket and picnicked on ham sandwiches Duncan brought from the embassy commissary and a rare bottle of Bordeaux Suzanne purloined from the French mission's stock.

As they gazed over the terraced rice paddies, Suzanne asked: "You're not married?"

"No," Duncan replied, as he filled their pewter cups with wine. "I have a fear of permanence."

Suzanne laughed, straightened her red cashmere sweater, and leaned back on her elbows. "You've not much to fear. There's very little of permanence in this world."

"You lost your husband?" Duncan asked.

Suzanne nodded, the gaiety gone. "Yes. His name was Max. I met him at at the University of Paris, where we were both studying philosophy." Suzanne sat up, lit one of her Chinese cigarettes and drew on it deeply. "Shall I tell you about him?" she asked.

"Please," Duncan said, refilling her wine cup.

"We lived in an apartment in the Rue Richelieu, a tiny one on the Left Bank. After a while, we married. We got jobs at about the same time. He worked as a reporter at *Le Figaro* and I at *Le Monde*. He was writing a novel when he was called up as a reservist." Suzanne stubbed out her cigarette and lay back looking at the rushing clouds.

"Max wanted so badly to finish the novel, but he didn't hesitate. He was a very serious guy … too damn serious. He became a lieutenant in the infantry. He was killed in June 1940 at Sedan when Guderian's panzer divisions broke through."

It had begun to rain lightly. Suzanne looked at the darkening sky and drained her wine. She turned to Duncan, wiping raindrops from her face. "Just before, he wrote to me. Said he could contemplate death in defense of France. But what made it so hard was the blundering of our politicians and generals. They made us so weak when we could have been strong. I suppose that's why I'm for De Gaulle, although I don't like his arrogance and some of his policies. He has the will to rebuild France."

"You fought for him," Duncan said quietly

"Yes," Suzanne said, rubbing her leg.

Unexpectedly a cloudburst and heavy rain swept the hillside. Suzanne and Duncan seized their things and ran stumbling to the jeep. Drenched and laughing, they settled into the jeep. Suzanne accepted a bandanna handkerchief from Duncan and when he kissed her she embraced him. They were together often thereafter.

Sitting one evening in the cliffside Hsin Hsin Café, one of the few Chinese spots frequented by foreigners in dreary Chungking, joking gaily about the political high jinks in the capital and complaining about the local beer, Suzanne impulsively invited Duncan to her apartment for drinks. They bedded that night without pretensions or questions, eager for pleasure and comfort in each other. She no longer spoke of Max, and he did not return to dream in Liao's divan.

At their parting this morning Duncan was more troubled about the possibility of a long separation than he had let on. He was in love with Suzanne. She was giving him happiness that had eluded him for so long. There'd been other affairs—the American embassy secretary in Peip'ing, the Eurasian in Hong Kong, and earlier in Chungking, the British doctor. He fled them when companionship and sex brought talk of permanence and marriage. Suzanne gave unconditional love, leaving room for the healing of the old wound. He was not yet rid of all that haunted him.

The prospect that he would not return to Chungking was very real. He was ready to resign from the State Department if he was ordered to withhold his open criticism of the official China policy. In October he'd thought of resigning when President Roosevelt recalled Joe Stillwell, commander of the China-Burma-India Theater. The general had quarreled with Chiang Kai-shek over his bungling war strategy. Duncan's father, a friend of Roosevelt and his former ambassador to France, dissuaded him.

There was another unspoken reason why Duncan was considering resigning. Years ago, after serving in Saigon, he had been barred from Vietnam by the French government. The State Department was holding him to the restriction. Once free of the Department's restraint he could return to Vietnam. His friends in the nationalist underground would smuggle him in. Help him search. Finally find out what happened to Mai. Be at peace at last.

In his quarters in the American Embassy compound, Duncan packed one suitcase and an overnight bag. He stored the rest of his belongings, readied for shipment, knowing he might not return to Chungking. In the late afternoon, an embassy chauffeur drove him to a dock on the Yangtze. It was linked by a footbridge to the airfield, which was no more than an island sandbar in the river, reinforced by stones and cement pilings. Clambering over the swaying bridge, followed by a coolie carrying his bags, Duncan noticed the river waters swollen by the heavy rains were lapping at the edges of the airstrip.

He boarded the C-46 supply transport which was deadheading nonstop southwest to Kunming. Sitting in a bucket seat, Duncan felt the plane shudder as the pilot revved the engines to their maximum and then accelerated down the runway illuminated by a double line of oil lamps. The aircraft lifted off at the very end of the runway and as it climbed the pilot switched off its lights.

At the first light of dawn the plane landed near Kunming at the principal base of General Claire Chennault's Fourteenth Air Force and taxied to the Quonset hut terminal past rows of Curtiss P-40 Warhawk fighters and twin-engined B-25 Mitchell bombers. Waiting on the tarmac for a bus, Duncan watched the planes lining up on the runways to take off for attack missions against the advancing Japanese columns.

In Kunming, Duncan checked into the Air Force transit hostel for flight clearance. He was put on a waiting list, though his orders specified priority, for one of the planes of the Air Transport Command flying ferry over The Hump of the towering Himalayas. Outgoing aircraft were often crowded with combat wounded. Two months earler America-backed Chinese troops had broken through the three-year Japanese blockade of the Burma Road, but the ATC Ferry was still the principal link for Nationalist China and Chennault's Fourteenth Air Force—the "Flying Tigers"—to allied supply bases in the outside world.

Three days after his arrival, sitting at the bar in the hostel, Duncan heard the Armed Forces Radio report that the Japanese had staged a coup in Indochina. For four years following the German occupation of France, the French Vichyite regime in Saigon, nominally in control of the country, had lived in uneasy coexistence with a Japanese occupation force. Now, alarmed about the growth of pro-Gaullist sentiment in the colony, Tokyo apparently had ordered a full takeover. Admiral Decoux, the Vichy governor-general, was under arrest. Japanese troops had seized public buildings, and overrun police stations and French military posts, including those along the frontier with China. Listening to the broadcast, Duncan speculated that the Japanese troops in Indochina would now drive north and join their columns pushing from the west in a pincer move on Kunming. A subsequent drive on Chungking had become more likely. Suzanne's fears were not misplaced.

As he waited for transport over The Hump, Duncan wandered restlessly through Kunming. It was a wide-open city, overrun by Americans busy carrying on the war or seeking relief from it. Young airmen on breaks from missions binged in the cafés and frequented the numerous taxi dance halls and brothels. At the bar in the Last Chance Café Duncan heard about the notorious Bordello Affair. An inspector-general had reprimanded pilots of the Fourteenth Air Force for hauling joy girls from other cities into Kunming for parties. Everywhere there was evidence of American civilian freebooters making fortunes black-markerting U.S. Army supplies and smuggling gold and drugs. Duncab was not surprised. Foreigners often sucumbed to the temptations of Chinas's endemic corruption.

One afternoon he wandered down the Street of Many Treasures, which was lined with shops catering mainly to American servicemen. He entered a jade shop and examined the pieces in a display case. They were of cheap or false jade. A tall elderly Chinese in a black mandarin gown greeted him in pidgin English. "Master, likee nice ring?"

Duncan took from his pocket a piece of precious white jade carved as a tiger, which he carried in the traditional Chinese manner to rub occasionally for tranquility and good luck. "Old Uncle," he said in Mandarin, "please bring me jade."

The Chinese looked at the white jade, bowed, and went silently to the rear of the shop and returned with a tray of green Imperial Jade.

Duncan smiled. "I likee," he said.

The Chinese laughed. "I apologize, Honorable Sir," he said in Mandarin.

As a gift for his mother, Duncan selected a pendant, which the shopkeeper sold to him at very low price.

Plagued by bad weather, Duncan waited ten days before climbing aboard a C-46 to fly The Hump. From the Yunnan plateau the plane labored at twenty thousand feet through the divide of the jagged Himalayas—dubbed by pilots the "Skyway to Hell." Always on the lookout for Japanese fighters, the pilot ducked through clouds hovering over the valleys. The plane, loaded with Chinese wounded and two coffins of Chennault's airmen killed in crashes, shook violently in the high winds. Duncan nervously looked out through a porthole at mountain peaks that seemed to loom only yards away. He rubbed his white jade as the plane leveled off after the five-hundred-mile flight for a landing at a base in a deep valley in India. Changing planes there and after hops across Africa, and a layover in Casablanca, Duncan landed at Andrews Air Force Base near Washington, D.C.

**Washington
March 27, 1945**

DUNCAN CHECKED INTO THE JEFFERSON HOTEL on Sixteenth Street and telephoned Henry Watson, head of the China Desk at the State Department, for an appointment. "Travis, dear boy, you're not for me," Watson told him. "You're upstairs. Nelson wants to see you, tomorrow at three." As he hung up the phone, Duncan thought: I've had it. If the Deputy Secretary of State was summoning him, it could only mean he was in trouble. He wouldn't see Chungking again.

Nelson, a gray-haired man wearing horn-rimmed glasses, was behind his desk in the large beige-carpeted office when Duncan entered. Smiling, Nelson came around the desk to shake hands with Duncan, waved him to a sofa and dropped into a chair beside him. "Welcome home," he said. "I'm having coffee. Join me." As a secretary brought in a tray, Nelson studied Duncan—the lean frame, the finely chiseled features and the dark blue pinstripe suit worn a bit casually in the manner of the well-bred New Englander who had been to the best schools and never lacked money. But this one, he thought, is not a patsy like some of those overly elegant gentlemen of the Department.

On Nelson's desk lay Duncan's personnel file, which contained commendations for gallantry from the British government and the Department.

In 1941, after Pearl Harbor, when the Japanese stormed ashore at Hong Kong, Duncan was serving in the colony as a consular officer. As the Japanese closed in, he refused to be evacuated on one of Chennault's transports, which were ferrying Americans out of Kai Tak Airport to the Kweilin air base on the China mainland. Instead, he donned a tin helmet and became a volunteer ambulance driver hauling wounded British and Canadian soldiers from the harbor front to St. Paul's Hospital in Happy Valley and Queen Mary Hospital in Pokfulam. At Aberdeen, while loading a wounded British sergeant into his ambulance, a shell exploded nearby and a shrapnel fragment gashed his chest. Duncan staunched the wound, drove to St. Paul's where he was bandaged, but then despite the protest of the hospital administrator insisted on continuing to work. When the Japanese finally overran the island, he hid for a week in the home of his devoted Chinese tailor near North Point at the edge of the harbor. One week later, in the night, he swam out to a Chinese fishing junk, bribed the boatmen, and was taken to Singapore. From there he made his way to Chungking.

Duncan drained his coffee, put down the cup, brushed back his straight black hair, and looked expectantly at Nelson. He'd never met the man, a respected career officer who administered the Department.

"I served under your father in the thirties, Travis, when he was ambassador to France," Nelson said. "I enjoyed working for him, unlike my experience with other political appointees."

Nelson took off his glasses and toyed with them. "You're wondering, of course, why we recalled you."

Duncan nodded.

"Our ambassador in Chungking hasn't been too happy with you." Duncan settled back in his chair. "He complained particularly about one of your cables to the Department. The one about the Generalissimo violating his truce agreement with Mao Tse-tung by diverting troops from the Japanese front to encircle Communist units. The ambassador said you're biased against Chiang Kai-shek … said he never signed off on that cable."

Duncan shrugged: "The ambassador normally doesn't sign off in advance on all traffic of the Political Section."

"Come now, Travis," Nelson said, laughing. "On a report that sensitive?"

Duncan frowned. "I don't have any ideological sympathy for Mao Tse-tung. I simply thought it crucial for the Department to have evidence that Chiang's first priority is not the war against the

Japanese but rather shutting the Communists out of a power-sharing deal. He's using some of his best troops to blockade the postwar Communists in violation of his agreement with Mao for a common front against the Japs. He's gambling we'll bail him out if the Japanese offensive closes in on Kunming or threatens Chungking."

Nelson nodded. "You're right about Chiang, of course. But the ambassador also complained that you've been consorting with Annamese exiles … some of them known Communists."

"Isn't that what the Department expects of an Annamese-language officer? If you've seen my cables you must know that the exiles passed on important information about developments in Indochina."

"Sorry, Travis," Nelson said with a tight smile. "I haven't read your cables. Indochina is not high on our list of priorities."

"I suppose this blow-up with the ambassador means I'm not returning to Chungking," Duncan said quietly.

"Not necessarily," Nelson said, cocking his head at Duncan. "In fact, we used your tiffs with the ambassador as a pretext for recalling you."

Duncan sat up erect. "I don't get it."

"Travis, I'm not able to enlighten you." Nelson rose from his chair, went to his desk, and rang a buzzer. A secretary brought Duncan's trench coat. "I'm told you have an appointment … an important one. Frankly, I don't know with whom, or when it will take place," Nelson said with a hint of annoyance. "You'll be contacted at your hotel. Expect to spend the night at your destination."

Six days later, at five-thirty in the morning, the concierge at Duncan's hotel telephoned to say a guest was waiting in the lobby. With his trench coat over his arm and carrying an overnight bag, Duncan went down. The concierge gestured toward a man in a black raincoat.

"My name's Freeman," the man said. "Mr. Nelson has told you about an appointment."

Freeman, a powerfully built man with cold eyes, led Duncan to a side entrance of the hotel and opened the rear door of a Packard limousine. Duncan got in and found a pillow and a folded blanket on the leather seat. Freeman drove out into the heavy rush hour traffic.

When the car stopped at a red light, Duncan leaned forward and asked: "Where are we going?"

"South … to Georgia," Freeman replied. "You'll find sandwiches and drinks on the folding sideboard."

"Do you mind easing my curiosity? Who do you work for?"

"OSS," Freeman said, as he slid the glass divider shut.

Duncan, frowning in puzzlement, fell back in the seat, thinking: OSS—the Office of Strategic Services—the intelligence agency. He was aware that the agency had hundreds of agents in covert operations in every war theater. He'd encountered several in China but knew little about their secretive work. What was the connection to him?

Duncan had been dozing, making use of the pillow, but when the car turned off the highway and went slowly down a dark side road he sat up alertly and looked out the window. The car passed a large illuminated building and Duncan saw a sign: "Georgia Hall, Georgia Warm Springs Foundation." Further down the road, the car stopped at a brilliantly lit barrier beside a guardhouse. A Marine Corps officer in khakis, wearing a .45 caliber sidearm, emerged from the guardhouse, conferred with Freeman and waved them through. The car continued down a winding driveway to a cottage agleam with lights beside a darkened larger house.

The door of the cottage was open and a smiling black man in butler livery greeted Duncan on the doorstep. "Welcome to the Little White House," he said. "I'm Henry," and led Duncan, with Freeman following, into a small pine-paneled foyer.

"Mr. Duncan," Freeman said, "I'll be taking you back to Washington," and handed him his overnight bag. The butler took the bag and escorted Duncan to a bedroom at the rear of the cottage.

"You have an appointment, sir, for breakfast at seven o'clock," the butler said as he closed the door.

Duncan, bewildered and exasperated by the hocus-pocus, threw the overnight bag on the four-poster bed and as he unpacked wondered who would be at breakfast. Why was he here? Incredibly, was he to meet President Roosevelt?

At seven in the morning, the butler knocked and Duncan, who had been waiting impatiently, followed him to a small dining room adjoining an open pantry. The man in a dark blue suit looking out the window turned and greeted him with outstretched hand. "I'm Bill Donovan," he said in a loud, vigorous voice, and grinned. "I hope you don't mind all the mystery. In the OSS we enjoy cloak-and-dagger."

Duncan recognized him immediately as General "Wild Bill" Donovan, the storied director of the Office of Strategic Services. He was a stocky gray-haired man, perhaps in his early sixties, with penetrating blue eyes and a pugnacious Irish look about him. A distinguished lawyer, diplomat and soldier, Donovan was a national hero. Wounded three times in combat in France during World War I, he was awarded the Congressional Medal of Honor. In his youth he studied for the Catholic priesthood before turning to the law. "Let's eat and talk," Donovan said, as Henry entered and poured coffee.

"I know your history," Donovan said, in the manner of a man who didn't have time to spare. "You were one of State's first Annamese-language officers. You studied Annamese in Paris at the Sorbonne. In those days we didn't pay much—if any—attention to that language. Your first post was in Saigon in 1935 as vice-consul at our consulate. It was then that you got into trouble with that Annamese woman. You were recalled and … "

Duncan stiffened and interrupted: "That was a long time ago. There was more to that than an affair with a woman." He leaned back in his chair, leaving the eggs on his plate untouched.

"I assume so," Donovan said softly. "But you've had other rather friendly contacts with Annamese since then. In Chungking, with some of the political exiles … revolutionaries."

"Routine isn't it for a Annamese-language officer?" Duncan said irritably.

Donovan pushed back his plate and put his elbows on the table, his hands clasped. "Obviously, we've brought you here for a special reason. We want you to undertake a mission. A very important one. You can refuse, of course. But, knowing your history, I don't think you will."

"General," Duncan said. "I can't imagine I'd refuse any mission you'd ask me to undertake."

Donovan smiled. "Good enough, Travis. This is the background. The war in Europe is about over. In the Pacific it won't be long. As you know, the president has been talking to Stalin, Churchill and Chiang about the future shape of the world. At the Cairo and Teheran conferences in 1943 and last month at Yalta, he raised the Indochina question. There was no agreement. The president is unalterably opposed to the French resuming their old colonial control. He's proposed a United Nations trusteeship and eventual independence. De Gaulle, who's back in Paris and feeling his oats, is fighting that idea. He's got the support of Churchill. The old boy wants to hold on to the British colonies. Introducing the idea of trusteeship would shake up the old Asian colonial system.

"More coffee?" Donovan asked, as he replenished his cup. Duncan shook his head impatiently.

"Before the president proceeds further, he needs more information. One of the central questions: If we bar the French and establish a trusteeship, who can we look to for leadership among the Indochinese?"

"I understand," Duncan said, an excited glint in his eyes. "What can I do?"

"Let me review the situation. Tell me if I'm wrong in any respect."

Duncan nodded.

"The Indochinese nationalists are scattered, hounded by the Japanese and the Vichy French collaborators. Most of them are hiding in the countryside. Others are in exile in South China. The puppet emperor in Annam, Bao Dai, installed by the French, is now propped up by the Japanese. He's a joke. He commands no support. The Indochinese nationalists are fragmented and squabbling among themselves. No single leader has yet emerged. Is that correct?"

"That's pretty much what I have been reporting to the Department," Duncan said, wondering if Donovan, unlike the Deputy Secretary of State, had read his cables.

"But we've come upon one possibility just in the last few days," Donovan said, leaning forward intently. "One of our agents, Charles Fenn, has been searching for an Annamese contact that would help us set up an intelligence network inside Indochina. The Gaullist Free French underground network we had there was wiped out by the Japanese after they seized full control of Indochina in their March 9 coup. Fenn was tipped off about an Annamite who heads an organization called the Vietminh—the Viet Nam Independence League. That's the guerrilla group which recently rescued and brought out Lieutenant Shaw, one of Chennault's pilots who was downed in Indochina. Fenn met with this Annamite on March 17 in—of all places—the American Office of War Information library in Kunming. This fellow visited the library often, reading everything from *Time Magazine* to the *Encyclopaedia Americana*. He's agreed to help us set up the Indochina network. Fenn quotes the French as saying he's a Communist. We're going ahead. We've worked with Communists before."

"What's his name? Duncan asked.

"Ho Chi Minh."

Duncan threw back his head and laughed. "What d'you know … the mysterious, elusive Ho Chi Minh pops up again! I've tracked him for years. I first learned about Ho in Chungking in 1942 when he was jailed by Marshal Chang Fa-kwei, the Kwangsi warlord. Chang was maneuvering for influence with the Indochinese guerrillas who operate along his border. He grabbed Ho as a bargaining ploy. When our military got interested in using Ho and his guerrillas in operations against the Japanese we tried to get him released. Chang let him go after making some kind of a deal with him. Then, incredibly, our Office of War Information people got interested in Ho. They made inquiries about hiring him to do broadcasts from San Francisco. He speaks good English as well several other languages. Ho responded by applying for a visa to the States at our consulate in Kunming in August 1944 under the Chinese name of Ho Ting-ching. The application died in Washington. What you tell me is the first word I've had about him since then. If we're going to use him, we ought to check out his background more thoroughly. We know nothing about his early years and connections."

Donovan nodded. "I'm trying to get the French files. We've had had a report about Ho from Chennault. Ho asked to meet with Chennault and the general agreed, just to thank him for bringing out Shaw."

Donovan glanced at his watch. "Enough," he said, rising. "The president wants to see you. He's on the sun porch of the main house going over his mail with his secretary, Grace Tully. We'll meet him as soon as Grace leaves."

Donovan led Duncan out of the cottage along a paved path past dogwoods in full bloom. As they walked toward the frame house, which stood on the brow of a hill overlooking a ravine, Donovan thought: It's too late now, but am I sure enough of Duncan to bring him to the president. Once again he turned his reservations over in his mind. Duncan speaks better Annamese and knows more about Indochina than anyone else in government service. But is he too wedded to the Annamese ... can we rely on him to be detached, impersonal? That old affair in Saigon. It also concerned him that Duncan had not been through one of his OSS schools, where agents learn the arts of spying, how to survive and, if need be, kill. Duncan might have need of these skills. There isn't enough time for that now.

The president was alone, seated in a wheelchair behind a card table in a sheltered corner of the colonnaded porch, examining documents. The sun shone bright and warm on this third day of April, but there was a stiff breeze in the pines and the president, dressed in a gray suit, had a light blanket tossed over his shoulders.

"Pull up those armchairs," the president said, extending his hand to Duncan. "Well, Travis, how's your dad?"

"Fine, sir. He's works with the War Resources Board ... leads the bond drive in Boston. Otherwise, he's on the golf course or on his boat off Cape Cod. My mother says he has no right to enjoy life so much."

The president chuckled. "Good. He was my first ambassadorial appointment and my best. The State Department resisted his appointment. They wanted a career officer, not a political appointee, not a Boston banker. France was falling apart. But nobody could have done better in those years than your father."

The president coughed and Duncan noticed a tremor in his hands. He was gaunt, and there were deep shadows under his eyes.

"Donovan has told you of our problem. I've proposed a trusteeship for Indochina and eventual independence. It could also be a model for dealing with the British and Dutch colonies. De Gaulle is resisting the idea, and he has Churchill's support. I haven't been able to persuade them to accept what should be apparent. There's no place for colonialism in the postwar world. At our conferences Stalin and Chiang Kai-shek seemed to agree with me. But lately, De Gaulle seems to have charmed them, and I'm not getting the support I need."

The president picked up a document from the table, glanced at it, and put it down. "I'm now drafting my speech before the first session of the United Nations at San Francisco on April 25. I intend to propose a trusteeship system for Indochina no matter what De Gaulle and Churchill say. The French have milked Indochina for eighty years. The people there are entitled to something better. I'll remain opposed to any return by the French to Indochina unless they agree to eventual independence. But first, we must be sure that Indochinese leaders exist who are able and willing to work with us. We get wildly conflicting evaluations of the Indochinese factions from French, British and Chinese intelligence. I don't trust any of them. Our own agencies know little."

The president coughed again and paused. He looked at Duncan and said softly: "Donovan has told me everything about you. You know the Indochinese. I have the same feeling about you as I did about your father. Go back and let me know if there are leaders with whom we could work out a trusteeship. Check on this fellow Ho, whoever and whatever he is. Donovan tells me General Chennault met with him five days ago to thank him for rescuing our pilot. Chennault liked him, although they didn't discuss politics. I'll wait for your report before I define my policy more clearly … publicly. Meanwhile, I've issued orders that we're not to assist the French military forces in Indochina in any way."

The president coughed again, raised his hand in farewell, and without waiting for Duncan's reply, rolled his wheelchair into the house. Grace Tully, who had been watching through the window, opened the door to let him in.

"He doesn't look too well," Duncan said hesitantly, as he walked with Donovan back to the cottage.

"No. You may not have much time if you're going to make a report to him," Donovan said, his eyes suddenly clouding. "I assume you're ready to do what he asks?"

"Of course," Duncan said. "Of course."

"All right. You'll be detailed from the State Department to the OSS as my special assistant. Return to Chungking. Pack up quickly. No need to report to the ambassador. He'll be told you've been transferred to us temporarily because we need your Indochina expertise. In Chungking check in at Detachment 202 with Colonel Richard Holdt, our regional director. He'll give you any help you need. He'll be fully briefed. But no one else must know about your meeting with the president. Then, without delay, go to Kunming. Our people will get you to the Indochina border. We think Ho Chi Minh is there, but we're not sure. He may have already crossed the border into Tonkin. If so, follow him. Find him wherever he is. Talk to him and his partners. Find out what he's all about. Find out if a trusteeship would be acceptable to him and his people."

Donovan led Duncan to the front door where the butler was waiting with his coat and overnight bag. "One other thing, Travis. Suzanne Dumont."

Duncan turned, startled.

"She's with M.5—the China unit of Free French intelligence. Before she went to China, our people cooperated with her in London. That was okay for European operations. But we're on another track in Indochina. Dumont does write for the *Observer*. But that's a cover. She comes under M.5 in Kunming and also reports to General Pechkov—you know him—the head of De Gaulle's mission in Chungking. If you have any more pillow talk with her, be careful."

At the front door Donovan put his hand on Duncan's shoulder. "You seem to have bad luck with women," he said chortling.

Forcing a smile, Duncan shook hands with Donovan and walked out.

Freeman was waiting in the limousine. As the car went down the driveway, Duncan sank back in the seat and pounded his fist into the palm of his hand. He should have known. She'd told him she was for De Gaulle. She didn't deny it when he joked about her being a French spy. *What a naïve sap.* Yet she hadn't pressed him for highly confidential information; nor had he leaked anything very significant to her. But the way she'd toyed with him. Unforgivable.

By the time the car reached the highway and turned north toward Washington, he had managed to put thoughts of Suzanne aside. He was sobered and wildly excited by the import of his meetings with the president and Donovan. For years he had been a maverick, a loner within the State Department. He had sent reports to the Department—which no one senior read—on the activities and attitudes of the Indochinese nationalists. Roosevelt and Donovan had made him a believer once again. He clasped his hands and raised them high.

Duncan took a notebook from his inside coat pocket and hunched over to jot down details of the conversations. Abruptly, he stopped and leaned back. Why had Donovan spoken to him of Saigon? Simply to impress on him that they'd taken everything into account before assigning him to the mission? He told Donovan the affair with the woman happened a long time ago. Yes, it had been ten years. Yet, yet, it was still as if it were yesterday. Mai Khang, so lovely, and then the horror … his guilt.

# -3-

**Saigon**
**November 1935**

IT WAS RAINING LIGHTLY, the waning of the wet season, when Duncan disembarked on the Saigon dock from the small British steamer out of Hong Kong. Attired in a white linen suit and brown pith helmet, which he thought was appropriate dress for an American vice-consul, he strode down the gangplank swinging a green umbrella cane. An Annamite clerk and a driver from the consulate, both smiling and bowing, were waiting for him, and having been cleared on board by an accommodating French customs official, he was driven in a Citroen sedan flying an American flag to his living quarters. It was a small three-room apartment with servants quarters at the rear in a narrow gray two-story building overlooking the flower market on Boulevard Charner in central Saigon.

Standing an hour later at the bamboo bar in a corner of the apartment's lounge, his luggage strewn about him, sipping a *Cinzanno* gin brought to him by Dinh, the cook-boy, Duncan could no longer contain his elation at being in Saigon. He popped on his pith helmet and hastened down the stairs for a quick look at the boulevard. In the flower market the carts were overflowing with chrysanthemums, orchids, roses and giant peonies. He strolled about enjoying the chance to exchange greetings in Annamese with astonished peasant vendors.

Duncan had yearned to return to Indochina since his first visit in February 1933. He was then a senior at Harvard and visited in the company of his father, the newly appointed ambassador to Paris, who was on a familiarization tour of parts of the French empire. In Saigon they had stayed at the massive palace of the French governor-general, shopped for silver ornaments on the fashionable Rue Catinat, and visited a French coffee plantation in the Mekong Delta. They motored up to the Dalat station in the central highlands for an audience with Bao Dai, emperor of Annam, in his summer palace and were waited upon by startlingly beautiful Eurasian women in silken *ao dai*. In Hanoi, the northern capital, they were installed in a lavish suite of the elegant Metropole Hotel, and hosted by French officials in the gardens of yellow stucco villas hidden behind high compound walls. Off the Tonkin coast they cruised the emerald waters of Ha Long Bay on a junk with red bat-like sails to view the grottos and jutting limestone formations.

Duncan was captivated by what he saw of the beauty of the country. But he came away aware that he and his father had been on very much of a Potemkin tour. When visiting a coffee plantation, before the planter quickly turned his car away, there was the sight of a white man lashing an Annamese worker with a bamboo rod. While speeding by villages on the mountain road to Dalat, he glimpsed ragged peasants with upraised pleading hands outside squalid thatch-roofed huts. He was shocked by the naked beggar children covered with sores, to whom he threw coins, on the streets of the fancy resort city of Hongay on Ha Long Bay, where the French colonials played.

When Duncan, upon graduation from Harvard, entered the Foreign Service, administrators at the State Department, after some delay, approved his request for Annamese language and area training in Paris at the Sorbonne. But they were somewhat incredulous that he elected Indochina as an area of specialization. In Washington there was little interest in the obscure colony; and there was no political reporting from Saigon to the Department. In Paris, Duncan was an ardent student at the Sorbonne, and he became friendly with Annamese exiles who spoke of another Indochina very different from what he and his father had been shown.

As Duncan wandered through the flower market on Boulevard Charner, his thoughts turned from contemplation of the delights about him to how he might find means of venturing into that other Indochina where foreign diplomats were not invited.

Three weeks after his arrival, Duncan was on one of his exploratory walks through the city. While strolling down Avenue Galieni, the shabby thoroughfare that extended to Cholon, the

Chinese twin city of Saigon, he paused at a small Annamese bookshop. Peering through the display window he saw an array of cheap Annamese paperbacks and magazines. But then he noticed among them what seemed to be a history of Saigon as capital of Cochin China, unlike anything he had come upon while rummaging in Portail, the French bookshop on Rue Catinat.

Duncan entered the shop eagerly. At a small counter in front of the cluttered bookshelves there was a young Annamese woman, obviously astonished at the sight of the tall foreigner in the black broad-brimmed hat and khaki bush jacket. Duncan added to her surprise by speaking Annamese: "May I look at your books?" She nodded, wide-eyed.

Browsing among the books, Duncan felt with mounting excitement he had chanced upon a research bonanza. There were tracts issued by obscure Annamese political groups, which he had not seen in State Department files in Washington, the Library of Congress or at the Sorbonne. He returned to the counter with several pamphlets, and stood there for a moment suddenly speechless as he looked upon the exquisite creature in the flowered cotton sheath with embroidered mandarin collar standing before him.

"How is it that you speak Annamese?" the woman said, her amber eyes alive with curiosity.

Duncan collected himself. "I studied in Paris at the Sorbonne."

"You're French?"

"No … American. I'm the vice-consul at the American Consulate in Saigon."

"American!" she exclaimed, and added delightedly. "I've never met an American before. Vice-consul … you're very important."

"No, no," Duncan said, laughing. "The consulate is very small … not important at all. There's only a consul and me. All we do is issue a few visas, look after our Christian missionaries in the countryside and the American businessmen who come to buy rubber at the plantations."

"Father!" the woman called out. A stooped man with a gray goatee emerged from the rear of the shop. "I heard," he said, examining Duncan over rimless spectacles. "You're American. I've read many books about your country. It's a wonderful country. A democracy, like, I hope, we'll be one day."

The daughter interrupted. "My father's name is Canh Dong. I am Mai Khang." She laughed gaily. "We don't have any foreign customers."

Duncan bowed. "You have one now. My name is Travis Duncan. I'll be back."

Mai handed Duncan change from the piaster notes he had put on the counter. "I hope so," she said shyly. "*Au revoir.*"

It was on his third visit that Duncan asked Mai to dine with him. He came the next day in his Citroen roadster and they drove to the Rue Catinat where they had dinner on the sidewalk terrace of the Bodega Restaurant. Mai was dressed in a light blue *ao dai*, slit at the sides to reveal white silk trousers. French couples seated at nearby tables glanced at them and whispered. Mai declined the offer of champagne and asked for a citronade; Duncan ordered a vermouth and soda. They chatted in Annamese and French.

"I know so little about you," Duncan said. "Tell me about your family. Your father is such a cultured man. He mentioned how much he enjoys reading Charles Dickens, though he must do so in French translation."

Mai stirred her drink slowly. "My father is the son of a middle school teacher. He reads many books, especially about problems of people in the oppressed classes. He is a graduate of a French school in Hanoi, the College Paul Bert. My grandfather believed Vietnamese must have a Western education if they are someday to become citizens of an independent country. So father took an entrance examination to the school and was admitted. After graduation he became an accountant at a big French coffee plantation, south of here on the Delta, where I was born. We were quite comfortable there. My mother was happy with her vegetable garden behind our little bamboo house. We also had a coconut palm in the garden."

Mai looked up at Duncan, her smooth golden brow becoming creased. "My father also taught mathematics in the middle school for

Vietnamese children. One day it was reported he had spoken after class to some boys about independence for Vietnam. The *Sûreté* came for him. He was sent to prison. We lost our house. Mother and I went to a rubber plantation where she worked along the rows of trees. She became ill. She wasn't accustomed to the labor—ten or twelve hours tapping and little food. Before she died she was able to put me into a Catholic convent here in Saigon. I was lucky. Many girls in Cochin China like me are sold to the Chinese in Cholon to work in brothels. When my father was released from prison, he worked on the docks unloading ships until friends lent him enough money to start up the bookshop."

Mai cast her eyes down upon seeing the expression of consternation on Duncan's face. "And where is your home?" she asked.

"Not a very interesting place," Duncan said, thinking, how could he speak to her of his comfortable life in the family mansion. "I'll tell you about it sometime."

"I don't come to the Rue Catinat often," Mai said, as they watched the early evening crowd of elegantly gowned French women in extravagant hats, army officers in smart khaki, Frenchmen in white suits, a few with beautiful Eurasian women on their arms. Their promenade along Rue Catinat was limited to a few hundred yards, past sidewalk cafés, the open terraces of the Continental Hotel, and the fancy shops with Parisian wares. "This is not part of our lives," Mai said, stirring her citronade. "My father would like to take you to a Vietnamese restaurant."

"I'd like that very much," Duncan said. "Tell me, Mai, I'm curious. Why do you always say *Vietnamese,* rather than *Annamese?*"

"Yes, the French always say *Annamese.* They forbid us to speak of our country as Vietnam. At my school in the French Catholic convent, the nuns made mention of us only as Annamites. But you should know—more than four-fifths of the people of Tonkin, Annam and Cochin China are of the same blood. We're a nation. Vietnam. We should call ourselves Vietnamese." That was the first political statement Duncan heard Mai utter.

Several days later, as the clock in the Notre Dame Cathedral tower chimed six, Duncan drove to the bookshop where Mai and her father awaited him. "Best we go by cyclo," Canh said. "We have two waiting." Canh and Mai mounted one of the pedicabs and Duncan followed in the other. The coolies pedaled rapidly into the port area, less than a mile away, past the grimy warehouses, the squat customs building and the principal docks to a stretch of the river where straw huts and shanties lined the banks.

The restaurant was in a corrugated-iron building facing out on a river inlet crowded with sampans, some with families living aboard. Canh led them into the restaurant, a noisy low-ceiling room filled with battered tables under slow-turning ceiling fans, the heavy air laden with tobacco smoke and the pungent odor of the *nuoc mam* fish sauce. A tall pocked-faced man, with a smudged white apron wrapped around his middle, greeted Canh warmly and led them to a corner table.

"He is from the north, a Tonkinese," Canh said, as he filled their glasses from a large bottle of Saigon beer. Duncan glanced about the room. At the other tables there were only men, most dressed in the black pajama-like clothes of the boat people. Duncan was the only foreigner.

As the meal progressed, Canh did most of the talking, pointing with his chopsticks to identify the various Annamese delicacies. He plied Duncan with questions about life in the United States, about how the country was governed, how Negroes and other minorities were treated.

The Tonkinese had just brought desert melons when Duncan asked: "Among the books in your shop I saw a tract of the Indochinese Communist Party. It was a copy of the 1930 program, which calls for the forced distribution of all land to the peasants. Don't the French object to you selling such pamphlets?"

Canh and Mai looked at each other silently. Mai nervously put down her chopsticks and folded her hands in her lap. Canh shrugged. "The French don't come into our shop. As for the pamphlet, it is only of historical interest. The Party is very weak now. It follows a changed political line. I'd forgotten that we still have a copy of the program. I didn't know it was on the shelf."

As Canh lapsed into silence, Duncan said: "I heard talk about the Party program in Paris when I studied at the Sorbonne. I was friendly with an Annamese student, Tran Huy Quat. He took me to meetings of the Association of Vietnamese Patriots."

Canh's eyes brightened and looked sharply at Duncan. "That Association was organized by one of our great revolutionary leaders—Nguyen Ai Quoc. He was a founder of the Indochinese Communist Party." Canh leaned back in his chair. "It's quite late. The riverfront is not too safe after dark. There are robbers. We should go."

After the meal at the river restaurant, Duncan saw Mai more often. Her father seemed to approve. They took drives along the gentle rise above central Saigon where many of the wealthy French lived in pastel-colored stucco villas with gardens shaded by magnolia and palm trees. They toured the port in a sampan and visited the fabric shops along the Rue Catinat. Once Mai came to Duncan's apartment on Boulevard Charner, and romped with his Siamese cat while Duncan played American songs for her on the phonograph. They danced. It was the first time that he held her in his arms.

"Not possible so soon … yet … I'm in love with her," Duncan thought, conveying his feelings only with his eyes and his gentle embrace.

The next day, in the blazing hot afternoon, Duncan went by the shop and asked if she would like to go for a swim in the pool at the French Cercle Sportif.

Mai's eyes closed for a moment. "You're not serious, Travis," she said. "Vietnamese are not permitted in that club. The women you've seen at the pool are Eurasians … *métis*. You and I do live in different worlds."

Duncan berated himself for days over his clumsiness. But when he next telephoned Mai, she agreed readily to see him and suggested the morning of the following day. He was puzzled when she told him to wear boots.

Mai was waiting outside the bookshop. She was dressed in black cotton and rubber sandals, not unlike the garb of the women venders in the flower market. "Come," Mai said gaily, "We shall go on a little tour, *d'accord*?"

Duncan followed Mai into the street where she hailed a cyclo and gave muted instructions. The coolie, a thin man in a torn shirt and a dirty towel wrapped about his head, pedaled into the French residential quarter through neat streets lined with plane trees out to the ring of squat cement block and corrugated-iron houses where many of the better-off Annamese dwelt, and then beyond to a canal filled with small sampans. Mai paid the sweating, panting pedicab man.

They were at the edge of a village, one of many in the wide shanty belt encircling Saigon. There were no streets, and Mai led Duncan down mud paths that ran beside straw huts crammed with starved-looking Annamese and naked children. The Annamese stared at them, gesturing wildly, and soon they were being followed by imploring beggars, cripples and children covered with sores. They wandered for hours, Duncan increasingly depressed by the misery he saw in the stinking hamlets.

"This is where they live," Mai said. "The common laborers, sampan folk, laborers on the docks, cyclo men and rickshaw pullers, and all the rootless ones. Hundreds of thousands of us live here, like this. My father lived here when he worked on the docks. This is my world."

In the following days, Duncan felt elated in that he was gaining insights into that other Indochina cited by the exiles in Paris. He pressed Mai to talk more freely about politics and the condition of her people. She did so willingly and in turn seemed intrigued by his comment at the restaurant that he had attended meetings in Paris of the Association of Vietnamese Patriots. She questioned him closely about what he had been told by the exiles, their hopes for Vietnamese independence, and how he responded. Encouraged by his sympathy, she spoke more openly.

As they walked one afternoon along a pretty stretch of the Saigon River front, past tiny stalls where clamoring vendors sold rice cakes, she said:   "My father told you in the restaurant that the Indochinese Communist Party is very weak now. That's true. It was wiped out after the peasants established Soviet communes four years ago in the provinces of Nghe An and Ha Tinh. The French sent in troops to suppress the peasants who had seized the lands of reactionary landlords. Many, many hundreds were executed. More than ten thousand political prisoners were sent to the penal settlements on the islands. The Party's secretary general, Tran Phu, was tortured to death in prison." She hesitated and then added firmly: "But the Party is rising again."

They paused on a riverbank to watch a Chinese junk slowly drift by as the crew hoisted yellow sails.

"I suppose you know," Mai said, "there were municipal elections in Saigon in May for the City Council. Two-thirds of the Council are French, but there are also Vietnamese elected on a 'worker's ticket.' Among them are several underground Communist Party members. The Party is following a legal line for the time being, but we still are preparing the people for land reform and the end of French colonialism."

Duncan noticed she said "we" and spoke as if she was quoting some document. "I'd like to know more about all this," Duncan said eagerly. "I heard nothing about it in Washington. Can we talk more about it … in my apartment? Tomorrow?"

"No. I have some matters to attend to," Mai said. "But I can visit you in five days, on Saturday or Sunday."

"Wonderful. Come for lunch on Saturday at one o'clock."

When Mai returned to the bookshop, her father was waiting for her. As she did after every meeting with Duncan, she reported on everything that had been said. Canh shut the door of the shop and they went into the back room.

"I worry," Canh said. "Perhaps you're meeting with Duncan too often. The *Sûreté* watches every foreigner. We may be drawing attention to ourselves. The *Sûreté* may begin to suspect you're having more than a romantic liaison with Duncan."

Mai listened silently, her eyes lowered.

Canh said: "We're playing a dangerous game, risking much in the hope that this American will pass our thoughts on to Washington." He sighed. "But what other way is there to tell the outside world about the condition of our people. No foreign journalists come here except the puppets of the French news agency. The missionaries and the businessmen accept things as they are."

Canh got up from the wooden stool on which he had been sitting, lit a cigarette, and paced the small room. "Is it worth it?" he asked in a querulous voice. "Can we trust this American? He's very young. There's an innocence about him."

"We can trust him," Mai said quietly, firmly. "I think he cares about our people."

Canh looked at his daughter sharply. "Do not become too attached to him. He's of another world."

"I know that," Mai said.

Four days later in the late afternoon Duncan was in his office in the consulate when one of the three Annamite clerks came in and said: *"Monsieur le consul* wishes to see you." Duncan put on his jacket and went down the hall, the floorboards creaking under his firm stride, to the consul's office. The consulate was housed in an old villa fronting on a square where children played in the Jardin d'Enfants under the care of *amah*s who sat gossiping under gaily colored parasols that shielded them from the blazing sun.

John Rivers, a tubby, genial man in his early sixties, was at his desk. This was Rivers' last post in a career spent mainly in the consular service handling commercial matters. Duncan liked the man but found him tiring.

"Ah! ... Travis, please sit down," Rivers said jovially, as he reclined in his leather chair. "That was an excellent report you did for the Department on the municipal elections, if you can call them that." He guffawed. "I don't think the Department has ever had any serious political reporting from here."

Duncan smiled politely. "I will be sending a more detailed report," he said.

"I had dinner last night with Monsieur Bollard, the counselor to the governor-general," Rivers said. "Quite unexpected. Interesting. He told me about the projected improvements to the port."

The consul leaned forward to fiddle with a crystal paperweight resting on a pile of visa applications. "Then we talked about you," he said hesitantly. "Monsieur Bollard thinks very highly of you. He also mentioned the Annamese woman you've been seeing. Her name escapes me at the moment."

"Mai Khang," Duncan said quietly.

"Oh, yes. That's it." He coughed. "The counselor says she's not trustworthy politically."

"What does that mean?" Duncan said with unconcealed irritation.

"Well … her father spent two years in prison here in Saigon for anti-French activities. You seeing his daughter, Bollard told me, is very unwise." Rivers spoke hurriedly, as if he hoped to end the conversation as quickly as possible.

Duncan breathed heavily. "I'm the Annamese-language officer here. I'm expected to have contacts with the Annamese, not only French officials. I don't think Monsieur Bollard should concern himself about my contacts with law abiding people."

Rivers flushed. "Travis, it's not our business to get mixed up in local politics. I think you should take Bollard's advice. Frankly, there was sort of a threat in the way he talked."

"Thank you, Mr. Rivers," Duncan said. "Is that all?"

Rivers nodded, looking unhappy.

Duncan strode back to his office. Sweating profusely, he stripped off his jacket, undid his tie and paced the office, flexing his fingers. Then he snatched up his jacket from the chair, ran down the stairs to his car and drove quickly, honking furiously to part the traffic, to his apartment.

At the apartment he hastily scrawled a note:

> Mai, dearest Mai. Best you not come
> to my apartment as planned. I will be in touch.
> Affectionately, Travis.

Duncan put the note in an envelope, wrote his name over the seal, and rang for Dinh, the cook-boy. "Take this letter quickly to my friend Mai Khang. You know where she lives. Be sure she receives it."

Dinh, a short, sharp-faced Annamese, bowed, took the letter with both hands, and hurried out.

Will she understand something is terribly amiss? Duncan wondered prayerfully.

Dinh returned two hours later, shaking his head apologetically, holding the undelivered note.

Duncan, in striped pajama bottoms, brandy glass in hand, sat in the sofa chair beneath the ceiling fan, which was doing little to relieve the oppressive heat. The only light in the lounge filtered in from the single bulb in the bedroom. Duncan had not slept. Through the night he had turned over in his mind what Dinh had reported. The bookshop was shuttered. Mai and her father were not in their room above the shop. The Chinese owner of the bar beside the shop told Dinh with a knowing nod he'd seen two French police vans in front of the building the previous evening. Duncan got up and went to the small bamboo bar in the corner of the lounge, poured another brandy, and went to the window. He opened the curtain and looked down at the flower mart where the peasant vendors in the first flush of dawn were bustling beside carts piled high with blossoms.

Taken by the *Sûreté* for sure, Duncan thought. Was Mai being interrogated in the notorious *Sûreté* building near Cathedral Square? Had she and her father been tortured? Everyone knew how the *Sûreté* abused Annamese political prisoners. Was this his fault? Of course it was. He should have anticipated that his association with Mai and her father would draw the scrutiny of the *Sûreté*.

In the morning, when the Cathedral clock struck eight, Duncan walked unsteadily, still not entirely sober, down the single flight of stairs to the street where his Citroen was parked. He was dressed in a dark blue suit with a neat white handkerchief in the breast pocket, but he was unshaven. He drove to the palace of the governor-general where Foreign Legionnaires in their white kepis and red epaulettes stood guard at the gate. At the entrance, he told the lieutenant, who spoke French with a Central European guttural accent, that he had an appointment with Monsieur Bollard. After a wait of fifteen minutes he was admitted to the courtyard. A Senegalese sergeant was waiting for Duncan at the door and led him to the second floor to a gilt-paneled room where Bollard, a hawk-faced man in a white suit, was waiting, standing under a crystal chandelier. "An unexpected, pleasure," Bollard said, waving him to a teak armchair. "Join me for coffee?"

Duncan shook his head. "You have Mai Khang," he said hoarsely.

Bollard sipped his coffee. "Yes," he said deliberately. "She and her father have been arrested."

"Why?" Duncan blurted. "Because she was seeing me, an American?"

"No," Monsieur Duncan. "Of course not. It is true that the *Sûreté* went to the book shop after noticing your last visit." Shaking his head and arching his heavy black eyebrows, Bollard said: "Negligent of the *Sûreté*. They should have paid attention to the shop earlier. You will be surprised to hear that at the rear of the shop, under the straw mat they found a trapdoor. It leads to an underground room. There was a printing press there. Astonishing? Yes? These Annamites are fantastic at tunneling. Also, piles of a pamphlet which demands an end to our French administration. It also calls upon the Annamite peasants to prepare to seize French plantations."

Duncan stared fixedly at Bollard. "What are you going to do with Mai Khang and her father? "

Bollard shrugged. "When the investigation is completed, it will be up to the court. If innocent, Mai Khang will be released. If not …" He pursed his lips. "Her father? Obviously guilty. He's known to us. If both are found guilty? Inciting antigovernment violence is punishable by imprisonment in a penal settlement or death."

Duncan leaped up. Standing over Bollard, swaying slightly, he shouted: "You can't do that!"

Bollard looked up coldly. "Your conduct, Monsieur Duncan, is unacceptable." He rose and opened the door. The Senegalese was waiting in the corridor.

Two weeks later, Rivers called Duncan into his office. "You've been recalled by the Department at the request of the French. I'm sorry. There's also a cable from your father, the ambassador. He suggests you return to Washington through Paris … spend a day at the residence."

Rivers sighed and looked relieved as Duncan walked out without pressing him with questions.

Duncan woke when the French maid came in at seven o'clock with orange juice, croissants and coffee. He had arrived in Paris late the night before and taken a taxi directly from Orly to the ambassadorial résidence.

"*Monsieur l'ambassadeur* would like to see you in the library at eight o'clock," the maid said.

The ambassador was at his desk reading *Le Monde* when Duncan entered the library. He dropped the newspaper onto his desk and embraced Duncan. The ambassador was a lean man, gray-haired, but with a youthful countenance very much like that of his son. The two settled in easy chairs near the fireplace.

"Bearing up?" the ambassador asked, smiling slightly.

"Fairly well, sir, under the circumstances. I suppose you're upset with me? You've reason enough."

The ambassador lit a cigarette and threw the match into the fireplace. "You really stumbled into it. I've had a fill-in from the Department. A contact at the Quai d'Orsay also gave me an earful. Apparently the *Sûreté* has now traced the paper trail from your friends' bookshop. Their tracts were going into those thousands of miserable shanties around Saigon." He shook his head. "No, I don't blame you for this whole mess ... except that you should have known, as my son, the *Sûreté* would be more interested in you than in any typical vice-consul."

Duncan clasped his hands and leaned forward. "Yes, I was naïve, innocent might be a better word. But so are all Americans—and our government—about Indochina. The French have locked up the country for eighty years. Well, now I've been there and experienced their colonialism. They've no intention, as some of us had hoped, of eventually transplanting democracy from Paris to Saigon. They're not packaging their homegrown revolution for export to their colonies. As a matter of conscience, I don't see how we Americans can tolerate that in silence."

The elder Duncan sighed. "I can't dispute what you say. But with Hitler acting up in Germany, Mussolini in Ethiopia, and the Japanese militarists in China, we're not in a position to begin challenging our allies about their colonial policies."

Duncan fell back in his chair, eyes closed. "What do you think they'll do with Mai Khang and her father?"

"You really care a lot for that woman?"

"Yes ... very much."

The ambassador drew heavily on his cigarette. "Her prospects are not very good. The French were frightened by the peasant uprisings in those two provinces—Ha Tinh and Nghe An. Their reaction has been merciless. There's been no let-up these past years in what has been a white counterterror against anyone suspected of trying to overthrow the colonial regime. The exiles here say that hundreds have been executed. It's still going on."

The ambassador mashed his cigarette in an ashtray and folded his arms. "Travis, listen," he said intently. "You're finished as far as service in France or in any of its territories is concerned. You're *persona non grata* to the Quai d'Orsay. You need time to pull yourself together. I don't like to ask favors of anyone in the Department, but I've made an exception for you. You're going back to Harvard to study Chinese for a year. You have an aptitude for languages, and the Department was glad to make the arrangements."

Duncan, his brow wrinkled, was about to speak when the ambassador rose. "I have an appointment at the chancery, Travis. Have lunch with your mother. We'll talk more at dinner. You must compose yourself for your debriefing in Washington."

Duncan, sighing heavily, rose slowly from his chair. "Okay Father, Harvard it is. I can't think of what else I might do. But about Indochina … the French can't keep me out forever. One way or another, I'll go back. I'll do whatever is possible for Mai Khang and for her people."

The ambassador shrugged.

In the afternoon Duncan located Tran, who had been his Annamese chum at the Sorbonne, and arranged to meet at a café on the Left Bank. Tran had left the university and was working in Paris as a clerk at the Banque d'Indochine. Tran, a slight man with bright inquisitive eyes, listened sympathetically over vermouth *aperitifs* as Duncan told him what happened in Saigon.

"Try to find out what they're doing with Mai Khang," Duncan begged. "You and the people in the Association have good sources everywhere in Indochina."

Duncan had been studying at Harvard for two months when the letter came from Tran. Mai Khang and her father had been sent to the Con Son Prison in the penal island settlement of Poulo Condore, tried by a French military tribunal, convicted of treason and executed.

Duncan fled Cambridge, isolating himself in his family's summer home on Cape Cod. He walked on the beach for hours, distraught and burdened by guilt. Watching the surf roll in, there were times when he thought of letting himself be engulfed, banishing all memory. After two weeks he returned to Harvard. He wrote to Tran: "Please, please, try to find out more about what's happened to Mai. I can't believe—I don't believe—that she's dead."

# -4-

**Washington**
**April 3, 1945**

DUNCAN WAS JOLTED when the limousine swung sharply into the semi-circular driveway of the Jefferson Hotel. He was unaware they were already in central Washington. He'd been bemused by the complexities of planning for his presidential mission, shocked by what he had learned about Suzanne, and had experienced a resurgence of agonizing memories of Saigon. As Freeman opened the limousine door, Duncan climbed out, thinking, I've got to collect myself.

In his room Duncan unpacked, leafed quickly through the *Washington Star*, had dinner brought in on a cart, and soon after went to bed. Weary as he was, he couldn't sleep. Thoughts and images of Suzanne intruded. She had given him comfort and happiness. Dreams of Mai had faded. *But a spy?* He recalled the way Donovan laughed. She had humiliated him. He became furious at the thought that he was still in love with Suzanne. He wished savagely she was in bed with him, that he was fucking her ... hurting her with his thrusts until she cried out. Restlessly, he swung out of bed, dressed and went down to the lobby bar.

There was a noisy crowd, most of them young and in uniform, jammed together at the small bar. Duncan went to an alcove adjacent to the bar and ordered a scotch. He was on his second when a young Army Air Force major with a black patch over his left eye walked into the bar. He was limping slightly. Something on his green tunic captured Duncan's attention. Above the array of ribbons and below his Air Force wings were the silver wings of the Chinese Nationalist Air Force. It signified he had been one of the Flying Tigers, the American Volunteer Group put together by Chennault before Pearl Harbor to help the Chinese resist the Japanese. The major looked about but there was no place at the bar or in the alcoves. Duncan waved, and the major approached.

"Thanks a lot," the major drawled as he took off his overseas cap and joined Duncan. "Name's Chris Chivers. From Jacksonville, Mississippi. I'm waiting for a friend."

"Travis Duncan. I'm in the embassy in Chungking ... been there four years. Saw those Chinese wings on you. Brother, I know what they mean."

The major laughed and asked the waiter for a bourbon on the rocks. "Yeah ... up until November I was still flying high."

"What happened? Mind telling me?"

The major knocked back his bourbon and signaled the waiter for a refill. "Real sad story, Mr. Duncan. I was flying a P-40 out of Kunming, just before the Japs took our base at Kweilin. I was covering the ATC transports ferrying out our portable equipment so we wouldn't lose it to the Japs. All that stuff brought in over The Hump ... *jeezez!*" He shook his head. "On the last day—when we were lifting out the local warlord, Chang Fa-kwei, and his staff—a Zero got on my tail and let me have it. Shouldn't have happened. The Zero is more maneuverable than our P-40s, but our planes are more high-powered and climb much better. Usually, we sit up high and dive down on them. This time I was just riding shotgun to protect the transport that Chang was on and I was easy. I crashed in a rice paddy. When I woke up, I was in a bamboo hammock being carried by a couple of peasants. They saw that inscription on the back of my flying jacket ... the one saying they'd be paid in gold if they turned me over to Chiang Kai-shek's boys. They did. The Nats hauled me to another one of our forward air bases."

The major's mouth tightened and he grimaced. "One leg broken in two places. One eye damaged. This is my first day out of Walter Reed. They operated on my eye. I'll be ready for a flight physical in another month. If the eye is okay, I'll go back."

"You want to go back after all that? "

"Mister, I was twenty-one when I joined the Flying Tigers. I don't know any other life. You see ... hey, there she is!"

Heads turned at the bar and there were whistles as a sergeant in a skirt and well-filled khaki blouse walked in. She was a petite brunette wearing a visor cap bearing the insignia of the Women's Auxiliary Corps over her bobbed hair.

Chivers embraced her. "Mister Duncan, meet Sergeant Sally O'Neil of the WACs. I trust you won't report me for running around with enlisted personnel."

"Major Chivers, I believe the Air Force chief-of-staff would break the rules if he had this chance. I've got to say good night."

Duncan went to bed more relaxed; grateful for the diversion in the bar. By comparison, the young major and his adventures made his problems seem less burdensome. He made a note of what Chivers told him about Chang Fa-kwei being plucked out of Kweilin just before the Japanese took the city. Useful to know. The Kwangsi warlord controlled the South China border area where Donovan said he might find Ho Chi Minh. Chang was now indebted to his American rescuers. If the Japanese had nabbed him, they would have beheaded him. I might cash in on that, Duncan speculated. Chinese usually repaid their debts.

Early the next morning, an Army Air Force captain knocked at Duncan's door and handed him a manila envelope and a black leather bag together with a key to open it. Enclosed in the envelope was a letter from the personnel office of the State Department detailing Duncan to the OSS and a set of military orders authorizing travel by Air Force transport to Chungking and then to Kunming. Opening the bag, tagged Top Secret, Duncan marveled at the contents. It contained a remarkable set of briefing books on the Indochinese nationalist movement.

Over the years Duncan had researched the movement extensively. Despite the meagerness of the official files in Washington, he had managed to collect considerable information by drawing on academic sources and interviews with exiles in France and China. But his findings were sketchy compared with what was in the black bag.

Donovan somehow had obtained the extensive files of the *Direction Generale des Etudes et Recherches* (DGER), the French counterpart of the OSS. Duncan spent the next hours perusing the DGER files. He was puzzled by the omission of any mention of Ho Chi Minh.

The black bag also included a detailed report by Fenn, the OSS agent, on his conversations with Ho Chi Minh. Not until he had studied the Fenn report did Duncan find the link. Fenn described Ho as a man of about fifty-five years of age, with a high forehead, receding black hairline, a wisp of a goatee turning gray and extraordinarily luminous eyes, who habitually dressed in a buttoned-to-the neck sand-colored jacket, cotton trousers and strap type sandals.

After reading the description and the record of Fenn's conversations, Duncan leaped up from the desk and went back to the DGER files. Unmistakably, Ho Chi Minh was Nguyen Ai Quoc—the phantom figure of the nationalist underground known to the *Sûreté* by as many as one hundred pseudonyms. The DGER file on Nguyen Ai Quoc contained highly detailed information. This was the odd little man in the rented morning coat who in June 1919 at the Versailles Conference was shunted aside when he tried to present a petition entitled *The Rights of Nations* to President Wilson. Duncan recalled seeing the spurned petition in the National Archives in Washington. Four years after being rebuffed by Wilson and other Western leaders, Ngyuen emerged in Moscow as a spokesman for the anticolonial struggle and a standing member of the Eastern Department of the Comintern. Since leaving the Soviet capital in December 1924, the DGER file stated, he had been tracked by the *Sûreté* on return visits to Moscow and on underground travels through Southeast Asia, Hong Kong, and South China. He had been condemned to death by the French *en absentia* for treason. The DGER file was closed on Ho in 1932 when he was reported to have died in the hospital ward of a British prison in Hong Kong. Obviously, he had escaped, Duncan surmised, and it seemed clear that the Comintern had published the report of his death as a cover to enable him to move about abroad clandestinely. This was "Nguyen the Patriot" now discovered by the Americans as Ho Chi Minh, in translation, "The One Who Shines."

Studying Fenn's report, Duncan was intrigued by Ho Chi Minh's response when asked if he was a Communist. Obviously eager to forge American allies he parried the question by saying that the French described all Annamites who want independence as Communists. Years ago Duncan had identified Nguyen Ai Quoc as one of the nationalists who in 1930 founded the Indochinese Communist Party at a secret meeting in Hong Kong. This was also the man that Mai's father said was the founder of the Association of Vietnamese Patriots in Paris. Now he knew. During his Sorbonne days he had been unknowingly linked through the Association to Ho Chi Minh.

Meticulously correlating the extensive files, Duncan wrote and underlined a note to himself: *Nguyen/Ho did serve as an agent of the Comintern. The files show, however, his political career has been devoted almost exclusively to opposing colonialism and crusading for an independent Vietnam. The Russians repeatedly have criticized him for being more nationalist than Communist.*

Duncan put aside the files and finished packing, but once again thoughts of Suzanne intruded. He could not simply turn his back on her. He must see her once more.

Duncan left Washington that night for China.

# -5-

**Chungking, China**
**March 9, 1945**

TWO DAYS AFTER DUNCAN DEPARTED CHUNGKING, Suzanne was awakened at 4:30 in the morning by the shrill ringing of the alarm clock beside her bed. Without opening her eyes, she silenced the alarm, and turning over, reached out beside her with a fumbling hand. Of course, he's gone, she thought as she became fully awake. She swung out of bed, switched on the lamp, and then sat back heavily on the edge of the bed, thinking of what she must do this day, wishing it was all a passing dream of the fitful night.

After a few minutes, Suzanne put on her dressing gown, went to the bathroom, and then breakfasted on coffee and sandwiches she'd prepared the night before. At the small vanity table with the cracked mirror in the alcove of the room, she combed her hair and then pinned it back in a bun. From an unmarked tube she applied a lotion to her face and neck that darkened her skin, and then did the same to her feet and ankles. She went to her closet, pulled out a suitcase. From it she took a black cotton blouse that buttoned down the front, a long black skirt with a green rope-like sash, and straw sandals. When she donned the clothes, she was in the dress of a peasant woman of the Tay minority people.

Precisely at 5:30, Suzanne slipped gingerly into a light raincoat and carrying a straw bag went down the stairs. A man in a black cap was holding open the door of a limousine.

"*Bon matin, madame,*" said the person reclining in the darkness of the back seat.

"*Bon matin*, Major Rems," Suzanne said, as she climbed in beside him.

The car wended through quiet streets and alleys, the headlights boring through the darkness, illuminating patrolling police and a few peddlers, to a dock on the Yangtze that was connected with a rope bridge to the airstrip. Suzanne and the major, who wore a trench coat and carried a small suitcase, crossed the bridge to a plane parked at the side of the narrow tarmac. Suzanne recognized the plane. It was a three-engined German Junker, which a French pilot defecting from the Vichy forces in Indochina had flown to Kunming and was now being used as a liaison plane by Zinovi Pechkov, the head of the French Military Mission.

At daylight the plane took off and Suzanne, settling back in her seat, focused her mind on the mission given to her by Pechkov five days earlier.

Suzanne was about to leave her apartment for the weekly press conference at the Chinese Foreign Office when the telephone buzzed. "The general will see you at eleven o'clock," the voice said and hung up. Suzanne knew that she was being summoned to see Pechkov at the mission, but she was puzzled. To avoid inviting suspicion that she was an agent, she met only infrequently with Pechkov and usually in a restaurant or at his home with French men and women attending, on the pretext of a social occasion. It must be something about Duncan, she speculated.

Suzanne was ushered into Pechkov's spacious office as soon as she arrived at the mission. When she entered, Pechkov was at his desk, behind which hung a large portrait of De Gaulle; he hurried to her side smiling and kissed her hand. A man of about fifty, with strong beaked features, he was dressed in a well-tailored gray pinstriped suit, the right sleeve pinned up.

Suzanne greeted Pechkov warmly, having always found him charming and extremely well-read—not surprising since she knew he was the bastard son of Maxim Gorki and had spent his youth traveling with the Russian writer.

"Come with me, dear," Pechkov said, as he picked up a file from his desk. He led her out of his office, up a winding staircase, to a room with cement walls that were bare except for maps of China and

Indochina. Pechkov seated himself at a table in the center of the room with Suzanne at his side. On it he placed a white envelope, a map and a package of Camel cigarettes. "My American friends are always very generous with their PX cigarettes," he said, laughing, offering one to Suzanne and lighting one for himself with one-handed dexterity.

"I must apologize for these rude surroundings, my dear Suzanne," Pechkov said. "My relations with Chiang Kai-shek are excellent, but his intelligence chief, Tai Li, has managed to put listening devices everywhere else in the building. But enough of that …

"You know Lang Son, of course, our principal military post in Indochina on the China frontier," Pechkov said. "Pleasant town for an army outpost. I visited it before the war. About ten thousand people live there apart from units of our frontier garrison of some twelve thousand troops. Many of them are engaged in supplying our other posts on the frontier along Route Coloniale Numero 4 which extends for seventy miles to Cao Bang."

Pechkov, with his finger on the map, traced the line of forts which commanded the four traditional invasion routes through the mountains into Tonkin from China.

With Suzanne increasingly puzzled as to the point of this briefing, Pechkov continued: "General Rene Lemonnier is in command of the Frontier Zone. His headquarters is in Lang Son and, unfortunately, he now reports to the Vichy governor-general in Saigon. The Japanese, who are collaborating with the Vichy traitors, are in control of the airfield at Lang Son. They also have a garrison nearby composed of elements of their 37th army division to keep an eye on the French troops and the border."

Pechkov tapped the white envelope on the table. "This is a personal message to Lemonnier from De Gaulle, actually signed and sealed by him. It calls on Lemonnier, immediately after the end of the war, to disarm the Japanese units on the frontier and declare allegiance to the Free French. This should be entirely possible once Tokyo surrenders. What is most important—absolutely crucial—for us is this: De Gaulle will be able at that moment to declare he's in control of the frontier and there is no need for the Chinese to cross over to disarm the Japanese." Pechkov smiled tightly. "We know the Chinese, especially the warlords in the provinces along the frontier. If they cross into Indochina, we may never get them out."

"I understand," Suzanne said, frowning. "But how can I help?"

Pechkov leaned toward Susan, no longer smiling, his eyes intent. "You will deliver the letter to Lemonnier. We've tried other means of getting this letter to him, without success. One officer stationed at Lang Son who secretly came over to us was to meet our people on the China side of the border to pick up the letter. He was intercepted by the Japanese and executed."

Suzanne fell back in her chair. "But how ..." she began. "Of course I'm ready to do what you ask. But why me?"

"Once you are briefed on our plan you will understand. We've worked out your assignment to the last detail," Pechkov said. "Major Rems of our mission will work with you. He knows Lang Son and the other posts on the frontier and speaks Chinese and also the language of the Tay people who live on both sides of the border. All is in place. Rems will explain everything to you in good time."

"I assume you agree," Pechkov said, standing up.

Suzanne rose slowly from her chair. "Yes," she said, and uncertainly accepted Pechkov's outstretched hand.

"One other thing I must tell you," Pechkov said. "We don't know what Lemonnier's reaction to the letter will be. He's been with Vichy for a long time. He might shoot you as a spy. But we think he'll cooperate—if for no other reason other than the letter promises him more than ample reward and a high post in the Free French Army. That's another reason why this letter, signed by De Gaulle himself, must be delivered directly to him."

As they walked down the winding staircase, Pechkov said: "You know, of course, that Duncan has been recalled to Washington."

"Yes," Suzanne said, her mind still reeling from what she had been told in the secure room.

Pechkov said: "It would useful to know before you leave for Lang Son, why he has been recalled. It may have something to do with Indochina."

Suzanne did not reply.

"He's quite an impressive fellow," Pechkov said. "Very clever but perhaps a bit too idealistic for his own good. Are you in love with him?"

"Yes," Suzanne said.

"I hope someday there'll be something for you and Duncan. These days love does not seem to have a high priority."

"Yes," Suzanne said.


The Junker was droning southeast into the dawn when Major Rems took the seat beside Suzanne. A youngish man with a gentle face, Rems looked more like a university professor than an army intelligence officer.

"Here's the letter," he said, handing an envelope wrapped in a cotton sheath to Suzanne. "Pin it to the inside of your dress by your bosom. If you are intercepted try to destroy it. Wear these beads. The bag at the end of the string should be between your breasts. In it is a special lighter which you can use to incinerate the envelope quickly. There is also a plastic vial, which the American OSS calls the Q-pill. Chewing and swallowing it will give you a better death than torture by the Japanese."

Suzanne frowned, shocked at the matter-of-fact tone in which Rems spoke to her of her possible extinction. She turned around and tucked away the articles given her.

Rems said, "We're heading for Lungchow in Kwangsi, which is about twenty-five miles from the Indochina border. When the Japanese drove into Kwangsi Province, they took Nanning and pushed on toward Kunming, bypassing the Lungchow region. The region is now controlled by a local Chinese nationalist warlord who profits by the smuggling of opium and other goods across the border. We've bribed him to cooperate with us. You and I will disembark when the plane lands, and it will take off immediately. There are

Japanese Zeros based at Lang Son which may attack if we are spotted, although they will be puzzled as to what a German Junker transport is doing in China."

The Junker descended to less than five hundred feet when still distant from Lungchow and then bumped to a hard landing on a grass-covered runway. With the engines still running, Suzanne and Rems scrambled down a ladder and ran across the airfield to where three Chinese in uniform stood beside two trucks. Rems said something to one of the Chinese, who handed keys to him, and the three left on the larger of the two trucks, both old Fords. Rems got into the cab of the small truck with Suzanne beside him. Suzanne discarded her raincoat and took a conical straw hat out of her basket and donned it.

"Let me review once again what I told you in Chungking," Rems said. "I'll take you down the road to within one mile of the border. We will meet a Tay tribesman driving a donkey cart. You'll sit beside the Tay as if you were his wife. He'll take you across the border through the Nam Quan Pass right past the French border post at Dong Dang. The French need food and they allow the Tay, the Nung and the The peasants to bring food across the border without much checking. About two miles south on the road to Lang Son, you'll stop at a Tay village where there is a marketplace. A Tay in the uniform of a sergeant of the French colonial infantry will meet you. He'll have further instructions and take you to our contact."

The Tay peasant with his small cart was there when Rems drove the truck on the rutted road through the low brush-covered hills to within a mile of the border, where the land sloped up to the mountains. A small boy was sitting in the cart on a pile of melons. Suzanne took her place on the driver's seat beside the Tay, who greeted her with a broad and nearly toothless smile. As the donkey pulled the cart down the road, Suzanne looked back at the truck vanishing in a cloud of dust. "In two days, I'll be here waiting for you," Rems had said, but Suzanne wondered if she would see him again.

At the road adjacent to the Dong Dang border post beyond the mist-shrouded mountain pass, three Foreign Legionnaires in khaki and broad-brimmed hats were checking the passing carts drawn by bullocks and donkeys and examining packs of foodstuffs being carried on the backs of peasants. One of the Legionnaires glanced into their donkey cart, reached in and picked up a melon as the driver cursed, and grinning waved the cart through. Suzanne, trembling, her head bowed, sighed heavily.

It was almost midday when the donkey cart reached the Tay marketplace. French military trucks and once a weapons carrier, loaded with Japanese soldiers, had passed them on the hard red clay road. No attention had been paid to the donkey cart. Just beyond the entrance to the marketplace, the Tay beckoned for her to get off the cart, and then, to her dismay, drove off.

"*Bon matin*," a voice said. She turned to a dark-skinned man in a blue beret, wearing the uniform of the French colonial infantry. "Follow," he said. They walked to an old, battered truck, loaded with foodstuffs. A Tay woman in dress identical to Suzanne's left the cab of the truck and walked away. "My wife," the sergeant said. "Come."

Suzanne climbed into the cab beside the sergeant and they drove off.

"My name is Binh," the sergeant said, in heavily accented French. "I work for Colonel Dubois. He's on the general's staff."

My contact, Suzanne surmised.

"We are going to the Citadel in Lang Son," the sergeant said. "It's seven miles from here. Please bow your head, Madame, when we go through the gates. The guards will think you are my wife. General Lemonnaire's headquarters is in the Citadel. There are also barracks there for a company of French soldiers and another barracks for my colonial company. I often carry food in for my company. There are also houses in the Citadel for the families of the colonial noncoms. I'll take you to my house. Colonel Dubois will come to see you this afternoon."

Binh drove into the town of Lang Son, down a wide street lined with yellow-ocher houses, to the Citadel, a massive stockade topped by guard towers. French sentries waved the sergeant's truck through the gate without checking its load. Binh parked beside one of a row of small adobe houses. He led Suzanne into the two-room house, seated her in a bamboo chair, brought her a jug of water and a bowl of rice flaked with bits of meat and spices, and said: "Please wait."

Half an hour later, a short man with a gray brush mustache, wearing military fatigues, followed by Binh, strode into the hut, took off his white pith helmet, bowed and kissed Suzanne's hand. "I am Colonel Dubois," he said. "You are very courageous, Madame," he said. Suzanne looked up at him with a half smile and nodded.

Binh drew a cotton curtain across the doorway, and left.

"We have very little time," Dubois said. "There've been some strange happenings here. You must return tonight. I'll explain later. The letter …"

Suzanne got up from the chair, turned around, reached into her bosom, unpinned the envelope, and wordlessly handed it to Dubois.

"Thank you, Madame," Dubois said. "I'll be back before evening. Frankly, I don't know how the general will react. He knows nothing of this." He tapped the envelope with a crooked smile. "As a matter of fact, I don't know precisely what's in the letter. Everything has been on a need to know basis. The Chinese agent who told me of your coming said very little."

Suzanne was about to speak, but then decided against it.

Dubois slipped the letter into a side pocket, bowed and departed.

It was evening when Dubois returned, accompanied by Binh. Suzanne, who had been waiting with growing anxiety, pacing about the room and the kitchen at the rear, was startled by Dubois's appearance. The colonel had changed into blue full-dress uniform. He pulled out a bottle of red wine and sandwiches from a sack. "You'll need these," he said, as he seated himself at the small bamboo table beside Suzanne. "The wine is excellent."

The colonel said: "General Lemonnaire asks you to convey the message that he is in entire agreement with everything that General De Gaulle proposes. But you must leave tonight. The Japanese are up to something. We observed them this morning moving heavy army reinforcements north up Route Coloniale Numero 1 for their garrison here. We've also had a radio message from Saigon saying something is going on there as well. The Japanese may be preparing to stage a coup. They posted a unit with tanks a few hours ago at the road junction leading to the Citadel. They've never done that before." Dubois chortled grimly. "The Japanese commander invited the general to dinner tonight at his garrison headquarters. The general will not go. He thinks it may be some kind of a ruse. But I and three other officers are going. We cannot refuse."

Dubois rose. "Sergeant Binh here will lead you tonight out of the Citadel through the Officers' Gate behind the headquarters. My staff car will be parked beside the wall. It is a Japanese-made car. I'll remove the French flag, so you should be able to slip away. Binh will drive you over the border at Dong Dang. I've given Binh a *laissez-passer* signed by the general which will get you past our border guards."

Dubois clapped on his kepi cap. "*Bon soir*, Madame, and *bon chance*."

"*Bon soir, mon colonel*," Suzanne said, and as he walked to the door called out: "*Bon chance*."

Binh said, "We'll leave at nine o'clock when there is a change of the guards in the watchtowers."

Suzanne shared her sandwiches and wine with Binh, and precisely at nine o'clock, they began walking across the open square toward the headquarters. They were midway to the two-story adobe building when gunfire broke out on all sides of the Citadel. Mortar shells exploded near the headquarters and the military barracks.

"The Japanese are attacking!" Binh shouted. He seized Suzanne by the hand and together they ran back to the house. As Suzanne watched with wild staring eyes, Binh stripped off his uniform, stuffed it under a mat, and put on the shorts, tunic and sandals of a Tay peasant. "We cannot hold them off," he said between gasps. "They'll break into the Citadel soon."

Suzanne and Binh waited tensely as the firing continued through the night. The French garrison was returning fire from the watchtowers and the ramparts. The firing lessened gradually, and at dawn as they peered from the doorway, a tank broke through the main gate followed by three weapons carriers with mounted machine guns firing as they were swiveled about. Suzanne and Binh ducked back into the house and sat there, looking at each other, saying little, waiting. The gunfire ceased soon after.

Suzanne sat in the bamboo chair, her hands clasped, wondering what the Japanese would do. Would they discover she was a white woman … torture her to learn why she was there in disguise? Would the soldiers rampage through all the houses raping the women? She reached into her bosom and fingered the bag with the Q-pill.

At noon they heard someone bellowing before the houses. "They are calling us out," Binh said, fright in his eyes. "We must go out."

Suzanne followed Binh from the house. They joined Tay families and Vietnamese civilians who were being herded toward the military barracks on the other side of the square. There were more than one hundred French soldiers kneeling with their hands on their heads in front of their barracks. Several hundred Colonials were doing the same before their barracks on the adjacent side. Machine guns had been set up pointing at both groups.

With Binh close at her side, Suzanne, head bowed, looked out from beneath the brim of her straw hat.

From Lemonnaire's headquarters, a Japanese officer followed by a squad of soldiers strode out to the center, which was now blazing hot in the midday sun. Binh gasped. Behind them, a French officer, followed by two others, bareheaded and disheveled, arms tied behind them, were being led out. Suzanne could hear that the three officers were singing the Marseillaise.

"General Lemonnaire … Colonel Dubois … and his chief of staff," Binh said, his voice shaking.

The Japanese officer drew his sword. General Lemonnaire was forced to his knees. The Japanese officer held his sword high with two hands. He beheaded the general with a single stroke.

Weeping softly, Suzanne averted her eyes as the other officers were beheaded in turn by others in the Japanese squad. The kneeling French soldiers were singing the Marseillaise, when machine guns opened up on them. Suzanne turned about, unable to bear the sight.

"It's a massacre," Binh cried.

With fixed bayonets the Japanese jabbed at the French soldiers lying in heaps where they had been gunned down.

They then herded the Colonial soldiers back into their barracks and the spectators into their houses.

Suzanne lay face down on a mat in Binh's house. He sat in a chair, stunned. After a time, Suzanne asked: "Why? Why?"

"Punishment for resisting them, I suppose," Binh said. "They also wanted us to see how white men can be put down."

It was in the late afternoon when they heard the first planes. Binh ran to his doorway. "American planes," he shouted. "They're attacking the airfield."

"Chennault ... the Fourteenth Air Force," Suzanne said. "Thank God!"

At that moment the first bombs struck the Citadel.

"No, no," Binh cried out in a pleading voice. "They're hitting the wrong target."

Another wave of B-25 bombers swept over the Citadel, and the military barracks exploded in flames.

"The men of my company are in that barracks. They've been killed," Binh sobbed.

Japanese soldiers were running out of the Citadel through the main gate as the bombers made another run.

"Come! Come!" Binh shouted to Suzanne. She stumbled after him across the empty square engulfed in smoke. The headquarters was partially destroyed. Binh took Suzanne by the hand and led her around the headquarters to the small Officer's Gate, which was intact, and unlocked it.

"The gods are with us. The car ... it's still here," Binh said, as he ran to the side of the ash-covered vehicle.

Binh drove the car along the wall and down a side road. There were Japanese milling about less than fifty yards from the Citadel, but none of them moved to stop the car. A P-40 swept low over them strafing a line of Japanese weapons carriers. With Suzanne crouching down so as not be seen, Binh drove out, twisting the car onto a back road skirting Lang Son to Route Colonial Numero 4.

"The Japanese will be moving up the road toward Dong Dang very soon," Binh said. "We'll try to cross the border before then. I have the *laissez-passer* the Colonel gave me to show to the French border guards."

"But your wife?" Suzanne asked.

"She'll be safe in the village ... safer than being with us."

There was no traffic on the road as the car approached Dong Dang. When they pulled up to the border crossing, they saw there were no guards at the post on the road.

"The Legionnaires have heard what's happened at Lang Son and pulled back into their fort to get ready for a Japanese attack," Binh said, as he gunned the car across the unguarded border.

Rehms was not at the designated place, a mile up the road, so they continued on to the airfield at Lungchow. The Junker was on the runway, about to take off, and Rems was getting into his truck when he saw the car wheel up, and ran toward it. Suzanne, limping heavily, walked to him, and fell into his arms sobbing.

# -6-

## Chungking
## April 6, 1945

UPON ARRIVING IN KUNMING, Duncan spent most of a restive day at the OSS Staff House waiting for a break in the fog enveloping Chungking. When his C-46 touched down at the flare-lit Chungking airfield after two failed passes, Duncan, bone weary and shaken by the precarious landing, went gratefully to his quarters in the American Embassy compound and straight to bed. He awoke early in the morning, his mind on Suzanne. At seven o'clock he telephoned her, thinking: This could be our last time together.

"Travis! It's you. You're back. Wonderful!" Suzanne exclaimed after a sleepy hello.

"Yes. Can I drop by?"

"Of course. Come for lunch."

"I can't. Can I just pop in ... say at nine o'clock?"

When Duncan knocked, Suzanne threw open the door and embraced him. She was in black silk pajamas, her hair tied back in a single braid. Taking his arm, she led him into the apartment. "I have coffee and toast ready." She disappeared and returned with a tray, which she placed on the chow table before the couch.

Duncan thought she looked very drawn, not her buoyant self. There were deep lines under her eyes.

Suzanne was pouring coffee into his cup when Duncan said, "You're an M.5 agent."

Her hand steady, Suzanne tilted the pot to her own cup, filling it to the brim. She picked it up, braced herself in a corner of the couch against a satin pillow, and said, "So, you're surprised? Shocked?"

"You surprised me once before … when you jumped into bed with me so quickly. I now understand why," Duncan said curtly.

Suzanne flushed, and lit a cigarette. "I don't know what you've been told. But it shouldn't have come as a shock that I do my bit for French intelligence. I've been with the Free French. You knew that. We all work for De Gaulle."

"Yes … and here you work to colonize Indochina once again."

Suzanne put out her cigarette, half-smoked, in the ashtray on the side table beside the couch and threw up her hands. "De Gaulle has his visions of empire," she said. "Some of us simply work to restore France itself."

Suzanne swung her legs off the couch and sat erect, her hands clasped, eyes flaring. "Travis, let me tell you what I'm all about. So get off your high horse and listen. Right now, I'm concerned only about rescuing our people in Indochina. You Americans could help us. There are forty thousand French civilians trapped there … men, women, children crying out for help. Since the March 9 coup, many of the men have been rounded up by the Japanese. Anyone suspected of Gaullist sympathies is beheaded. On the China border our forts have been overrun by the Japanese. At Lang Son the commanding general and his deputies were beheaded … their French soldiers massacred. Chennault's planes intervened, but too late. In any case they struck the wrong targets in the Citadel and killed hundreds of our colonial infantry. I know because … "

Suzanne hesitated. Pechkov had sworn her to silence about her mission to Lang Son so as to guard against revelation of the De Gaulle letter. She leaped up and paced the room, her lips compressed, and then wheeled about to Duncan: "Our troops are now in retreat from the other frontier forts and from the Hanoi sector, thousands of them trying to escape to China. They're being cut to pieces by the Japanese. But that doesn't seem to concern your president. He denies help to our people because of his frustration with De Gaulle. Our troops are getting no cover from Chennault's air force. Chennault isn't even permitted to drop supplies to them!"

Taken aback by Suzanne's outburst, Duncan shifted about uneasily on the couch and then raised his hand to still her tirade. He said, "I can tell you the president would lift the ban on military support if De Gaulle agreed to independence for Indochina. The president imposed it simply because he doesn't want to have anything to do with restoring French colonialism."

"Yes, he debates with De Gaulle while thousands of our people are dying," Suzanne said bitterly. "As for De Gaulle? Our savior. The cables from Paris are unbelievable. What does he say about the massacre of our troops? *The shedding of French blood will reinforce our claim to Indochina.* My God! All he seems to worry about now is that conference of the United Nations in three weeks—afraid your president will insist on a trusteeship for Indochina."

Suzanne picked up the pillow lying beside her and hurled it across the room. "As for me, I'm going to do anything … anything I can to help our people."

Duncan, calmer, gulped his coffee, and looked intently at Suzanne. "Okay, okay. But why were you assigned to me? Why did I become a target for M.5?"

Suzanne sighed, her eyes averted. "Of course the mission was interested in you, what with Washington deciding our future in Indochina. Pechkov knew—as head of the Political Section at the embassy—you were seeing the cable traffic with Washington. You're also well informed about developments inside Indochina. You've had contacts with the Annamese exiles. You were an obvious key source. Pechkov pressed me. But I didn't go back to him with anything that might embarrass you. You must know that." Suzanne searched Duncan's features for understanding.

Duncan nodded.

"All right, now I'm going to tell you something about yourself," Suzanne said in a lowered voice. "If the *Sûreté* learns I've leaked this to you, I'm in very great trouble. Never mind that." Standing before Duncan, hands on her hips, she said, "Travis, the *Sûreté* has been keeping tabs on you for years. When our Free French took Paris at the end of August they confiscated the files at the *Sûreté Generale*. Your file was sent here. The dossier is very detailed—everything about your contacts with Annamese exiles while you were studying at the Sorbonne. Of course the *Sûreté* was watching you, the son of the

American ambassador." She lifted an eyebrow. "And there were also details about the episode in Saigon in 1935 ... the affair with the Annamese woman."

His eyes narrowing, Duncan jumped up. "I don't care to hear about that," he said roughly. "I'll go now. Goodbye, Madame Dumont."

"Wait, Travis, just one moment more," Suzanne said, holding up her hand. "For me it doesn't end so easily. Yes, I misled you about some things. But I didn't mislead you when I gave you my love. Yes, I jumped into bed with you, as you put it," she said with a twisted smile. "I enjoyed it. You're a good lover, Travis. It was my first sex in a long time. But it was more than that. I ... "

Duncan was walking toward the door when Suzanne called out: "Wait. there's one other thing, something important I must tell you. Travis, Mai Khang is alive."

Duncan spun about.

"She was released from Poulo Condore in the general amnesty of 1936 decreed by the Popular Front Government. The information given you that she'd been executed was planted by the *Sûreté* so you wouldn't try to contact her again."

"My God, Suzanne, is this true? Not a trick? The exiles here knew nothing of her. There was nothing about her in the archives."

"It's true. Mai Khang has been tracked by the *Sûreté* for years. When she was released, she was exiled to Madagascar with the other political prisoners. But she escaped. She now goes by the name of Trinh Mai. She's a senior cadre of the Indochinese Communist Party. The exiles you talked to ... even if they knew, they wouldn't reveal anything to you—a foreigner—about one of their top leaders in the underground."

"Where is she?" Duncan asked, his eyes wide and staring, "What about her father?"

"Her father died in prison. Our people don't know where she is. They think she's in South China with other Annamese revolutionaries."

"Suzanne ... how I can find her? "

Suzanne shook her head. "I don't know. The French have no information. If she's in China, there's only one source who could help you find her quickly. That's Tai Li, of course."

Duncan nodded. He went to Suzanne; kissed her on the forehead, and breathing heavily, without speaking, walked out of the apartment.

As the door closed on Duncan, Suzanne sat bent over on the couch, with fingertips on her lips. She'd lost him, she thought. Despite Pechkov's demands, possibly out of guilt or maybe because she loved him and was afraid of losing him, she had never probed deeply into his embassy affairs. He seemed to realize that. He might have forgiven her deception. But why ... why then had she felt compelled to tell him about Mai? Why awaken his old desire?

Agitated, Suzanne lit a cigarette and went to the sideboard where she poured a glass of red wine. She raised the glass but then put it down, spilling some. Perhaps it was because she knew instinctively it was better this way. She'd never questioned him about the past, but she knew that no matter what he told her, there was a part of Duncan she didn't possess. The pain on those two nights when, in his sleep, she heard him mutter Mai's name. Better that he meet Mai and exorcise the ghost. Perhaps ... perhaps he'll come back. She lifted the glass and drained the remaining wine. Was Mai still so beautiful after running in the underground all these years?

In the afternoon, at his embassy quarters, acting on Donovan's instructions, Duncan telephoned for an appointment with Colonel Holdt, the OSS chief. Before picking up the phone, he had wandered about the apartment, gazed out the windows muttering: *"All those years."* As he went to his meeting with Holdt, he agonized; he would not divert himself from tracking Ho Chi Minh to search for Mai. Yet there was a link. If Mai was in South China, perhaps she could lead him to Ho. But how to find her? Obtaining the help of Tai Li, the chief of Chiang Kai-shek's secret police, wouldn't be easy. He'd never met Tai Li, a remote, feared figure. Officially, Tai Li's was the director of the Bureau of Investigation and Statistics, but in fact, he was much more. He disposed thousands of heavily armed agents at more than four hundred stations throughout what remained of Nationalist China. With Chiang Kai-shek's license, he'd converted the truncated nation into a virtual police state.

Colonel Holdt, an imposing man with thin blonde hair graying at the temples, greeted Duncan warmly in his office in the hostel of Detachment 202. Duncan knew Holdt slightly, having met him at embassy meetings at which chiefs of the American agencies in the Chinese capital coordinated their activities. He glanced at a picture of Donovan on Holdt's desk.

"My law partner before the war … quite a guy," Holdt said as he waved Duncan to a chair. They all seem to be lawyers, Duncan thought.

"All this is a little different from the diplomatic life," Holdt said grinning as he took Duncan's measure. "You've really taken on a tough one. Getting to Ho Chi Minh won't be easy. We've arranged for you to fly to Kunming tomorrow. Our people there will get you to Ch'ing Hsi on the border. We flew Ho there after he met with Chennault. He agreed to set up an intelligence network for us. But then we lost trace of him. He may have crossed the border into Tonkin. You'll have to pick up his trail in Ch'ing Hsi."

"Here's a photograph of him taken when he met with Chennault," Holdt said, leaning across his desk to show Duncan the print. "He's a funny, skinny little guy. In return for rescuing that pilot, Shaw, he asked for only two things: A signed photograph of Chennault and six new Colt .45 caliber pistols in their original wrappings. Why in their original wrappings I don't know."

Duncan said, "Thanks, Colonel. That's very helpful." He hesitated and then said, "Colonel, I need your help in locating a contact who could lead us to Ho Chi Minh. She's an Annamese woman I knew in Saigon in 1935. She's now known as Trinh Mai."

Holdt nodded and leaned back in his swivel chair.

He knows about Mai, Duncan guessed, and went on: "I believe she's somewhere in South China. I'm told she's now a senior cadre of the Indochinese Communist Party. She would know how I could get to Ho Chi Minh."

"If she's in China, she's probably in Kwangsi, somewhere close to the Indochina border," Holdt said reflectively. "The warlord there, Marshal Chang Fa-kwei, has been sheltering some of the Annamese nationalists. With the Japs now in occupation of the French posts, he needs the help of the Annamese guerrillas operating along the border."

Duncan nodded. "I know something about Chang. He's played a double game with the Annamese and the French. There's a link between him and Ho Chi Minh. In 1942 he put Ho—who was then known as Nguyen Ai Quoc—into his Tienpao Prison, claiming he was a spy. Ho was kept in chains and almost died there. That made the French happy. But the next year Chang released Ho in return for help in organizing a puppet outfit, the Viet Nam Revolutionary League—the Dong Minh Hoi. The League has been his lever in dealing with the Annamese nationalists. Can we get Chang's help?"

"Possibly, through Tai Li. He works closely with Chang. They're in cahoots on the opium traffic coming through Burma and Thailand. He keeps tabs on the Annamese nationalists through Chang. If Tai Li wanted to find this Annamese woman, he would go to Chang."

"Can we get to Tai Li?"

"We don't deal directly with him in this screwed-up Allied intelligence set-up. We do liaison with him through SACO, the coordinating agency for intelligence operations. It's crazy but Tai Li is director of the agency. Captain Miles of the U.S. Naval Group is deputy director. Miles keeps him happy with plenty of supplies for his police units, a lot of which probably goes into the black market. I'll talk to Miles for you."

When Duncan left his office, Holdt swiveled his chair around and chuckled as he thought, the guy is flipping between Dumont and that Annamese woman. But he'll be okay as long as he keeps his cock in his pants. He's green, but learning fast, impressive dossier. And he's right. Trinh Mai might be very helpful. We don't have any other lead to Ho. Holdt picked up his phone and called Captain Miles.

Holdt telephoned Duncan in the afternoon. "Tai Li will see you. Miles told His Excellency that you're a special assistant to Donovan. Tai Li was impressed. Agreed to see you. Surprised the hell out of Miles. Tai Li rarely sees foreigners. A driver from the U.S. Naval Group will pick up you up at 9 o'clock tonight and take you to Tai Li's residence. Check with me afterward."

Duncan sat beside the Navy driver as he drove the jeep on a circle road up to one of the city's mountain peaks. They passed through a concrete tunnel and parked before the spiked iron gate of a walled compound, guarded by two soldiers carrying Thompson submachine guns and an officer with sidearms. Duncan was escorted into a foreign-style house, along a thickly carpeted corridor lined with huge porcelain vases, to a mahogany paneled drawing room, and seated before a charcoal fire. Tai Li entered a few minutes later. He was a rather tubby man, who looked to be in his late forties. He was dressed in a satin fur-lined gown, over which he wore the traditional wide-sleeved jacket.

"Please be seated," he said in Chinese as Duncan rose to greet him. "Do you speak German?" he asked.

"Unfortunately, no," Duncan said.

"You probably know I took my early military training in China under German instructors," Tai Li said. A white-gowned servant entered with tea. "Lung-ching tea," Tai Li said, sniffing his cup. "Difficult to get these days. Grown in the Japanese-occupied areas." He sipped his tea and studied Duncan. "Captain Miles told me of your interest in making certain contacts. Before we discuss that matter, please come with me."

Tai Li led Duncan into an adjoining room, an office where there was a large wall map of the Far East. He picked up a pointer from a redwood desk and turned to Duncan.

"Advancing from East China, the Japanese have attained the goals of their Ichigo offensive," Tai Li said as he pointed at the map. "They've taken Kweilin and Chennault's other forward air bases. Now they're pushing through Kwangsi. Their target is Kunming and then Chungking. The Generalissimo is already making plans to move the capital. Also, we're in danger of being overwhelmed from another direction. We have intelligence reports that Tokyo intends to withdraw their Southern Area forces into China. About seven hundred thousand troops from Thailand, Burma, Malaya and Indonesia will pass through Indochina and link up with their China command. China will become the center of their operations on the Asian continent. The March 9 coup that General Tsuchihashi staged in Indochina was designed to prepare the way."

Tai Li put down his pointer. "There doesn't seem to be any realization in Washington of the gravity of our situation. We're in danger of total collapse."

Tai Li tucked his hands into the sleeves of his jacket and confronted Duncan, his dark eyes hard and cold: "Meanwhile, you Americans are concentrating all your military efforts in the Pacific. If we're to hold off the Japanese, we need reinforcements. A diversionary American landing on the South China coast would strengthen our position immeasurably. Chennault's Fourteenth Air Force must be reinforced so he can give us more support in defense of Kunming. Your B-29 bombers based in the islands should strike at the Japanese columns coming south and west from Hankow. This is of paramount importance."

Tai Li leaned back, his eyes narrowed. "Do you follow me, Mr. Duncan?"

Duncan glanced at the map, nodded, took out a notebook and busily made notes. He had listened, not believing much of what he had been told, and decided he must play the gullible American.

"Mr. Duncan, your General Donovan is very influential with the president. It would be helpful if you reported our situation directly to him. Your embassy doesn't seem to be conveying our warning forcefully enough. This is a time for action by the president, not debate within the State Department. Can you give me your assurance, Mr. Duncan, that you will do this for us?"

"I understand, sir. I will pass your message directly to General Donovan," Duncan said.

"Come then," Tai Li said, and led Duncan back to the reception room. "As for this other matter, Mr. Duncan. If he can, Marshal

Chang Fa-kwei will be of assistance to you. I understand you are going to Kunming. Wait there until you receive a message from me or the general."

Holdt listened with a trace of amusement to Duncan's account of his meeting with Tai Li, and then extended his hand. "Travis, you handled it just right," he said. "You must know. We have the same intelligence reports as Tai Li about the possibility of a withdrawal of the Japanese Southern Area troops into China. So far there's been no sign of such a move. Chennault has bombed out the rail line from Hanoi to Nanning in South China. The Japs would need the railroad to make such a huge move. As for the Jap push toward Kunming, Tai Li is just making another end run around our embassy. We won't buy it, of course. We have no intention of diverting forces needed more urgently elsewhere." He laughed. "Fortunately, Tai Li doesn't know it's you who persuaded Washington that the Nationalists can stop the Jap offensive, if they commit those troops the Gimmo is using to blockade the Communists."

Holdt got up from behind his desk and walked around to face Duncan. "Do as you promised. Pass Tai Li's message to Donovan," he said. "He'll know how to deal with it. That's Tai Li's price for putting you on the trail to Trinh Mai and Ho Chi Minh." Holdt looked keenly at Duncan. "Trinh Mai may be of help to us. But don't confuse your priorities. Your job is to get to Ho."

"I know that," Duncan snapped back, flushing.

"Okay … okay …" Holdt said. "We booked you on a plane leaving in the morning. On arrival in Kunming contact the OSS detachment commander, Colonel Hopkins. He's been in contact with the Vietminh."

In the evening, at his quarters in the embassy compound, Duncan stretched out on his bed and fingering his white jade tried to calm himself and sort out the tumble of events. He regretted his outburst at Suzanne. His anger had stemmed more from bruised ego than from proof she'd betrayed him. By revealing that Mai lived, she'd exposed herself to retribution by the *Sûreté*. He was indebted to her and in a rush of emotion thought of holding her once more in his arms. He was overjoyed by the revelation that Mai Khang was alive. He had been so eager for the long-sought reunion, but now suddenly he was apprehensive. Would she be forgiving of his failure to shield her from the *Sûreté*? What would she be like after that hellish year of imprisonment at Poulo Condore followed by the harsh life in the Communist underground? Over the years Mai had become more of a figure of his dreams than real. Was he still in love with her or had she become simply an icon in his obsession with Vietnam?

Duncan poured himself a brandy, but left it untouched; he put on his trench coat and went out into the compound, which was shrouded in fog off the river. Walking about, he waved to the Marine guard stationed inside the gate. He had become friendly with the guard on duty, Corporal Elmer McCloskey. The young Marine had been wounded in the landing of the Second Marine Division on Tarawa in Novenber 1943; more than one thousand marines had been killed and two thousand wounded taking the Pacific atoll. Yet McCloskey had volunteered to return to duty in the Pacific. Duncan paused to look out over the river, and he thought about McCloskey and what the marine had been through. When Duncan boarded the plane in the morning his mind was more ordered, fixed on his mission.

# - 7 -

**Kunming**
**April 8, 1945**

AIRCRAFT WERE STACKED OVER the base of the Fourteenth Air Force waiting to land when Duncan's transport circled over Kunming. His transport was diverted to a holding pattern to the northwest over Lake Tianchih on the hilly plateau. After fifteen minutes the C-46 received clearance and glided past the tower on West Mountain, the home safe marker for transports coming over The Hump and pilots returning from combat missions. As his plane touched down, Duncan saw B-25 bombers and P-40 fighters in tight formations lined up on the runways, taking off in quick succession to attack the Japanese columns pushing west from Kweilin.

A driver in an army jeep was waiting and Duncan was taken to the OSS Staff Hostel, a converted university dormitory northwest of walled Kunming, where he dropped his baggage before being driven to the mud-walled compound of OSS headquarters.

In an office on the second floor of a tile-roofed building, Colonel Hopkins, a tall, pleasant-faced man, rose from behind his battered wooden desk and greeted Duncan genially. He got straight down to business in a summary manner that smacked of his lawyerly background.

"We don't know where Ho Chi Minh is," Hopkins said. "We took him down to Ch'ing Hsi near the border on an L-5 taxi plane. We gave him a Chinese radio operator and equipment, including a hundred and fifty pound hand-crank-powered radio, for use in setting up an intelligence network. But then Ho, with his guerrillas and the radio operator, disappeared. They may have crossed the border into Tonkin."

Hopkins tossed a manila file to Duncan. "As you'll see from that, we know virtually nothing about Ho Chi Minh. We did have a contact here last year with the Vietminh. It was with an Annamese, Pham Viet Tu. According to Pham, the Vietminh is a coalition of Vietnamese nationalist parties. It was formed in 1941 by a Nguyen Ai Quoc."

"That's Ho Chi Minh," Duncan said.

"Okay. Pham begged us to forward a letter to Washington with two requests: Show sympathy for their independence movement and give them arms for guerrilla operations against the Japanese. We agreed to do that—off the record we helped them draft the letter— and we delivered it to Bill Langdon, our consul-general here. After we prodded Langdon, he talked to Pham. Langdon told him he'd pass along their letter. But then he knocked Pham on his ass by saying that it didn't make sense for the United States while rescuing France from the Germans to undermine its Empire. As for arms, we didn't give them any because headquarters was afraid they'd use them against the French."

Hopkins snorted: "But as a token for rescuing Shaw, we did give Ho Chi Minh those six Colt .45 caliber pistols he asked for—with twenty thousand rounds of ammunition."

Duncan closed the file and asked: "What do I do now?"

"We've asked Chang Fa-kwei to clear you for Ch'ing Hsi. I expect Chang will agree. He owes us plenty. We lifted him and his staff out of Kweilin just before the Japs took the city. We lost two fighter pilots on that operation."

Duncan said, "I know. I met one of them in Washington … a Major Chivers. He's pretty bunged up, but recovering and hot to come back."

"These kids flying with Chennault are all like that," Hopkins said. He extended his hand. I'll call you as soon as we hear from Chang. There's nothing you can do except wait. Right now I think you could use a little diversion. I'll pick you up tonight at the hostel at about six o'clock."

Duncan agreed gratefully. Leaving the headquarters, he asked to be dropped off in the center of Kunming. Duncan walked restlessly through the shabby streets lined with tin-roofed shacks and then walked up Five Flowers Hill to the ancient Wu Hua Si temple. He sat cross-legged before a towering golden Buddha and was moved to say a short prayer that he would find Ho and somehow his search would lead to Mai.

Duncan, in a new suit of khakis without insignia, climbed in beside Colonel Hopkins at the wheel of his jeep, and they drove into Kunming, turning off onto one of the few paved roads and parked before a modern building surrounded by a tall wooden fence topped with spikes. "This is Mei Yuan, where the women OSS agents live," Hopkins said.

"Women OSS ... here?" Duncan exclaimed.

"Yup ... ladies of the Women's Army Auxiliary Corps— WACS—detailed to us. They work in our radio-monitoring center. They correlate enemy transmissions, fix map coordinates of Jap targets for our bombers and transmit weather reports. Right now there's a special team triangulating Japanese POW camps on the mainland so we can pick up our guys fast when the war ends. Almost all these gals read Chinese. Some know Japanese."

Hopkins honked the horn and drove into the compound as two Chinese with rifles slung over their shoulders opened the gate. Hopkins led the way through a garden with stands of bamboo and fragrant with blossoming plum trees into a reception hall, where they were seated by a Chinese woman servant in a long white gown.

Hopkins rose calling out: "Hi Betty," as a young blonde woman in khakis wearing the WAC shoulder patch came skipping down the stairs and embraced him. Obviously, Sergeant Betty Hutchinson was Hopkins' steady girlfriend, Duncan thought, as he smiled at her during the introduction.

On a large veranda on the upper floor, there was a dancing party in progress, and Duncan, charmed, listened to phonograph records of popular tunes current in the States which he had never heard. As he circulated, he found that several of the women, like Betty, were daughters of China missionaries, and he joked with them gaily in colloquial Chinese.

"You made a big hit," Hopkins told him as they left Mei Yuan. "Ginny—the tall one with the great shape—asked if you'd like to go out on the lake on one of those pleasure junks. Those are great parties. Chinese flutes ... noodles and beer ... and you can never tell what other action. I told her and Betty we'd check back tomorrow."

At noon the next day, Hopkins came to his room at the hostel. "We're in luck," he said. No, not the lake ... you've got clearance from Chang's headquarters. We're to fly you to Tepao. We have an Air-Ground Aid Section there that monitors Japanese movements in Indochina. It's in the western corner of Kwangsi, about thirty miles from the Tonkin border. The Tepao airstrip is not far from Ch'ing Hsi. The AGAS people will pick you up."

The C-47 bumped down on the short dirt airstrip in the jungle at Tepao. A weapons carrier came alongside the plane as it landed. Duncan threw his duffel into the rear of the truck and climbed in. The driver, a slender young man in camouflage fatigues wearing horned-rimmed glasses, stuck out his hand. "Welcome, Mr. Duncan, to the bung hole end-of-the-line. I'm Major Jim Roberts, CO of the AGAS unit."

As they bounced over a rough grass track toward the AGAS camp, Duncan clutched the side of the truck and asked: "How are things?"

"Lousy," Roberts said. "Before the Jap coup, we were getting beautiful intelligence from Free French agents ... Jap troop movements, bombing targets, weather. The British were dropping supplies to the agents. But we've heard nothing from them for a couple of weeks. I guess they got wiped out. We're hoping the Vietminh will set up a new network. Their guerrillas are now in control of six provinces of Tonkin."

As the jeep turned into the tent encampment, the major said: "There's a Chinese officer waiting to see you. He's one of our liaisons with Marshal Chang."

The major led Duncan to his headquarters tent where a round-faced Chinese, dressed in a blue civilian tunic and baggy pants, was leaning against a radio stack smoking a limp cigarette. "This is Marshal Lee of the Special Forces," the major said to Duncan. "I'll be back for you."

"Welcome," Lee said in Chinese. "Marshal Chang Fa-kwei sends his greetings. He's been very busy. Otherwise, he would be here to welcome you. We know that General Donovan is a great friend of China."

Duncan bowed slightly. "Thank you. Please convey the respects of General Donovan to General Chang Fa-kwei, as well as my own."

"Good," Lee said, smiling broadly. "We understand you wish to meet with certain Annamites. This has been arranged. Our Dong Minh Hoi will be there. We will leave tomorrow night at five o'clock for Ch'ing Hsi. It is about twelve miles from here, quite close to the border."

"Thank you," Duncan said, wondering if members of the Dong Minh Hoi, the nationalist faction fostered by the Chinese, would be the only Annamites at the meeting. Would they lead him to Ho or Mai?

Promptly at five, Duncan was picked up by Lee in an American jeep and they drove south on the narrow muddy road to Ch'ing Hsi, weaving past black-clad peasants in conical straw hats, some in donkey carts and others leading water buffalo or pushing wheelbarrows. It was twilight when they approached the old dingy city. Ch'ing Hsi was enshrouded in the *crachin*, the almost continuous drizzle just before the onset of the hot season.

"The Annamese nationalists work in Ch'ing Hsi under our protection," Lee said.

"Ho Chi Minh is here?" Duncan asked.

Lee laughed. "Ho Chi Minh? We have known him as Nguyen Ai Quoc. No. Ho crossed the border several days ago with some of his guerrillas. Mac Sin, a Chinese radio operator who works for your OSS, went with him. The AGAS major gave them radio equipment and other supplies."

Lee drove through the dark twisting alleys of Ch'ing Hsi, past open shops lit with oil lanterns, and parked outside a two-story wooden building on Chin Pi Street. "This is the Indochina Café," Lee said, as he chained the wheel of the jeep. "It is owned by Sung Minh Fang, a good friend of Ho Chi Minh."

In the café Chinese soldiers and civilians sat at small round tables drinking beer and tea. An elderly Chinese waiter seated them, bowed and said to Lee with a knowing smile: "Sung Minh Fang has prepared your special menu."

Lee nodded, and said to Duncan: "I'll return soon." He was back in a few minutes, and led Duncan up the back stairs to a room illuminated only by two oil lamps set on an oblong table behind which Duncan made out three figures who rose as he entered. Duncan tensed as he recognized Mai standing there between two men. She extended her hand to him across the table.

Since Suzanne's revelation, this was the moment he had played over and over in his imagination, but so differently from this reality. A quick handshake across a table, not an embrace, not the intimate moment in which to tell her of how he had longed to be with her again, to beg forgiveness for failing to safeguard her.

"Welcome," Mai said. "These are my comrades, Duc Hien Tuong and Tran Huy Khang." As Duncan shook hands with the two men, he glanced at Mai, his eyes becoming more accustomed to the dim light. She was in Annamese peasant dress, her hair tied back in a thick ponytail. The oval face with its exquisite profile and luminous eyes seemed unchanged, but a fierce beauty had replaced the delicate demeanor.

"You are well, Travis?" Mai asked in a soft voice, as Duncan and Lee seated themselves opposite.

"Yes, and you? Your father ...?"

"I'm well. My father is dead. He was executed by the French on Poulo Condore."

"I grieve for him. I'm grateful that you escaped."

"My father and I were tried by a French military tribunal. We were sentenced to death. We were offered our freedom if we would expose our network in Saigon. But my father did not bend. I was spared by the amnesty arranged by the Popular Front government."

Truong, leaning across the table, interrupted: "It was very good that Trinh Mai was saved. But the amnesty came as a consequence of one of our most serious mistakes." His voice took on a liturgical quality. "We followed the Comintern's Dimitrov Line. We accepted promises made by the Popular Front for reforms in our country. We gave up our anti-colonial struggle for three years to make common cause with the French Communist Party. The reforms were a farce. We will not make such a mistake again."

"My comrade is correct," Mai said. "But now, Mr. Duncan, we've been told you wish to meet with Ho Chi Minh. Please tell us why."

"I'm a special assistant to General Donovan, the head of the Office of Strategic Services. He reports to our president. Your representatives have been in touch with the OSS and asked the United States for assistance. General Donovan cannot make a recommendation without further information. It would be useful if we knew your leaders better. Our agents have met with Ho Chi Minh. Yet we wish to know him even better and more about his policies. As the representative of General Donovan, I'd like to meet with him. Hear his views in greater detail."

Mai glanced at her companions, who nodded. "We know of you from our Vietnamese comrades in Chungking," Truong said.

"Yes, I have spoken to them quite often," Duncan replied, wondering with a stab of anguish why Mai had not contacted him.

"You will have an answer in two days," Mai said, and stood up, signaling an end to the meeting. Duncan thought her smile was less perfunctory when she took his hand once again to say goodbye. Would he see her again? Would they ever be alone? These questions tormented Duncan as he followed Lee down the stairs, stumbling on the bottom step.

At their table, Lee lit a cigarette and ordered two bottles of Kunming Beer and pork dumplings. "You have met three very senior Vietminh cadres tonight. I trust you are pleased?"

"Yes ... yes, thank you," Duncan said, collecting himself. "I suppose they're members of the Indochinese Communist Party?"

"Not all of them. Trinh Mai and Duc Hien Truong are members of the central committee of the Communist Party. Tran Huy Khang is a member of our Dong Minh Hoi. There are several factions in the Vietminh." He puffed several times on his cigarette before adding: "I suppose the Communists are now in control."

"Does Ho Chi Minh head the Vietminh?"

"That is unclear. Ho concerns himself mainly with political affairs. Vo Nguyen Giap runs the guerrilla operations. They have their differences. Truong, who you met tonight, is one of his men. Mai is close to Ho."

"Does Chiang Kai-shek approve of you working with the Communists? It seems strange."

Lee shrugged. "Marshal Chang Fa-kwei has his own views. He thinks only of driving the Japanese and the French out of Indochina ... of protecting his province. The Annamites have a right to independence. We've had enough of colonialism in Asia."

Duncan was not surprised by Lee's remarks. The embassy in Chungking had received reports of a growing separatist movement among the warlords in the south. "Do you think Ho will receive me?" he asked.

Lee picked at a dumpling with his chopsticks. "Try one, Mr. Duncan. These *chiao-tze* are excellent. A specialty of the teahouse. Oh, yes. Ho Chi Minh will do anything to get American support. Others in the Vietminh, I am told, doubt that it is possible. You will see for yourself."

# -8-

TEPAO
APRIL 11, 1945

SHORTLY AFTER DAWN, Duncan was awakened in his tent in the Tepao compound by Major Roberts shaking his shoulder. The major handed him a mug of steaming coffee. "I have orders to get you ready to cross the border. Get breakfast in the mess and come to my quarters. When Duncan entered the major's tent, he found that Roberts had already laid out a black Chinese peasant shirt and pants, rubber-soled sandals, a small backpack and other gear. "Ever been camping?" the major asked, chuckling.

"I was an Eagle Scout," Duncan said grinning. "Done a lot of cross-country skiing in Colorado," he added hastily.

Roberts sighed. "They tell me you have a long, hard walk ahead of you. You'll have to travel light. So I'm giving you this poncho. It unbuttons into a mat. You'll want to sleep under it. This fucking drizzle will keep up for the next couple of weeks." He held up a carbine. "Know how to use this?"

Duncan shook his head. "I've used a shotgun ... hunted quail in Virginia." Seeing the expression on Roberts' face, he said reassuringly: "I was a good shot."

The Major stared at Duncan incredulously. "I'm not asking any questions. But I don't get it. Why in hell did they pick you for a border crossing in this god-awful sector?" He shook his head. "I'll show you how to handle the carbine. This baby may be handy if you run into bandits. And there are plenty of murderous types roaming the border. Some of them operate in gangs of as many as three or four hundred, mostly Chinese army deserters and Annamite renegades. The big gangs are well armed."

"What about the Japanese?" Duncan asked.

"Not a great problem right now. Their closest post is at Cao Bang, about thirty miles southwest of where you'll cross the border. The Japs usually don't venture into where you're going. It's dense jungle country. The French call it the Mountain Citadel."

"Do you know when I'm supposed to take off?" Duncan asked.

"No. I was told you don't have clearance yet."

Early in the morning of April 12 Colonel Lee arrived at the Tepao compound in his jeep with two soldiers in the back seat toting machine pistols. He found Duncan in his tent sitting on his cot garbed in his peasant outfit. "Not entirely convincing," the Chinese said, unsuccessfully suppressing a laugh as he surveyed him. "But good enough, I suppose. Come, we have an appointment."

Lee maneuvered the jeep expertly over the rutted road, which grew progressively worse as they bypassed Ch'ing Hsi and entered a thatched hut village surrounded by a low mud wall. Naked children and barking dogs swarmed about as Lee climbed down. "This is Tichou," Lee said "The road ends here. We're ten miles from the border." Suddenly, a group of men in black wearing conical straw hats and carrying rifles materialized around the jeep. Lee smiled broadly. "Our Annamite friends," he said. "Mr. Duncan, go with them. I leave you here."

Duncan got out of the jeep, strapped on his backpack and, carrying his carbine, smiled at the guerrillas and greeted them in Vietnamese. One of the guerrillas, who seemed to be the leader, gestured and Duncan followed the group to a house on bamboo stilts, which stood at the center of the village. The leader invited him to climb the bamboo ladder. He gasped when he came to the top rung.

Mai was seated cross-legged on a straw mat in the center of a bare room, which was open at the sides. With her were Truong and Khang, who had been with her at the Ch'ing Hsi meeting. The three rose, smiling.

"Welcome," Mai said. In the daylight Duncan saw the lovely amber eyes and the oval face he remembered so well, but the features now were gaunt and there was a thin scar on her left cheek. Her hair was tied back with string, and she was dressed in a black shirt over baggy pants and rubber-soled sandals. Duncan shook hands with her and then with the others, who were obviously amused by his outfit.

Duncan put down his equipment and seated himself beside Mai as two Chinese women entered carrying bowls of food. "Share our food," Mai said, "and I will tell you of our plans. We must leave soon." Duncan bowed and accepted a bowl of rice sprinkled with pork bits and red pepper.

"You are now known as Trinh Mai," Duncan said, as he picked up his chopsticks.

"That is my name," Mai said. "Please call me Mai as before." She put down her bowl. "We're going to Pac Bo, our headquarters in the forest. Ho Chi Minh and other Vietminh leaders are there. It's a hard march. Many dangers. Many bandits raid along the border. I've made the march once. We lost two comrades in an ambush by bandits. Are you sure you wish to come with us?"

"I'm ready," Duncan said, as he scooped the last of the rice from his bowl.

"Good. Let's go now," Mai said, rising. "We must go south to the border and then march northwest to the crossing place."

The four joined the guerrillas outside the house. Lying on the ground were six shoulder yo-poles with baskets tied to the ends. The guerrillas were putting their guns and other equipment into the baskets.

"Put your carbine into that basket," Mai said, pointing one out to Duncan. "We must go along the border in disguise. The villages we'll pass are heavily armed to guard against bandits. If they see us approach with rifles, their people will attack us. When they see us carrying only baskets, they'll think we are smugglers and let us pass peacefully. Many smugglers pass their way. They bribe the villagers."

Mai beckoned to a stocky, dark-skinned man dressed in a black jacket and shorts. "This is our friend, Chu Van Tan. He is a Nung. The minority peoples are our friends and help us. Tan will guide us to his village on the other side of the border." Mai handed a straw hat to

Duncan with a smile and donned one herself. She was carrying a knapsack slung over her shoulder.

The Nung guide, barefoot and carrying a machete, led the party out at fast clip along a narrow forest trail where chattering monkeys swinging in towering trees scolded them. The trail wound through narrow valleys between low-lying green hills. In the distance beyond the Tonkin border loomed the forested highlands of the Mountain Citadel. After ten miles Duncan, who had been pressed to keep up, was relieved when they halted near a village at the foot of a hill terraced with brilliant green rice paddies. Tan disappeared into the village and returned with three boys carrying earthen jugs of water. It began to drizzle once again as they resumed the march.

The party bypassed a succession of villages, each visited in advance by Tan. They arrived at the border crossing point after dark. Tan had arranged shelter at a nearby Nung village. Damp and exhausted, Duncan followed Mai and her comrades up a ladder to the platform of a straw-thatched hut. "We'll rest here for a few hours and at daylight we'll cross the border," Mai told him.

It was pitch-dark when Truong, holding a small flashlight, shook Duncan awake. When Duncan climbed down the ladder he found the guerrillas by the light of dried grass fires busily emptying the baskets they had carried on the yo-poles. They were donning cotton field hats and fastening webbed belts from which hung knives and canteens. Narrow bags of rice were draped across their chests. Some were drying ammunition clips and loading them into bolt-action Chinese rifles.

Truong handed Duncan his carbine, one of the soft gray field hats and a bowl of spiced barley gruel, which the villagers had prepared. "Eat all of it," he advised Duncan. "It may be some time before we can eat again."

At dawn Tan led the way out of the village. Six of the guerrilla fighters followed the Nung in single file. Mai and Duncan came close behind. Truong, Khang and the six other guerrillas brought up the rear.

The trail across the unmarked border was sodden from the continual drizzle, slowing their pace. They plodded through ravines choked with jungle growth and scrub grass. Tan and the guerrillas hacked with their machetes at vines that intruded on the trail. Once they heard the distant roar of a mountain leopard.

Mai said encouragingly to Duncan: "On the other side of this forest, there is a belt of open land. Beyond that is Tan's village, where guides are waiting to lead us to Pac Bo."

As they came into the more open country the sun broke through clouds. The party halted and Tan, smiling, pointed to a flat-topped hill. "My village is there, on the other side of that hill." The sun was high when they reached the crest.

Suddenly, Tan, sniffing the air, began to run and disappeared over the crest. Mai, followed by Duncan, went to the head of the halted column and signaled for a quick march down the terraced hill into the valley. Halfway down, she raised her hand for a halt.

"Dear God," whispered Duncan in anguish. The village of some forty huts was in blackened ruins, some of the burned thatched roofs were still smoldering.

The guerrillas, their rifles at the ready, fanned out and moved down the slope toward the village, which lay in a box canyon. On the west the land dropped away into a river ravine. On the open end of the valley, the Nungs had erected a mud and bamboo wall, which was now in ruins. Bodies were strewn along the wall and near the huts. Three dead water buffalo, two of them butchered with their intestines spilling out, lay at the foot of the hill.

Mai and Duncan followed the guerrillas into the devastated village. They came upon Tan crouched over the bodies of a woman and young girl crumpled before the entrance to a hut. "My wife and daughter," he sobbed. "It must be Luc Van Loi ... the bandit ... the one they call General." Tan tore at his tunic and rocked over the bodies. "A curse upon that demon," he cried out. "My people had no chance. Luc Van Loi has so many men and so many guns. They must have come for our grain and animals."

"How can we help you?" Mai said, tears in her eyes.

Duncan, groping for words, put his hand on Tan's shoulder,.

"There's nothing you can do," Tan said, standing up. "Everyone here is dead. Some of my people must have run into the forest. I must look for them. My son may be with them." He picked up his rifle and machete. "You must go now. The bandits cannot be far away. They may come back for our grain and the rest of the buffalo meat. I am no longer able to guide you. Go to the river. Follow the trail on the near side until you come to the waterfall. Cross the river there where it is shallow. The trail to Pac Bo begins on the other side."

Mai nodded. "I remember." She embraced Tan and the others shook his hand in turn. Truong handed sack of piaster notes to the Nung and then impulsively pulled his pistol from its holster and gave it to him. Tan, with hands pressed together, bowed.

As they were turning to go, Tan shouted: "Look!" and pointed. A skirmish line of men had come over the crest of the hill and were scrambling down the slope. "The bandits ... run."

With Tan leading them, they ran toward the river. When they reached the ravine, Truong shouted to Mai: "Go with the American! We'll hold them off!"

Mai took her rifle off her shoulder. "No," she said.

Truong gasped: "The American must get to Pac Bo. Go!"

Mai hesitated, bowed her head despairingly, and said to Duncan: "Come."

Duncan shook his head. "No. No. I'm not going to run away. Let's stick together and fight them off."

Mai seized his hand. "Truong is right. Come ..." Then more urgently: "You must come."

Duncan, glancing back at the guerrillas spread out on the ground with cocked rifles, followed Mai reluctantly as she ran to the ravine. He followed her down a steep, winding path to the riverbank. As they came to the rock-strewn trail bordering the river, they heard bursts of gunfire. They began to run, hopping among the rocks. Several hundred yards along, exhausted, they slowed to a walk, panting.

"The gunfire has stopped," Mai gasped as soon as she could speak. "I hope the comrades escaped. I fear for them. There were so many bandits." She sighed heavily and tugged at her cap. "There's nothing we can do. We must cross the river now. We'll be safe on the other side."

With Duncan close behind, Mai began to run again, slipping at times on the trail made wet by the spray of the swift flowing river. Not long after, they came to the waterfall spilling over a limestone cliff. "This is the place," she exclaimed. She gazed over the turbulent waters of the river and then turned to Duncan in dismay. "I don't see it!" she cried out. The river, swollen by the continual rains, was no longer shallow. Mai couldn't locate the sandbar on which she had crossed on the previous march.

Duncan came up beside Mai. "The sandbar is submerged," he said, "Can you guess where it might be?" Mai pointed. Duncan went to the spot. "Let's try it," he said. "Come." He stepped onto the riverbed, facing downstream, and stretched out his hand to Mai. They braced against the current and waded out. In a moment, the water was up to Duncan's chin and he was struggling to keep Mai from being swept downstream. Duncan felt his carbine slip off his shoulder as he reached out to grasp Mai with his other hand. She was dangling from his outstretched hand when he found footing and he dragged her after him onto the far bank. They lay there panting. Duncan flopped over and smiled weakly at Mai.

"I'm ashamed," Mai said. "I lost my rifle. Our fighters die rather than give up their weapons."

Duncan dismissed the thought with a wave of the hand. "Not your fault. I lost mine too. No big loss for me. I really didn't know how to use the damn thing. Where's the trail?"

Mai got to her feet and pointed up. "We must go up that little path to the top of the cliff. We can wait there to see if any of our comrades come. The trail to Pac Bo begins beyond the cliff at the edge of the forest."

# -9-

THE SKIES WERE DARKENING when Mai and Duncan reached the top of the cliff. They waited for an hour but then gave up hope of locating any surviving comrades before morning. They settled at nightfall beneath the shelter of a stand of low mangrove trees at the edge of the forest. Duncan, groaning with weariness, dropped his damp backpack, pulled out his poncho and spread it on the grass between two large surface tree roots. He smiled at Mai, who was observing him uncertainly. "Dinner time, " he announced cheerfully.

Mai frowned and sighed. "My rice was in my knapsack. I lost it in the river."

Duncan reached into his backpack. "No rice, but ..." he said, and triumphantly held up two Hershey chocolate bars.

"Miraculous, indeed," Mai said, as she took off her wet drooping hat, brushed back her hair and retied it with the string. "We'll find food in the forest. But it won't be as tasty as your chocolate." She accepted a bar with a slight smile.

Duncan squinted at the sky as the drizzle resumed after a brief let up. "Will it never stop?"

Mai shook her head. "Not until the hot season. We call this 'rain dust.' It should end in a week or two."

Duncan lifted up the poncho, trampled the stubborn grass beneath it, and said: "We can sleep under this."

Mai glanced about and nodded.

They crept under the poncho and lay there resting side-by-side with their hats tipped over their brows against the drizzle.

"I'm so sad ... so sad for my comrades," Mai said softly. "I'll not forget them ... never. They sacrificed themselves for us, for the revolution. They knew how important it is for you to reach Pac Bo ... to meet with Ho Chi Minh."

Duncan said, "I too will honor them forever."

"Poor Tan ... his village, his wife and daughter," Mai said. "Someday ... someday we'll hunt down those bandits." She turned on her side, away from Duncan, hiding her tears.

Duncan listened to the swelling night noises of the jungle without speaking. He felt strangely at home and separated from everyone and everything beyond the forest. After a time, he said: "Mai, I'm to blame for what happened to you in Saigon. I should have known that seeing you so often would make the *Sûreté* suspicious. I was a fool! Such a damnable fool! Can you forgive me?"

Mai turned over, facing Duncan. "I was the one who accepted the risk," she said sadly. "My father warned me. He said the *Sûreté* kept watch on all foreigners. But I thought it would help our people if you—someone from the American consulate—understood us better. That perhaps you would tell your government in Washington about us. That's why I took you out to the villages, to show you how our people suffer, why we must be our own masters and make a new kind of life."

"I have not forgotten," Duncan said. After a few moments of silence, he whispered, "In those last days there was no chance to tell you how much—how deeply—I care for you." He turned his head and looked at Mai, who faced him with her eyes closed. "My feelings for you are unchanged." He bit his lip. "And you? After Poulo Condore ... did you resent me, a blunderer, a foolish American?"

"No, Travis, no. You were not to blame," Mai said. "Please, we have to rest now. We have a hard march ahead."

It was the first time since their encounter in Ch'ing Hsi that she had spoken his given name. Duncan reached out to hold her hand. She drew her hand away, but in the night, as the damp cold penetrated, she huddled closer to him.

At the first glimmer of daylight Mai went to the edge of the cliff and sat there on a rock, waiting. No one came. It was noon when she went to Duncan and said: "They are gone. Let us go. There's nothing ... nothing we can do for them."

Mai led Duncan along the rim of the cliff. When they came upon a small pyramid of stones, she looked about and then pointed to an opening in the tangle of jungle foliage, "There, there!" she cried, "That's the beginning of the trail." They entered the forest single file with Mai leading. They trudged for hours, making agonizingly slow progress over the narrow vine-clogged trail. The way might have been near impassable if Ho Chi Minh's party preceding them had not freshened the path by slashing the virulent impinging brush.

Coming upon a thick clump of dwarf bamboo Mai excitedly called a halt. With her knife she dug around the base of a cane and brought it down. From the top, she pulled off young bamboo shoots and handed them to Duncan. "Lunch," she said. Duncan obediently chewed and found the shoots stringy but moist and edible. They stuffed a supply in Duncan's backpack. When they resumed their march with Duncan leading the way, they both carried bamboo poles, which they used to beat back overhanging vines.

The drizzle resumed, adding to their discomfort. Mai stopped when they came to an old palm tree that had been toppled in the wind. She stripped some palm fronds, broke off some small branches, and with rope-like vines fashioned two peasant rain capes, which they threw over their shoulders.

Once, clambering up a rock-strewn hummock, Duncan peered ahead and wondered if they could make it to Pac Bo. The trail wound through limestone gorges and over the slopes of hills covered with scrub brush and through tall stands of pines on jagged mountains.

As they tramped along, Mai, always on the lookout for food, discovered black yam sprouts beside the trail. She dug up the roots and stuffed them into Duncan's backpack. Later, she added to the larder by scraping the yellowish bark off a cinnamon tree.

As the sun was dipping low, they forded a stream, filled their water bottles and sat down exhausted under the overhanging rock of a small grotto. Duncan gathered dried grasses from inside the grotto, took out his packet of matches from inside his shirt where he had stored them to dry, and built a fire over which Mai heated the cinnamon bark and yam roots on a thin flat rock.

Turning over the roots on the rock, Mai said, "Many of the peasants have been living for months on food like this. Most of their crops were destroyed last year by typhoons and floods. More than a million of our people have died in the famine. The French and Japanese have made it much worse," she said, stoking the fire hard with her bamboo stick. "Families have been forced to deliver quotas of grain to them from what little they had while their children starve to death. Our peasants will never forget that."

As they sat eating, picking at the food with bamboo splinters, Duncan asked gently: "The scar?"

Mai ran her fingers over the scar on her cheek. "The French in the prison at Poulo Condore. They tortured us." Her eyes became vacant. "They put father and me in cells beside the courtyard so we could hear the firing squads executing Vietnamese martyrs. We heard the martyrs crying out for our independence before they were shot. First, they tortured father. I could hear his cries. He was in the cell next to mine. I'm sure he did not betray our comrades. Then they came for me. They told me to listen … father was going to be shot. I heard the firing squad." She wrapped her arms about her knees and looked into the sky. "The next day, they came again … a French *Sûreté* officer with two Eurasians. When I would not tell them about our network in Saigon, they slashed my cheek and whipped me. They stripped me naked and humiliated me. They said they would be back the next day, but they never returned. The news must have come about the amnesty. I was freed with the other political prisoners. We were sent into exile in Madagascar. I escaped from there on a Chinese ship that went to Shanghai."

Duncan listened, his eyes closing at times, suppressing an impulse to cry out, yet not knowing what he could say that would be sufficient.

In the night, Mai slept on his shoulder while he lay awake. I love her … I love her … he thought. I'll make everything right.

They continued the march early the next morning and lunched on a small python, which Duncan had battered to death with his walking stick when he came upon it coiled on the trail. Mai expertly slit the python's belly, skinned it, and cooked strips of the white meat atop a sliver of rock.

"Tastes like chicken," said Duncan, complimenting Mai on her jungle culinary art.

Toward sunset they came to a waterfall spilling over a very large grotto in a ravine. Along the shore of the pond beneath the waterfall and beside the placid stream, there was a profusion of wild rhododendrons. Mai exclaimed in delight and Duncan felt his spirits lifted by the beauty. They slept that night beside the waterfall, lulled by its murmurs. Duncan awoke with a start when he suddenly felt Mai no longer beside him. He threw aside the poncho and sprang up.

Mai was swimming in the pond. She had washed her clothes and spread them out to dry on the shore. She beckoned to him. Duncan undressed, gingerly made his way into the pond over the sharp rocks, and swam out to Mai. He followed her under the waterfall, raising his face joyfully to the cascading water. He reached out for Mai but she eluded him. She swam back to the shore, and sat there nude with her arms locked about her knees. The drizzle had finally stopped, and she was enjoying the sun which had come up, bright and hot, over the mountain. She laughed as she watched Duncan wade out of the pond, his arms crossed before him concealing a stubborn erection. He flopped down beside her thinking how wonderful it was to see her laugh.

"Perhaps we can rest here for a day," Duncan said.

"Only this morning," Mai said. "We must find food and go on."

"Why must we hurry?"

"Let's talk about that later."

She stood and picked up her still damp clothes, uninhibited by Duncan's frank gaze. Beautiful, Duncan thought. She was slim with perfectly shaped small breasts, her shining black hair falling nearly to her waist. When she gathered up her hair, Duncan saw the scars on her back, and he was gripped by guilt once again.

While returning to the campsite, they saw a large black bear drinking downstream. "There may be berries or other food on the other side of the stream near where the bear is drinking," Mai said.

They waited until the bear had lumbered off and then waded through the shallow rapids to the far bank. As they searched along the tree-lined shore, Duncan plucked an orchid from a vine and with a bow presented it to Mai. She put it in her hair, smiling her thanks. They were about to turn back when Mai said excitedly: "There!" Leaning above them on a slope was a tall banana plant. The bear had done the work for them. Strewn on the slope were bunches of green-skinned bananas that it had knocked down, some of the fruit stripped and eaten, but many others whole. They gathered armfuls while glancing about for the bear.

Sitting by the waterfall, eating bananas, Mai said: "You asked why we must hurry."

"Yes," Duncan said, as he heaved a handful of banana peels into the stream.

"Ho Chi Minh is assembling Vietminh leaders in Pac Bo for a conference. They must decide what to do next. The French are already plotting to restore their colonial control. We need help. Ho Chi Minh has been telling the comrades that if President Roosevelt has promised the Philippines independence how can the Americans not do the same for us. But not all the comrades believe you Americans will support us. Others wish to rely on Mao Tse-tung and Stalin. Vo Nguyen Giap tells our fighters to believe only in armed struggle. Ho Chi Minh wants to use your presence in Pac Bo and your message from Donovan as proof that Americans will help us."

"I understand," Duncan said, thinking uneasily that Ho Chi Minh might be depending too much on what he could say.

Mai rose and began to fasten her web belt. "The trail is easier from here on," she said. "Pac Bo is not too far."

Refreshed by their idyll at the waterfall, Duncan and Mai strode out. Beyond the stream there was a fork in the trail, but a pyramid of stones pointed the way. They camped that night on a limestone cliff, ate bananas, and watched as the stony landscape was softened by the golden and crimson sunset.

In the morning, as he was putting on his backpack, Duncan glanced up and shouted: "Look!" pointing to the horizon where there was a faint column of rising smoke.

"Pac Bo," Mai said, sighing gratefully.

An hour later, as they tramped along the broadening trail, there was a whistle. On all sides, figures in black shirts and white pith helmets, guns in hand, rose out of the jungle. "Our people!" Mai cried out.

In a moment, more than a dozen guerrillas surrounded them. A young man wearing spectacles, carrying a British Sten submachine gun, who seemed to be the leader, shouted: "Welcome Comrade Trinh Mai. We've been waiting for you. I am Tao Boi Tau. But where are the other comrades?"

"Lost to bandits," Mai said, grasping Tao's outstretched hand. "We were ambushed in the Nung village."

"For the revolution!" Tao said sorrowfully. "We will honor them." He offered his hand to Duncan. "Welcome. Uncle Ho will be happy to see you."

Duncan looked more closely at the guerrillas as they followed Tao down the trail. Most were little more than boys and they carried a strange collection of French, Chinese, British and Japanese weapons. One bore an ancient flintlock.

"They're fighters of the new unified Liberation Army, " Mai said.

The column had just descended the lower slope of a mountain when Mai exclaimed: "Pac Bo!"

Duncan was astonished. Somehow he had imagined Pac Bo as a sizable village. But all he saw were four huts with thatched roofs which stood on bamboo stilts near a stream. Tao led Mai and Duncan to the hut nearest the stream. "This is where Uncle Ho lives," Tao said, and climbed up the ladder into the hut, which stood some four feet off the ground.

After a few minutes, a frail, slender man with a graying wispy goatee, wearing a faded Nung jacket, khaki shorts and rubber sandals, came down the ladder unsteadily, Tao assisting him. He put out his hand to Duncan.

"Welcome," he said in English, his eyes bright in gaunt features. "I'm Ho Chi Minh. You've had a hard journey. I'm grateful that you have come." He reached out with both hands to Mai. "Welcome. I grieve for our comrades." Turning back to Duncan, he said: "I have very sad news. We've received a radio message. President Roosevelt died on April twelfth."

Duncan's eyes widened, his features ashen. "Dear Lord," he said, his hands clasped tightly, shoulders hunched.

"We wept at the news," Ho said. "The world has lost a very great man. Our people were depending on him for help in our struggle." He shook his head, thin lips pressed together. "You must rest now, Mr. Duncan. Tao will take you to the place where you will stay. There is a radio message for you."

Duncan murmured his thanks, waved to Mai, and followed Tao, who led him into one of the huts where he dropped his backpack on a straw sleeping mat. Apart from the mat, there was only a bamboo table and two pine stools in the hut.

"We'll bring you blankets," Tao said, switching from Vietnamese to heavily accented French. He lowered his head. "I'm sorry about your president. He was for all peoples."

Duncan managed an appreciative smile.

"Uncle Ho will see you soon. He's not too well ... still very tired after the march from the border. After all, he's not young. He's fifty-five years old. Now, have a good rest. There's your radio message," Tao said, gesturing to a handwritten note on the bamboo table. "Your Chinese radio operator who came from the border with Uncle Ho is in contact with Kunming."

Duncan sat on one of the stools and studied the Washington message which had been relayed from Kunming: *President Roosevelt died at Warm Springs on April 12 of stroke. Truman is president. Indochina policy unclear. Continue as before. Will keep you posted. Donovan.*

Duncan lay down on the straw mat, the backpack under his head, his mind reeling in shock and grief. No one can take his place, he thought. Truman. He couldn't recall anything about him except that he was vice-president and before that a senator from Missouri.

There were so many questions. Would Truman stand up to De Gaulle on Indochina policy like Roosevelt? He thought of the president, his face gaunt and pale, speaking to him, sending him on his mission. He scrambled up from the mat, leaned over the table, his eyes damp, and banged his fist down and then again. He put his hand to his brow, eyes closed, and whispered: "Yes, Sir, yes."

The bamboo hanging at the door rustled and Duncan turned about, his eyes glazed. Mai entered carrying a jug and a cotton bag. She put the jug on the table. "Beer, made in a village not far from here. Not very good, but strong," she said. "I thought you might need it." She took out two bowls wrapped in palm leaves filled with rice and chunks of meat. "Better than what we've been eating. Pork. The comrades shot a wild boar yesterday." She looked at Duncan with a gentle smile. "I have not prayed since I left the Catholic school. But I prayed today for your president."

Duncan embraced her.

# -10-

## Pac Bo
## April 18, 1945

DUNCAN WAS AWAKENED from a deep sleep of exhaustion late the next morning by Tao, who came into the hut followed by a Vietnamese woman with a pan of steaming hot water. "Good morning, Mr. Duncan," Tao said with a broad smile, seemingly ever cheerful and exuberant. He was now bareheaded, wearing blue shorts, and no longer carrying the Sten gun. "This is Dinh, one of our Nung friends, who will help you. Uncle Ho invites you to lunch. I will come for you in two hours." As Duncan threw aside his blanket, Dinh, a shy dark-skinned girl with long braided hair, reentered the hut with a bowl of rice gruel and a pitcher of hot green tea. Smiling shyly, she produced a bar of yellow soap from her blue jacket.

Duncan washed, felt his beard, and decided to let it grow rather than use the razor which he carried in his backpack. He breakfasted and then climbed down the ladder, looking about with great curiosity. There was considerable activity. Squads of soldiers were bivouacked along the permeter of the village. As Mai had apprised him, Vietminh leaders were gathering for a conference. Unperturbed by the bustle, a boy carrying a bamboo stick rode calmly through the village clearing astride a water buffalo.

Tao came at noon and escorted him to Ho Chi Minh's hut. Ho and Mai awaited him there. The hut was as bare as the one in which Duncan had slept, except that there was a rude open cabinet with books and pamphlets spilling out.

"You slept okay?" Ho asked in English as he invited Duncan to join him and Mai at the table.

"Yes, thank you," Duncan replied.

"I'm sorry I can't offer you a better meal," Ho said, casting a gentle smile at Duncan. On the table lay a platter with chunks of barbecued meat, corn with red pepper bits, rice, green bananas and a jug of beer. "The meat is venison. Our people were lucky enough to shoot a deer. Please," he invited, picking up his chopsticks. "Too bad, we don't have more things. I'm quite a good cook. When I was very young, only twenty-one, I signed on as an assistant cook on a French ship, the *Admiral Latouche Treville*. Later on, when I lived in London, I worked at the Carlton House for the famous chef Escoffier, washing dishes in the kitchen. But later," Ho said, flourishing his beer mug, "I was promoted to assistant pastry cook."

"I suppose that's where you learned your very good English," Duncan said. "You also employ American slang very well."

"My English isn't that good," Ho said laughing. "Before going to London I visited New York ... saw the Statue of Liberty. It inspired me. Gave me hope for the future of our country. I admire your Declaration of Independence very much. I can recall some of the phrases. I'm using some of the expressions ..."

"How do the ideas in the Declaration of Independence—and words like freedom—fit with your Communist ideology?" Duncan interjected, with a challenging tone in his voice. He immediately regretted his remark as inopportune and overly aggressive.

But Ho laughed. "I suppose you're asking me the question that foreigners—even the Russians—often put to me. Am I a Communist or a nationalist? My comrades in the Comintern have accused me at times of being too much of a nationalist. I'll say to you in truth: I'm first a nationalist and then a member of the Communist Party. Independence is my paramount goal. After independence I'll leave it to the Vietnamese people to find their way according to their needs."

Ho lit a cigarette, tilting it up in his long slender fingers, and said: "You have a message from General Donovan?"

Duncan put down his earthen beer mug. "General Donovan isn't in a position to make political commitments," he said deliberately. "He wishes to learn more about your views and intentions. He'd like your reaction to the possibility of Vietnam becoming a trusteeship after the defeat of Japan. You may know, that was President Roosevelt's idea. He looked upon trusteeship as a step toward full independence."

Duncan paused and then added uneasily: "Frankly, we have not yet had word as to whether President Truman will support the idea."

Ho leaned back in his chair, inhaling his cigarette deeply. After a few moments, he said, "I can't give you an answer at this moment. The leading cadres of our Vietminh will be conferring here in the next days. We don't as yet have an agreed policy. Vo Nguyen Giap, our military commander, is in favor of calling on our people to rise in an armed general insurrection. Many believe as Giap does that that's the only way we can gain our independence. I don't agree. The time is not right. We're not yet strong enough for a military offensive. The French would come back in great strength and, as before, they'd crush us. To succeed in our struggle for independence we need the help of your country."

Ho stubbed out his cigarette. He reached over for two of the large serving chopsticks and put some venison on Duncan's plate. "Please have some more," he said in an appealing manner. Duncan dutifully tasted a chunk, wishing that the meat hadn't been so strongly flavored with the *nuoc mam* sauce.

"I'd like you to meet with my comrades," Ho said. "It might make it easier for me to convince them we should try to obtain help from America."

After lunch, Mai, who had remained silent through the discussion, led Duncan down to the stream near Ho's hut. In bright sunshine they seated themselves on a bench enjoying the respite from the *crachin*.

"Comrade Ho has given this stream the name of Lenin Creek, and the mountain there, Karl Marx Peak," Mai said. "When he is well, he sometimes bathes in this stream in the early morning."

"Ho Chi Minh was deeply influenced by Lenin, wasn't he?"

"Yes. For many years he couldn't see a clear path to our independence. At the Versailles Conference in 1919, your President Wilson, like the other Westerners, refused to even talk to him when he was appealing for our right to self-government. The next year he read Lenin's *Preliminary Draft Theses on the The National and The Colonial Questions*, and for the first time he felt he had found a means—through Marxism-Leninism—of bringing about our liberation."

Raising her voice, her features flushed, Mai said: "But now Ho Chi Minh believes only you Americans can help. The Soviet Union has suffered too much in the war to give us aid. We don't trust the Chinese, who dominated us for almost a thousand years. Only you have the power and the economic resources to help us."

Duncan reached down, picked up a stone and skidded it across the surface of the stream. "We'll do what we can," he said, wishing that he could say more.

The sun was shining hot in their eyes and Mai said: "Let's walk to the waterfall near the grotto." They walked up a path overlooking a ravine where the stream frothed through. "These cliffs have given us good protection against any surprise French attacks," Mai said, leaning against a boulder. "That's why Comrade Ho put the camp in this area. In the forest, not far, there are huts for our fighters who come to train and hear political lectures."

"When did you and your father join the Communist Party?" Duncan asked.

Mai laughed. "I wasn't entirely open with you in Saigon. I told you that my father was arrested when the *Sûreté* learned he spoke to students about independence. That was true. What I didn't tell you—the *Sûreté* found copies of Lenin's *Selected Works* in his desk. Father spent two years in the Saigon Central Prison. He always counted himself lucky he wasn't guillotined like many other Vietnamese nationalists. After he was released he worked on the docks until the Party gave him money to open a bookshop. I left school to help him. Later, the comrades installed a printing press in the cellar of the shop."

As they walked back to the camp, Duncan said: "During our last talk in Saigon, listening to you, I began to suspect that you were a member of the Party. Having seen the poverty in the villages on the outskirts of Saigon, which you showed me, I could understand why you might be working in the underground."

Mai laughed and linked her arm in his as they strolled on.

Outside his hut, Mac Sin, the Chinese radio operator, a round-faced Cantonese dressed in khaki shirt and shorts, was waiting. "A message, sir, from General Donovan," he said soberly, handing over a handwritten note. "It was relayed from Kunming. I'm in that hut," Mac Sin said pointing, "if you need me."

Duncan took the note into the hut, studied it, and then slammed his fist on the table. It was a three-sentence message: *Truman supports trusteeship subject French consent. We will provide assistance to Vietminh in return for intelligence and action against Japanese. Advise their position Donovan.*

Duncan sagged onto a stool. "Subject to French consent," he muttered. It was obvious Truman had yielded to De Gaulle. The French would never agree to a trusteeship that provided for eventual independence as envisioned by Roosevelt. What am I going to tell Ho? He must have seen Donovan's message. Mac Sin wouldn't risk withholding any radio traffic from the Vietminh.

Duncan stewed for two days over the Donovan message before Tao came with a summons from Ho Chi Minh. "Uncle Ho would like you to meet his comrades at two o'clock," he said, his cheery manner subdued.

When Duncan entered Ho's hut he found him sitting cross-legged with six other men on straw mats. His companions were lean men, whose hard, deeply bronzed features bespoke years in the field. Each of them shook hands, smiling as they were introduced. Duncan was seated facing them. Vo Nguyen Giap, the guerrilla commander, was on Ho's right and Truong Chinh, whom he knew as the secretary-general of the Communist Party, on his left.

"We're grateful that you have come," Truong said. "Your journey to Pac Bo was a hard one."

"Trinh Mai guided me very well," Duncan said.

Truong nodded. "She's one of our most trusted cadres. Comrade Ho tells us you bring a message from General Donovan."

"Yes. He wishes to cooperate with you and asks what would be your terms."

"What kind of help can we expect?" Giap asked. "Weapons? Training of our soldiers?"

"The OSS is ready to provide assistance to you in return for intelligence information and for your cooperation in operations against the Japanese. I am prepared to report your needs to General Donovan."

"And is America ready to support our fight for independence?" Truong asked.

"The United States is in favor of your eventual independence."

"Eventual?" Truong asked, with a forced smile.

"The question of a trusteeship leading to independence is being discussed among the Allies," Duncan said, feeling guilty that he was not being entirely open about the diminished prospects of a trusteeship.

"With French consent?" Giap asked bitterly.

Obviously, he had seen Donovan's telegram, Duncan thought.

Ho interrupted: "Let the other comrades speak," he said.

For the next hour, Duncan heard litanies about the abuses of the French over decades from each of the others. Glancing around at the men, toughened by years in the jungle battling the French and their native allies, he thought, I would hate to have them as enemies.

When the last of them had spoken, Ho Chi Minh said: "General Donovan is not the only important American friend we have." From his bookcase, he took out a large manila envelope. "This was presented to me when General Chennault thanked us for rescuing the American pilot, Lieutenant Shaw." He passed around an eight-by-ten glossy photograph of the general signed: "Yours Sincerely, Claire L. Chennault."

As the others examined the photograph, Ho went to a corner of the hut and dragged forth a wooden case. "The Americans have also sent us gifts," he said. Out of the case he took six .45 caliber Colt pistols in their original wrappings and distributed them to his six comrades.

Duncan glanced about. The six seemed impressed, although several cast questioning glances at Ho.

"Thank you, Mr. Duncan," Ho said, as his companions were inspecting their new pistols. "We'll speak again soon."

Dismissed, Duncan rose, bowed, and feeling relieved scrambled down the hut's ladder. A master politician, he thought, as he walked back to his hut, reflecting on how Ho had handled the meeting. But he was not yet prepared to commend Ho to Donovan as someone who could be trusted to lead a Vietnam trusteeship. There was no certainty Ho could retain control of the radical Giap and those factional leaders under his influence. Duncan was also not yet persuaded that Ho was entirely free of binding commitments to Moscow.

WHILE DUNCAN WAITED FOR HO to summon him again, Tao ceremoniously brought him a thick pamphlet of Ho's writings. Duncan read them eagerly, wanting to know more about this man who was just beginning to be known to Americans. Surprisingly, there were few ideological tirades or references to world revolution in the essays and speeches. To Duncan, the writings conveyed a portrait of a highly cultured intellectual with a pragmatic grasp of international politics, a leader deeply concerned about the condition of his people and relentlessly dedicated to their independence. Yet Ho left no doubt that it was his intention to transform Vietnam into a Communist society of some sort. Not elaborated were his current ties with Stalin and Mao.

The pamphlet contained Vietnamese translations of poems written in 1942 by Ho in classical Chinese when he was held in prison, sometimes in shackles, in Ch'ing Hsi by Chang Fa-kwei. Most were simply descriptive of Vietnamese life and aspirations, but there was one that impelled Duncan to copy into his notebook:

> *The ancients used to like to sing about natural beauty:*
> *Snow and flowers, moon and wind, mists, mountains and*
> *rivers.*
> *Today we should make poems including iron and steel*
> *And the poet also should know how to lead an attack.*

Mai was absent from the camp during the five days that Duncan waited to hear from Ho Chi Minh. Tao said she was giving lectures at a nearby village in an education center for peasants who came to study from many parts of Cao Bang Province. Uncle Ho himself, Tao said, often gave lectures at the center in Vietnamese, Chinese and French, at times reciting his poems to illustrate his lessons. Many of the people trained there went out into villages throughout Tonkin to recruit for the Vietminh.

Duncan was reading in his hut when the slats of the hanging bamboo door were gently parted and Ho Chi Minh entered. Duncan leaped up, flustered. "Sir ...," he began. Ho held up his hand and gestured for Duncan to be seated and then took the other stool.

Ho appeared tired. His high forehead was creased and his large eyes, usually so bright, were clouded. He was in his faded Nung jacket. "I'm sorry to have kept you waiting so long," he said. "It must be very boring for you."

"No, no," Duncan said quickly, putting his hand on the pamphlet of Ho's works which lay on the table. Ho smiled, pleased.

"We've had hard talks. But the comrades are now agreed," Ho said. "We saw, of course, your telegram from General Donovan. We've also had messages from our comrades in Chungking about the disappointing talks on trusteeship at the UN conference in San Francisco." He sighed. "We didn't expect the French to yield easily."

Reaching into a pocket of his jacket, Ho withdrew a wrinkled sheet of paper folded in four. "This is our proposal to the French government for the future of Vietnam," he said, and read from the statement, which was in French:

*That there be universal suffrage to elect a parliament for the governing of the country, that there be a French Governor-General as President until such time as independence be granted us. That he choose a cabinet or group of advisors acceptable to that parliament. Exact powers of all these officers may be discussed in the future. That independence be given to this country, in not less than five years and not more than ten. That natural resources of this country be returned to the people of the country by just payment to the present owners and that France be granted economic concessions. That all freedoms outlined by the United Nations will be granted to the Indochinese. That the sale of opium be prohibited.*

Ho handed the paper to Duncan. "We ask General Donovan to transmit this proposal urgently to the government of General De Gaulle."

"It will be radioed at once to the general," Duncan said, accepting the sheet of paper with both hands.

Ho said: "As for General Donovan's proposal, we welcome it. We agree to supply the OSS with intelligence reports and cooperate in operations against the Japanese in exchange for arms and training."

Ho stood up. "That's all I can say. We'll await further word from General Donovan. You may wish to consult with your people. You can leave whenever you choose. We'll give you quite a large escort to the border. There is always the danger that you will come upon a Japanese patrol or bandits. Tao will go with you. We are grateful for your help."

When Ho left, Duncan sat at the table turning pages of Ho's works. The import of the message was pretty clear, he thought. This was Ho's final effort to reach a political compromise with the French that would preserve the country from a costly conflict. From Ho's demeanor he guessed that Vo Nguyen Giap and the other militants had only reluctantly agreed, doubting that De Gaulle would accept the compromise proposal. What Giap wanted more than anything else was arms from the United States to carry on the struggle for independence. Yes, in exchange they would provide intelligence information. They might mount guerrilla attacks against the Japanese. But Ho had not specified that. More likely, Duncan speculated, Giap would husband their military strength for an ultimate bid for power after the Allies had defeated the Japanese.

After taking Ho's message to the radio operator, Duncan decided he would leave for the border in two days. It was better that he return quickly to Kunming, where he could communicate with Donovan more freely.

In response to Duncan's repeated inquiries, Tao had told him Mai would be returning to Pac Bo tomorrow afternoon. There would be time for a last meeting with her.

Mai came to Duncan's hut late in the afternoon carrying a jug of coconut juice. "A gift from the people," she said, holding it aloft. She looked happy, her features glowing. "I would like to be a teacher someday in a village school," she said. "The people want to learn. They are so grateful to anyone who gives them knowledge."

Duncan took the jug, delighted to see Mai liberated from her usual somber mood.

"Let's go to the bench by the stream," Mai said. "I'll take the jug and you bring the cups."

Reflections of the orange setting sun were shimmering off the placid waters of the stream. "Summer has come," Mai said, as she poured the milky juice into the mugs.

"Thanks for that," Duncan said, but then added with a grin: "But I'll miss our poncho."

Mai laughed. "How was the meeting with the comrades?" she asked.

Duncan sipped his drink and told her of what had transpired. "It's the best that I could have hoped for," he said. "But Giap was so hard, so bitter."

"He has reason to be bitter," Mai said. "His sister, Minh Khai, was guillotined by the French for conspiracy. His wife, Minh Giang, and their little son died in Hanoi Central Prison."

"It's time to end this horror," Duncan said, angrily kicking the pebbles at his feet.

"We've waited more than eighty years," Mai said. "We believe the time is approaching." She refilled Duncan's cup. "Tao told me he's leaving with you tomorrow morning, that you are carrying a message for us to Donovan. We're grateful."

"Yes. But I'll come back, Mai. I want to be with you."

"You'll always be welcome," Mai said, her eyes lowered.

Duncan searched her features, waiting for her to say more. "Mai, do you care for me?" he burst out.

"Yes," Mai said softly.

"Do you love me?"

"Yes ... in a special way."

Impatiently, wanting her to say more, Duncan leaned toward her. "Mai, do you have a lover?"

"Yes," Mai answered, and looked at Duncan with a frown. "There's a man I love. He's not here now. He's a party cadre. He's in the South. Ho Chi Minh sent him there to persuade other Vietnamese parties to join the Vietminh."

"You never told me," Duncan said.

"There was no reason to tell you. It doesn't affect what we are to each other."

"I wish you well," Duncan said stiffly and stood up. They walked to the camp, not speaking. When they came to Duncan's hut, Mai handed him the jug and said: "You'll always be in my heart."

Duncan offered her his hand. "Goodbye," he said, and scrambled up the ladder into his hut. He threw the jug into a corner and slumped in the chair, thinking, she's misled me ... concealing that she had a lover ... encouraging me in small ways to believe that one day we might become lovers. Well, at least it's over ... this damn obsession of mine. Damn it! Damn it!

The Nung woman entered the hut and began arranging the blanket on his straw mat. She looked up smiling, and Duncan morosely thought for an instant of asking her to return for the night. He sat at the table hands locked together and then took his tranquility jade from his breast pocket. After a time he asked himself: Why would I even assume that she'd been without a man all these years? He shook his head. He'd been a fool. Locked in the forest he had once again become a prisoner of his opium dreams of Mai. He thought of how uncaring he'd been of Suzanne. He slammed his backpack on the table to make ready for his departure early the next morning.

Duncan was lying awake in the night when he heard the rustle of the hanging bamboo. A figure was silhouetted against the moonlight shining through the open side of the hut. Duncan rose, clad only in his shorts. The figure approached. It was Mai. Duncan stood transfixed, unbelieving, as she reached behind her head, untied the string, and let her hair tumble. She undressed and came to him, nude. Duncan embraced her, whispering her name, but she silenced him with her fingers on his lips. Mai smoothed the blanket over the straw mat, lay on it and reached up, inviting him. Duncan embraced her, pressing her close. After a few moments he turned away and lay trembling, his hand fumbling for hers. She stroked his chest, fondled him, and then mounted him, slowly rocking. She kissed him and he roughly turned her about, and thrust into her.

When they lay resting, Duncan asked: "Do you love me?"

"I must go," Mai said. "You must prepare for your march."

Mai rose and dressed. When Duncan tried to speak, she placed her fingertips on her lips and disappeared into the darkness.

# -12-

TAO WAS AT DUNCAN'S SIDE when the march began at daybreak. It was a large party. Apart from some thirty guerrilla fighters, there were Nung guides and bearers. "The bearers will bring supplies back from the border," Tao explained. Baked by the hot sun of the season, the trail was easier than when Mai and Duncan had traversed it.

At the end of the first day, the column camped at the waterfall where Duncan and Mai had cavorted. Tao built a small fire of pine branches and dried grasses. As they partook of their meal of hard rice cakes and dried fish, Duncan studied Tao with growing curiosity. He had a youngish face but there were tinges of gray in the mop of black hair, strands of which hung over his dark brown forehead. His right cheek was scarred, likely from a knife thrust. Despite his apparent youth, he was very much in command, and among the fighters he was the only one to carry a coveted British Sten gun.

"How long have you been with the guerrillas?" Duncan asked.

"Many years," Tao said. "Since I was fifteen."

"The guerrillas let you join when you were so young?" Duncan asked.

Tao laughed. "I was special. I ran away from Hai Duong … the town where my family lived for many generations. It is not far from Hanoi."

"Why did you leave?"

"The French were after me. My head would have been cut off if they'd found me," Tao said, swiping at his throat. Seeing that Duncan was curious, he said with a grimace: "Want to know the whole story? It's ugly."

"Tell me," Duncan said, putting down his bowl.

"I was a student in the middle school. One day the French *résident* came into my classroom. He was a tall, fat man with eyes that frightened me. We were told he was inspecting the school. Afterward, our Vietnamese schoolmaster called me into his office. He was very nervous. He said the *résident* would like me to work for him as a houseboy. 'You'll be very well paid,' he said. 'You'll eat good food,' " Tao stirred the fire with a pine twig. "I didn't want to do it because it meant leaving school. But my father—he was a poor candlemaker— told me to do it. 'We mustn't refuse the *résident*,' he said, 'You can send us money.' "

Tao wrapped his arms about his knees and stared into the fire. "The *résident* had a very big house and garden. It was in a compound guarded by soldiers. I wasn't allowed to leave the compound. But at Tet, our lunar new year, they let me go home for a day. That night two men came into our home. My father was very humble before them. They said they were fighters for independence. They asked me what I did in the *résident*'s house. I told them how I served the *résident*, and that sometimes at siesta time he would tell me to take off my clothes and tell me to do what he commanded.

"The men then talked with my father and afterward they told me: 'You must do something for your people … for your country.' One of the men lay down on a mat and the other showed me how I could kill the *résident* with a knife, stabbing him first in the throat so he would not cry out. They showed me how to fold the knife and hide it below the arch of my foot in my sandal. I was frightened but I agreed.

"Just beyond the wall at the rear of the *résident*'s house, there is a tall tree. They said a rope ladder would be thrown from it to me and that after I'd killed the *résident*, I was to climb up the ladder and down into the marsh, where they would be waiting for me."

Tao rose, gathered some dried grass, and threw it on the fire, which flared up. "Two days later, at siesta time," he said, "the *résident* called me into his bedroom, made me undress, and had his way with me. Afterward, I went into the next room beyond the beaded curtain and waited. When I heard the *résident* snoring, I went in. I could see him on the bed through the gauze mosquito netting. He was on his back and wearing only the bottom of his silk pajamas. I took the knife out of my sandal. I slowly parted the netting. He didn't move. I stabbed him in the throat, cut it, and when he lifted up with blood running from his mouth, I stabbed him in the heart again and again … just as I was told to do. When he lay still, I went into the bathroom and washed the blood off my hands and arms. I put the knife back in my sandal."

Tao laughed. "I was so scared—I was just a kid—I became paralyzed … my body covered with sweat. I was afraid to go out. But after awhile, just as I usually did, carrying my bowl of rice, I went into the garden. I was lucky. There, I saw a man up in the tree which stood high on the other side of the wall. He dropped the rope ladder to me."

Tao looked somberly at Duncan. "I escaped. But the French shot my father in the town square. They gathered all the people to watch." He picked up the Sten gun and examined it. "We have a hard march tomorrow. I must look after my comrades now."

Duncan, too appalled to say anything, watched Tao leave to check on the other guerrillas, who were gathered around fires or sleeping.

Duncan sat beside the fire, staring into the embers, thinking about what the Vietnamese endured.

When the fire was low Duncan kicked up the earth beside it to soften it, spread his poncho and lay down, the backpack under his head, and looked up at the sky. The moon was full. Its pale light slanting through the trees evoked the image of Mai's silhouette in the hut. He recalled how she embraced him, the smoothness of her body, the hard fullness of her breasts, of the moment when he possessed her. He closed his eyes, thinking: I'm still not free of wanting her. Why did she come to me? Why didn't she speak? Was she promising we'd become lovers when I returned? Or was it out of pity? Or was it to bind me even closer to her people? The questions churned until he slept.

Two days later they were at the Nung village, which had been overrun and torched by the raiders of the bandit general. Duncan gazed sorrowfully into the ravine where he and Mai had fled while the Vietminh guerrillas held off the bandits. The few villagers who escaped had returned but only to mourn and bury their dead. Behind the village were burial mounds under which the slain Vietminh guerrillas rested. The village was now deserted. Skeletons of the three buffalo, bones picked clean by scavengers, lay where they had been butchered.

Tao and the other guerrillas watched silently as Duncan went into the nearby forest and fetched purple rhododendron blossoms. On each of the mounds he dropped a blossom. "For Mai and for me," he said as he came to the last of them. He waited until his eyes were no longer moist before he rejoined Tao at the edge of the clearing.

"How can these bandits ... this General ... roam free?" Duncan asked bitterly.

Tao shrugged. "The French, the Japanese and the Chinese—all have tried to clear them from the border. They've captured a few. Executed them on the spot. We've killed some. But the country is rough. It's very hard to track them. The one they call the General is the most cunning. He's of mixed Annamese and Chinese blood, a deserter from the Chinese army. He often raids across the border. He must have been desperate for food to attack a Nung village. The Nung people do not forget. He won't be able to hide from them forever."

The column made camp at night in the abandoned village. Duncan rested beside Tao in one of the huts. An opening in the scorched thatched roof allowed him a view of jewel-like stars and of the moon as it made its passage.

Duncan had been sleeping no more than an hour when he was awakened by shouts. Tao leaped up, seized his Sten gun, and ran barefoot from the hut. When Duncan emerged from the hut, he saw the guerrillas gathered in the center of the village. Tao, his eyes alight with excitement, came running to him.

"It's Tan, our Nung friend, and one of our comrades. They escaped from the bandits. They hid among the bodies of villagers in one of the huts and at night ran into the forest. They were not able to follow you and Mai into the river ravine."

"Truong and Khang?" Duncan asked, his hands clenched.

"They were killed. Tan and our comrade Dang were the only ones who escaped. When Dang, who was wounded, could march, they went to the Nungs. Now Tan has been sent by his people to ask for our help. They have tracked the General and his bandits, who destroyed this village. Nung tribes are gathering to attack them. They want us to join them. It will be a great battle. There are many bandits and they are very well armed."

Duncan strode to where Tan and his Vietminh comrade, Dang, were standing. Tan turned to him, smiling broadly. He was carrying a rifle, a machete slung across his back, and stuck in his belt was the .45 caliber pistol which Truong had given him just before the bandits swarmed down the mountainside. Duncan embraced him and then Dang, whose arm was still in a sling.

"I'll march with you," Duncan said. "Give me a gun."

Tan held up his rifle and shook it at the heavens. He then bowed, pulled Truong's pistol from his belt and handed it to Duncan with a half-filled clip of bullets. "Our Vietminh fighters leave tonight," Tao said. "The General is camped in a valley about a day's march from here. We must go quickly. He is too cunning to stay in one place too long."

Less than an hour later, the Vietminh guerrilla column with Tan and five other Nungs in the lead was on the march along a trail that led northwest along the border. In bright moonlight the column trudged through mostly open country between low hills, slowing at times to allow the Nungs to hack vines which obstructed the trail.

Striding behind Tan, Duncan struggled to keep up with the forced pace. Whenever the column stopped, he would lean against a tree, panting. The column halted for the night under a thick jungle canopy that shut out the moonlight. Duncan lay down on the spiny grass with his backpack under his head and reached into his jacket pocket to make sure the pistol was still there. Apart from a knife, he had not carried a weapon since losing his carbine in the river crossing with Mai.

The march resumed at dawn and except for a brief halt at a stream to take water continued until midday when the column came into a clearing where, it seemed to Duncan, about two hundred Nung tribesmen, most of them naked except for loincloths and sandals, were gathered. There were no women. Apart from machetes, with which all the Nungs were armed, some carried spears and and others a strange assortment of Chinese, Japanese and French rifles, ranging from ancient flintlocks to bolt-action guns.

Tan led Duncan and Tao to a gray-bearded tribesman with scarred cheeks, sitting cross-legged under a pine tree with a Chinese rifle across his lap. They bowed to the tribesman, evidently a chief, who, welcoming them in his native dialect, bid them sit before him. With Tan translating the guttural Nung dialect into Vietnamese, the chief outlined his strategy for the assault on the bandits.

Three days earlier the General had made a raid across the border on a Chinese village, and his band was now camped in a valley less than a half-day's march from where the Nungs were assembled. The plan was to attack that night. With a pine twig, the chief traced the oval shape of the small valley and described what his scouts had seen. On the floor of the valley, beside a stream, there was a tent, evidently the headquarters of the General. Clustered about it were the tents and lean-tos of some one hundred of the General's men. Mules were tethered nearby. Sentries were posted along the crests of the surrounding hills, but vigilance seemed lax because the bandits returning from their raid loaded with loot were celebrating.

"We hope they are drinking much wine," the chief said with a cackling laugh. "Their celebration will become ours." He poked at the drawing on the earth. "After we have taken out the sentries on the hills, our people will attack just before dawn from the south side of the valley. We ask that you silence the sentries on the northern crest. Wait there until we drive the bandits up the slope toward you. Then open fire and advance down the hill, killing all you find."

The chief looked at Duncan and then at Tao, waiting for their response.

"A good plan," Tao said. "We are with you, elder brother."

Duncan nodded approvingly.

The chief said, "Tan and some of my people will go with you." He rose, shook his rifle in the air and called out to some of his men, who were squatting nearby, waiting for the order to move out.

With their chief in the lead, the Nungs left the clearing and moved into the forest to infiltrate in a broad arc onto to the southern side of the valley in which the bandits were camped. Tao, with Duncan at his side, accompanied by Tan with twenty of his Nungs, led his column along the trail leading to the northern heights above the valley. At dusk, on reaching the reverse slope of the northern hill, Tao deployed his Vietminh along the base while Tan led his Nungs up toward the crest.

At the first glimmer of dawn, gunfire erupted in the valley. Duncan followed Tao and his guerrillas up the wooded slope. At the top of the hill they saw the Nungs standing over six bodies which had been disemboweled. Lying around the cold embers of a fire were jugs of Chinese wine.

Tan grinned at Duncan. "They were drunk. It was the same at their other sentry posts. Listen! My people are attacking from the south hill. The bandits will retreat toward us soon."

The Vietminh took up positions along the crest and waited. Duncan lay beside Tao. The dawn was full on the valley when Tao shouted: "Here they come." Duncan could see figures carrying guns struggling up the slope toward them. He gripped his pistol more tightly, resting his elbows on the slope to steady himself. His throat was constricted. He'd never been in face-to-face combat. The Vietminh waited until the bandits were almost at the crest before opening fire. Some of the bandits toppled over. Others took cover in the brush and returned fire. Duncan could make out their contorted faces. The Vietminh heaved grenades and then charged down the slope. Suddenly, a figure loomed up before Duncan pointing a Sten gun. Duncan held up his pistol with two hands and fired twice directly into the face of the man, who pitched forward. Duncan looked down at the body crumpled before him. "Jesus, Jesus," he muttered laughing, elation replacing fear. His .45 had split the head of the bandit and brains mixed with blood were oozing out. Duncan bent over staring, making the man out to be Chinese. Abruptly, he stopped laughing, turned around and walked away unsteadily.

Duncan was sitting on a limestone rock just below the crest, looking about with vacant eyes when he saw Tao and a group of guerrillas herding eight men, their hands tied. He climbed up the hill toward them. The gunfire had broken off, except for an occasional distant shot.

On a command from Tao the prisoners fell to their knees. When Duncan approached, the prisoners looked up at him with evident relief, as if this white man might be a kinder captor. Bloodied, dirty, with hair drooping over their features, Duncan had difficulty distinguishing each of them by ethnic origin. Several seemed to be of tribal origin. But most apparently were Vietnamese or Chinese. They wore black peasant dress or military shirts, except for one large Chinese-looking man, stripped to the waist, his powerful body glistening with sweat, who did not look up. Duncan smelled the stink of sweat and fear.

Tan appeared, holding a bloodied machete, trailed by his fellow Nungs. Wild-eyed he surveyed the prisoners and walked among them, looking closely at each. When he came to the man stripped to the waist, he took hold of his black ponytail, yanked his head back, and bent over to look into his face. "Ah yah!" he shouted. "The General ..."

Duncan guessed that the General had discarded his shirt possibly because he had worn epaulettes.

Tan looked silently at Tao, waiting.

"They are yours," Tao said.

Tan put his machete to the throat of the General. "Get up," he said in Vietnamese, and motioned him aside, apart from the other prisoners. He then shouted in his native dialect.

The Nungs with machetes swinging charged onto to the kneeling prisoners. As Duncan watched he saw that the Nungs were not killing the whimpering prisoners at once, but were hacking at their limbs, gouging their eyes, prolonging their agony as much as they could.

Duncan turned to Tao, intending to protest, but his mouth filled with vomit. The General, still standing untouched, cried out to Duncan in French. "You're a civilized man. Shoot me!"

Duncan looked into the man's fear-crazed eyes. Then he glanced about at the Nungs standing among the tortured dead, holding their bloodied machetes.

I'm for them, but I'm not one of them, Duncan thought, and reached for the pistol in his belt. As he took hold of the .45, Tao clutched his hand, restraining him. Suddenly Nungs were in a tight circle around them.

Duncan shook his head and wiped his mouth with the back of his hand.

"Come," Tao said. "He belongs to Tan. He's the murderer of his children."

Duncan was walking down the slope when the screams began. He put his hands over his ears and kept walking.

# -13-

WITH THE BATTLE OVER, the Vietminh column rested at the foot of the northern hill while Tao, accompanied by Tan, went into the valley to meet with the Nung chieftain. Duncan sat apart from the guerrillas. He refused the rice ration that was being doled out. He walked to a nearby stream, sat on a limestone outcropping, and fingering his white jade gazed up the hill. He thought back on the massacre of the bandit prisoners on the hilltop and how Tao restrained him when he was moved to shoot the General. All that horror amid the glory of the dawn and in a field of fragrant mountain lilies. But that's their way of life, he thought. If I must work with them for a better future, there's no choice now but to abide by their tactics. It's enough to warp the soul, he sighed, as he returned to the Vietminh encampment.

In the morning, Tao marched the guerrilla column back to the ruined Nung village. Two Nung guides accompanied them, but Tan and the other Nungs remained in the valley to bury their dead and to pick over the bandit loot. The Nungs suffered numerous dead and wounded in the firefight on the valley floor, but the Vietminh had not suffered casualties.

After a night in the village, the column crossed the border and bivouacked at Tichou, where Duncan had been brought by the Chinese major to meet Mai. "Someone will come for you tomorrow," Tao told Duncan after speaking to the village chief.

A jeep bumped into the village the next morning with Roberts, the major commanding the Air-Ground Aid Section, at the wheel and another American soldier seated beside him with a Thompson submachine gun at the ready on his his lap. "Greetings!" the major hailed Duncan, who had just come out of the hut where he had spent the night. The major laughed as he shook Duncan's hand, "Brother," he said, "you look like something dragged out of a cave. But you made it. Good deal."

Duncan smiled wanly. He shook hands with Tao and the other Vietminh who had lined up to say farewell. "Let's go," he said, climbing into the jeep. "I can smell the coffee."

On the road to Tepao, the major said: "We've had a message from Colonel Hopkins in Kunming. They're sending a plane for you. And oh yes! Don't know if you want to talk to them, but there are two French correspondents at my camp. One's from the Agence France–Presse and the other—a good looking French dame—she works for the *Observer* in London."

"Really ... really," Duncan said, his jaw slack. "The lady's name is Suzanne Dumont?"

"That's right," the Major said. "You know her?

"I knew Dumont and that AFP man, Jacques Marcuse, in Chungking," Duncan said, affecting a casual tone. "How about that Marcuse? How do you like the monocle? What are they doing here?"

"They're waiting to interview French survivors of the Jap coup who are heading for the border," the major said. "One column— Foreign Legionnaires from the frontier post at Cao Bang under a Colonel Reul—should reach this sector soon. So damn sorry for them. It's tough going. Jap planes have been strafing them."

"The poor bastards ... I know now what it's like making it through that frontier terrain," Duncan said, while trying to gather his thoughts about what he would say to Suzanne. He had looked forward to a reunion—but here? Now? Yes, he wanted to see her. Try to make up for his clumsiness in Chungking. But what could he tell her about Mai ... that he was rid of his obsession? That last night with Mai ...

In the AGAS camp the major dropped Duncan off at the tent he had occupied previously and where his clothes were being kept. "Coffee will be on the way in no time," the major called out. "I'll have water heated for washing. We'll have lunch in my tent at noon with the correspondents."

A mirror hung on the tent pole and Duncan grimaced at his reflection. A bearded gaunt face with bloodshot eyes stared back at him. His black hair, usually slicked back, hung in curls about his ears. Only a month, he thought, but everything is changed—the world and me.

The major and the two correspondents were already at the folding table in the major's tent drinking beer when Duncan walked in, shaven and in his khakis. Jacques Marcuse, a tall, thin man, monocle cocked on his left eye, rose and extended his hand. "Travis, old boy, how nice to see you again," he said, in an accent redolent of British schooling. Duncan shook his hand and went to Suzanne, who wore an excited smile, kissing her on both cheeks.

"Quite a reunion," Duncan said, his hand resting on Suzanne's shoulder. She reached up and grasped his hand tightly.

Marcuse lit a curved pipe and said: "You've been across the border. Met with the Vietminh ... with the one they call Ho Chi Minh?"

"Yes," Duncan said, as he took a chair and reached for the beer.

"What's he like?"

"Impressive," Duncan said, thinking it best not to say too much before being debriefed by Donovan's people. "He says he'll never stop fighting for independence and I don't doubt it. He's a tough old Communist, but humane."

"Humane?" Marcuse said, in a skeptical tone. "More so, I trust, than his Vietminh comrades. I don't hold any brief for what the French have done in this country, but the Vietminh are now outdoing them. I've seen reliable reports about what's been happening in the Tonkin countryside. Vietminh assassination teams—they call them Honor Squads—are systemically eliminating Annamese village officials and others accused of collaborating with the French or the Japanese ... anyone who opposes them. Hundreds have been killed. They're tightening their control of the region."

Suzanne interjected: "It's true ... a horrifying purge."

Duncan listened silently. Recalling the bitterness and anger of the Vietminh leaders he'd met in the Pac Bo hut with Ho and what he'd seen on the hilltop, he didn't doubt what he was being told.

"Here we go," the major said, as a Vietnamese woman entered carrying a platter of steaks. "Buffalo, but good." Platters of rice, corn and bamboo shoots followed. Marcuse wrinkled his nose, but Duncan attacked the food with a relish that evoked laughter from Suzanne. "You've not eaten too well these past weeks," she said.

"The bananas were superb," Duncan said. "But what's the story about the French troops coming up to the border?"

Suzanne said, "You've heard about Lang Son." She closed her eyes for a moment. "The garrison at Dong Dang did little better. After Lang Son, the Japanese sent a couple of regiments against the Dong Dang forts. The troops there fought hard. They surrendered only after they ran out of ammunition. The Japanese—they must have been infuriated because of their heavy casualties—beheaded the French commander in front of his assembled colonial troops. They shot and bayoneted others in the garrison. Not many got away. But thank God … the garrison at Cao Bang escaped. We're waiting for them here. As for General Sabbatier's troops—thousands of them retreated from the forts around Hanoi and are now fighting their way toward the Yunnan border."

Marcuse interrupted: "Sabbatier's troops could have made it to Yunnan by now, but De Gaulle instructed Sabbatier to hang on in Tonkin to retain—as he put it—a presence that would symbolize continued French sovereignty over Indochina." Marcuse puffed furiously on his pipe. "So ridiculous. We're being led by a pompous ass." He looked around the table. "Don't quote me," he muttered.

"The delay gave the Japanese time to close in on Sabbatier's units," Suzanne said. "They've been badly cut up. What's left of his force may not reach the border for some time, but at least Chennault is giving them some cover … dropping supplies to them."

"So it's been lifted," Duncan exclaimed, "Roosevelt's order against assistance to French troops?"

"Yes, by Truman," Suzanne said, "but late … so very late."

As a pall settled over the table, the major said cheerfully: "Well, the good news is that the Japs are being whacked in the Pacific. Home by Christmas. Wow!"

"How long will you be here, Suzanne?" Duncan asked.

"Until Colonel Reul's Legionnaires arrive from Cao Bang and we can interview them. And you?"

"I expect to leave tomorrow."

"Early," the major said. "A taxi-plane, an L-5, is coming in for you just after daylight, unless Jap Zeros are up."

Duncan turned to Suzanne: "May I come by your tent later to say goodbye?"

"I'm sure you two have much to say to each other," Marcuse injected mischievously, his monocle fixed and his bushy eyebrows raised.

Suzanne glared at Marcuse. "Of course, Travis," she said.

Suzanne was sitting on her cot reading by the light of an oil lamp nailed to the tent pole when Duncan ducked in. She had discarded her bush jacket for a pink blouse with ruffles, which by some mysterious intuition she had been moved to bring to the primitive border.

Duncan felt the old stirring. She's so damn beautiful, he thought.

"Come sit beside me," Suzanne said. "You look a bit thin. Malaria? Dysentery?" She tugged playfully at his curls.

Duncan shook his head. "And you," he said, "Everything going well?"

"Surviving," she said with a toss of her head. "In Chungking, at the Mission, Pechkov guessed I told you about Mai. But he forgave me. He owes me something." As Duncan listened astounded, she told him of her mission to Lang Son. "All in the dustbin now," she said.

"So you're still working for M.5?"

Suzanne laughed. "One doesn't resign easily from M.5. I'm going to file a story from here to the *Observer* on Roberts' radio. But that's not why I am here. I'm carrying instructions for Colonel Reul. De Gaulle wishes to reorganize all the French troops that make it over the border into a new unit. The Americans have agreed to reequip them for operations against the Japanese."

Suzanne lit a cigarette and looked at Duncan through a puff of smoke. "Tell me, you found Mai?" she asked with a faint smile.

Duncan nodded.

"She's well?"

"Yes, she is."

"And your romance?" Suzanne asked, and touching Duncan's hand, said. "You can understand my curiosity." She smiled, a bit imploringly.

"Romance?" Duncan said with an abrupt shrug. He stood up, lifted Suzanne into his arms and kissed her on both cheeks. "I'll look for you. Don't forget me."

"I'm a patient woman," Suzanne said, and kissed him hard on the lips.

"GOOD LUCK ON THE FLIGHT," Major Roberts said, as they watched the L-5 bounce to a halt on the grass strip. "You've had the Lord with you all the way through that terrain where nobody sane ought to go."

Duncan laughed, took the white jade out of his pocket and held it up. "My good luck piece," he said rubbing it.

The propeller was still spinning when Duncan climbed into the plane beside the pilot, who extended his hand and shouted: "Cummings from South Dakota ... and praying that I get back there right soon!" They took off, skimming over the banyan trees towering up to one hundred feet at the end of the strip.

As the plane barely cleared the jungle canopy, Duncan wondered: What if the single engine on this jalopy goes out? Once, when the engine coughed, Duncan tensed but the pilot laughed, "Don't get edgy. We'll be okay. These jobs are more reliable than the C-47s. Got to fly this low to avoid being spotted. The Japs run air patrols out of Lang Son." He glanced up over the horizon. "My last time down to the border I hauled that skinny little Viet ... Ho what's his name. Spunky character ... never blinked when a wheel grazed one of those banyan trees as we were coming in."

At the Kunming airfield, a soldier in a jeep took Duncan to Colonel Hopkins' office.

"How about a drink before lunch?" Hopkins asked, as he welcomed Duncan. "Bet you haven't seen real booze for a long time."

"Sure, I could use a bourbon on the rocks," Duncan said.

Hopkins went to a sideboard, poured drinks and joined Duncan on the leather sofa. "I'm sure you've got quite a story to tell," he said. "But first, Travis, you're going back to Washington. Donovan wants to talk to you face-to-face."

Duncan straightened up, startled, and frowning asked: "Will I be coming back?"

"I don't know. It's Donovan's call. He wants a preliminary report from you immediately. We'll radio your report tonight if you can write it after lunch."

Duncan drained his glass. "I could use another one of these," he said, still shaken by news of the recall. I'll get back to Vietnam, one way or another, he thought.

Hopkins fetched another drink. "There'll be a bottle in your hostel room," he said grinning, "but only after you write that report. We'll put you on a flight over The Hump as soon as possible. The message from Donovan said he wants to meet you without delay, but not at the E Street Headquarters in Washington. He wants to talk to you privately, at his home."

"At the Georgetown house?"

"No. In his apartment on Sutton Place in New York. It's where he lived when he was practicing law in New York."

Duncan shook his head. "I don't get it," he said. "Why all the hush-hush?"

"You've been out of touch," Hopkins said. "You're not going to get any medals pinned on you in Washington for hooking up with Ho Chi Minh. Things have been moving fast and are not the same as when you left. We worked all through the war with Communists in Europe ... like Tito in Yugoslavia ... and we swapped intelligence with the Soviet NKVD. It paid off in operations against the Germans and Italians. But now with the war over in Europe Donovan is catching some flak from certain types in the Senate and in the press about our links with the Commies. You'll hear more from Donovan."

Duncan was on an ATC flight over The Hump two days later. At Andrews Air Force Base a young army lieutenant met him and he was taken to a Fairchild liaison plane. Several hours later he was at the military airfield at Fort Dix in New Jersey where Freeman, the OSS driver who had taken him to Warm Springs, was waiting with his Packard limousine.

"You've joined the club," Freeman said grinning as he stowed Duncan's bags.

At Sutton Place on Manhattan's East Side Freeman parked at the end of the cul-de-sac and led him to Donovan's apartment. An elderly woman in a black-trimmed apron responded to the bell and led Duncan through the spacious apartment to the library where Donovan, in white civilian shirtsleeves, greeted him.

"Travis, good to have you here," Donovan said, grasping Duncan's hand. He gestured to a sofa chair near a window looking out on the East River and called out: "Emma, bring us coffee, please." As he took a chair near Duncan, Donovan said: "I don't use this apartment very often since leaving Wall Street ... traveling too much. Emma, my housekeeper, looks after it."

Duncan glanced at the antique figurines around the library standing before shelves spilling over with books and manuscripts. "You have some rare things," he said.

"Oh yes," Donovan said absentmindedly as Emma brought in a tray: "Have some coffee." He settled back, stirring his coffee. "Your report, Travis, was most interesting ... more for what you told us about Ho Chi Minh than what he said. His proposal for a transition to independence in five to ten years within the French Union won't fly, of course. De Gaulle would never agree. I tried it out on the French ambassador here, and he just laughed. I suppose, you anticipated that?"

Duncan nodded. "I think Ho Chi Minh also anticipated that."

Donovan said: "Since Roosevelt's death, De Gaulle has become confident he can hold onto Indochina. If FDR had lived, I'm sure he'd have carried through his idea of a trusteeship, possibly with some kind of transition to independence not unlike what Ho proposes. Ho's plan fits in pretty well with what FDR was thinking not long before he died. Quentin Roosevelt, Teddy Roosevelt's grandson, who works with us, and is well plugged in, told us: Rather than buck Churchill and De Gaulle—what with Stalin and Chiang Kai-shek indifferent about Indochina—the president was thinking of a compromise. He wouldn't object to France acting as trustee if De

Gaulle pledged eventual full independence." Donovan snorted: "Well, that's water over the dam."

"Where do we go from here?" Duncan asked. "The Vietminh won't accept whatever the Allies find convenient. The French are in for a fight if they push back into Vietnam."

"I agree. But no one is taking hold of the problem. Right now, the situation is status quo. President Truman is so preoccupied with winding up the war with Japan and putting together Europe that he's not paying attention. He favors self-government for Indochina. But the State Department has persuaded him not to go ahead on a trusteeship arrangement without French consent. That just about kills the trustee idea. But we're not making any long-term commitments to the French. We've agreed to aid the forces they have on the ground in Indochina but only for action against the Japanese. As for the Vietminh, we can give them limited assistance in return for their help in operations against the Japanese. We can't promise them anything beyond that. We may not have an agreement on the political future of Indochina until after the war."

"That's a nothing policy," Duncan said, putting his cup down so hard that the coffee spilled onto the silver serving tray.

Donovan shrugged. "There's nothing more we can do for now. But, Travis, we've got to keep the Vietminh working with us. It's essential. Ho's guerrillas are in control of all Tonkin except for Hanoi and the few other areas held by the Japanese. We depend on them for intelligence on Jap movements, targets for Chennault planes, weather, and rescue of any of our air crews shot down."

Donovan got up and stood before the mantelpiece, hands thrust into his pants pockets. "Travis, I want you to go back to Pac Bo. Be open with Ho. Tell him where things stand. Promise him we'll give him what help we can. Hold on in Pac Bo until the political situation clarifies. We'll keep you informed."

Donovan folded his arms and cocked his head at Duncan. "Well?"

"I'm ready to go back, General," Duncan said tightly. "But you've got to know what you've got in me. I'm still committed to the mission President Roosevelt gave me. Identify a leader in Indochina who'd serve us well under a trusteeship. I'm not ready to say it's Ho. I must find out more about him. But right now I think he's the best bet."

"It doesn't worry you that he's a Communist?" Donovan asked in an even voice.

Duncan laughed sardonically. "Sure, I'd be happier with Ho if he were a Jeffersonian democrat. But you don't have to be in Indochina very long before you find out there are no democratic leaders. The French did nothing to prepare Indochina for democratic self-rule. That's why a trusteeship is needed. It would be a chance to turn that benighted country into a more humane society ... eventually into a democracy."

Donovan dropped back in his chair. "When we sent you to Indochina—and asked you to check out Ho—I told you we've been working with Communists. It didn't worry us all that much that Ho was said by the French to be a Communist. But the situation has changed. Washington is very edgy now about Stalin's moves in Eastern Europe and his flirtations with De Gaulle. Our contacts with Communists everywhere are being scrutinized by Congress and the press. We are reevaluating those old connections. So, this is the deal, Travis. Go back. Work with Ho according to my instructions. But remember: For the long haul we've got to know where Ho stands in relation to the Russians. Nail that down. Am I understood?"

"Yes, Sir," Duncan said.

"Okay," Donovan said. He poured himself another cup of coffee. "I have a message from your father. He wants you to visit him and your mother at their vacation house on the Cape. That might be good for you after what you've been through. One other thing. I want you to spend some time at our Special Techniques School. It's at the Marine base at Fort Belvoir in Virginia. I worry about sending you into Tonkin without any military schooling. You don't have much time. But at least Belvoir will give you some familiarization with weapons. We'll arrange some parachute training for you as well. You may have to drop into Pac Bo. It'll be easier than the trail from the border. We want you back in Pac Bo by mid-July."

"Diplomacy never prepared me for this," Duncan said with a sigh. "Okay, General."

"You'll go back to Kunming in the temporary grade of lieutenant colonel. A uniform will do more for you than that wrinkled suit you've got on."

After checking in at the Waldorf Hotel, Duncan telephoned the house at Hyannis and spoke to his mother.

"Oh Travis, how wonderful to have you back. Come here at once. We're dying to see you."

"I'll come for the weekend, Mother. I need a couple of days to work things out. I'm at the Waldorf."

"That's fine. We've invited the Sullivans for the weekend. You remember, they have a house down the beach. Their daughter, Nora, your old flame, will be with them. Poor thing. She lost her husband three years ago. Johnny was killed in the Pacific. He was a naval officer on the *Yorktown* when it was sunk. You remember Johnny, of course."

"Of course, Mother," Duncan said.

After he hung up the phone, Duncan went into the sitting room, looked out the window, and thought about Johnny, that freckled-faced kid with red hair. They'd been at school together, with the other rich kids, at the Noble and Greenough School in Brookline, and then at Choate. Johnny wasn't the first. How many of his classmates had already been killed in the war? For the last three years he'd suffered spasms of guilt. He with a relatively safe diplomatic job while the others were getting killed. Not like Dad—a major in the First World War—commanding that infantry battalion in the hellish fighting through the Argonne Forest.

But now he felt more at peace with himself. Roosevelt and Donovan had given him work that counted. Duncan sat down on the sofa and picked up the *New York Herald Tribune*. Crumpled at his feet lay the *Washington Star* and the *New York Times*, already read. In perusing the papers for news of Indochina, Duncan found nothing.

On Saturday morning Duncan took the train to Boston, rented a car and drove to Hyannis. Growing up he had spent most of his summers at the big wood-shingled house on the beach. As he pulled up before the pillared verandah of the white mansion, he felt a surge of nostalgia for the old days of play. Vera Duncan, his mother, came running down the steps and they embraced. She will be delighted, he thought, with the jade pendant I bought for her in Kunming.

"You look beautiful as always," Duncan said. She was a fine featured, youthful woman with dark bobbed hair, slim in a white blouse and skirt. "Come," she said, taking his arm. "Your father is waiting for you in his study. The Sullivans will be here for dinner."

Duncan dropped his bag in the hallway and went upstairs to the study, a small room off the master bedroom. Michael Duncan, pen in hand, was bent over his massive old desk, writing amid a clutter of books and paper binders. He jumped up when Travis knocked at the doorway, took off his pince-nez glasses, and hugged him. "So good to have you home, Son." he said, in a voice heavy with emotion. He cleared a pile of books from the chair beside the desk. "Sit down. You've really had a time. Donovan told me about your trek to Ho Chi Minh. I'll want to hear more. I'm glad all that's over."

"Not over yet, Father. I'm going back."

Michael fell back in the swivel chair. "Oh … Donovan didn't tell me. What is it this time?"

"We need the help of the Vietminh in operations against the Japanese."

"Isn't there anybody else Donovan can send?"

"I know Ho Chi Minh better than anybody else in the OSS."

"Son, you know best what you have to do. But I hate to see you taking these risks. I'd find it easier to live with that if I saw that people in this country cared more about Indochina. At the State Department, Indochina isn't on anybody's priority list. The Secretary of State is telling the president we can't afford to antagonize De Gaulle by harping on Indochina. The Congress, the newspapers and the public couldn't care less."

"We'll regret that deeply someday," Travis said. He paused. "Father, do you know about my meeting with Roosevelt?"

"Yes. The president wrote to me in confidence after you left for Indochina."

"Well?"

"I understand, Travis. But the policy has changed … what with the fear of Stalin. You could become a scapegoat if you bucked the French and became too friendly with Ho Chi Minh."

"Father … when Roosevelt asked you to go to Paris in 1933, with France falling apart and the State Department fighting your appointment, you didn't balk."

Michael studied his son's features and smiled. "Come," he said, rising. "I want to show you our new German shepherd pup."

Duncan joined his parents at the front door to greet the Sullivans when they arrived, their chauffeur trailing behind with the baggage.

"Travis, and handsome as ever," Nora said as she came into his arms. She was a slender woman with a tilted Irish nose, flirtatious blue eyes and upswept blonde hair. Like her mother, she was in a flowered chiffon dress.

"And you, beautiful as ever," Duncan said, pleasantly surprised at her undiminished good looks. "So very sorry about Johnny."

"Travis, great to see you," Drew Sullivan boomed. "Just back from Indonesia?"

"Indochina," Duncan said sourly.

"Same part of the world, I suppose," Sullivan guffawed. He was dressed, like Michael, in a blue blazer and white trousers and wore a foulard.

Duncan felt underdressed in his open-necked white silk shirt and wrinkled seersucker trousers. Duncan had never particularly liked Nora's parents. Her father, a balding heavyset man, who was not shy about letting it be known he was a very successful banker. His wife, a stout woman, was a self-satisfied matron not untypical of pretentious Beacon Hill. Once, they'd assumed Duncan would marry Nora.

Dinner was agonizing for Duncan. Michael tried to turn the conversation to his son's experiences. Sullivan listened politely, but quickly reverted to speculation about what the end of the war would mean for Boston's economy and politics. Nora, exchanging quick smiles with Duncan, said little during dinner.

As the men were going into the lounge for cigars and liquor, Nora said to Duncan: "Swim in the morning?"

Just after nine, they were walking along the beach. "Just like old times," Nora said.

"That was hard, losing Johnny," Duncan said. He had not attended their marriage at the Sacred Heart Church in Boston. They married four months after his departure for Paris to study at the Sorbonne. Not long before that, he'd broken up with Nora, whom he had dated for years.

"Yes," Nora said. "We didn't have many years together. We didn't have any kids. I had a miscarriage." They walked on in silence. As she bent over to examine a seashell, Nora asked: "Married? Girl friend?"

"Never married," Duncan replied.

"Well, all's not lost," Nora said laughing and ran into the surf.

In the afternoon, they lounged on the beach near the white picket fence. Nora had changed into a black low-cut bathing suit and Duncan took in her figure appreciatively.

"Why don't we skip dinner here and go out on the highway?" Nora proposed. "Bunny's is still there. It's sleazy as ever, but fun."

"Sure."

They sat in a wooden booth at the roadside café, and Duncan talked about Indochina, disjointedly at first and then ever more passionately as the night went on, recalling everything except Mai. He didn't seem to be aware of the lively chatter at the bar or the blaring jukebox. Nora was attentive, encouraging Duncan with an occasional question. She had read little in the newspapers about Southeast Asia nor remembered anything about Indochina from her years at Smith, although she had graduated with honors in European history. When Duncan paused, sloshing his drink about, she asked: "Are you going back?"

Duncan nodded.

"For how long?"

"I don't know," he said. "Our war will be over soon, but not the one in Vietnam … the long war." He tossed back the rest of his drink.

"It's late," Nora said. "Mind if I drive?" Duncan shrugged. They were almost at the house when Nora said. "I'm staying in that room just down the hall from yours … where I used to stay on weekends." She laughed.

"I remember," Duncan said thickly. They'd had their first fumbling sex there.

At the house Duncan went unsteadily up the stairs grasping the banister and on the landing they said goodnight in a close embrace.

In his room Duncan stripped and fell naked into bed. He lay awake and once again memories of Mai stubbornly intruded, confusing and depressing him. She didn't say she loved me, he thought. God, why can't I get her out of my mind? He tore aside the sheet covering him, went to the closet and put on his old silk dressing gown. He walked down the dimly lit hall to Nora's room and knocked on the door. Faintly, he heard: "Come." When he opened the door, Nora said, "I've been waiting."

As the Sullivans were saying goodbye in the morning, Nora kissed Duncan gently. "Let's keep in touch," she said and laughed.

"You're still wonderful as ever," Duncan said. Out on the verandah he waved to her as the Sullivans' car drove out.

Duncan spent the next two weeks in the OSS Special Techniques School at Fort Belvoir learning spy craft, how to survive and how to kill. Surveying his classmates, Duncan marveled at the types Donovan had selected for his clandestine missions. They ranged from Wall Street lawyers and graduate students fresh from Japanese studies at the Army language school at Berkeley, to an aristocratic Russian émigré, an anthropologist and a man whom Duncan recognized as a Hollywood actor.

Wearing green fatigues they were up every morning doing push-ups and running under the scrutiny of a merciless Marine drill sergeant. The AGAS major at Tepao would be pleased, Duncan thought, knowing that here he was learning how to rapid-fire a carbine, an M-1 rifle and the folding paratrooper submachine gun. Duncan worked at molding plastic demolition explosives, and came under the tutelage of the celebrated Colonel Fairburn, a brutish, muscular Briton. Fairburn once headed the police in Shanghai where he had developed the Fairburn knife, a perfectly balanced six-inch blade for killing. Duncan was taught how to slash, slit a throat, whip the knife from inside his trouser leg, armpit or back and throw it with deadly effectiveness. When the course ended, Duncan was issued a kit, which among other things contained a plastic vial. "This is a Q-pill," he was told. "If the alternative is worse, crush it between your teeth and you'll die quick."

Duncan was in the barracks packing, hoping for another weekend at Hyannis and play with Nora, when he was handed an order to report to the paratrooper training center at Fort Benning, Georgia. Dismayed, he sat on his cot and wondered momentarily if his father had not been right about the wisdom of a return to the more sedentary arts of diplomacy. He didn't savor the idea of jumping out of an airplane at all. As a child he had been nervous about heights. He remembered once when he was eleven going to the edge of a high diving board on a dare and then backing off.

At Fort Benning, Duncan reported to an army paratrooper colonel who seemed seven feet tall in his highly polished boots. The colonel didn't conceal his distaste for the odd types the OSS sent him. "I have orders to get you out of here in a week," he said. "We generally require five jumps, but you'll have time for only two by day and one at night. Good luck."

At the end of the week, Duncan limped back into the colonel's office. "Sprained my leg on the night jump." Duncan said, half apologetically.

The colonel rose chuckling from behind his desk. "You did okay," he said. "They tell me you got a little nudge from the jump master the first time. Not unusual. But you behaved like a pro on the night jump."

The colonel handed over a large sealed Manila envelope. "Your orders, I guess," he said, shaking his head. "Always a lot of hocus pocus with you guys. You're to pick up uniforms here and go to Washington in two days."

In the barracks Duncan opened the envelope. It contained flight orders from Washington to Kunming. There was a note from Donovan. "Proceed at once to Kunming. We have made new arrangements for the Vietminh. Hopkins will brief you."

Duncan, in the uniform of an army lieutenant colonel, left Washington for Kunming on July 15.

# -15-

**Kunming**
**July 18, 1945**

HOPKINS THREW A MOCK SALUTE when Duncan walked into his office. "Welcome, Colonel," he said grinning. "That rank will get you better grub, booze and transportation. But the insurance policy is still only for ten thousand bucks. Drink? You've been busy. Jumping out of airplanes. Enjoyed it, I'm sure."

"I can think of better ways to spend my time," Duncan said, as he accepted the bourbon and settled on the leather sofa.

"I don't think you'll regret the training," Hopkins said. "It looks like you'll have to parachute in somewhere near Pac Bo. The Japs have begun sending big patrols out of Cao Bang along the border. It would be too risky to try that trail again."

"I look forward to it," Duncan said with a sigh, and knocked back most of his drink. "Any good news?"

"Yes. We've been authorized to drop weapons, ammunition and other supplies to the Vietminh. We'll also parachute in a training team. The Viets have been giving us excellent intelligence. We're now fulfilling our part of the deal. There's a training team about ready to go. It's commanded by a very good guy, Major Jeb Trivers. The code name is Deer Team. You'll parachute in ahead. We'll count on you to coordinate with the Vietminh and stake out a drop zone for the team."

"When do I leave?" Duncan asked.

"In two days. We'll message the Vietminh you're coming and ask them to specify a drop area. We haven't been in contact with them for some time. Chennault's headquarters is supplying a C-47 with a jumpmaster."

I wonder if Mai will be in Pac Bo, Duncan thought, as he said goodbye to Hopkins.

Two days later, at 3 AM, Duncan was driven to a briefing room in a building just off the tarmac at the Fourteenth Air Force base. He was surprised to see Hopkins there, having already taken leave of him. Hopkins was standing with four other men: an Air Force major, two lieutenants in flight garb—presumably the pilots of the C-47 drop aircraft—and a sergeant, the jumpmaster. After introducing them, Hopkins said: "There's a switch in plans. We've had a message from the Vietminh. They're ready to receive you, but they've moved their headquarters."

"And that's our problem," the Air Corps major said, as he mounted the platform and went to one of the maps. "Originally," he said, pointing, "we were asked to drop you here near Pac Bo, just over the China border. Easy. Now we're ordered to drop you at a placed called Kim Lung, which is about three hundred miles from here. Okay. But here's the problem. It's only forty miles northwest of Hanoi. The Japs have an air base at Hanoi with a lot of nasty Zeros. They run air patrols out of there to cover their big outpost at Thai Nguyen on the highway running north. And also, to cover Route Colonial Numero 1 running northeast, their supply route for Lang Son and the other frontier posts. They now control all those posts clear to Cao Bang. We've asked that our B-29s based in the islands knock out the Jap base at Hanoi—something we haven't been able to do from here. As yet, the B-29s haven't been diverted for that job."

"We don't know why Ho has relocated to Kim Lung," Hopkins said. "It's so damn close to that Jap outpost at Thai Nguyen."

The major said, "Ordinarily, we wouldn't attempt a drop at Kim Lung. But given the importance of your mission, we've agreed to drop you there at daybreak. For cover, three of our fighter planes will rendezvous with your C-47 over the drop zone. But with their limited fuel, they'll be there only for a few minutes. Pray you're not spotted and, if you are, that the Japs haven't scrambled too many Zeros."

The pilots looked at each other, but said nothing.

Duncan shook hands with Hopkins. "Only ten thousand bucks?" he said. Hopkins just grinned.

Duncan boarded the C-47 as it was being refueled. The jumpmaster, Sergeant Casey, and two army privates were already aboard. Casey was a fresh-faced youngster who looked to be just out of high school. Oh brother, my life in the hands of a kid, Duncan thought. Lashed down in the cabin were canvas-wrapped bales, each with a parachute attached. Duncan saw that his own duffel was hooked onto one of them.

Duncan shook hands with Casey and waved to the other soldiers. "They'll be pushing out those supply bales and your stuff," the sergeant said as he unfolded a map.

"Colonel, here's Kim Lung. As you can see, it's in a mountain valley. We should be over it at the crack of dawn. We've been told to make the drop in the rice paddies near a village that's not far from Kim Lung. The Viets have told us they'll build fires as markers."

"At what altitude do I jump?"

"That's tough," the sergeant said grimacing. "The drop area is probably no more than a small opening in the jungle. We'll have to come in pretty low. We'll try to drop you at about eight hundred feet, but it may be lower." He folded the map. "There's no reason for it to happen, but if the static line doesn't open your chute, you'll need to pull that rip cord mighty quick."

"I get it, thanks," Duncan said stiffly, and settled back in the bucket seat as the twin motors coughed and started.

At daybreak the transport began to circle, and ten minutes later one of the pilots called back: "Village down there ... columns of smoke. Must be Kim Lung."

The sergeant put on his earphones, opened the hatch, looked down and began talking to the pilot. "Got it," he said and motioned for the soldiers to push out the supply bales. As the plane circled for a second time, Casey said to Duncan: "We're going in at one thousand. Stand. Hook your static line. Wait. There's the rice field." Suddenly, Casey clapped his hands to his earphones, his eyes wide.

"Hold it," he said. "Aircraft approaching. They may be ours. No. Japs!" he shouted. As the C-47 veered sharply, the pilots taking evasive action, the jump master was sent sprawling and Duncan, standing in the open hatchway, saw a Zero hurtle by, its guns firing. He looked down. Seeing the aircraft was not far from the drop zone, he muttered: "Better go for it." He leaped out of the plane.

Thankfully, Duncan heard the thud of the parachute opening and then felt himself being jerked around. Descending, he looked up, saw that the three covering American fighters had dived down and were tangled in a dogfight with two Zeros. The C-47 was distant on the horizon, trailing black smoke. As he floated down he could see he was at a considerable distance from the rice field. He began working his lines to slip toward it but came down short, crashing into a towering banyan tree. When he recovered from the jolt he found he was suspended from a large branch. Duncan hung there quietly for a time and then reached down and took the Fairburn knife out of his leg holster and held it aloft to slash the parachute lines. But then, looking down through a hole in the foliage canopy below him, he saw he was up probably about ninety feet. If he cut the lines he'd be killed in the fall. Duncan wiped away the gnats that had settled on the scratches on his face and looked around. Birds fluttered about him chirping. Two monkeys squatting on a branch were solemnly observing him. He could see patches of the sky but no longer heard the drone of aircraft. He wondered what had happened in the dogfight and if the C-47 had made it home.

It was some time before he decided what he must do. Certainly, the Vietminh and villagers had seen him float down and must be beating through the forest looking for him. They might be nearby, although he had not heard any calls. He unsnapped the carbine from his shoulder, loaded it, and fired a shot. He was not sure who or what the sound would attract, but there was no alternative. He fired three more shots at fifteen minute intervals before he heard cries and thrashing below the tree. He heard a guttural voice, and peering down saw a dark face grinning up at him. Duncan held his carbine on the ready, wondering if this was a friendly type. A figure in a loin cloth with a machete slung over his back climbed nimbly up the trunk of the tree onto the branch from which Duncan was suspended. He took hold of the parachute lines and began to swing Duncan side-to-side as two other natives below poked through the foliage. One reached out and grabbed Duncan and soon he was being eased down the tree by a relay of men shouting at each other. About the base of the tree, there was a cluster of villagers, and Duncan gasped in relief when he saw that standing among them was Tao and several of his guerrillas, cheering as he was let down.

"Welcome, American comrade," Tao said smiling as he helped Duncan free himself from the parachute harness.

Duncan rubbed his scraped cheeks and embraced Tao, who was carrying his familiar Sten gun. "I'm glad to be with you again," he said glancing at the villagers, who were speaking excitedly and pointing at the sky, and asked: "What are they saying?"

Tao laughed. "They're saying Ho Chi Minh has worked more of his magic and brought a man from the sky."

Duncan asked tensely: "What happened in the battle between the American fighters and the Japanese Zeros?"

"The Japanese planes were shot down. The villagers are looking for their wreckage."

Duncan sighed in relief: "And the big plane—the transport?"

"We don't know. It disappeared. We have the bales which fell from the plane."

Duncan looked about. "Is the village over there Kim Lung?"

"No. Our friends, the Tay people, live in that village. Kim Lung is on the other side of the mountain. Our new headquarters is there. We moved to Kim Lung not long ago. From there we have better communication with our units throughout Tonkin. We've given Kim Lung the new name of Tan Trao, which means New Tide in English. Uncle Ho is in Tan Trao. I must tell you. He's sick," Tao said worriedly. "Very sick."

Duncan frowned. "That's very bad news. I must see him as soon as possible."

"We'll march quickly to Tan Trao. It's not too far."

"Is Trinh Mai in Tan Trao?"

"No. She's in the south—in Cochin China—trying to rally the other nationalist parties to us. So far we haven't succeeded in uniting the parties. The Trotskyites especially are opposing us ... very strongly. They accuse us of being too willing to compromise with the French."

"Mai is doing dangerous work," Duncan said, thinking: She's with her old lover. Hopefully, he'll care for her.

Tao said: "Yes. Very dangerous. The parties sometimes fight among themselves. There have been assassinations. It's very sad. Not only that. Mai must also watch out for the *Kempeitai*, the Japanese security police, who are everywhere. Any Vietnamese suspected of being in the resistance is beheaded ... no matter what the party. No trials. Frenchmen too have been executed—many of them—anyone accused of being Gaullist. No one is safe there."

With Duncan at his side, Tao signaled to his guerrillas and they moved in a column through the Tay village, waving to its inhabitants as they entered the forest. The trail curved over the slope of a cedar-covered mountain. Hardened by his training at the OSS and parachute schools, Duncan was able to keep up with the fast pace of the march. As the column began the descent on the far slope through a low-hanging mist, Duncan could glimpse Tan Trao, a cluster of huts in a lush valley, considerably larger than the Pac Bo encampment. Just outside the village Duncan saw a field laid out with man-made obstacles on which squads of men and women were drilling.

Entering the village, Tao led Duncan at once into Ho Chi Minh's palm-thatched hut. Ho was huddled under a blanket on a mat resting on a bed of leaves and splintered tree branches. Beside him was a small table on which stood a teapot and next to it a dish in which there seemed to be mashed herbs. Ho propped himself up as Duncan entered and raised a quivering hand in greeting. Duncan took his dry fevered hand between both of his, concealing his shock at Ho's emaciated condition. The man is dying, he thought.

"Welcome, my friend," Ho said in English. "I'm sorry I can't greet you properly. But as you can see, I'm quite ill. Malaria, and other things I suppose. How's General Donovan?"

"He's well. Sends his greetings. He passed your message on to the French. They haven't yet replied."

"I'm not surprised."

"The general thanks you for the intelligence your people have been giving us on Japanese operations. The Fourteenth Air Force has been able to strike many targets. Your people have brought out some of our downed pilots."

"Good!" Ho exclaimed.

His eyes are still bright, Duncan thought, somewhat relieved. "We're now ready to do our part," Duncan said. "If you agree, we'll send a small team here to train your fighters with American weapons."

"Of course, we agree. Thank you. Make arrangements with Vo Nguyen Giap," Ho whispered and lay back on his mat. "We'll talk more when I'm better. There's much to discuss."

Tao led Duncan to a bamboo shelter where Vo Nguyen Giap was meeting with three of his guerrilla commanders. Giap, a short, wiry man with calculating eyes, greeted Duncan coolly. "We've been waiting," he said. His manner warmed as Duncan told him of the planned drop of weapons and the training team. "I'll bring in about two hundred of the best cadres in our units for the training," he said with a rare smile.

An hour later, Duncan handed a message to Mac Sin, the radio operator who had come from Pac Bo, to be sent in code to Hopkins in Kunming. *Inform Donovan Ho agreeable, Drop Deer Team at Kim Lung with equipment. Urgently include a medic with kit for jungle diseases. Ho critically ill. Advise schedule for drops. Will mark zone. Duncan.*

It was a week before Duncan received a reply: *Jap air base at Hanoi knocked out. Expect drop at noon in two days. Hopkins.*

Duncan was in the drop zone when six members of the Deer Team parachuted in. Major Trivers was the first to land, and Duncan ran to him. The major, a youngish looking man in camouflage dress, disengaged from the parachute harness, glanced about and said as he shook hands with Duncan: "I'm not sure this is better than practicing law in Michigan."

As he was being introduced to other members of the team, which included two Vietnamese sergeants, Duncan asked anxiously: "Who's the medic?"

"He's coming on the next drop," Trivers said. "We had trouble finding one with the right jungle know-how."

"I hope he won't be too late."

"That bad?" Trivers asked, his brow knitted.

"Yes. What happened to my C-47?"

"Bad news," Trivers said. "The plane crashed. The P-40s shot down the two Jap planes. On the way back they passed over the C-47's wreckage. It was gone ... burning."

The cherubic face of the jumpmaster passed through Duncan's mind.

In the Tay village the Deer Team was ceremonially offered fruit and tea before the departure for Tan Trao. Duncan declined with bows. Then, escorted by Tao and his guerrillas, the party slogged along paths bordering the rice fields, trailed by Tay tribesmen carrying the bales dropped from Trivers' transport. Entering Tan Trao, Trivers whooped when he saw a flower-bedecked archway with the inscription: *Welcome to Our American Friends.*

The following day, in the next drop, four more members of the Deer Team, among them, a medic, Paul Hoagland, parachuted in. Giving Hoagland no more time than it took to retrieve his medicine kit from one of the supply bales, Duncan led him to Ho Chi Minh's hut. Ho greeted them weakly and lay prone on his mat, shaking with fever, his eyes closed as Hoagland examined him and injected him with quinine and sulfa drugs.

Outside the hut Hoagland slung his medicine kit over his shoulder, and said: "This man doesn't have long for the world. But

I'll take care of him. He looks as if he's got malaria, dysentery and other tropical diseases."

Over the following days the Vietminh camp erupted into intense activity as guerrilla cadres arrived. The Deer Team made ready for their training as American transports parachuted in rifles, machine guns, mortars, grenades and bazookas, enough for an enlarged infantry company. The two hundred elite fighters assembled by Vo Nguyen Giap joyously caressed their new American weapons, putting aside their captured French weapons, badly worn Chinese bolt-action rifles and an assortment of other antique firearms.

As the training went forward, Duncan, who was acting as an interpreter, was astonished at the speed at which the eager guerrillas became schooled in American weapons and tactics. When Vo Nguyen Giap approached him to ask if the Americans would expand their aid even more, Duncan simply shrugged. Watching Giap at a distance talking to his men, Duncan wondered if he was indoctrinating them to battle the Japanese, as Washington intended, or mainly for action against the French.

Tao was usually with Duncan during the training classes. Twice, Duncan asked him if there was any word from Mai. "Nothing," Tao replied. "The situation is not good in the South." He did not press Tao again.

After an exhausting day under a burning sun on the drill field, Duncan was lying on the cot in his bamboo shelter when he heard Tao excitedly summoning him. He went out into the village square and saw that Ho Chi Minh had emerged from his hut. Dressed in a long-sleeved white shirt and khaki shorts, he was walking about the camp, somewhat unsteadily on his spindly legs, greeting a gathering crowd.

"Your people saved his life," Tao said to Duncan.

Duncan joined the crowd around Ho who, upon seeing him, motioned for him to come closer. "You see, Travis, I'm well again, thanks to Sergeant Hoagland," he said, his voice still quavering. "Let's have a talk soon." It was the first time that Ho addressed him by his given name.

Two days later in the evening Ho invited Duncan to his hut, which was illuminated by two oil lamps. There was a jug of beer on the table and Ho was once again smoking. "Major Trivers is very kind," Ho said, holding up a pack of cigarettes. "Chesterfields, my favorite." He inhaled deeply. "I asked the major if his men would like to meet some of the girls in the entertainment group which has just arrived." He laughed. "You know, we have very good aphrodisiac herbs in our forests." He poured beer into Duncan's mug. "The major wasn't interested. How about you, Travis?"

"No, Sir," Duncan said smiling, and treating the offer as a joke, but wondering how Mai would feel about the suggestion, even if made in jest.

"I'd like to hear more about your talk with General Donovan," Ho said, his mood sobered. "Was there any support in the Truman Administration for my proposal to the French?"

"President Truman has declared he's in favor of self-government for Indochina," Duncan said, and then remembering Donovan's injunction that he be open with Ho, added: "But he looks to the French to take the initiative."

With a sigh, Ho said: "We'll keep trying for an agreement with the French, but we have no illusions. Without the help of you Americans, there will be no agreement." Raising his voice, he said: "Travis, your people are against colonialism. You've promised independence to the Philippines. Why not us?"

Duncan had been looking for an opening to press Donovan's question about Ho's relations with the Russians. During his first extended talk with Ho he had tentatively raised the question of communism versus nationalism, now he felt that he must do Donovan's bidding and probe deeper.

"About independence, Sir," Duncan said, "you've worked for the Comintern. It's well known that Stalin demands that members of the Comintern swear loyalty to him before anything else. Frankly, we would like to know where you stand."

Ho sighed. "I suppose you're putting that question to me again. *Am I a nationalist or an agent of the Comintern?* Let's go back to the beginning. Three decades ago, when the West did not heed our appeals, we turned to Lenin, who taught us that liberation from colonialism is unobtainable without revolution. The only ideological home at that time for Indochinese like me—nationalists struggling for independence—was in the international Communist movement. But Travis, we now recognize that this is another age ... that the world situation has changed."

Ho filled Duncan's beer mug, lit another cigarette and, in the same intense tone, continued: "At the 1941 plenum of the Indochinese Communist Party in Pac Bo—when the Vietminh was founded—we did not follow the Comintern line in support of Stalin's nonaggression pact with Hitler. We went our own way. Yes, since then we have been aligned with the Soviet Union, like you Americans, in the fight against fascism. But we're not getting any help now from the Russians in our struggle. They've got their problems and we have ours. Our present contacts with them are direct, not through the Comintern. Am I a Communist? Yes ... but I think of myself more as a national-socialist than a Communist. I was trained in Moscow. But, I repaid that debt with fifteen years of work in the international Communist movement. I have no further commitment. I consider myself a free agent."

Ho looked beseechingly at Duncan: "What we want most is friendship with your country—your help in winning our independence—and later, your economic help in rescuing our people from poverty."

Ho leaned back in his chair wearily, closing his eyes. "I've said that so often. When will your people hear me?"

Duncan said, "It's late, Sir, and you need your rest. May I come back soon?"

"Yes, do ... often."

During the next weeks Duncan returned frequently to Ho's hut. Ho spoke of his boyhood as the son of a disaffected mandarin, of how he scratched out a living as a photo retoucher and revolutionary journalist in Paris, of his lonely pilgrimage around the world seeking support for Indochina's independence, and years in Chinese and Hong Kong prisons. The two debated about ideology and culture, making their points in several languages. Ho held forth in colloquial English and fluent Chinese and French. Once he lapsed into Russian as he spoke critically of how Marxism-Leninism had been corrupted in the Soviet Union into Stalinism. As Duncan was bidding him goodnight, Ho went to a corner of the room where there was a battered portable typewriter and fetched typewritten pages of his poetry, which had been translated into English, and presented them to him.

One afternoon, walking with Trivers from the training grounds back to the village, the major remarked casually: "You're spending a lot of time with Ho?"

"Yes, I am."

"What's the little guy like?"

"Clever, cultured … committed to independence for his people whatever it takes. I have no illusions about what he says. He speaks in several voices—to his own people, to the French, to the Russians, and to us. He'd make a pact with the devil to win independence. When I think of how the French have screwed his people, if I were Vietnamese, I'd likely be out on your drill field among Giap's men, learning how to throw grenades."

Trivers squinted at Duncan.

Duncan studied the expression on Trivers' face. "Well, Jeb, imagine it's 1775. You've refused to pay taxes to the British because you thought their demands were unfair. The Brits have now moved into your town and shot some of your neighbors. Would you join the Minutemen?"

"Sure," Trivers said.

"That's how Ho makes his case to me."

# -16-

Tan Trao
**August 6, 1945**

STUNNED AND STRUGGLING TO GRASP its implications, Duncan read
and reread the cryptic message scrawled on rice paper brought to him
by the radio operator. It was August 6. The message said: *FYI Air
Force today dropped atomic bomb on Hiroshima. Hopkins.*

Duncan jumped off the platform of his shelter and ran to Ho
Chi Minh's hut. He found Ho speaking to four men and a woman
seated cross-legged before him on straw mats.

Ho greeted Duncan warmly. "These are comrades from the
South," he said as the Vietnamese stood up bowing. "They're here
for a meeting of our Communist Party leaders. We're preparing for
the convening of the National People's Congress on August
sixteenth."

Introductions completed, Duncan handed Ho the radio message.

Ho read it, glanced up at Duncan, and then studied the message
again. His hand grasping the crumpled sheet fell to his side. He tilted
his head high, eyes gleaming. "They'll surrender," he whispered in
English. "This is our opportunity. We must move quickly."

Early in the morning of August 16 Duncan entered the Tan Trao
community hall, a large bamboo structure on stilts with thatched roof
where the National People's Congress was in its opening session.
There were sixty delegates of Communist and allied political parties
in the hall; Pham Van Dong, the second man in the Communist
politburo was speaking on a raised platform. Duncan seated himself
on one of the straw mats in the rear row.

There was a great stirring in the hall when Dong introduced Ho
Chi Minh. Most of the delegates knew of the legendary revolutionary,

founder of the Communist Party, only as Nguyen Ai Quoc. Now they would know him as Ho Chi Minh. As Duncan craned to watch Ho, a frail figure in a khaki tunic and shorts mount the platform, he drew a sharp breath. Unmistakably, although somewhat obscured, there on the platform seated in a row of leaders behind the rostrum, was Mai. The delegate sitting beside Duncan, a dark-skinned man in a Nung jacket, grunted irritably as Duncan leaned out in front of him to get a better view. Duncan sat back, thinking: She must have seen me come into the hall, yet no gesture of recognition? I'll go to her when the session ends.

Duncan had been listening for almost three hours to a succession of speeches and reports when Trivers came into the hall, tapped him the shoulder, and beckoned for him to follow. Outside the hall, Trivers grinned at him: "The Japs have surrendered. The war's over. I guess dropping the bomb on Nagasaki did it. Michigan here I come!"

"Hallelujah! It's so hard to believe," Duncan said, as he grasped Trivers' outstretched hand. "I must tell Ho."

"No need. The radio operator is passing him a note. Let him be happy. Later, we'll tell him the other news, which ain't good," Trivers said, grimacing. "Hopkins' telegram also gave us a fill-in on the Potsdam Conference. After Truman, Churchill and Stalin met, our Joint Chiefs of Staff and the British Joint Chiefs decided to divide Indochina for operational purposes along the Sixteenth Parallel. Chinese troops will occupy the North. The Brits will take over in the South—meaning all of Cochin China, including Saigon. The Chinese and the Brits will accept the surrender of the Japanese troops and disarm them."

Duncan's jaw fell. "That's insane," he said furiously. "Chiang Kai-shek will occupy North Vietnam with troops from South China—those divisions under that gangster warlord in Yunnan, Lu Han. They're the worst rabble. They'll loot the North. And the South, well, the damn Brits will let the French sneak back into Cochin China."

"You got it right, chum," Trivers said. "You're elected to tell Ho. But come on now," he said, tugging Duncan's arm. "The team is celebrating at lunch. We're cracking open the last bottles of bourbon."

Duncan looked back at the Congress hall, wondering as he trailed after Trivers how he might arrange to meet Mai.

Duncan left Deer Team's party in Trivers' hut at noon. Looking for Mai, he walked through a crowd of Congress delegates who were emerging from the hall. During his speech, Ho Chi Minh had spoken of the presence of the Americans and delegates turned to smile and bow before the tall foreigner in khaki uniform and combat boots. Not seeing Mai, Duncan impatiently strode back to his hut at the edge of the village. Mai was there, sitting on a ladder propped against the hut's platform. She rose, smiling as Duncan approached.

"Mai!" Duncan shouted and extended his arms. Mai accepted his embrace but stepped back quickly. "I'm happy to see you, Travis," she said. "Are you well?"

"Yes, of course," Duncan replied, looking searchingly into her eyes. "Mai, it was so good to see you in the hall. You've been in the South for many weeks. I wasn't sure we'd meet again."

Smiling gently, Mai said, "I saw you come into the hall. Ho Chi Minh spoke very well of you. You're a true friend of the Vietnamese."

"Come," Duncan said, and helped her up the ladder into the hut. He seated Mai on a stool, shoved aside the pile of books on the table, and perching there, looked eagerly at her. She had changed. Her features were pinched and burned darker; her eyes were still luminous but there were heavy lines under them. Her black cotton tunic was frayed, and Duncan could see calluses on the toes of her feet protruding from her worn rubber sandals. Duncan asked softly, "You're very tired?"

"Yes," Mai said. "I came here yesterday. I've been on a march with other comrades—from the South—for many days. We started out as soon as the call came for the Congess. There were many obstacles. We lost three comrades in an ambush by Civil Guards, led by a Frenchman."

Duncan said, "Things aren't going well in the South, are they?"

"There's much work to be done," Mai said. " The people are confused. They're misled by supporters of that puppet of the French and now of the Japanese—Emperor Bao Dai—and by other corrupt Vietnamese parties … like the Trotskyites. But we'll rally all the people once we establish a government."

Mai lifted her face to Duncan pleadingly. "Travis, we need your help urgently. Here's our situation. Ho Chi Minh has been authorized by the Congress to set up a provisional government in Hanoi. We must get him to Hanoi as quickly as possible, before the French can interfere, before they can persuade the Japanese to let them take control. The British are supporting the French. They are parachuting Gaullist agents into some parts of Vietnam. Our people have intercepted some of them."

"I understand what you're saying," Duncan said. "But how do I fit in?"

Mai snatched a map from the pocket of her tunic, spread it on the table, and pointed. "Here is Thai Nguyen," she said, "the nearest junction on the road to Hanoi. It's a two-day march on the trail from Tan Trao. There's a large Japanese garrison at Thai Nguyen. The garrison controls the road to Hanoi, which is forty miles to the south." Mai straightened up and faced Duncan. "Ho Chi Minh asks that you and the Deer Team go with him and our Liberation Army soldiers to Thai Nguyen. Now that the war is over, you Americans can demand that the Japanese there surrender to you. It is likely they'll do so. If the Japanese refuse, Vo Nguyen Giap will attack with the weapons you've given us. But it would be a very hard fight. Once the road is open, we'll escort Ho Chi Minh to Hanoi. Tao has already left for Hanoi to tell our underground workers there of our plans."

Duncan examined the map. "Possible," he said, tracing with his finger the crooked mountainous trail to Thai Nguyen. "All right. I'll do what I can. I'll talk to Major Trivers. I'll need his agreement "

Mai sighed deeply, her eyes alight. "Thank you. Thank you. Ho Chi Minh wishes to see you tonight. Will you be able to give him an answer then?"

Duncan said, "I'll try." He hesitated, tightened his mouth. "Mai, something else. Forgive me for speaking about it at this time, but I'm troubled. There's something I must know." He bent to her. "That night in Pac Bo ... you came to me. Was it because you're in love with me?"

Mai closed her eyes for a moment. "My heart is full of love for you," she whispered." You have been so kind to me. You're doing so much for my people." She hesitated. "That afternoon, when we spoke at the riverbank before you left for the border, you were so sad. I wanted you to be happy. I wanted to give you a gift." She regarded Duncan sorrowfully. "I had nothing to give you except myself."

Duncan folded his arms tightly. "Mai, tell me. It's that other man, isn't it? The one you told me about in Pac Bo when we sat beside the river. It's him you really love."

"Yes," Mai said. "You'll meet him soon. He came with me from the South." Shyly she went to Duncan, kissed him on the cheek and left the hut.

That evening Tan Trao was illuminated by huge bonfires as the guerrillas, joined by delegates to the Congress, gathered to celebrate the Japanese surrender. A Tay female dance troupe garbed in their long swirling black skirts performed in the center of the camp. Loud cheers erupted with each burst of light as the Deer Team fired off its stock of red and white signal flares.

Duncan walked restlessly about the village, and paused at a campfire, where he greeted the soldiers who were drinking beer and cooking rice. For a time, he stood there staring at the fire licking at the blackened iron pots, turning over in his mind what Mai had said to him. He thought: I've been unfair to her. Blinded by the illusion she's still the girl I knew in Saigon I pressed my unwanted self on her. I should have understood why she came to me that night.

When the celebration was over, Duncan went to Trivers' hut.

Trivers was dozing on a straw mattress under a mosquito tent, stripped to his brown shorts. The other members of the Deer Team had left. He awoke as Duncan came into the hut. "What's up," he mumbled.

"We need to talk."

"Can't it wait?"

"No."

Trivers groaned, rolled off the mattress, and emerged sleepy-eyed from the mosquito net. He reached for a clay pitcher and splashed water over his face. "Great celebration," he said. "The boys ... all they talk about: When do we go home?"

Duncan said, "Jeb, Ho Chi Minh and Vo Nguyen Giap are leaving for Hanoi. They're going with the guerrillas we trained. They want us to go with them."

"Why not?" Trivers said brightening. "It's the only way out of this jungle. The Japs have surrendered. Our mission is over. When do we leave?"

"In the next couple of days ... they're in a hurry. Ho Chi Minh plans to set up a provisional government in Hanoi."

"I'm ready to hit the trail for Hanoi," Trivers said. "But that provisional government business or what have you, I don't know about that, Travis. We can't get mixed up in Ho's politics. Mind you, I like the little guy. He may be a Communist, but honestly, some of us guys think of him as some sort of George Washington fighting for independence. But we do have strict orders—no politics."

"Affirmative," Duncan said. "They only want one thing from us. Help in getting to Hanoi. This is what they plan: We head for the road junction at Thai Nguyen. You know it. It was the base point on your parachute drops."

"Sounds good," Trivers said, standing up and pulling on a khaki shirt.

"One big problem: There's a sizable Japanese garrison at Thai Nguyen that controls the road. That's where they need us. Ho figures the Japs will surrender to us, Americans, now that the war is over. If not, Giap intends to attack the garrison. We'd go down the road to Hanoi as soon as it's cleared."

Trivers sat on a packing case and lit a cigarette. "That worries me," Trivers said. "Attack the Japs?" He shook his head. "You know these guys we've been training are fantastic guerrillas. They can mop up the French and those mercenary Civil Guards. But the Japanese? I don't know about that. We'd better think more in terms of palaver with the Japs. Get them to let us go down the road without a fight. Brother, I want to get back to Michigan."

"I'm with you, Jeb," Duncan said, pleased and somewhat surprised by Trivers' ready acquiescence. "Do you have to clear all this with Kunming?"

"I'm not going to ask them," Trivers said with a wicked grin. "I want out of here. Our last orders were to stick with Ho and work with him against the Japs. Well," Trivers shredded his cigarette, "you can tell Ho we're ready to march." With lifted eyebrows, he leaned toward Duncan. "And Colonel, sir, remember Kunming's orders … no politics."

Duncan nodded: "I'll go to Ho now," he said and departed with Trivers watching him with a skeptical smile.

In Ho's hut, Mai and a slender Vietnamese man wearing rimless spectacles were seated with Ho on straw mats. They were dipping into bowls of *pho* noodle soup.

"Welcome," Ho said. "It has been a joyous day. Share our dinner."

Mai went to the door of the hut, called out, and a woman came with another bowl of soup, spoon and chopsticks. Duncan accepted with a bow.

"You know our traditional soup," the slender Vietnamese said with a smile, speaking in unaccented French. He had fine, well-cut features, and was unusually light-skinned for a Vietnamese.

"Yes, I like it very much," Duncan replied, wondering if the man was a *métis* of Vietnamese and French blood.

Ho said, "You know Mai, of course, and this is Hoang Minh Cong. He's also a member of our Party's central committee. They've come together from the South."

Duncan glanced at Cong, forcing a smile and thinking: So this is the man. He glanced at Mai who was sitting with eyes lowered and hands folded in her lap. I must speak to her, he thought. Tell her everything is all right between us.

"This is a great day," Ho said. "Our people are celebrating both the end of the war against Japan and the decision at the Congress to establish a provisional government."

Duncan put his bowl aside. "Major Trivers and I are agreeable to going with you to Hanoi. At Thai Nguyen we'll do as you ask—try to persuade the Japanese to open the road."

Ho clapped his hands. "Ah! We thank you!"

Duncan bowed. "I have other news that's not so good. At the Potsdam Conference the military chiefs of staff decided to divide Vietnam for operational purposes at the Sixteenth Parallel. Chinese troops will come into the North to accept the surrender of the Japanese. The British will disarm them in the South."

Cong slammed down his bowl. "How could they do that?" he exclaimed, speaking in Vietnamese. "Don't we have any rights? The Chinese will come in like locusts. They may not leave. As for the British ... they are already helping the French return."

Ho, his brow deeply creased, raised his hand. "This is very disappointing. It complicates our struggle. It's all the more necessary that we move swiftly. We must get to Hanoi before the Chinese. There is no telling what they may do once they occupy the North. Mr. Duncan, if you're agreeable, we'll set out the day after tomorrow for Thai Nguyen."

"Of course," Duncan said, wondering if Ho, who still seemed frail, could survive the tortuous mountain trails to the highway junction.

Ho said, "Good." He took two handwritten sheets from his desk. "We have prepared two important messages," he said. "We ask that you transmit them through your radio. This one, addressed to the French government, renews our offer to join the French Union and accept a French president if we are guaranteed full independence within ten years. The proposal is similar to that forwarded previously through General Donovan. The provisional government we will form in Hanoi will be ready to negotiate on that basis."

Ho glanced at Cong, who was staring stonily straight ahead, before continuing: "When I told our Congress of this proposal some comrades criticized me. Many called for a general armed uprising if the Allies make any attempt to bring back the French. But the Congress finally approved my proposal after I persuaded them we're not yet ready for such an armed uprising. I reminded them of Lenin's warning against launching a revolution before all conditions are favorable. Our moment hasn't arrived yet. Too many forces are arrayed against us. Now, from what you tell us, we shall have to deal not only with the French and Japanese, but also with the Chinese and the British."

Duncan saw that Cong was about to take issue with Ho when Mai's eyes blazed, silencing him.

Ho said, "Here is the other message, Mr. Duncan. It's an appeal to the United Nations by our National Liberation Committee. It asks that they stand by their solemn promise to support independence of all nationalities."

Duncan carried the two messages to the radio installation and then returned to his hut, sat on the packing case, sipped water from a canteen and reviewed Ho's latest appeals. Ho had been persuasive at dinner, as he had been over these last weeks in all matters. But he appeared physically so frail. Could he make it to Hanoi? Did he have the force to hold together the Vietminh coalition? Cong evoked the image of Vo Nguyen Giap, who might assume power. Would Giap lean to Mao, his revolutionary model, and take an uncompromising line? On reaching Hanoi, Duncan decided, he would put his findings together without delay and report definitively to Donovan as to whether they could rely on Ho. There were unanswered questions, but he couldn't hold off any longer on his recommendation. Donovan told him in Washington that a political decision on the future of Indochina was likely to be taken when the war ended.

A MONSOON RAIN WAS WHIPPING TAN TRAO when Giap's elite two hundred lined up before the Community Hall for the march to Thai Nguyen. While their shining American weapons were impressive, they were otherwise a ragged looking lot dressed in odd bits of uniform, some barefoot. Giap was in baggy trousers, a short-sleeved white shirt, and wore the brown fedora, which he habitually affected, an odd contrast to the pith helmets and soft field hats of the others.

In the ranks, dressed in black, there were nine women, all veteran *tieudoi*—platoon leaders. Duncan had watched these women in training: crawling with their rifles and machetes through the mud between bamboo spikes. Once, the sight made him shake his head as he compared the *tieudoi* to Nora in her chiffon dress at the Cape.

Members of The Deer Team, in their khakis and wearing backpacks, stood beside Giap at the head of the column; their radio equipment and other baggage carried by Tay bearers. Cong, in the black shirt and shorts he had worn in Ho's hut, but shouldering a Thompson submachine gun, came up beside Duncan.

"Let's march together," Cong said, smiling. "On this trail we'll come to know each other much better. Ho Chi Minh will join us when we have secured the trail and taken Thai Nguyen. Mai will come with him."

As the troop moved out, Ho and Congress delegates stood under the shelter of the Community Hall waving and cheering.

In a narrow file the troop marched at a fast clip through the valley and over the mountain into the village at the bottom of the Kim Lung ravine where Tay guides in loincloths and carrying machetes joined them. They were soon in heavy jungle. The guides widened the trail by hacking at overhanging creepers and giant ferns. The trail wended over limestone cliffs on mountain slopes and across streams swollen by the rains. On paths soggy from the heavy monsoon downpours, the marchers sometimes sank to their knees in mud. Wading through fetid swamps they stopped at times to scrape leeches from their legs

Wading across a rocky riverbed, breasting the high water with his carbine held over his head, Duncan became increasingly puzzled as to how Ho, weak and sickly, could be expected to make this trek.

Giap marched at the head of the column with some of the fighters scouting ahead. Cong stayed behind with Duncan, once steadying him when he slipped as they crossed a rocky streambed. "Thanks," Duncan said, when they rested on the grassy far bank.

Cong chuckled. "We must look after you. Uncle Ho told us you may be the only *laissez passer* we can show the Japanese on the road to Hanoi." Cong drank from his canteen and looked at Duncan as he tightened the cap. "Uncle Ho hopes for a lot of help from you Americans. That would be good if it happens." He stood up and adjusted the straps on his backpack. "But this is what I depend on most," Cong said, patting his submachine gun. "Vo Nguyen Giap taught me that."

On the first night, the troop rested in a clearing among pines on a mountain slope. Exhausted, Duncan leaned his back against a tree and wrapped himself in his poncho to ward off the rain and clouds of insects. Cong, draped in a sheet of soft black plastic, came up beside him, spread a light fiber mat on the ground and dropped his backpack. He looked down at Duncan, smiling. "Come, sit on the mat," he said. "I'll get our rations." He returned a few minutes later with a pot of rice and dried fish. Duncan grunted his thanks, accepted a pair of chopsticks and speared a bit of fish in the pot. He wrinkled his nose. Cong laughed. "You haven't yet acquired a taste for our *nuoc mam* sauce—too strong for you," he said, speaking in French.

Duncan shrugged, scooped up some of the cold rice and glanced at Cong. "You speak French without an accent."

"Naturally," Cong said. "I was born in France. My father was a translator for the Indochina Desk of the Quai d'Orsay. His grandmother was French."

Duncan stared at Cong. "And you've been a guerrilla for years, ambushing and killing Frenchmen. Doesn't that depress you?"

"No. That's not so unusual," Cong said. "There are many others among the comrades like me who have known France very well." He put his chopsticks down. "I studied at the University of Paris. Loved living in Paris. Why not? Such a beautiful city—the galleries, the wine and ... ah yes, the girls. Annamese, but I was accepted ... no discrimination." He laughed. "A bit of discrimination, perhaps. A French girl with whom I slept was guilty of that. She said she preferred Vietnamese men because they have better bodies and are more grateful lovers. Wonderful, yes? I had nothing to do with the Vietnamese exiles in Paris who were always complaining about the French." The rain became heavier and Cong drew the plastic sheet more tightly about him, made a hood of it over his head.

"What brought you to Vietnam, to this?" Duncan said, gesturing elaborately at the muddy hillside.

"Excellent question," Cong said, smiling grimly. "Here is the obedient son. Pity me. After graduating from the university—and only because father insisted on it—I came to Vietnam, to a school in Hue that trained Vietnamese for government positions. Everything looked pretty good to me—after all, one could see that the French had built schools, great roads, hospitals and factories. Also, life was comfortable at the school. Then I went out on my first assignment. I became an assistant to the French governor at Bien Hoa in Cochin China. I learned then the *colons* were not like the French I knew in Paris. I discovered ... ," Cong grimaced, "what it meant to be a Vietnamese here in my own country. I was paid less than the Frenchmen who did the same job. Every day was a day of new humiliations, of being treated like shit. Crawling to the governor to get anything done for my people. Seeing how peasants were ground down, beaten by French plantation owners. And, yes, it was true what the exiles in Paris said about the French monopoly on salt, opium and alcohol—about villages forced by the French to take quotas from the monopoly—poisoning my people with opium and alcohol."

Cong took off his glasses and wiped off the rain. "I wanted to do something about it. At least talk about it. So I joined a discussion club. One day the *Sûreté* broke up our meeting. They beat the hell out of us. Our leader was taken off to prison. That's when I went underground. I linked up with Communist fighters. At first they gave me a piece of wood carved like a pistol; it was all they could spare. I got a French rifle after I killed a Civil Guard with a knife in an ambush. Stabbed him, cut his throat. And that night I wept about it. I don't anymore. After that I started killing Frenchmen whenever they got in my way. I've made a choice between being a slave or a killer. Does that answer your question, Colonel?"

The march resumed at dawn and by nightfall the troop was at the northern outskirts of Thai Nguyen. Giap deployed his men along the crest of a hill which overlooked the town. Crouching in the brush on the crest Duncan could make out a watchtower looming over the Hanoi road. Made of bricks, it stood on stilts, the ladder—which extended up to a narrow door—had been pulled up for the night. The light of an oil lamp flickered through one of the apertures. There was no telling how many Civil Guards were in the tower.

Duncan returned to the base of the hill where, beneath a mangrove tree, Trivers was being briefed by Giap. Duncan joined them. Giap had spread out a crude map of Thai Nguyen on a plastic sheet and was tracing positions in the town by the light of a single candle.

Speaking in French, which Trivers understood, Giap said: "We have agents in the town. The Vietnamese mandarin is ready to surrender. He's trying to persuade the Civil Guards to give up. But we aren't sure if they will. They still take their orders from the Japanese troops who occupy the official French *résidence* and the surrounding grounds. The French are gone. They were rounded up by the Japanese after the March 9 coup and sent to the Citadel prison in Hanoi."

Stabbing his finger at the map, Giap said: "The main Japanese encampment is here, on the southern edge of the town. It comprises a fort protected by four concrete emplacements which command the Hanoi road."

Giap, smiling broadly, glanced around at the faces of the others. Obviously enjoying himself, he said: "At four AM we'll open fire on the watchtower with one of those beautiful bazookas you gave us. After we knock out the tower, we'll advance into the town. We may have to wipe out the small Japanese garrison. Once we take control of the town, we'll move on the big Japanese encampment to the south which controls the road."

Trivers asked tightly, "What if the Japs counterattack?"

Giap arched his eyebrows and smiled. "The war is over, Major. We trust that you and Colonel Duncan will convince them of that."

Duncan crawled back up to the top of the hill, following Trivers, and waited for the signal to open fire. He unlimbered his carbine and cocked it. There was no telling what lay ahead, perhaps a Japanese ambush. How distant from the Cape, he thought. What a place to die —in an obscure town in the heart of what was nowhere for most Americans.

A bazooka flamed precisely at 4 AM and the Vietminh opened up on the tower with rifle and machine gun fire. The bazooka missed its target, and Giap—not wishing to waste another precious rocket— ordered his fighters forward. There was no return fire from the tower. Instead, the ladder was let down from the doorway and six frightened Civil Guards, hands up and without weapons, clambered down. They were dragged to Giap who questioned them roughly. Turning to Duncan and Trivers, who had been watching, Giap said, "They were told by the mandarin not to resist. The Japanese units at the *résidence* left the town yesterday, pulled back to the main encampment. I've ordered the Civil Guards to bring the mandarin to us. We'll go into the town and wait for him."

Duncan and the Deer Team followed Giap down a deserted street lined with darkened mud brick houses and thatched huts. "I think Giap's disappointed that he didn't have more of a chance to use his new toys," Trivers said to Duncan. "The Japs at the big fort may give him the fight he's hankering for."

Just after dawn, the four Civil Guards reappeared leading a man in a white suit who bowed obsequiously on approaching Giap. The mandarin was an elderly man with chin whiskers, dressed in a starched high-collared shirt with a black string tie. "Welcome to the Liberation Army," he said in a trembling voice.

Giap nodded curtly. "Where are the other Civil Guards?"

"They are gathered before the old house of the French *résident.*"

"Their weapons?"

"Piled before the *résidence.*"

"And the Japanese?"

"They retreated to the fort south of town. Japanese soldiers from all the posts nearby have been concentrated there. They know of your coming."

In the town square, before the walled yellow stucco house of the French *résident,* the troop found about one hundred and fifty Civil Guards sitting in rows with their French and Japanese weapons stacked to one side. The *résidence,* its gates dangling open, had already been looted and stripped down to the toilet bowls and bidets in the bathrooms. The square was filling up with cheering Vietnamese, who were hailing the arrival of the Liberation Army. Miraculously, crude red flags with a five-pointed gold star at the center, the emblem of the Vietminh, had appeared on every street together with welcoming placards. Jugs of tea and beer were being offered to the new masters. Members of the Vietminh underground wearing armbands had emerged and were picking up the surrendered weapons.

Duncan and Trivers were seated on splintered furniture in the *résidence* drinking beer when Giap came to them with paper and pen. He said, "We must send a letter to the Japanese commander at the fort telling him we'll attack if he does not surrender." Giap spread his hands. "The Japanese have surrendered to you Americans in the Pacific. Why not in Thai Nguyen?" Giap laughed. "Write them a note, please."

Trivers hesitated but Duncan took the pen and paper offered by Giap and hastily wrote out an ultimatum, signing it with his military title.

The mandarin was dispatched with the message. By early evening, he had returned with the terse refusal of the Japanese to surrender.

Moments after receiving the mandarin's report, Giap sent out reconnaissance patrols to the south of the town and began preparing to assault the Japanese fort.

"We're in for it," Trivers said. "Better check our weapons."

In the early morning darkness the troop, led by the reconnaissance scouts, moved through the town and took up concealed positions at the base of the hill on which the Japanese encampment stood.

At dawn Trivers surveyed the Japanese positions with his binoculars and groaned. "Hopeless," he said. "We don't have anything powerful enough to penetrate the fort's concrete bunkers. They've also cleared fields of fire all around them."

Giap scowled. "Well, let's shoot and see how they react."

A few minutes later the Vietminh opened fire with their entire arsenal of weapons. There was no counterfire from the Japanese emplacements—only an eerie quiet on the hill.

When Giap ordered the shooting stopped, Trivers examined the Japanese positions once again with his field glasses. "You're wasting your ammunition," he said to Giap, who glared at him in frustration. Suddenly, there was a shout along the Vietminh skirmish line. A white flag had gone up above the fort.

"You spoke too soon," Giap snapped at Trivers.

Out of the main bunker stepped a Japanese soldier, apparently unarmed, holding a white flag, behind him a Vietnamese civilian. They walked zigzag down the hill and Giap, followed by the Americans, went out to meet him. While the Japanese soldier stood silently by, the Vietnamese, a frightened official in a bedraggled white suit, offered a letter held clenched in his two hands.

"It's addressed to you," Giap said irritably, handing the envelope to Duncan, who ripped it open.

"It's from the commanding officer, a Colonel Utashi," Duncan said. "He wants to talk to me. The soldier will lead me up the hill." He glanced at the others. "I'm going," he said, handing his carbine to Trivers and signaling his assent to the Japanese soldier, who saluted.

Duncan followed the soldier up the hill, and halfway up began to wonder if he had been too impulsive. What if the Japanese planned simply to hold him hostage or torture him for information? They were dug into impenetrable fortifications. They outnumbered Giap's troop. There was no need for them to be accommodating. He rubbed his chin nervously. No going back now, he thought, as they passed through an open gate in a barbed wire entanglement and entered the main bunker. He was led into small room with whitewashed concrete walls where a Japanese officer was waiting.

The officer, hatless, dressed in a crisp khaki uniform with a row of campaign ribbons on his chest, smiled and offered his hand. "Colonel Utashi," he said in English. "Harvard, Class of 'twenty-nine." Too astonished to speak, Duncan took the Colonel's hand and accepted a wicker chair beside a small table on which stood a bottle of brandy, two glasses and his opened letter. The Japanese, who looked to be in his late thirties, was a strongly built man, square-jawed with dark eyes in which there was a glint of amusement.

"Welcome, Colonel Duncan," he said, filling the glasses. "Napoleon Brandy, a gift from the French *résident*'s cellar. I'd have preferred to receive you in my more comfortable quarters further up the hill in the encampment, but these are not ordinary times.

"As for your letter," the Japanese said, picking it up: "I'd be delighted to surrender to you, rather than the Chinese, who will be beastly. But I have my orders from General Tsuchihashi in Hanoi. We'll allow you to pass freely on the road here and at our other posts. But we'll not give up our arms." He sighed. "Tokyo has not yet formally surrendered.

"As for your Annamese friends," Utashi continued in a rather impatient tone, "tell them not to try anything by force. We're well entrenched. I have excellent troops, arms and plenty of ammunition. The areas around our emplacements are mined. If provoked, we'll teach them a lesson."

Utashi downed his brandy and leaned forward eagerly, "Now, tell me, Colonel: How are the Boston Red Sox doing this season?"

Duncan, struggling to engage the Japanese with some comparable degree of savoir-faire, said coolly: "The Red Sox? When I was in the States in June they were in second place, doing well."

"That's great," Colonel Utashi said. "It'll be some time before I can see them play again. Let me tell you about the last game I saw at Fenway Park ..."

Listening with a slight smile, Duncan wondered if Utashi, this sophisticated man, this graduate of Harvard, Class of '29, had been in Nanking in late 1937 when Japanese troops seized the city, raped perhaps twenty thousand or more women, massacred some two hundred thousand people. He felt an urge to say: I know about Nanking. I was there. Were you there? In his every encounter with the Japanese, memories of Nanking always returned—the anguish he felt for the victims and his feelings of guilt. He had been a vice-consul at the American embassy. On December 9—four days before the Japanese troops entered Nanking—he and the rest of the staff of the American embassy departed down the Yangtze on the gunboat *Panay*. It was left to American missionaries, a German Nazi diplomat, an American surgeon and a few others to create the Nanking Safety Zone, which sheltered hundreds of thousands of Chinese from Japanese abuse. Then to return—a survivor after the Japanese bombed the *Panay*—to learn of the horrors: thousands decapitated by the Japanese or buried alive for sport, young men used for bayonet practice, the sobbing missionary telling of the body of the girl in the sand pit with the bamboo cane protruding from her vagina. Why had he fled on the *Panay*—not stayed to be witness, to help somehow?

"I accept your terms," Duncan said to Utashi. "We have no other option."

Duncan followed the Japanese soldier down the hill, zigzagging through the minefield. Rejoining Giap and the Deer Team, he made his report without telling them of Utashi's fascination with the Boston Red Sox. Giap listened sourly and then led the troop back to the town square to await Ho Chi Minh.

# -18-

JUST BEFORE DAWN ON AUGUST 10, four days after the atomic bombing of Hiroshima, Tao left Tan Trao on a mission known only to Ho Chi Minh and Vo Nguyen Giap. He was ordered to hasten to Hanoi, bearing instructions for the Vietminh underground: When the Japanese surrender, make preparations for the entry of the Liberation Army into Hanoi and the arrival of Ho Chi Minh, who will establish a provisional government.

Tao and two other guerrillas, dressed as peasants, wearing conical straw hats and fiber palm rain capes, led by a Tay guide, marched swiftly along the trail to Thai Nguyen. They bore no weapons; Tao reluctantly had left behind his beloved Sten gun. In a belt under his cotton shorts, Tao wore a money belt containing a thousand French piasters.

In a day and a half, they were at the junction with the road which led to Hanoi. Bidding farewell to the Tay guide, they joined a throng of peasants who were entering Thai Nguyen by foot, on bicycles and by bullock carts en route to the morning market. As they walked through the open market in the town square, the posted Civil Guards and a passing Japanese army patrol took no notice of Tao and his companions. There was no food on sale in the market save for some green bananas and strips of fish hanging up to dry. Most farm crops in the region, as in all of Tonkin, had been destroyed in the cruel monsoon. The year-long famine had been so severe that there was common talk of cases of cannibalism.

Tao approached a table on which lay iron pots, scythe blades and machetes. Behind a spinning sharpening stone sat the broad-shouldered ironmonger, his head wrapped in a white cotton cloth. Beside him sat a woman and a young girl. Tao picked up a machete, examined it, and put it on the table with the blade pointing at him. He selected another, and put it down, arranging the two so that they formed a V.

"Do you wish to buy two for the price of one?" asked the peddler.

"I need many more than two," Tao replied. "Do you know of a place where I can buy them?"

The peddler looked closely at Tao and then whispered to the woman beside him. "She knows of such a place," he said.

The woman and the girl, carrying iron pots, went into the crowded square. Tao followed at a distance while his companions stayed behind. Tao was led to the entrance to a decaying two-story yellow plaster house the bottom floor of which was occupied by a shop for *au baba* costumes, pants and shirts made of silk and cotton, formal clothes worn by some of the more affluent Vietnamese. Whispering to the merchant behind the counter, who kept looking about furtively, Tao made arrangements for a rendezvous at dusk.

In the twilight, on the outskirts of Thai Nguyen, off the road and just short of the Japanese concrete emplacements atop the hill, local partisans were waiting for Tao and his companions. Three bicycles were stacked nearby. At nightfall the partisans led them, walking the bicycles, along a trail parallel to the road. Once beyond the Japanese fort the partisans vanished into the darkness, leaving the bicycles to their visitors. Through the night Tao and his companions pedaled down the clay road toward Hanoi, skirting village watchtowers by ducking off the road into the jungle. During daylight they rested in the forest.

Beyond Dong Anh they found that the road had become a quagmire. The Lich River dikes had burst under the weight of the monsoon downpours, flooding the countryside. The trio abandoned their bicycles and struck off to the southeast, treading on the rises between the rice paddies until they came to a village beside an inlet of a Red River tributary. Fishing sampans, some with families aboard, were anchored near the shore amid protruding thatched roofs of huts inundated by the floodwaters. The next morning, in a small sampan with a single boatman at the rear oar, they floated downriver to Hanoi. The sampan drifted to a spot on the shore where there was a path through tall reeds, and the three clambered up a steep bank outside the city's Old Quarter. It was August 14.

As rumors spread of imminent Japanese capitulation, Hanoi turned into a tumultuous, feverish city. Joyfully, the Vietnamese awaited liberation without knowing who would be their next master. Nationalist parties were staging impassioned demonstrations, united against the return of the French colonialists, but militantly divided as to which faction should rule. The French community, panicked by the violent threats against them, stayed in their barricaded homes. Within the walls of the old military Citadel, four thousand restive French solders and officials imprisoned by the Japanese prayed for release.

At the Japanese General Staff Headquarters on the River Front, General Tsuchihashi, awaiting orders from Tokyo, prepared his staff for the agony of the surrender ritual. His garrison of thirty-five thousand troops was deployed to keep a semblance of order. Heavily armed patrols on foot and in weapon carriers circulated through the Old Quarter along its narrow bustling streets and alleys. In the strangely desolate French quarter, tanks rumbled continually along the broad boulevards lined with palatial yellow stucco buildings.

On the day Tao arrived, the Hanoi newspapers carried the news that Tsuchihashi had yielded civil authority to delegates of Bao Dai, the puppet emperor residing in Hue, who had been subservient to the Japanese since their March 9 coup. But the royal delegates, fearful of a Vietminh insurrection and assassinations, cowered in the Kham Sai Palace, afraid to occupy the mayor's office.

At the riverbank Tao, his clothes still splattered with the mud of the Red River delta, mounted a pedicab and went directly to a house in the Old Quarter, a faded blue two-story building, a *tube*, so-called because of its narrow length, where the Vietminh Revolutionary Military Committee had its headquarters. There was a great swirl of activity about the house. Young men holding swords stood at the entrance.

Not long after Tao's arrival, members of the Revolutionary Committee were assembled to hear the report of the emissary from Tan Trao. Six Tonkinese, three attired in white linen suits and the others in black peasant garb, were seated in a small windowless room around a battered table laid out with green tea, rice cakes and papayas. A haze of tobacco smoke enveloped them.

Nguyen Khang, a thin-faced man dressed in black, poured tea into the porcelain cup before Tao. "Welcome, dear Comrade, we've waited anxiously for news from Tan Trao," he said.

Tao bowed and said: "I bring you greetings, Comrades, from Ho Chi Minh and Vo Nguyen Giap. What is your situation?"

"It is very good." Khang replied. "Our comrades have taken control of most of the villages around Hanoi. They've seized some arms. They are ready to come into the city when we call. We've been acting on the instructions of March 12—prepare to order a general insurrection when the time is right. We think the time is right now."

Tao emptied his teacup. "There are new instructions," he said, glancing around the table. "You are asked to wait until Vo Nguyen Giap and the fighters of the Liberation Army reach the city. There will be less risk then. There are Americans with them who are helping us."

"Americans?" Khang exclaimed.

"Yes. They've trained our soldiers and given us weapons."

There were excited murmurs around the table.

Khang put out his cigarette and lit another. "It may not be wise to wait," he said, his eyes suddenly heavy-lidded. "Bao Dai's supporters and other political parties—the Dai Viets and the Trotskyites—are maneuvering for power. Our people are ready to rise."

There were grunts of assent around the table.

"And what of the Japanese?" Tao said sharply. "They may support Bao Dai. They could slaughter our people."

Khang gestured toward a portly man who was wearing a white fedora and puffing on a curved pipe. "Comrade Phan has been speaking these last days to a Japanese."

Phan leaned forward. "His name is Nishimura. He arrested me during our demonstration against Bao Dai before the Kham Sai Palace; took me to the *Kempeitai* headquarters. He questioned me. But he did not torture me. He became friendly and talked a lot. He spoke of Asia for the Asians; denounced the French. When I asked about Bao Dai, he laughed, and said: 'We're tired of supplying him with money and girls.' "

Tao interrupted. "He was friendly. But for whom does he speak?"

Phan was silent, his eyes darting apprehensively to Khang.

"You do not know," Tao interjected. "Yes, he is of the *Kempeitai*, but the security police are not the army. The risks are too great." His eyebrows twitching, Tao studied the faces as the Tonkinese looked at each other.

Khang broke the silence. "Phan may be able to arrange a meeting for you with Nishimura."

Tao frowned, then nodded.

Khang said, "We'll tell the Armed Propaganda Brigade to wait, not to act as arranged."

The next day, Tao met with a succession of local Vietminh commanders as he waited word from Phan about the possibility of a meeting with Nishimura. When there was no news by evening, he became firmer in his resolve to delay the uprising until Giap's troops reached the city.

On the morning of the sixteenth came the news that Tokyo had surrendered. The streets of the Old Quarter became alive with festive demonstrations. University students carrying banners marched through the Old Quarter and paraded into the French sector shouting independence slogans. Japanese patrols nervously clutched their weapons as firecrackers exploded. The tanks withdrew to side streets.

At noon Phan came for Tao. An appointment had been arranged with Nishimura at the *Kempeitai* headquarters. Phan and Tao took a double pedicab. Phan wore a white suit. Tao had changed reluctantly from his peasant clothes into *au baba* tunic and new leather shoes, complaining about the fit. The cyclo went south into the French quarter, past the Returned Sword Lake and west into Hoa Lo Street.

The pedicab man stopped there, refusing to go further. They were about fifty yards from the Hoa Lo Prison, an old yellow plastered hulk, once jokingly called *La Maison Centrale* by French officials. This was now the *Kempeitai* headquarters.

At the iron gate Phan showed his identity card to a Japanese army officer who then escorted them into the prison. As he entered a dank corridor, Tao recalled the layout of the prison described to him by Vietnamese nationalists who had survived incarceration by the French. He wondered if Vo Nguyen Giap would come here when the Liberation Army took the city. At the southern end of the prison was the room in which stood the guillotine that ended the life of his sister, Minh Khan. Just beyond the former warden's office, into which they were now being conducted, were the interrogation rooms and the tiny dark cells where Giap's wife, Minh Giang, and their infant son had died of neglect. Glancing about, Tao felt enveloped with a sickening sense of pity and anger that brought tears to his eyes.

The Japanese officer opened a metal door for Tao and Phan, admitting them to a large office with bare whitewashed walls and barred windows. There was a stepladder at one end before a large wall map of Hanoi and its environs studded with black and red pins.

Phan bowed to Nishimura, who was seated behind an oblong hardwood conference table, flanked by two Japanese army colonels. The Japanese rose and shook hands stiffly with their guests. Nishimura, a thin man with high cheekbones and a shaven head, was wearing a black tunic buttoned to the throat. He introduced the army officers, who were in khaki uniforms with open-collared white shirts.

Nishimura, speaking in French, said to Tao: "So you've come from the Kim Lung valley, from Ho Chi Minh. Interesting man, your Ho Chi Minh, as he now calls himself. We have quite a dossier on him."

Surprised by Nishimura's reference to Ho, Tao thought irritably he'd not authorized Phan to reveal so much. "Thank you for receiving us," he said.

"Yes," Nishimura said. "We wanted to speak to someone of authority in the Vietminh. Coffee?" He gestured to a silver pot and tray on the table. "You grow very good coffee in Cochin China."

Tao accepted a cup as Nishimura continued: "Your units around Hanoi are very active. They've killed Tonkinese Civil Guards and seized their weapons, and there have been other incidents, even more troublesome. One Japanese soldier has been killed. We've not retaliated, not yet."

Tao thought of Japanese reprisal raids in which hundreds of peasants had been massacred.

Nishimura said, "Asians should not be killing Asians—especially in these difficult times. Japan has lost the war, a war the emperor fought for the co-prosperity of all Asians. We should stand together against the white imperialists—Asia for the Asians. Don't you agree?"

"Yes," Tao said warily. "Asia should be free of colonialism. We hope you'll help us establish an independent Vietnam."

"We are in favor of Indochinese independence," Nishimura replied. "That's why Tokyo ordered us to turn over civilian authority to the Bao Dai government." He laughed. "Of course—here—-we know Bao Dai. He never took up arms against the French. He *has* used arms … but only for the pleasure of hunting tigers."

The Japanese colonels who had been listening stone-faced joined in the laughter.

"Unfortunately, Monsieur Tao, we cannot help you," Nishimura said, a look of sadness crossing his face. "We have our orders. We must respect the royal government."

Tao threw an angry glance at Phan as if to say: There you have it.

"However," Nishimura said, "it's not for us to tell the Indochinese people what they should or should not do. Naturally, we must keep order in Hanoi. We cannot permit attacks on installations where Japanese troops are on duty. We will not allow any one to molest our General Staff Headquarters, the Citadel, the Metropole Hotel—where foreigners are quartered—or the Bank of Indochina."

Tao looked in turn at the army colonels who had not spoken. They simply nodded.

Phan said cautiously, "We understand. But the Bank? It belongs to the Vietnamese people. We're told your army withdrew sixty million piasters only a few days ago."

Nishimura snapped impatiently: "We need local currency to provision our troops, who after all are maintaining order."

Tao stood up: "*D'accord*, Monsieur Nishimura," he said with a polite smile.

Nishimura extended his hand to Tao. "Convey my greetings to Ho Chi Minh. As for his politics ..." He shrugged. "The situation has changed. We now find his politics tolerable."

Outside the prison, walking back to the cyclo, Tao said: "Their troops will not interfere. The colonels were there to tell us Nishimura was speaking for the army as well as the security police. The conditions do appear right for a general insurrection."

On the morning of August 17, Kang sent out word to the Armed Propaganda Brigade that the time for action was at hand. Responding that afternoon, members of the Brigade infiltrated a mass meeting in the square before the Opera House. The royalists had convened it to rally support for Bao Dai. As a royalist leader rose to speak, a Brigade team brandishing pistols seized the microphone while another member standing on a high balustrade unfurled a huge Vietminh flag over the facade of the Opera House. In the uproar that followed, Kang went to the rostrum and exhorted the crowd to parade for independence. The aroused crowd eagerly joined in a march behind a Vietminh flag through the Vietnamese neighborhoods of the city. Tens of thousands poured into the streets to cheer.

Tao, standing apart, watched the coup at the Opera House and the street demonstration. It had been a final test. The Japanese had not intervened. The Revolutionary Military Committee met through the night of the eighteenth to make preparations for a general uprising. Ten companies, mainly students, comprising some eight hundred men and women, were marshaled. A few were armed with rifles and pistols, but most with machetes, spears and swords. Early on the morning of the nineteenth, thousands of peasants, bearing scythes and other crude weapons, led by Vietminh partisans, converged on the city.

At a mass rally before the Opera House, the Committee proclaimed the August Revolution and thousands poured out of the square to seize the Civil Guards Barracks, the Mayor's Office, and the Kham Sai Palace. By the morning of the twentieth, the Committee was in control of Hanoi, save for the Japanese-guarded installations.

Tao quickly left the city to report victory to Ho Chi Minh and Vo Nguyen Giap.

# -19-

Thai Nguyen
August 21, 1945

DUNCAN WAS AWAKENED in the French *résidence* on the morning of
August 21 by great shouts in the town square. He snatched up the
carbine leaning against the wall of the wrecked dining room. His first
reaction was that he'd been deceived by Utashi and the Japanese were
attacking. Outside, from the verandah, he saw a squad of Vietminh
fighters crossing the square. Walking slowly behind them was Ho Chi
Minh with Mai at his side. Duncan hastened out through the gate.

Ho beckoned to Duncan, and the crowd parted to let him
through. Clasping Ho's hand, Duncan tried to conceal his sense of
shock. Ho was even more shriveled than when he last saw him in
Tan Trao. His Nung jacket hung loosely on his emaciated frame, and
his hand felt skeletal. "I'm so very relieved that you're here," Duncan
said, his brow furrowed. "You've had a hard journey."

"Yes, it's been a hard journey," Mai interposed, as Ho turned to
greet others in the gathering crowd. She was haggard, her eyes dull
with exhaustion. "Where's Vo Nguyen Giap?"

"He's with his men securing the villages along on the road,"
Duncan replied. "Cong is with him." Mai evinced no interest at the
mention of Cong's name.

"We'll need a day's rest before going on to Hanoi," Mai said
wearily. She turned to look at the four Tay tribesmen trotting into the
square, carrying a crude replica of the closed sedan chair in which
mandarins and other high officials had once made their rounds. Mai
inclined her head toward the chair. "It was the only way we could
bring him here. He walked a bit. We cannot let him die before we
reach Hanoi. Do we have any cars or trucks?"

Duncan replied, "Giap found two trucks and a car. But there's no gasoline, only rice alcohol. The alcohol works okay, but we may not have enough to reach to Hanoi."

"All we need is enough to get Ho to Hanoi," Mai said. "The rest of us can walk."

Duncan watched her go wearily toward the *résidence* with Ho. I'd like to take her in my arms, he thought, wipe the sweat off her face, tuck back those strands of hair.

A jubilant Giap returned that afternoon to the town square. Tao was at his side. Riding a bicycle along the road, alone and exhausted, Tao, to his great relief, had encountered one of Giap's patrols. Triumphantly, he held aloft a copy of the Hanoi newspaper *Tin Moi*, describing the events in Hanoi and telling of the forthcoming proclamation of a Vietnamese provisional government. This was Giap's first word of the Vietminh coup.

The Vietminh celebrated the Hanoi victory that night in the town square. Ho appeared briefly before the enthusiastic throng. Standing on a platform of logs he hailed this first success of the August Revolution.

Duncan glanced several times at Mai sitting with Cong beside one of the bonfires and then morosely watched the two go into the *résidence*, side-by-side. Although he disliked the taste of the maize beer, he accompanied Trivers in downing several mugs.

Not long after, sleeping fitfully on his straw mat in the *résidence*, Duncan was awakened by muted but clearly angry voices. He listened intently. He couldn't make out what was being said, but he recognized the voices as being those of Mai and Cong.

On the morning of August 23, a large crowd of cheering peasants gathered in the town square and the streets to say goodbye to Ho Chi Minh as he left for Hanoi. On Ho's orders, stocks of rice cached in the houses of the mandarin and other rich townspeople were distributed to the hungry peasants. One of the trucks was loaded with bags of grain that were to be doled out along the way.

Ho rode with Mai and Duncan in an ancient French sedan, which the mandarin sadly relinquished. "Please come sit in the back seat with me," Ho said to Duncan. "I have some questions."

At the wheel was a foreigner Duncan had not seen before. He was a muscular bearded man with a mop of blonde hair who spoke French largely in monosyllables. He was dressed in the black garments of the guerrillas and wore an iron crucifix attached to a string of red beads around his thick neck.

"This is Joseph Pulaski, our Polish comrade," Mai said. "He defected to us from the Foreign Legion. There are other Legionnaires like him with us ... good friends. They train our people and fight beside us. He came with me from Tan Trao. He has many friends among the Legionnaires who are imprisoned by the Japanese in the Citadel in Hanoi. He hopes to liberate them."

Pulaski grunted a greeting, put a Sten gun at his side, and turned on the ignition. The engine barked several times before it started. Behind the car came the truck carrying the Deer Team with a jovial Trivers at the wheel, happy to be on the way home. Vo Nguyen Giap, accompanied by Cong, had gone forward in the other truck, pressing on toward Hanoi.

As the car sputtered down the road, Ho said to Duncan: "I've been thinking about what I shall say to the people in Hanoi. As I told you in Tan Trao, many, many years ago I read your Declaration of Independence. I still can recall many of the words. I thought it was a very inspiring revolutionary document. Do you remember any of the lines?"

"I don't recall many exactly," Duncan said with an embarrassed smile.

"One line especially impressed me," Ho said. "*All men are created equal.* I live by that idea. Could you get me a text of the Declaration?"

Duncan said: "When we get to Hanoi and set up our radio, I'll ask for one."

On the first day the convoy covered about twelve miles and halted near a village beside a crumbled watchtower, which had been demolished by Giap's guerrillas. Campfires were lit to cook the evening meal. Duncan took a pot of heated water and was washing under a guava tree when Trivers, who had been exploring the village with his two Vietnamese sergeants, sat down beside him.

"Not a pretty scene in that village," Trivers said grimly. "The Community Hall is burned down."

"The Japanese?" Duncan asked, frowning.

"No. My sergeants spoke to the villagers. It was Giap's men. They shot some of the Civil Guards after they surrendered. They also executed the village chief and burned down his house. All of them were accused of being too buddy buddy with the French and the Japanese." Trivers picked up a twig and snapped it. "That's what Giap calls securing the road. What a load of shit! We've been told that other villages along the road got the same treatment. Your Uncle Ho," Trivers said, his mouth twisted, "playing Santa Claus to the peasants, handing out rice while Giap goes about killing."

Duncan dried his face and threw down the cloth. "I'm going to ask Ho about this," he said angrily.

Ho was stretched out on a straw mat atop a bed of leaves beside a fire, with Mai sitting beside him. Pulaski was sitting nearby in the shadows with the Sten gun across his lap. Ho sat up as Duncan approached. "Have you had food?" he asked solicitously.

Duncan squatted beside him. "There've been many killings in the village. The village chief and some of the civil guards have been executed."

Ho frowned. "The Japanese ..." he began.

"No," Duncan interrupted sharply. "The villagers say it was Giap's men. No question. And I don't understand. Giap told us he was making the villages secure. Well, that's not security. That's terror."

As Duncan spoke, Ho folded his hands and looked at him steadily. "On the battlefield, Giap makes the decisions," he said quietly.

"But it's your struggle as well," Duncan said, breathing heavily.

"Travis, I'm sure you will recall what Lenin once said about revolution. You can't make an omelet without cracking eggs. That's sad but true." He lay back on the mat and closed his eyes.

Duncan stalked away and for the next few hours, lying under his poncho unable to sleep, brooded about his exchange with Ho Chi Minh. What was he? Mai and others spoke of him as some kind of Mahatma Gandhi. Yes, he'd seen Ho dispense rice to the poor, read poetry to the children, lecture to villagers about love of country and, surprisingly, speak tolerantly of some of the French. Yet there was the other side: the unrelenting denunciation of traitors, giving license to Giap's assassination squads in their purging of the villages and the killing of opposition leaders. Was Ho simply a superb actor, playing the father figure in one act and in the next, the merciless unforgiving revolutionary?

Tossing about, Duncan wiped the splattering rain from his face and asked himself: But how much choice did Ho have? How should he cope with the Vietnamese Civil Guards—who were serving as mercenaries for the French and the Japanese—and the clashing factions? He ticked them off in his mind: that puppet Bao Dai, the Dai Viets who were following the antiwhite banner of the Japanese, the gangster Binh Xuyen, the fanatical Cao Dai with their crazy Pope, the pro-Chinese Dong Minh Hoi, the others, all competing for power. Yet it was time, yes, it was time, for Ho to restrain Giap. You can't build a united nation on corpses. "We can't support that kind of a regime," he muttered as he shut his eyes and pulled the poncho tighter around him.

In the morning, as they prepared to resume the journey, Mai came to Duncan.

"Please understand," she said softly. "We do what we must. I too have killed. If need be I will do it again ... for the revolution. What you said last night to Ho Chi Minh caused him much pain. Understand, please. Ho is searching for a way to stop the killing, to end this struggle that goes on and on. He's offered to compromise with the French and invited the other Vietnamese parties into a coalition. But until we are at peace, he must let Giap have his way.

Giap is not an immoral man. You know, he's a Doctor of Laws. But he became convinced when he stayed with Mao Tse-tung in Yenan that power comes out of the barrel of a gun. Before Ho Chi Minh decides finally who possesses the right strategy—he or Giap—he must know if he can depend on your people for help."

Duncan said, "The other night—in the French *résidence*—you were quarreling with Cong. I heard your voices. Was it about differences between Ho and Giap?"

Mai frowned. "Yes," she said, biting her lip. "Cong was objecting to the message Ho sent to the French offering to compromise. Cong thinks like Giap: Rely on the gun."

Duncan smiled. "So it was about politics, not a lovers' quarrel?"

Mai nodded.

Duncan asked impulsively, "Do you really love him, Mai?"

Mai frowned, startled at the question. "Yes," she said firmly. "He's my comrade, at my side. He's a brave fighter. "Also ..." and she sighed, "he gives me what I need. This life ... there are times when I need some tenderness and comfort. He gives me that."

"I understand, Mai." Duncan went to her and kissed her on both cheeks.

Mai smiled gently. "It's good that we've opened our hearts to each other."

Duncan watched Mai go to the car and join Ho in the back seat. When he climbed in beside Pulaski at the wheel, Mai smiled at him with a new intimacy. As the sedan jolted along on the muddy road, Pulaski began to sing in Polish. Ho clapped his hands. "I once heard that song in Warsaw," he said. "I spent some happy days there."

Duncan said cheerily to Pulaski: "When I was a university student in Paris I visited Warsaw ... beautiful city. Where are you from?"

"Lutsk," Pulaski replied.

"Long way from Paris. How did you ever get into the French Foreign Legion?"

Pulaski laughed loudly, muttering a curse in Polish as he shook his head, and said in French: "I had no choice. I killed a man in Lutsk—found him with my wife. Not a big crime in Lutsk, except he was the son of a very rich man. I suppose that's why my wife bedded with the little grasshopper, surely not because he had a better cock." He twisted the wheel sharply to avoid a pothole and uttered another oath in Polish. "I left Lutsk on a freight train; got across the French border hiding in the back of a truck. I went to Paris. But I had no money. The police caught me when I tried to rob a restaurant. The judge said to me: 'Prison or the Legion.' "

Ho said, "The Japanese are holding hundreds of Legionnaires in the Citadel in Hanoi. Comrade Pulaski will try to rally them to us. He's already brought over many Legionnaires to our side."

"Why not?" Pulaski said. "They hate the French. Most of them—like me—can't go home." He laughed as he wiped the mud-splattered windshield. "They like Vietnamese girls—they take wives, *congais*."

"Don't some want to go home eventually?" Duncan asked.

Pulaski grimaced. "Yes, a few."

"We execute them," Ho Chi Minh said curtly, speaking in a manner that Duncan had not heard before. "They know too much about us. It would be dangerous for us to let them go free. They might go back to the French. There are bad ones among the Legionnaires. I cannot forget that a Legionnaire unit wiped out my native village in Annam."

Suddenly, Pulaski brought the car to a grinding halt and grabbed his Sten gun. A group of figures, holding rifles, dimly visible, stood on the road ahead. Duncan reached for the carbine at his feet.

Pulaski put a round into the chamber of the Sten gun and stuck his head out the driver's window. "It's all right," he said, turning to Ho. "They're our people."

One of the figures, emerging from the mist came up to the car. It was Cong with a plastic sheet around his shoulders. He held his hand up in salute. "We've been waiting for you," he said smiling. "The road is flooded. The car and truck will never get through. Vo

Nguyen Giap and our soldiers have already gone ahead. They're walking and using boats on the canals. The column must be close to Hanoi by now. Many of our units in the villages along the way have joined them. They've secured the route by which we will go."

Cong helped Ho from the car. Turning to Duncan, he said: "Tell your comrades to follow us."

When Duncan returned with the Deer Team, Ho was already propped up on a litter of bamboo poles and strips, carried by four of the guerrillas, with a plastic cover against the rain. "He wanted to walk," Mai said, "but Cong insisted. It's Giap's orders."

Marching on the road and skirting flooded sections by beating through the forest to high ground, the party reached the town of Yen Vien at nightfall. Local Vietminh partisans waiting on the road escorted them to huts on stilts above the waterlogged earth. In the morning they were led to a village on the Duong River where a small flotilla of sampans was tied up. With two sampans of guerrillas preceding, the boats floated down the Duong to where it joined the Red River. By afternoon the boats were alongside a quay near the Chuong Duong Bridge, which linked Hanoi to the road to the Gia Lam Airfield. Duncan saw Giap standing on the quay. He was wearing a white suit and the familiar fedora. Behind him were parked a black limousine and two smaller cars.

Giap helped Ho into the Citroen limousine. He strode over to Duncan and speaking rapidly in French said: "Those other cars will take you and the Deer Team to the Metropole Hotel. An American military mission is already there. We haven't met them yet. We'll send a car in the next few days to bring you to our house in the Old Quarter. In just five days—on September second—Ho Chi Minh will proclaim our provisional government. We're acting as quickly as we can. The Chinese have already crossed the border. They'll soon be in Hanoi. We don't know what their attitude toward us will be. The French are trying to take power again. Three days ago, we captured Pierre Messmer and two other French officers. The British dropped them at Phuc Yen northwest of here. Messmer admitted that he was appointed commissioner for Tonkin by De Gaulle with the mission of restoring French control."

"What about the Japanese?" Duncan asked.

"They don't interfere as long as we stay away from their protected zones." Giap chuckled. "Their puppet, Bao Dai, abdicated two days ago. He's joined our government as supreme counselor. *Au revoir!*"

As the Vietnamese driver took them into central Hanoi, Duncan looked about amazed. The streets were festooned with Vietminh flags and placards, which denounced the French, while others were inscribed: "Welcome American Friends." It was only a few blocks to the Metropole Hotel, a large yellow building with side balconies and a green copper dome, erected in the grandeur architecture of the turn-of-the-century. The hotel was cordoned off by Japanese soldiers, who were letting only foreigners enter. Hanging over the stone portico was a Vietminh flag beside an American flag.

# -20-

Hanoi
**August 26, 1945**

A BULLNECKED MAN IN A WRINKLED seersucker suit greeted Duncan as he crossed the lobby of the hotel. "I'm Monsieur Tolner, manager of the hotel," he said in heavily accented English, as his pale gray eyes ran over Duncan's soiled khaki uniform, and then, in obvious chagrin, took in the ten members of the Deer Team trailing behind. "You're the Americans, no? I was told of your coming."

Duncan said: "Yes, I'm Colonel Duncan and this is Major Trivers. We'll need rooms for our entire group."

The manager's gaze shifted to the two Vietnamese sergeants of the Deer Team. "Of course," he said with pursed lips. "We're happy to have Americans here. I have a room for you on the second floor. Your friends will have to wait a few minutes. We're crowded. Some French families have been staying here since the Annamese seized their houses. I must ask them to leave and then make ready some rooms." He snapped his fingers at a Vietnamese in a white tunic and shorts. "Boy, take the colonel to room 234. But first, show him where Colonel Hopkins is staying."

Duncan glanced at the manager in surprise. Hopkins, the OSS guy in Kunming ... here? But why? Duncan shrugged and picked up his backpack. "Thanks, Monsieur Tolner. Shall I register?" he asked.

Tolner sniffed. "Unfortunately, we've given up such formalities."

The men and women seated at wicker tables at the far end of the ornate lobby, all of them whites, turned to stare as Duncan followed the bowing Vietnamese up the stairs.

In his room Duncan dropped his backpack and carbine. The servant pointed out Hopkins' room, a corner suite at the front of the hotel. Duncan knocked on the door and entered at the brusque

"*Entrée.*" Hopkins was seated in the corner of a sofa writing on a clipboard. It was a very large room with a tall arched window overlooking Ba Dinh Square with a view beyond of Restored Sword Lake.

Hopkins jumped up. "Travis, you made it!" he cried, grabbing Duncan by the shoulders.

"Yes," Duncan said, "along with the Deer Team, and would you believe it, Ho Chi Minh and company. When did you get here?"

"Landed at Gia Lam four days ago," Hopkins said, as he and Duncan settled on the sofa. "Technically, I'm on a mercy mission to look after POWs. The Japs are holding about three hundred British POWs in a stockade near Gia Lam. They're Gurkhas captured in Malaya in 1942. But actually, my job is to report on what's going on and to monitor the arrival of the Chinese occupation force." He scrambled to his feet. "Hey, you must need a drink." He went to a side table.

"Here you go," Hopkins said, handing a tall glass to Duncan. "Brandy. It's the only hard stuff you can get here." He cocked his head with a teasing expression. "Boy, do I have a surprise for you," he said. "Suzanne Dumont is here."

Duncan glass almost slipped from his hand and he brushed his trouser leg where drops of brandy had spilled. "What's she doing here? Covering for the *Observer*?"

"No. I think she's dropped that correspondent cover. She's here with her boss, Jean Sainteny, the major who runs M.5 in Kunming. They came on my plane with two other Frenchmen. I was ordered to take them with me. Sainteny is supposed to be looking after the French community. Boy, did they cause trouble when we got here. Another drink?"

Duncan, his mind on the presence of Suzanne in Hanoi, shook his head.

"I tell you, Travis," Hopkins said, "our landing here was something unbelievable—like a Cecil B. De Mille movie."

Hopkins sat down beside Duncan, chortling. "We parachuted four agents from our C-46 to reconnoiter Gia Lam Airport before landing. One of our guys, Bob Maisonpierre, was getting out of his harness, when he was approached by a Jap officer in shiny boots and jodhpurs who said in perfect English: 'Welcome. The war is over. It's time again for baseball and whiskey.' He then took the four agents over to one of the hangers and broke out—would you believe it—a bottle of Johnny Walker. Now where in hell would he get that booze?" Hopkins asked, shaking his head.

"When our plane landed and we came into the city, the Annamese gave me and my gang a big welcome, cheering like mad. They found an American flag somewhere and draped it outside of the hotel. They must have thought we were here to celebrate their independence. But when they found out that a French mission—Sainteny and his aides—was with us, there was a near riot around the hotel. The Japs had to call in more troops to put it down. These people aren' t going to tolerate any return of the French."

Hopkins stood up. "Look, you must be exhausted. Go to your room and get some rest. I'll bring you one of my uniforms—we're about the same size—while yours get washed. We'll have dinner downstairs at eight o'clock. The food's good."

"Okay," Duncan said, "but there's one other thing you can do for me. You've got a radio team with you?"

"Of course."

"Get me the text of the Declaration of Independence."

"The what?" Hopkins asked, his mouth agape.

"The Declaration of Independence. I promised Ho Chi Minh I'd get it for him."

"I suppose there's a text lying around Kunming or Chungking," Hopkins said, as he opened the door for Duncan. "If I have to, I'll go to Washington. Why not? They already think the OSS out here is nuts."

At eight-thirty Duncan entered the dining room, which was furnished in old world style with heavy crystal chandeliers. He had begun writing his report to Donovan and was late for dinner, having lost track of the time. As he threaded past tables fully occupied with foreigners, among them Americans in uniform, he saw Suzanne sitting with a French army officer. She was wearing her bush jacket but he noticed that the shoulder patch identifying her as a correspondent had been removed. She stood up, her eyes widening, and reached back to adjust her hair as she exclaimed: "Travis! It's really you. I heard that some Americans had come from the interior."

Duncan kissed Suzanne on the cheek and shook hands with the French officer, who rose to greet him. He was a ramrod straight, dark-haired man, who looked to be in his mid-thirties, with a small mustache and an imperious expression.

"This is Major Sainteny," Suzanne said, looking flustered.

"I've heard about you," Sainteny said, as he shook hands. "Colonel Hopkins shared some of your reports with me in Kunming."

Duncan bowed slightly. Smiling at Suzanne, he said: "I'm sure we'll be seeing each other. Colonel Hopkins is waiting for me. I'm terribly late."

"So you've seen her," Hopkins said as Duncan came to the table. "What a dish! Donovan got a big laugh out of it when he heard you were playing around with her in Chungking."

"What are you drinking?" Duncan said, ignoring Hopkins's sally.

Hopkins poured red wine into Duncan's glass. "I sent a message to Donovan about your arrival," he said. "There's a coded radio message from him. He wants you to contact a Russian who's surfaced here. He's an NKVD agent who worked closely with Donovan in London during the war in Europe. His name is Stephan Solosieff. He represents himself as liaison to the Japanese for purposes of caring for Soviet citizens in Indochina. That includes the Russians among the Foreign Legionnaires imprisoned in the Citadel. Donovan says you can be reasonably open with him. Mention his name. Exchange information about Ho Chi Minh. Find out, if you can, what Moscow's attitude toward Ho is."

"I'll work on it," Duncan said. "But what about the Chinese?"

"They're on the way … Lord help us. I've just sent a message to the embassy in Chungking asking the ambassador to protest to

Chiang Kai-shek. Lu Han's troops are raising hell. Since crossing the border, they've been stealing everything in sight—food, money, even the furnishings of French houses. They've beaten up both French civilians and Annamese. There are reports of rapes. Nothing we can do beyond protest. While moving this way, Lu Han—in compliance with the Potsdam agreement—is disarming the Japanese."

"How long will the Chinese be in the country?" Duncan asked, a brooding expression settling over his features.

"There's no saying. At Potsdam it was simply agreed they'd accept the surrender of the Japanese in the North. Nothing was said explicitly about how long they will stay or who'll take over from them. They might stay for a good while. There's a pro-Chinese underground here—the Dong Minh Hoi—that's been putting out propaganda hailing the Chinese as liberators of Vietnam and denouncing both the French and the Vietminh."

Duncan did little more than toy with his food, although it was the first Western fare he had eaten in weeks. Over coffee, he interrupted Hopkins, who was chatting about the Japanese surrender to Douglas MacArthur. "John, I'm writing a report about Ho Chi Minh, about what he's trying to do. It's for Donovan. I'd like you to send it, if you think it's okay."

"That's fine," Hopkins said, studying Duncan's tense features. "You know, Travis, like most of us here I'm sympathetic to Ho. We know what's going on. But don't go overboard. Washington and Chungking are a long way off. Their slant is different and Vietnam isn't their highest priority. They're not looking to us to call the shots."

"That's my impression," Duncan said. "Thanks for dinner. I'll see you at noon."


Duncan was in his room sitting on the badly scuffed chaise longue writing his report under dim lamplight when the telephone beside the bed rang. It was Suzanne: "May I come to your room?"

At the door, Duncan drew Suzanne quickly into the room, and she, saying not a word, yielded to his embrace. Duncan kissed her hard, ran his hands down her back and drew her close. She leaned away from him and laughed: "Not tonight. And not before you tell me: What of your Mai?"

"Is that why you've come? To ask me that question?"

"No. Not entirely." She walked to the center of room, and turned around, smiling. "When we last met I told you I was a patient woman. Well, I am. You can see that. Yet you shouldn't find it surprising that I ask."

Duncan went to Suzanne and took both her hands. "Mai—yes, I've been with her. She's been kind, very kind … freed me from the guilt I've felt since Saigon. We're now very good friends only. No more than that. Believe me. And you … I've never stopped loving you."

Suzanne looked up at Duncan with a quizzical expression, tousled his hair, and then pushed him away, laughing.

Duncan, shaking his head, led Suzanne to the chaise. "Okay, okay, but now tell me what you're doing here?"

"My assignment? Do everything I can for the French civilians in Hanoi and the French military prisoners in the Citadel."

"And Sainteny, your M.5 boss?"

"More complicated." Oh dear God … if he knew I was here, Suzanne thought.

"What's he up to, Suzanne?"

"He's preparing for the return of a French administration."

"Return of the *colons!* " Duncan spat out.

"No. Not just that. He's not such a bad man … not simply a servant of the *colons*. He wants to help the Annamese, give them a lot more rights."

"But on French terms."

"Yes," Suzanne said.

"What does he think of Ho Chi Minh's offer?"

"He knows it's not acceptable to De Gaulle. Sainteny may negotiate with Ho. But independence? Never. Autonomy? Yes, perhaps. But only for Tonkin, certainly not for Cochin China."

"Never give up Cochin China—the South—the rubber and coffee plantations … where the money is. *Right?*"

Suzanne shrugged. "I didn't come here to ask you to help Sainteny in his mission. I came to ask you to help me in mine." She withdrew her hand from Duncan. "The Japanese won't let us leave the hotel. They say the Annamese would kill us. I need your help. The French military prisoners in the Citadel are in desperate condition. Help us, Travis. Please, ask the Japanese—General Tsuchihashi—to allow me to visit the Citadel. Also, if you can, speak to him about what can be done for the prisoners. Colonel Hopkins is caring for the British POWs. Why couldn't he make that request for us?"

Duncan listened silently, then went to the sideboard in the corner and came back with a bottle of brandy and two glasses. He poured the brandy and offered a glass to Suzanne. She shook her head. Duncan downed his brandy and put the glass on the floor beside the bottle.

"All right," he said, "I'll talk to Hopkins."

Suzanne stood up, put her hands on Duncan's cheeks and kissed him on the forehead. "Thank you," she said.

Duncan followed Suzanne to the door. She looked up as he opened the door for her, put a hand on his chest, and whispered: "Travis, I shouldn't tell you this. Sainteny could have me shot. There are French troops on a ship bound for Haiphong. They'll arrive soon. De Gaulle doesn't seem to understand what this will lead to. The Vietnamese will rise and run amok. There'll be terrible fighting. French civilians will be massacred. You Americans must do something to prevent a bloodbath."

She closed the door gently behind her.

At noon Duncan went to Hopkins's room and found him in a foul temper. Pacing agitatedly about the room Hopkins said: "I've just got back from the POW stockade at Gia Lam. The Gurkhas are in awful shape ... sick ... some dying from malaria, beri beri and I don't know what else. The Japs haven't given them adequate medical care. I'm going to protest to Tsuchihashi. I've got an appointment with him in an hour," he said, glancing at his wristwatch.

Duncan said: "I need to brief you on a couple of matters. I met with Suzanne Dumont last night after dinner."

"My God, Travis, are you still involved with that woman?"

"If you're asking me if I slept with her, the answer is no. She passed on some important information, said Sainteny could have her shot if he knew what she was doing. She told me there's a ship with French troops bound for Haiphong."

"That's in violation of the Potsdam Agreement," Hopkins said angrily. "But I don't get it. Why did Dumont leak that information to you?"

"She said the landing of French troops would touch off a Vietnamese uprising—that French civilians would be massacred. She said we must do something to head off what could be a bloodbath. I believe her."

"I'll check this out with Tsuchihashi," Hopkins said. "He should know. The Chinese would have briefed him if they've given clearance for a French landing at Haiphong. If it's true, we'll ask the embassy in Chungking to protest to Chiang Kai-shek."

"Dumont raised one other thing," Duncan said. "She's concerned about the French military prisoners in the Citadel. There are four thousand of them packed in there since the March coup. It must be a mess. Dumont wants to visit the Citadel. Get in and find out what's going on, then talk to Tsuchihashi about improving conditions for the soldiers. That's why she's here. To care for the prisoners and for French civilians in the city. She's asking for your help in persuading the Japanese to allow her to see the prisoners in the Citadel."

Hopkins said: "Sainteny has already made that request. I don't know why Dumont is making the same pitch. But there's no reason why we shouldn't try to help their people. I'll ask Tsuchihashi. He's in full control of the prisoners until the Chinese arrive."

Hopkins put on his cap and straightened it. "I'm due for that meeting with Tsuchihashi," he said. "What about your report to Donovan?"

Duncan nodded. "I'll finish writing it after I've talked to that NKVD guy ... Solosieff. He may add something."

"When you get to it, remember what I told you," Hopkins said. "Don't get too far out on a limb."

# -21-

SUZANNE WAS AT THE DESK of the concierge in the lobby of the
Metropole when the manager approached her: "Good evening,
Madame." She glanced at Tolner with thinly concealed distaste. She'd
heard about the Corsican—his dealings in the black market, how he
supplied women for Japanese officers.

"I believe Major Sainteny is looking for you," Tolner said. "He's
in the bar."

Suzanne nodded curtly. She had hoped to run into Duncan,
perhaps dine with him. Last night she had tossed sleeplessly for hours
yearning for him. She was wearing her favorite dress, a black gown
she had brought from London, and Cambodian silver earrings.

Suzanne found Sainteny at a corner table beside a drooping
potted palm.

"Ah! Suzanne, come join me. Somewhere, Tolner found a bottle
of excellent Bordeaux." He signaled a waiter for a glass. "You look
ravishing. Are you having dinner with Colonel Duncan?"

Suzanne shook her head.

"Ah! But you saw him last night—late, in fact after midnight.
Rather indiscreet, my dear, for a member of my staff."

Tolner, Suzanne surmised. One of his staff most have seen her
leave Duncan's room. She said: "I went to ask if he would arrange a
visit to the Citadel."

"Without consulting me?"

"You said it was urgent we find a means of getting into the
Citadel," Suzanne said coolly.

"Well, I must congratulate you. I've received a message from
Colonel Hopkins. The Japanese have agreed to allow you to visit the
Citadel. A humanitarian gesture on the part of General Tsuchihashi.

Also, I assume he wants to keep the Americans happy. He must think they can protect him from the Chinese."

Suzanne said eagerly: "When can we go?"

"Tomorrow morning. But only you. Not me, not the head of the mission," he said irritably. "The visit is unofficial. Technically, they say, only the Chinese can grant official access. Also, Tsuchihashi refuses to receive you. He said you can write out any requests. A doctor may accompany you when you visit the Citadel, but no one else. Doctor Clos will go with you," Sainteny said, cocking his head with a playful expression.

Suzanne looked puzzled: "Clos?" She grew tense. "You mean Francois Clos of the *Sûreté*?"

Sainteny glanced about at the neighboring tables, lowered his voice, and bent forward. "Precisely. And you'll carry a little present for General Mordant. Just a little gift from his wife—a locket with her picture inside. Quite naturally, you'll ask to see Mordant. He's the senior French officer among the prisoners. You need to know a bit more about this locket." Sainteny said, and tasted his wine. "The picture in the locket is not of the general's wife. But only he will know it. It's a signal, a signal that the French underground in Hanoi is ready and weapons have been stored for him in the agreed places. If the picture in the locket were of his wife, it would mean that the underground was not yet ready. This locket signal was agreed upon as part of a contingency plan before Mordant was put in solitary confinement. Mordant plans an uprising in the Citadel when French troops land at the port of Haiphong. He intends to retake Hanoi from the Vietminh. Quite daring. I have doubts that it will work," he said with a shrug. "But the general is determined, and he is too influential to oppose. He was De Gaulle's man in Cochin China before the Japanese coup."

Suzanne whispered: "But the Chinese? They'll be taking over Haiphong. Will they permit our troops to land?"

"Pechkov is negotiating with Chiang Kai-shek in Chungking. The Generalissimo has a price: We hand over our concessions in China, especially in Shanghai, and also ownership of the Hanoi-

Nanning Railroad. He'll get all of it, of course. We'll give him anything to get the Chinese out of Tonkin."

"I'm not sure …" Suzanne blurted out.

Sainteny silenced her with an upraised hand and slipped a small black leather case to her. "You have your orders. The hotel manager is loaning us his car and driver. Hopkins has arranged for a *laissez passer* to get you by the Japanese at the hotel gate. Clos will meet you in the lobby tomorrow morning at seven o'clock. Now for some dinner. No? Oh, too bad. Good evening."

Suzanne walked up the stairs to her room, thinking: Shall I go to Duncan? She picked up her telephone but then decided not to call him.

Clos was sitting in one of the wicker chairs in the lobby, and he rose as Suzanne, limping more heavily than usual, came down the stairs. She was wearing a khaki jacket and trousers with a cap that bore a French army cockade. Suzanne greeted Clos with a grudging smile and a crisp "Good morning." He was a fat man with heavy jowls, thinning blonde hair and a livid scar above his left eye. Suzanne had met him previously in the hotel where he was housed. When the Vietminh took possession of the city, he managed to escape alive from the mob that attacked the *Sûreté* headquarters but had been badly beaten and slashed over the eye with a machete. Obviously, Sainteny selected him to make sure the locket was delivered.

"Good morning, Madame, Doctor Clos at your service," the Frenchman said with a smirk, as he doffed his white pith helmet. He wore a brown gabardine suit and was carrying a black bag. "I'm sure you have the case."

Suzanne didn't reply and led the way out of the hotel to the driveway where Tolner was waiting beside a very old, but highly polished Citroen sedan. The manager bowed and then saluted as Suzanne and Clos got into the car.

The Citadel was in the Old Quarter of the city near the sports arena where the usual soccer matches had been displaced by political demonstrations. In its entirety, the Citadel cantonment embraced some one hundred dilapidated buildings, most of them used in the past as barracks for French troops. In a corner, overlooking the cantonment, was a hexagonal-shaped tower, a relic of the Imperial City of the nineteenth-century Nguyen dynasty.

Suzanne and Clos were admitted to the Citadel through the bronze gate and taken to an office where a Japanese colonel in a khaki uniform and wearing a holstered pistol stood behind a desk awaiting them. He was a solidly built man, with short cropped graying hair, and his hard eyes suggested he was not pleased about receiving the visitors.

"I am Colonel Kamiya," he said in French. "I've been ordered to show you about. There are many buildings. I'll take you through a few. You will not be allowed to speak to the prisoners. We must maintain discipline." He glanced at Clos' bag. "You must leave that case here. We have Japanese doctors who care for the prisoners." He ignored Suzanne's shoulder handbag.

The tour took them through dimly lit, stifling hot barracks along passages so clogged that they could scarcely pass. Sitting on the cots jammed together were gaunt, bearded men, most of them in odd bits of uniforms. Suzanne saw that most of the military were Foreign Legionnaires, but there also were French soldiers as well as colonial Senegalese and Moroccan Goumiers. Apparently, all had been ordered to keep silent. But after Suzanne and Clos had passed through with the colonel and his squad, who were armed with machine pistols, they heard subdued cries of "*Vive la France!*" and "*Vive De Gaulle!*"

"May we see a hospital ward?" Clos asked.

The colonel hesitated and then assented.

In the barracks, which had been converted into hospital wards, Suzanne paled at the sight of hundreds of emaciated patients lying on filthy bed linen. Her eyes moistened as she touched a few of the hands stretched out to her. And we're being shown the best of things, she thought angrily.

At one bed an unkempt wasted man painfully raised up and called out: "Madame, Madame … you are French?"

"May I speak to him?" Suzanne said to the colonel, and went to the patient without waiting for a reply. The patient grasped her hand, stared at her with wild eyes and began to sob.

"My friend, soon you'll be going home," Suzanne said. "The war is over."

The patient, his mouth gaping, regarded her in disbelief. "The war is over," he whispered, and then shouted: "The war is over!"

There was excited murmuring at the other beds. Several of the patients sat up. "When can we go home?" a soldier with bandaged eyes cried out.

Suzanne turned to the colonel: "Haven't they been told?"

The colonel said calmly: "We have nothing to say to them. Tokyo has ordered General Tsuchihashi to cease combat operations. But there has been no official surrender in Hanoi." He frowned impatiently. *"Come now."*

Returning to the prison office, Suzanne, barely able to contain her outrage at what she had seen, managed a faint smile at the colonel as she said: "We'd be grateful if we could see the senior French officer, General Mordant. I have a gift for him … from his wife." She took the black leather case from her handbag and handed it to the major. He opened the case, took out the turquoise locket, snapped it open and looked at the picture. Holding up the locket by its gold chain, he said: "She's very pretty. His wife?"

Suzanne nodded, once again forcing a smile.

"Very young for him?" The Colonel said. "The general is at least sixty."

Clos said hastily: "His second marriage. His first wife died of cancer, I think it was, before the war."

Clumsy, Suzanne thought, guardedly watching the colonel.

The colonel said: "The general is in a special barracks in another part of the Citadel. I'll pass the locket along."

Clos looked at Suzanne, his eyebrows lifted. She said, "We would like to see him, Colonel, just for a moment or two?"

"The general is in a high security area," the major said. "I'm sorry."

In the car, as they were returning to the hotel, Clos asked worriedly: "Do you think he'll give the locket to Mordant?"

Suzanne, propped in the corner of the leather seat, responded sullenly: "He said he'd pass it along. But I don't see what difference it makes. Did you see the condition of those soldiers? What kind of an uprising could Mordant lead?"

At the hotel Suzanne went to Duncan's room, but there was no response to her knock on the door. She had hoped to meet with him, thinking she should—in defiance of Sainteny—tell him about the Mordant affair. She felt remorse. Duncan had accepted her word that her visit to the Citadel would be no more than an effort to relieve the sufferings of the French prisoners.

In her room Suzanne found an urgent summons from Sainteny to a dinner meeting.

In the early evening, Duncan was in his room, preparing to go to dinner with Hopkins at a sidewalk café beside Restored Sword Lake, when there was a rapping at the door. He was surprised to find it was Pulaski, the former Legionnaire who had accompanied Ho Chi Minh from Tan Trao.

"Good evening, my Colonel. May I have a word with you?"

Duncan seated Pulaski at the small table in the center of the room, put a brandy bottle and a glass before him, and smiling said: "So?"

Pulaski reached into his black tunic and pulled out the black leather case that Suzanne had asked the Japanese that morning to be given to Mordant. He snapped open the case, took out the locket, opened it, and showed the photograph to Duncan.

"Your friend told Colonel Kamiya that it was a photograph of Mordant's wife," Pulaski said, speaking in French. "It is not. The

Japanese knew that in less than an hour after Madame Dumont left the prison. The Japanese do not know what the photograph was supposed to signify. But they assume it was a signal, perhaps for an uprising. They are returning the case so that the French know they are aware of what might be planned. Please give the case back to your friend."

"I don't understand," Duncan said, filling Pulaski's glass. "What do you have to do with all this?"

"We've had contacts with the *Kempeitai* since our Vietminh took over the city government. There is a Communist cell among the Legionnaires in the Citadel. Most of them are Russians but there are also Germans, Hungarians, Austrians, and some French. They are my friends. They've infiltrated the Mordant organization in the Citadel. I have been passing their information to the Japanese. This cooperation is good for everyone, except the French," he added with a chuckle.

"But why are you asking me to return the locket to Madame Dumont?"

"The *Kempeitai* know you came to Hanoi with me. Your Colonel Hopkins arranged for the visit of Madame Dumont to the prison. The *Kempeitai* believe you and Madame Dumont are lovers. The clerk at the hotel desk—the Eurasian—told them of her visit to your room. He's a *Kempeitai* agent."

Duncan settled back in his chair and looked at Pulaski with a smile. "Interesting," he said. "All right. I'll return the locket to Madame Dumont. Now tell me: You have Russian friends. Do you know a Soviet official named Solosieff?"

"Of course," Pulaski said. "He's very interested in the Russians in the Citadel. He was especially interested in one of them."

"What do you mean?"

"Andrei Voskressenski, a defector from the NKVD who worked in Hanoi. He went over to the Vichy French and then leaked information, which was passed to the Japanese. He was a Eurasian— Japanese mother—but the *Kempeitai* didn't trust him."

"What do you mean: 'was?' " Duncan asked.

"We performed a service for Solosieff. One morning Voskressenski was found in his bunk with his throat cut. In return, my Russian friends in the Citadel hope they'll be more welcome when they are shipped home."

"Can you arrange a meeting for me with Solosieff?"

"Certainly, I will contact him tonight."

When Suzanne entered the hotel dining room for dinner with Sainteny she was surprised to see men in the uniform of the British Royal Air Force sitting at two tables. They were the first Britons she'd seen in Hanoi.

With Sainteny at his table was another Frenchman, whom she immediately recognized, although he was not in uniform, as Captain Bertrand, a member of the M.5 intelligence unit in Kunming. Just as she was being seated at the table, she saw Duncan approaching the table in a grim, purposeful manner. She felt a sense of panic.

Duncan ignored Sainteny's jovial invitation to join them, acknowledged an introduction to Bertrand, and nodded curtly to Suzanne.

"I had a visitor this evening," Duncan said, visibly angry. "A friend, a former Legionnaire ... a Pole. He works with the Japanese at the Citadel in caring for Legionnaire prisoners. He asked me to give this to Suzanne." Duncan put the black leather case on the table in front of Suzanne. "My friend said: 'The Japanese are not fools'." Duncan spun about and strode away.

Suzanne, dismayed, rose to follow Duncan who was leaving the dining room, but then fell back in her chair.

Sainteny, arching an eyebrow, picked up the leather case and snapped it open. "The locket is still there," he said. With a smile, he offered the case to Suzanne. "It's yours, my dear."

Suzanne raised a restraining hand, shook her head, and looked at Sainteny in surprise. He doesn't seem to be disturbed, she thought, watching him slip the case into his jacket pocket.

"It makes no difference," Sainteny said. "Bertrand here, who arrived this afternoon on the RAF plane—you see the crew over there—tells me that French troops will not be coming into Haiphong anytime soon. Alas, poor Mordant, what a disappointment for him. We've not yet reached an agreement with Chiang Kai-shek. It seems that his General Lu Han is not entirely disposed to obeying instructions from Chungking. The old warlord wants time to collect more loot in Tonkin, and especially those rich custom duties at Haiphong."

Sainteny signaled to a waiter for the wine glasses to be filled. "Bertrand has brought us the details of another plan—a much better one—and you, Suzanne," he said smiling at her, "have an important part in it."

Sainteny continued in a low voice. "General Gracey, the British commander of the Twentieth Indian Division in Burma, will arrive in Saigon on September twenty-second with one of his Gurkha units. He is to accept the surrender of the Japanese. We have managed to persuade Gracey, who is very friendly to us, to bring along one company of our Colonial infantry regiment stationed at Rangoon. That this French unit will be with Gracey is top secret. It may not even be known to Lord Mountbatten's headquarters at Kandy, Ceylon, to which Gracey reports. Your duty, Suzanne, will be to get word of these arrangements to Jean Cedile, our commissioner for Cochin China."

Suzanne wrinkled her brow in puzzlement. "I don't understand. Why me? Why not Captain Bertrand here, who is fully briefed?"

Sainteny chortled. "I would prefer that. Unfortunately, Bertrand and the others in our group here are too French. Until Gracey arrives and approves, the Japanese won't permit any French people to pass through the airport. With your impeccable English, that British passport, which your devoted mother bestowed on you, and if necessary, your *Observer* press credentials, they should allow you to pass. I have arranged a place for you on the RAF plane, which is leaving here tomorrow. It carries an advance party for Gracey. You'll simply mingle with the British upon arrival in Saigon."

Suzanne settled back in her chair, straining to keep her composure, as Sainteny elaborated the plan. Her assignment at the start had been to do what she could to safeguard French civilians and care for imprisoned soldiers. Now, she was being drawn into a plot for which she had no taste.

"Contacting Cedile won't be easy," Sainteny said. "He was parachuted south of Saigon on August twenty-second, the same day Pierre Messner was dropped near here. Messner was supposed to become commissioner for Tonkin." Sainteny sniffed: "Stupid bureaucrats in Paris—they thought both of them would be welcomed. Cedile was luckier than Messner, who was captured by the Vietminh. It was the Japanese who found Cedile and his aides. Cedile was taken to Saigon, but we don't know where he is being held. You must find him. When you do, tell him he'll be freed just as soon as Gracey arrives. He's then to lead our Colonial unit to the internment camps where our troops are held, release them, and take them to the munitions depots to pick up weapons. They'll then seize the Saigon municipal installations. We have reason to believe that the Japanese will not interfere—assuming Gracey approves."

Sainteny topped off the wine in Suzanne's glass. "Come now, my dear, you've hardly tasted this superb wine which Bertrand brought. I've ordered an excellent dinner. You've plenty of time to pack. The RAF plane doesn't leave Gia Lam until three o'clock tomorrow afternoon. And, ah yes, important. In Saigon, go to the Continental Hotel. The manager there may be able to help you. His name is Rene Giscard. He's a survivor. He's hung on under many regimes; once worked for M.5. Tell him Guillermaz sent you. Guillermaz was his handler. Guillermaz is dead—but never mind. Giscard is well connected. He's been in the opium trade. He used to bring in girls from Paris for Bao Dai. He may be useful. But do not trust him too much."

DUNCAN WAS LEAVING THE HOTEL in the morning when Suzanne ran across the lobby to him. She touched his arm. "Travis, I'm sorry. Believe me. I had no choice."

Duncan turned on her furiously: "I don't know precisely what game you tried to play with Mordant," he whispered, his voice hoarse. "And I don't have time to discuss it right now. You became involved in something so dangerously stupid. The Japanese know what Mordant's up to. That's why they've kept him in solitary confinement for weeks in the old military prison in the Citadel. They know—even Giap knows—where the French underground has stored those weapons." Duncan breathed heavily. "Mordant is a fool. If there were an uprising, the Vietnamese would butcher every Frenchman in sight. The Japanese would watch with pleasure."

Suzanne said frantically: "I know. I know. Travis, believe me, the only possible explanation: Mordant is very powerful. He's De Gaulle's man. Sainteny is afraid to oppose him. The French who support Mordant are desperate. They'll try anything to take the city back from the Vietminh. But Travis ... that ship, the one I told you about loaded with French troops, has been diverted from Haiphong."

"Where's it headed now?

"I don't know."

Duncan collected himself. "All right ... I've got to go. I've got a meeting with Ho Chi Minh. I'll see you tonight."

Suzanne shook her head, and closed her eyes: "No, I'm leaving this afternoon for Saigon."

"Saigon?"

"Yes. The city is in chaos. The Japanese are losing control. They've turned civilian authority over to the Vietminh's Committee of the South. But the other Annamese factions—the Trotskyites, the Dai Viets and the Cao Dai—are maneuvering for power. The Binh

Xuyen gangsters are attacking French families. The British are going in. Sainteny has arranged for me to liaison with them. Get them to protect French civilians. A Royal Air Force plane is leaving here at three for Saigon. There's an advance party on board for General Gracey's British Occupation Force. They've agreed to take me."

Duncan stared at Suzanne in consternation. "So it's goodbye again," he said, fumbling for words—only the most worn clichés occurring to him. "We didn't have much time together." His face tightened. "Well, when you get to Saigon keep your head down."

Suzanne took both of Duncan's hands tightly in hers, "I'll see you somewhere." She walked off quickly, her eyes moist, berating herself for having misled him yet again.

Duncan hurried out of the hotel, nervously thinking: That night in my room—grabbing her, trying to bed her even before I told her how much I love her. I should have said to her then—straight out—that I want to be with her after we're out of this mess. Make some kind of commitment. Make up for the pain I've caused her—that craziness about Mai. He bit his lip. If something happens to her in Saigon …

The car and driver sent by Giap were waiting. As they drove off, Duncan wrenched his thoughts from Suzanne to the impending meeting with Ho Chi Minh. He would help him, if he could. In only two days Ho would proclaim Vietnamese independence and the establishment of a provisional government. Yet in reality the proclamation would be little more than rhetoric. The Chinese were swarming into Tonkin like locusts. The South was in turmoil. The Vietminh were struggling to consolidate power there before Gracey arrived in Saigon with his occupation force. Ho's Committee of the South had staged a successful coup on August 25 in Saigon, assuming control of city hall with Japanese consent, but now they were being challenged violently by the Trotskyites and other nationalist parties. The disorder in Saigon could give the British an excuse to return administrative control of the city to the French. Yesterday, at the hotel, when he came with the locket, Pulaski told him that Mai and Cong had left for Haiphong, where they would board a junk sailing to Saigon. Evidently Mai and Cong had been dispatched to deal with the conflict in the South. They would invoke Ho's authority in trying to weld all the nationalist parties into the Committee of the South.

The car took Duncan to Hang Nhgang Street, to a spacious three-story house which a wealthy supporter had recently donated to the Vietminh. Ho and Giap were waiting for him in a cluttered sitting room on the second floor, which appeared to be serving as both work and dining space. Duncan saw Ho's portable typewriter on a small table in a corner.

Arms outstretched, Ho welcomed Duncan. Although now removed from the jungle to the capital, Ho was still wearing his habitual faded khaki jacket, shorts and sandals. By contrast, Giap was in a white linen suit, white shirt with a black tie and black shoes. Duncan saw that Ho was painfully thin, not yet fully recovered from his illnesses. The three sat around the dining table, which was covered with documents. A shy Vietnamese girl brought a porcelain pitcher on a tray with brown sugar and milk. "Have some coffee, Travis," Ho said in a feeble voice.

Duncan reached into his breast pocket and produced several sheets of typewritten paper. "As promised, the text of the Declaration of Independence," he said, handing the pages to Ho, who accepted them eagerly with both hands.

"I'll make good use of these words," Ho said. "They will be inspiring for us in these difficult times." He rose and placed the sheets on his typewriter, which was covered with a frayed green cloth.

"We feel abandoned by everyone," Ho said, speaking in French. "The Allies are not preventing the Chinese troops from looting our countryside ... robbing the peasants of what little food they have left after the floods. Their advance units may reach Hanoi in a week's time. What will happen then? Do you know, Colonel, how many Chinese are coming? How long will they stay?"

Duncan put down his cup, feeling the anguish of the man acutely. "At Potsdam it was agreed only that the Chinese would take the Japanese surrender in the North. No date was set for their withdrawal. We estimate that the Chinese are bringing in one hundred and fifty thousand troops comprising Lu Han's divisions from Yunnan and Chang Fa-kwei's units coming from Kwangsi. We've asked our embassy in Chungking to protest their behavior."

"We're grateful," Ho said. "We have no influence with them. Has there been any reply from the French about my offer to accept a French president?"

Duncan shook his head.

Giap, who had been leaning on the table with his arms folded, straightened up abruptly, his eyes afire. "Why must we wait on the French?" he demanded in a loud voice. "They'll only betray us. We cannot expect help from anyone—even from the Communist Party in France. You've heard what Maurice Thorez, who's running the party now, said about you. 'We cannot trust Ho. He is a Trotskyite at heart.' Those are his exact words. Thorez is Stalin's man—and Stalin is interested now only in getting De Gaulle's support for his plans in Europe. Why tie our hands by negotiating with the French?"

Duncan was shocked. He'd never heard Giap speak to Ho in anything but deferential tones.

There was only silence for what seemed to Duncan a very long time. Giap fell back in his chair, seemingly surprised by his own audacity.

Then, in a low deliberate voice, Ho said: "I prefer to smell French shit for five years, rather than Chinese shit for the rest of my life."

Turning back to Duncan, Ho said calmly, "Have another cup of coffee."

Duncan, thinking it was time to leave, said, "No thank you."

Ho lit a cigarette, inhaled deeply, then said, "We now find ourselves in a situation in which only you Americans can help us. There will be a special place for you in Ba Dinh Square on September 2, when we celebrate our Independence Day and I present my government."

When he left the house on Hang Nhgang Street Duncan carried with him a message from Ho to President Truman appealing for Allied recognition of his provisional government as the only legal body in Vietnam.

At the hotel, Duncan was checking for messages at the concierge's desk when he was told that a gentleman was waiting to see him at the corner table in the lobby, under the painting of Napoleon at the Battle of the Pyramids. The man in the white suit rose to greet him as he approached the table on which rested a white Panama hat and a silver headed cane. "Colonel Duncan, what a pleasure—Solosieff, " he said, speaking in English.

"My pleasure," Duncan said as he shook hands. He signaled for a waiter as he joined Solosieff at the table. The Russian hooked his cane on the back of his chair. "Coffee?" Solosieff, a paunchy man, with bushy brown eyebrows over pale blue eyes, nodded, smiling.

"General Donovan sends you his greetings," Duncan said.

"Ah! Wonderful man, General Donovan, great friend. I last saw him in London," Solosieff said. "We had very useful exchanges of information during the war." He sipped his coffee. "Pulaski tells me you've been with the Vietminh."

"Yes," Duncan said, recalling Donovan's instructions that he be open with Solosieff. "I was with a team that trained some of Giap's cadres."

"You dropped guns and ammunition to them?" Solosieff asked, wearing an expression that suggested he already knew the answer.

"Yes. For use against the Japanese."

Solosieff laughed. "I'm sure they had no intention of wasting much of your ammunition on the Japanese. They had the French in mind."

"I don't doubt it," Duncan said. "What's your impression of Ho Chi Minh and his people?"

"A very clever man, Ho, but too impatient."

"Impatient?"

"We think Indochina should remain under the French for some time," Solosieff said. "Rather than under you or the Chinese," he added with a twinkling smile. "Let General De Gaulle guide them to eventual self-rule. We have great respect for the general. You know, of course, he signed a Treaty of Alliance and Mutual Assistance with Stalin in December."

"I don't think Ho will agree to wait too long for independence," Duncan said.

"Are Ho Chi Minh and his Vietminh now under American protection?"

Duncan shrugged. "We collaborated with him against the Japanese, but we've made no political commitment."

"Good. I would advise you Americans not to get involved politically. You've had very little experience in this country. It could become a quagmire for you."

"More coffee?" Duncan asked, thinking that both of them now had the information they wanted.

"No thanks," Solosieff said, picking up his hat. "I must be off. Convey my best wishes to General Donovan."

Duncan telephoned Hopkins in the morning and went to his room with Ho's message for President Truman and his own finished report.

Hopkins greeted Duncan warmly. "What Dumont told you checked out," he said. "Tsuchihashi told me that the ship is the *Triomphant* with one thousand French troops aboard. But the Chinese so far have refused to grant permission for a landing at Haiphong. De Gaulle is now holding the ship at sea waiting for clearance to land at Haiphong or some other port on the Indochina coast."

Duncan nodded and handed over Ho's message and his report.

Hopkins accepted the two documents, glanced at Ho Chi Minh's message to Truman and sank into the couch to read Duncan's lengthy report. Duncan stood, thumbs stuck into his belt, watching him read the report and then leaf back through it.

Hopkins looked up and said quietly: "You're proposing that the United States back Ho's provisional government. Never mind De Gaulle ... or that Ho is a Communist ... that he worked for the Comintern. All this against the background of the worry in

Washington over Stalin's moves in Eastern Europe and the Middle East. Travis, you're really going out on a limb."

Duncan flushed. "Roosevelt asked me to find someone we could rely on as a leader in a trustee arrangement," he said tautly. 'That was my assignment. Well? It's Ho Chi Minh. I'm suggesting that we support Ho's proposal—that Vietnam enter into the French Union under a French president for a period of five to ten years after which Vietnam would become independent. That fits right into Roosevelt's approach."

Hopkins listened quietly, the pages of Duncan's report scattered beside him.

Duncan folded his arms. "Is Ho a Communist? Yes, but he says—and I believe him—he's a nationalist first. All the files, including those of French intelligence, show he's always been devoted before anything else to furthering independence for Indochina, even in the years he worked for the Comintern. We know that the Russians have complained in the past of his nationalist tendencies. What Solosieff told me of their support of De Gaulle is further proof we can attract Ho away from the Russians. Ho won't become a satellite of Stalin or Mao unless we drive him into their arms by ignoring his appeals. He's ready to enter into an agreement with us for economic cooperation. He's searching for a unique place in the world and he's looking to us."

Duncan sat down beside Hopkins, leaning toward him, hands clasped. "John, the French are not going to stop Ho's people from getting their independence. I've been with them … lived with them in the field. I'm convinced Vo Nguyen Giap will turn this country into a death trap for anyone—including us—who gets in their way."

Hopkins stood up, walked to the window, and gazed out. "Travis, I don't have the guts to put down on paper what I feel about your report," he said, "Not with the current mood in Washington."

Then Duncan stood up. "John, I know there are characters who'll yell I'm a patsy for the Communists. For me there's something worse than being smeared—backing off from what I've found here and what I believe is good for our country as well as the Vietnamese. We're going to need friends in Southeast Asia."

Hopkins turned around. "I'll send Ho's message and your report to Donovan without comment. One other thing … Dumont."

"Yes," Duncan said stiffening. "She's leaving for Saigon."

"What for?" Hopkins said, frowning.

"She says the city's in chaos and she's to work with the British to safeguard the French civilian population."

Hopkins said: "I don't have any objections to you continuing your relationship with Dumont. She may be a useful source of information as to what the French are up to. But be careful. She seems to be playing all sides. As for your report, we'll wait for Donovan's reaction. Until then, don't get any more involved with Ho than you already are."

"Yes, Sir," Duncan said.

# -23-

**Hanoi**
**September 2, 1945**

ON INDEPENDENCE DAY, Duncan and Hopkins, accompanied by Trivers and the other members of the Deer Team, strolled through friendly crowds to Ba Dinh Square where they were seated at places reserved for them before the speakers' platform. Vo Nguyen Giap himself had delivered their formal invitation at the walled Gautier Villa on Avenue Beauchamp, where Hopkins's delegation was now housed. Giap made his visit the occasion for a public ceremony. Accompanied by an honor guard that bore an American flag and a brass band which played the "Star Spangled Banner," Giap formally welcomed the Americans to Vietnam and extended the invitation.

The square was packed with hundreds of thousands of celebrating Vietnamese; among them were village elders in traditional green sashes and yellow turbans mixing with city workers in white shirts and blue trousers, young women in their flowing *ao dai* silks, and schoolchildren waving flags and singing revolutionary songs.

Ho Chi Minh arrived in the square in an early-thirties vintage Ford. Duncan watched in wonderment as Ho, despite his ailments, nimbly mounted the high speakers' platform. The platform was wrapped in red and white bunting and encircled by soldiers in brown pith helmets holding pistols. At a microphone, hatless and dressed in a high-collared khaki suit and white sandals, Ho Chi Minh read his proclamation of independence.

Translating for Hopkins, Duncan' voice quavered as Ho Chi Minh delivered the first lines of his address:

> *All men are created equal. The Creator has given us certain inviolable Rights: the right to Life, the right to be Free, and the right to achieve Happiness. These immortal*

*words are taken from the Declaration of Independence of the United States of America in 1776. In a larger sense, this means that: All the people on earth are born equal; All the people have the right to live, to be happy, to be free.*

As Ho continued, appealing for world recognition of his new provisional government, Hopkins, grinning, said to Duncan: "He's made pretty good use of that text you gave him." Duncan, visibly moved, didn't respond.

As Ho concluded his address, two planes with U.S. Air Force markings clearly visible, droned over the city and then swooped low over the square. There was a roar from the crowd.

Hopkins shouted: "Those were P-38 Lightnings. What in hell are they doing here?"

Laughing, Duncan said, "The crowd must think it's a salute to Vietnamese independence."

"I don't think it's so funny, Travis," Hopkins grumbled. "Those P-38s must have been on reconnaissance. But look around. We're here in front of the speaker's platform in uniform. Uncle Ho is spouting from our Declaration of Independence. And our planes are overflying. Maybe, we're giving these people the wrong idea—that the United States is backing their government. Well, I don't see any evidence of that in the message traffic from Chungking and Kunming."

Duncan, sobered, said quietly. "You're right."

"Speaking of traffic from Chungking," Hopkins said, "you and I have to talk when we get back to the villa. We got a response this morning on your report to Donovan."

At the villa Duncan and Hopkins were alone at lunch, seated at a long redwood table in the dining room. Like the other reception rooms in the luxurious stucco house, once occupied by the French manager of a coal mine, the dining hall was done entirely in French period furnishings. The Japanese had moved the Americans into the villa because of the increasingly violent anti-French demonstrations around the Metropole Hotel.

"You're leaving Hanoi," Hopkins said abruptly, as they were served coffee in small Chinese porcelain cups.

"I'm being recalled?" Duncan asked, frowning. "Donovan didn't approve of my report—my suggestion we support Ho's government?"

"No. Donovan hasn't commented as yet on your recommendations. The problem is with Chungking. Your report was copied to the embassy. The ambassador says you've been seduced by the Communists."

As Duncan shook his head impatiently, Hopkins said: "The ambassador doesn't have the authority to order you back to the States. Only Donovan can do that since you're detailed to him on a special mission. What the ambassador is insisting on immediately is that you be separated from direct contacts with Ho. It would be troublesome to buck him on that."

"And what does that mean?" Duncan asked with a twisted smile. "Are you going to lock me up in the Citadel or in one of those cushy whorehouses in the Old Quarter? I would prefer the latter."

Hopkins smiled. "If you're hot for a classy French brothel, I can recommend one. But no. Donovan is sending you to Saigon. We need you there."

Duncan gulped his coffee and regarded Hopkins more hopefully.

Hopkins said: "The Brits—a regiment of Gurkha troops—are due in Saigon twelve days from now. Gracey, their commanding officer, is a stiff-necked colonial India type, who like Churchill thinks colonialism is godly and sacrosanct. Under the Potsdam Agreement, Gracey's mission is restricted solely to disarming the Japanese. He has no authority to restore French administration of Cochin China. He's been told that by Lord Mountbatten at Southeast Asia Headquarters in Kandy. But given Gracey's inclinations, he might give the French an opening, perhaps with the excuse of restoring order if there's Annamese unrest. He might even allow the French to bring in that troopship, the *Triomphant*, which was diverted from Haiphong. Right now, there's plenty of unrest in Saigon. As in Hanoi, the Japanese have turned over civilian authority to the Annamese—a Committee of the South—that's run by Ho Chi Minh's people. But its Vietminh leadership is being denounced by the Trotskyite party and some of the other bomb-throwing nationalist factions."

Duncan looked puzzled. "How do I fit into all of this?" he asked.

"You fit in, brother, but in a pretty tricky way," Hopkins said. "Your mission is to do whatever you can to hold Gracey to the Potsdam Agreement. As Donovan puts it: 'Do whatever is possible to deter the British from turning over Cochin China to the French before there is Allied agreement on the future of all Indochina.' Do you follow me?"

"I get it," Duncan said.

"We're telling the British simply that you'll be representing American interests in Cochin China and that you have an immediate assignment. There are two Allied teams going to Saigon to evacuate POWs being held by the Japs in Cochin China. One is the British Force 136. The other is our OSS team of seventeen people, which has the code name Project Embankment. And you, buddy, will be in command of the Embankment team."

Hopkins left the table and returned with a briefcase, opened it, and handed a file to Duncan. "That's the list of the people in your OSS complement. Your second-in-command is Lieutenant Charles Conroy. He's a smart tough Texan. He'll do the legwork on getting our POWs evacuated, leaving you free to watch Gracey. Conroy is leaving today for Saigon with most of the team. We'll have another aircraft for you in a few days. I'm also giving you a noncom, one of my people—Sergeant Saul Jacobson, a terrific kid who picked up a Silver Star for a parachute mission behind the German lines in France. He'll stick with you and guard your backside."

Hopkins leaned back in his chair, folded his arms and studied Duncan. "Well?" he said.

Duncan put his elbows on the table with fingers locked. "I love it," he replied.

"It's a tough one, Travis. Gracey is unhappy about Americans operating in his zone. He may claim you have no business there once the American POWs are evacuated—that the South is entirely a British show. He has declined to provide Project Embankment with logistical support or security. There's a terrorist free-for-all in Saigon—a lot of killings back-and-forth by assassination squads of the Vietnamese factions and by the French underground. Binh Xuyen gangs are raiding in the Saigon suburbs for loot. Take your issue weapons with you." He laughed. "Don't forget your Fairburn throw knife."

Duncan listened, thinking: Suzanne is in that maelstrom. I'll look for her as soon as I get to Saigon.

Hopkins extended his hand. "Good luck, buddy."

"Thanks," Duncan said. "One question: Why hasn't Donovan commented on my report. Does that mean he disapproves?"

Hopkins raised his hands in a gesture of frustration. "Donovan probably doesn't know what to tell you. The policy is in play. Truman is still trying to nudge De Gaulle toward self-government for the Indochinese, but he doesn't seem ready to insist on it. The State Department is afraid of putting De Gaulle's nose out of joint while we maneuver with Stalin. Publicly, we're holding in a neutral position. Donovan keeps checking out the White House, but the staff types aren't paying much attention to this part of the world. Donovan will respond when there's some decision."

# -24-

Saigon
**August 31, 1945**

FOLLOWING A YOUNG BRITISH LIEUTENANT carrying her bags, Suzanne entered the lobby of the Continental Hotel and approached the reception desk. The lieutenant dropped her bags, saluted and left with a cheery wave. Suzanne had chosen to stay at the Continental rather than at the villa set aside by the Japanese for the British advance party. She assumed the villa would be closely guarded and therefore she would be hampered in her movements. At Tan Son Nhut Airport, she experienced no serious difficulty with the *Kempeitai*. The Japanese major was curious about her, since she was the only woman on the RAF plane. He meticulously scrutinized her British passport and the *Observer* press pass—her French identity papers had been left in Hanoi—before stamping her entrance permit. She assumed the *Kempeitai* would keep track of her in Saigon.

The clerk at the reception desk was obviously puzzled by the unexpected arrival of Suzanne and the quick exit of the British lieutenant. "Madame, we're not admitting new guests," he said in French. The clerk was a young man, whose olive complexion and the cast of his eyes, marked him as Eurasian.

"May I speak with Monsieur Giscard?" Suzanne inquired.

The clerk vanished and returned a few minutes later with a large man with gray hair, beady dark eyes and a bulbous nose lined with protruding veins. "Madame," he said, bowing, his eyes flicking over the well-fitted khaki blouse and trousers and the leather luggage.

"I'm Suzanne Dumont. May I have a private word with you, Monsieur Giscard?

"Certainly, please come with me," the Frenchman said, with a slight accent but sufficient for Suzanne to guess at his Corsican origin. The manager led Suzanne to a small round table in a corner of the lobby, which was seedy and no longer resplendent as in the days of colonial grandeur.

"I have two requests," Suzanne said, as Giscard fixed her with an inquiring gaze. "First, a room." This elicited no response from the manager. "Second, I wish to contact Jean Cedile."

Giscard shifted heavily in his wrought iron chair, its legs screeching on the marble floor, but there was no change of facial expression. "I do not know Jean Cedile," he said coldly. "As for the room, I'm sorry. The hotel is full."

Suzanne said quietly: "Guillermaz sent me."

Giscard's brow wrinkled. "Guillermaz?"

"Yes. Guillermaz sent me."

"And how is he?"

"As well, as you might expect, at his age."

Giscard snapped his fingers at a passing waiter. "Have a vermouth with me. Two vermouth and soda, the Italian," he said to the Vietnamese waiter while surveying Suzanne with a raised eyebrow. "It's been many years since I've heard that name."

"You've not been forgotten," Suzanne said. "I've been told—if you like—it's possible for you to return to the old arrangement."

Giscard sat back in his chair, folded his arms, studied Suzanne and then said: "I know of someone who is acquainted with Monsieur Cedile. I will ask him to call upon you. As for the room, it will not be the best , but adequate."

In the afternoon of the next day, Suzanne was in her room moodily looking out the window at the heavy traffic on Rue Catinat when the clerk at the reception desk telephoned to say she had a visitor. Suzanne hurried down two flights of stairs to the reception desk but found no one there except the Eurasian clerk. She was turning away impatiently when a deep voice said: "Madame Dumont." It was a bearded man in clerical garb holding a broad-brimmed black hat. "I am Father Tricoire. I understand you wish to contact a mutual friend."

"Yes, Father," Suzanne said, as she accepted the extended hand, concealing her surprise that Giscard had chosen to work through a Catholic priest. In a few moments she and the priest were regarding each other over lemonades at a table on the hotel's broad open verandah.

"My Vietminh friends have changed the name of this street," the priest said, smiling and gesturing to the street before the hotel, "from Rue Catinat to Paris Commune Street. No one takes it seriously, not even the Annamese."

"You're French?" Suzanne asked.

"Yes, but I've been here so many years I feel more like an Annamite. I'm the chaplain at the old *Sûreté* prison. It's where the Japanese have interned some of the French soldiers. I was the chaplain at the prison when it was filled with Annamese political prisoners. The Japanese saw no reason to dismiss me. You see," the priest said laughing. "Some things don't change."

Suzanne, instinctively warming to this burly, gray-haired clergyman with lively blue eyes, said: "So you have friends on all sides."

"Yes, isn't that the role of a priest? Perhaps that's why that wayward son of mine, Giscard—whom I have not seen at mass in more than two decades—asked me to put you in contact with Jean Cedile. Jean is not too popular with the *colons*, but he is a good man. I brought him together with the Vietminh leaders of the Committee of the South—people I knew when they were in the *Sûreté* prison."

"Have they come to any kind of an agreement?" Suzanne asked.

The priest shook his head. "Jean is seeking peace, but he doesn't have much to offer the Vietminh. De Gaulle is willing to make some concessions to Annamese autonomy, but he is insisting on separating Cochin China from Tonkin. The Annamese will never agree to that. Jean is negotiating as a private French citizen, saying only that he has connections in Paris. He's keeping it a secret that De Gaulle appointed him officially as commissioner for Cochin China. He's afraid of being assassinated by any one of the Annamese factions. Something entirely possible."

"When can I meet him? " Suzanne asked.

"I'm seeing him tonight. I'll ask him to see you. I trust it's for a good purpose."

"I have a confidential message for him from Paris," Suzanne said, wondering if the priest would be so helpful if he knew the contents of the message.

The priest said, "Jean is now in good enough condition to meet with you. The Japanese treated him roughly when they found him. He was dropped with three others in Tay Ninh Province, fifty miles northwest of here. The Japanese stripped him naked. An officer questioned him and played the game of pretending he was going to decapitate him with his sword. But Jean didn't show fear. They took him to Saigon for further questioning. He told them only he was on a fact-finding mission, not that he had been appointed commissioner. They've released him. But he's keeping out of sight. He's been threatened by some of the hotheads among the French *colons* who are angry about his contacts with the Vietminh."

Suzanne pressed: "Father, when will I know about the meeting?"

The priest said, "I'm celebrating Sunday mass the day after tomorrow in the Central Prison and then I'll go to Norodom Square … to the presbytery of the cathedral on the square to watch the Vietminh's Independence Day ceremonies. It will be a great demonstration. Many thousands of Annamites will be there. It is taking place at the same time as the Independence ceremonies in Hanoi. We may be able to hear the speech of Ho Chi Minh, which is being broadcast here. Meet me on the upper floor of the presbytery at about one o'clock. I should have an answer from Cedile and also we can watch the ceremonies from the presbytery."

"Marvelous," Suzanne said. "I'll be there."

The priest extended his hand to Suzanne, threw some piasters on the table, put on his hat, and rose to go. He hesitated. "Madame, there's a possibility of trouble in the square at the time of the ceremonies. The French *colons* are not happy about this Vietminh independence talk. I hope for a peaceful day. But please, take care. These are dangerous times."

At noon on Sunday the crowds streaming up Rue Catinat toward the Notre Dame Cathedral, only three short blocks from the Continental, were already so dense that Suzanne decided to set out early for the presbytery. Amid the great throng, there were city dwellers in holiday dress mingling with bare-footed peasants. Columns of young men paraded, bearing banners denouncing French colonialism, some of them armed with clubs and spears. Suzanne felt uneasy threading through the crowds, as hostile glances were leveled at her by Vietnamese who apparently took her to be French, although she wore no markings on her khakis. Scores of thousands were already massed in Norodom Square behind the red-brick cathedral when Suzanne entered the large plaza and walked up the steps of the two-story presbytery just after one o'clock.

Father Tricoire, with open arms and a genial expression, greeted Suzanne at the arched doorway of the presbytery. The priest led her up winding stone steps into a small chapel on the upper floor to a chair before a corner window overlooking the square. Then ducking behind the altar the priest came up with two small communion cups and, with a wink, pulled a flask out of his cassock and poured two drinks. "We'll need a drop of cognac to endure all the speeches," he said, smiling.

Suzanne thanked the priest with a gay smile.

"Cedile invites you to dinner Tuesday at nine o'clock in the Bodega Restaurant," the priest said. "It is the only good French restaurant still open in Saigon. It's not far from the Continental. Giscard will take you there." He stood up and peered through the window. "Ah, the ceremonies have begun. I will translate for you."

From a platform decorated with Vietminh flags, a succession of speakers summoned the demonstrators to the defense of the independence and unity of the new Democratic Republic. The crowd stirred restlessly when it was told that they would not hear—because of a suspicious technical failure—the promised broadcast of the speech being made in Hanoi by Ho Chi Minh. The Vietminh president of the Committee of the South, Tran Van Giau, exhorted the crowd to be on guard against traitors who were creating incidents to justify the return of French troops. Arms in the air, he signaled the start of the parade, which was to wind through the city. It was then that the first shots were fired.

"Dear God," the priest cried, and ran to the far window. "Someone is shooting from the Jean Compte Building—the automobile building ... just beside us—its garage doors have been opened."

There was another fusillade and an immense roar went up from the crowd. Suzanne could hear return fire from the square.

"Come, Suzanne, we must go," the priest shouted. "The people will attack all the buildings on this side of the square. They'll kill every white they find."

The priest hurried down the narrow steps clutching Suzanne's hand. As they ran out the front entry, there was a burst of shots and the priest stumbled. "I'm hurt," the priest whispered. Suzanne drew his arm over her shoulders and half-dragging him led him into the garden at the side of the building to a cluster of rhododendron bushes where they both collapsed. A screaming mob was already charging into the presbytery. Suzanne, panting, pushed the heavy body of the priest under the bushes and lay there with her arm thrown over his chest.

"You must go, child," the priest gasped, his eyes closed. "There is nothing you can do for me. I'm dying."

Suzanne could see that he had been struck in the chest by more than one bullet. He had begun to bleed heavily.

"Father, I'll get help," Suzanne said, her hand on his cheek. "The Vietnamese know you."

The priest did not respond. When Suzanne realized that he was already dead, she lowered her head, sobbing. There were screams and she could see French women and children being dragged out of the presbytery by Vietnamese youths. They must have killed the men, Suzanne thought.

Suzanne lay for hours beside the body of the priest, listening to the tumult on the square, which quieted as it began to rain heavily. At dark she kissed the hand of the priest and crawled to the front gate of the presbytery. The square was virtually deserted except for three Japanese weapons carriers and some trucks filled with troops. Unsteadily, she walked to Rue Catinat. Her mind was frozen with the horror of the priest's death, her mouth slack, and it did not occur to her that she was in any danger. She walked past a Japanese patrol who looked with curiosity at this woman in torn, soiled clothing, but did not challenge her. In the hotel lobby, the Eurasian clerk ran to her side, but she waved him away. In her room, Suzanne clung to a bedpost and wept. He had friends on all sides, she thought, and they killed him.

Suzanne did not venture out of the hotel during the next two days. Heavily armed Japanese troops were on the streets trying to restore order as Vietnamese mobs roamed the city, breaking into French and Chinese shops, attacking French civilians wherever they could find them. The Committee of the South, to whom the Japanese had turned over civilian police powers, was unable to control the mobs, some of them organized by competing nationalist factions.

On Tuesday, at 6 PM, Giscard telephoned Suzanne in her room. "It is safe to go now. Monsieur Cedile must not be disappointed," he said. "I'll be waiting for you in the lobby at eight-thirty." This was her first word that the appointment would be kept despite the death of the priest.

Giscard led Suzanne out of the hotel to a cyclo waiting outside a side door on a dark street. "Safer than a car," Giscard said as he buttoned up the cyclo's plastic rain cover. Suzanne could see that Giscard was extremely nervous, not relishing his role as guide.

In less than ten minutes the cyclo was at the Bodega Restaurant on a corner of the Rue Catinat. No one was seated at the restaurant's outside verandah tables, which were screened by metal mesh to ward off any hurled grenade. Two Vietnamese and a foreigner in white shirt and shorts, cradling carbines, stood as sentries, at the front of the restaurant. Giscard quickly ushered Suzanne into the restaurant, brightly lit by crystal chandeliers. The French *maitre d'hôte* greeted Giscard and took them to a corner table set for two. Suzanne let her red silk shawl fall from her black dress and looked about, thinking she had not seen such a pretentious café since Paris. Giscard rose a moment later as a man in a straw hat and black raincoat with collar drawn up approached the table, followed by two others with machine pistols slung over their shoulders.

"Madame … Jean Cedile," the new arrival said. He shook hands with Giscard who quickly left the restaurant while the two bodyguards went to a nearby table. Cedile was a portly man with thinning blonde hair and fine aquiline features. Noting his ample girth, Suzanne thought he seemed an improbable parachutist.

"I understand you were with Father Tricoire when he was killed," Cedile said with a pained expression.

Suzanne nodded, her eyes moistening.

"We all suffer from his death," Cedile said. "Anyone who works for peace in this accursed country becomes a victim."

Suzanne sighed. "Do you know who fired those first shots in the square?"

Cedile shrugged. "Almost certainly, some of the French *colons*. The fools are convinced that life here can be made to be as it was before. They've been provoking the Vietminh and threatening anyone who tries to negotiate with the Annamese. Their strategy is to create enough disorder so that the Allies will believe the Vietminh are not fit to govern."

A waiter brought a menu and a wine list, both of which Cedile put aside. "The menu is a limited one, as are the wines," he said. "However, the *escargot* is always excellent and I took it upon myself to order our dinner."

"I'm grateful," Suzanne said. "I've eaten very little these past days."

"You're from Paris?"

"No. I'm M.5 in Kunming with Jean Sainteny. We've been in Hanoi since August twenty-second. I came here four days ago with the British advance party."

"I know Sainteny. You have a message?"

"Yes, from Paris. Sainteny received it by courier five days ago with instructions that it be delivered to you orally."

Cedile listened, frowning, with an expression of growing disbelief as Suzanne imparted the details of the plan for release of the interned French troops and the takeover of the city, which he was ordered to put into effect after the British landed.

"Those idiots in Paris," Cedille said angrily, his voice trembling. "They cannot comprehend the situation here. They disregard my reports about the power of the Vietminh, the extent of their popular support. You saw evidence of that support in Norodom Square. Bringing in a few French troops now, before we've come to some kind of an understanding with the Committee of the South, trying to take over this city ... my God!" Cedile lowered his head and shook it. "We'll be inviting civil war, a terrible conflict."

Suzanne regarded Cedile with surprise. She hadn't expected this kind of a reaction from him. She had thought of him simply as another functionary who would obey orders. What he was saying confirmed her own growing apprehension that Paris was blundering into catastrophe.

Cedile gathered himself. "Have some wine," he said, pouring champagne. "When are you returning to Hanoi?"

"As soon as I have your reply and I can arrange a flight with the British."

Cedile said, "I need time to think things through. Perhaps talk again to the Committee of the South. Find out more about the attitude of this Ho Chi Minh. I'll have a reply for you before the British troops arrive ten days from now."

Suzanne returned to the Continental with Cedile in his Citroen. As she left the car, Cedile said: "You'd be wise, Madame, to take precautions for your own safety. We're being drawn into a bloodbath."

MAI CLUTCHED THE EDGE of her wooden slatted seat as the train jolted along the rough roadbed. During the war Vietminh guerrillas had repeatedly sabotaged the sixty-mile-long rail line to Haiphong, and the repairs had left the roadbed only barely passable. Cong, who had been peering out the window as the train was pulling out of the Hanoi station, was now more relaxed, and he smiled at her. At the *Kempeitai* station checkpoint, Cong had displayed forged French identity papers identifying himself as a submanager in a textile plant in Haiphong, and Mai as his wife. The Japanese had passed them through after searching their two small valises.

They were sharing a third class compartment with a large pot-bellied Chinese, a prosperous merchant, who was accompanied by his wife, dressed in a flowered *cheongsam*, and two small children. The soft-seat compartments and the first-class Wagon-Lits cars up ahead were filled with Japanese military.

Mai could not restrain herself from laughing as she watched Cong, who was attired in a white suit, struggle with bent finger to loosen his stiff collar. Mai was in a beige *ao dai* gown, slit modestly low at the sides revealing her silk trousers. They had not been so formally dressed for many months.

The two, although lovers, were not traveling together simply by their own choice. As on other key political missions, Ho Chi Minh had insisted that Mai, his close associate, pair with Cong, one of Giap's most trusted deputies. They would report individually to their superiors. On this mission, they were to attempt, where they had failed in the spring, to bring as many of the nationalist parties as possible into the Vietminh fold. It was of the highest importance, Cong and Mai were instructed, that the Committee of the South present a united front when British troops landed in Saigon so that there could be no pretext for General Gracey to invite French administration. Giap had authorized Cong, if need be, to employ

Honor Squads—the Vietminh assassins—to eliminate leaders of factions who violently resisted the Vietminh fiat. In the Hanoi area, such resisters had already been dealt with. Since seizing control of the municipal installations, Honor Squads had killed hundreds of opponents.

Mai was grateful for this interlude away from the strife. She and Cong would have some time together alone, before plunging into the Saigon imbroglio. We've not made love for many weeks, she thought, as she gazed at him. She had not yielded to him often enough. Cong had become impatient at times. Only a few days ago he shouted at her that he'd been to a brothel. Yet the next moment he was tender and understanding. The curse upon them was that of her torture in the prison at Poulo Condore. The memory kept returning: The Eurasians attacking her with a maize cob as she lay bound with legs apart. The French *Sûreté* officer laughing after saying to her that rape was forbidden by regulations but nothing else. Her ripped hymen and vagina were still bleeding the next day when she was told of the amnesty. It was the price she paid for refusing to name members of the Saigon underground. Now she endured the physical pain of making love only when her whole being impelled her. There were times—was it the memory of Poulo Condore?—when she would become strangely lustful, like that night in July after the ambush during the march north—the last time they made love. The forward scouts of their column were ambushed by a company of Civil Guards who were unaware that the main Vietminh force was only several hundred yards behind. The Vietminh column descended on the Civil Guards, most of whom fled, leaving behind their officer, a Frenchman, who lay wounded, moaning on the ground. She watched Cong fire a pistol into the head of the Frenchman. That night, she invited Cong, and they made love with unrestrained passion.

Mai thought of her affair with Duncan. She regretted confusing him by going to his hut that night in Tan Trao. It was an impulse after he turned away from her earlier in the day, looking so unhappy. She didn't want him him to leave embittered, feeling that she had misled him. Perhaps she should have told him earlier about Cong. Now, all was right with him. He was no longer a prisoner of the memory of what happened in Saigon. But she felt a need to tell Cong everything. Explain to him. She glanced at Cong. Should she? He would be enraged.

At the Haiphong station, Mai and Cong passed through the police checkpoint and then went to a food cart where a Nung woman peddler sold them cold tea and bowls of rice and dried fish. On the street they hailed a pedicab and Cong directed the cyclo man, a ragged oldster wearing a jute rain cape, to the Thang Nam Hotel, near the harbor. The port had been heavily bombed by Chennault's Fourteenth Air Force, but the center of the city through which they rode was largely untouched. The cyclo man pedaled along wide boulevards lined with plane trees, past the classic City Theater and the other pink-plastered municipal buildings glowing in the sunset, to the shabby harbor front. The hotel, like most commercial establishments in the city, was Chinese-owned, and a young Cantonese with close cropped hair, wearing a long gray gown, checked them in without asking to see identity papers after Cong had paid in advance for the night.

"Friends will come to pick us up in the morning," Cong told him.

A small boy led them up to their room, which had a single narrow window, a slowly turning ceiling fan and a four-poster bed hung with white gauze mosquito netting. Cong locked the door and hooked a chair under its knob, remembering how the Chinese clerk had eyed his roll of piaster bills. Because of the risk of being searched by the Japanese police at the Hanoi station, they carried no weapons. They slept that night in close embrace; Cong kissed her breasts but did not press himself upon her.

In the morning, Danh came for them. He was a muscular young man with smiling eyes, who walked with a limp. Four fingers of his right hand were missing—from a demolition charge that had exploded too soon. From a knapsack, he pulled out a .38 caliber automatic pistol, which he handed to Mai, and a Japanese machine pistol with a folded handle, which he gave to Cong. "I took the machine pistol from a French planter after I cut his throat," Danh said. "We ambushed his truck on a bridge over a river gully on the

Delta ... killed the four Civil Guards with him. Some of the comrades wanted to slit the throat of his wife, but we left her."

Mai and Cong, having changed into their customary black clothing, followed Danh along the waterfront to a small sampan tied up at a dock for fishing vessels. They walked by French custom officials in white uniforms, who ignored them. The Japanese had allowed the French to continue running the port, which before the Allied blockade had done a brisk trade with Japan in manufactures from the Haiphong factories. The sampan took them out into the harbor to a large Chinese wooden junk with an orange bamboo-ribbed sail rigged to a towering mast. A red-blue-and-white Chinese Nationalist flag hung limply from the flat stern high off the water. They climbed up a rope ladder to the deck.

On board, Danh introduced Mai and Cong to the *lao-pan*, the junk master, a shifty-eyed Cantonese wearing a cap and a black jacket.

Before leaving on the sampan, Dahn whispered: "Safer to go on this Chinese junk. There are two French patrol ships—they've defected to De Gaulle—running along the coast. They sometimes stop and search Vietnamese boats. But be careful. These Chinese sometimes rob passengers and throw them overboard."

Mai and Cong were led below to a tiny cabin with a narrow bunk for one person. It smelled of the charcoal that the junk carted to Saigon in exchange for rice.

The junk sailed before the afternoon wind through the silted channel to the Gulf of Tonkin, past huge sandstone rocks jutting from the water, and down the coast toward Saigon. At sunset, Mai and Cong took bowls of rice and pork, given to them by the cook, the fat wife of the *lao-pan*, and went up on the deck where they sat on a bulkhead. The crew of six were having their meal below. The wind had calmed and the junk's motor was running.

Mai put down her chopsticks. She began: "One night I was with the American, Duncan. It was before I went to the south, before he left for the border with Tao."

Cong continued to eat. Then he put his chopsticks and half-filled bowl on the bulkhead cover, folded his arms and looked toward the darkening coastline. "Why?" he asked. "Do you love him?"

"Not as I love you. I really didn't want to make love with him," Mai said. "But he'd been so caring of me and he's helping our people so much. He didn't ask, but I knew he wanted me. I thought I would never see him again." She paused and examined Cong's features worriedly. "I'm telling you this because I love you and I want nothing bad between us."

Cong said bitterly: "If you did this for the Party it was for nothing. Duncan is a good man. But we Vietnamese cannot rely on Duncan or any American. The Americans will never fully know our pain and accept what we must do. We Vietnamese can only depend on ourselves. We, you, have given enough to white men."

Cong jumped off the bulkhead and went below, followed by Mai. Cong slept that night on the floor of their room beside the bunk where Mai lay. Once, Mai reached down to grasp Cong's hand, but he pulled it away.

Two days later, in the twilight, the junk was idling in a light breeze at the mouth of the Saigon River, as the crew waited for daylight to enter the port. Mai was walking down the narrow passageway to the kitchen to be doled the evening meal when there was a shout. Chinese crewmen had leaped on Cong, who had been walking just behind her. One of them tore at the machine pistol slung over his shoulder and another came at him with a knife as he lay sprawled on the passageway. Mai, taking her pistol from beneath her tunic, fired into the chest of the man with the knife. The other Chinese who was pinning Cong to the deck looked up in terror. Mai calmly aimed and shot him in the forehead as the two other crewmen fled. Cong recovered his Bren gun, went into the kitchen and herded the master and his quivering wife over the bodies of the two dead men up to the deck. While Mai guarded them, Cong found all the other crewmen and lined them up on the deck.

Cong and Mai squatted on the deck until dawn. With Cong standing over him, the master started the motor and steered the junk down the Saigon River past the sunken hulks of merchant vessels.

Planes off American aircraft carriers operating in the Yellow Sea had bombed the port and made it unusable for larger ships. The master brought the junk alongside a partially demolished wharf, anchoring it among a flotilla of small boats. Mai hailed a taxi sampan, which came alongside.

Before going down the ladder to the sampan, Cong ordered the master to stand up. "You Chinese are no longer masters of the Vietnamese," he said, "and so that you do not forget this …" With a knife he slashed the cheek of the *lao-pan*.

Mai and Cong found Saigon in turmoil. The Japanese had done little to curb the violence that followed the shootings in Norodom Square. The Committee of the South had not been able to galvanize the Vietnamese police into restraining action. Vietnamese militants were harassing the terrified civilians of the French community and also turning on each other in a struggle for power. Armed *colons* of the French underground were striking back at Vietnamese civilians with reprisal killings.

Within hours after landing at the Saigon dock, Mai and Cong were meeting with Tran Van Giau, the Vietminh head of the Committee of the South, in the governor- general's palace, which had been turned over to him by the Japanese. They conferred in an ornate drawing room where Giau camped, his belongings scattered about in a disarray that would have dismayed the former French occupants.

Mai conveyed Ho Chi Minh's instructions: Do everything possible to maintain order and a cooperative spirit with the British, so as not to provoke a challenge to the legitimacy of our government. Avoid clashes with the French community. Once the British have left Cochin China, the revolution will then go forward.

Giau, a scholarly looking man in a stiff-collared white shirt, listened to Mai with a frown that betrayed impatience. "That's been my policy," he said sharply, "but there are problems. The Japanese aren't doing enough to keep order. Marshal Terauchi seems to enjoy watching us stew with the French. But it's the Trotskyites who are giving us the most serious trouble. They've denounced me as a traitor for advocating peace and cooperation. They will not join our committee so that we can present a united front to the British. They won't give up their arms, and they've been inciting the mobs. They're now calling for an general uprising and confiscation of the French plantations."

Giau cast a sidelong look at Cong with narrowed eyes. "They must be silenced."

Cong said: "Contact Ta Thu Thau—I assume he still heads the Trotskyite Party—tell him Mai and I wish to meet with him, that we have a message from Ho Chi Minh."

"It will be difficult to persuade Thau to meet," Giau said. "He fears our Honor Squads."

"We'll meet him wherever he prefers." Cong said.

Mai and Cong were taken by a Vietnamese driver in a rented car to the end of Avenue Gallieni and then another mile and a half into the center of Cholon, Saigon's twin Chinese city. At Thau's suggestion, it had been agreed that they meet in the Paradis dance hall.

"Dance hall!" Mai exclaimed when told of the arrangement with the Trotskyite chief.

Giau smiled. "Why not? He thinks it's safe for him. They collect weapons at the door. There are armed guards on the inside to keep order. Besides, Thau goes there often. He likes the taxi dancers. It is also convenient for us."

The driver dropped them off in front of the Paradis, a one-story stucco building painted a garish blue on a cobbled street in the center of the pleasure district. Gambling establishments, opium dens, fancy brothels, and the cheaper bawdy houses whose prostitutes waited on stools before the doorways surrounded the dance hall. The district was ruled by Chinese gangs that had emigrated years ago from Macao. At the entrance to the Paradis, young Chinese men in black shirts with machine pistols slung over their shoulders checked customers for hidden guns, knives and grenades.

A five-piece Vietnamese band was playing American jazz when Mai and Cong entered the dimly lit hall heavy with a haze of tobacco smoke. Armed guards leaned against walls that were covered with obscene drawings. Mai drew glances from all sides as she entered. She was wearing a flowing *ao dai*, like the taxi dancers, but she was without their garish makeup. Among the patrons, well-dressed Vietnamese and Chinese—there were only a few French—she was the only woman. Chinese house hustlers were circulating among the men selling tickets for dances with taxi girls who waited at corner tables.

Mai and Cong were escorted to a table, which Thau had reserved near the round dance floor. A few minutes later, Thau entered the hall followed by three men. Thau came directly to the table while the others sat at another not far away. Thau was a tall, slender man with furtive eyes, graying hair, and only one ear, the other seemingly sliced away.

Mai greeted Thau familiarly. "Good evening, Comrade Thau," she said. "We've not met for many years. But I still remember how our comrades praised your courage at Poulo Condore."

"I grieve for your father, Comrade Khang," Thau replied with a small bow. "He was a true patriot who never compromised with the French."

Thau ordered a goblet of yellow wine but did not lift his cup as he listened to Mai detail Ho Chi Minh's proposals for restraint, negotiation and a common front. Mai could tell by his dark expression—as she spoke—that Thau was not being swayed.

"The French have subjugated and abused us for eighty years," Thau said. "They won't let go. To negotiate with them is to be betrayed. Any Vietnamese who compromises with them is a traitor. This is the time—while the Japanese are passive and the French are weak—to rise up and take back our country. That's what we Trotskyites intend to do. Tell that to Ho Chi Minh. He does not seem to believe anymore in world revolution."

Cong said: "Perhaps we should talk again."

Thau signaled for the bill. "There's no use," he said, and made ready to leave.

Mai and Cong stood up to say goodbye as Thau bowed and left. They sat down again and waited without speaking until they heard the sound of gunfire outside the dance hall. The jazz band stopped playing and there was a hush in the hall. When the gunfire ceased, Mai and Cong went out to the street. No one followed them. The car in which Thau and his bodyguards were riding had gone only a few yards from the dance hall when the Honor Squad opened fire. Thau's body had been dragged from the car and lay in the gutter. The plan had been a simple one: When Thau left the table, and if Mai stood up, that was the signal that there had been no agreement and Thau was to be assassinated. A member of the Honor Squad, standing at the rear of the hall, had conveyed the signal.

On a side street Cong and Mai found a cyclo which took them to the Grand Hotel in Cholon, where they were to report to Giau in the morning. They went into the bar where wealthy Vietnamese and Chinese were loudly entertaining their courtesans. They drank many cups of strong Mongolian *paikareh*. At midnight they went to their room and made love.

# -26-

**Saigon**
**September 8, 1945**

LEANING BACK IN THE BUCKET SEAT of the throbbing C-46, his eyes closed, Duncan mulled over what it would be like—this return to Saigon after ten years. Jacobson, the young sergeant assigned to him by Hopkins dozed beside him, snoring unobtrusively. Duncan thought of Saigon, the excitement of his first meeting with Mai at the bookshop, how she showed him the shockingly squalid Vietnamese villages, dancing with her in his apartment overlooking the flower market. The youthful innocence of it. Then, the horror and torment, his ceaseless search for her. Mai was no longer at the center of his life, but her Vietnam still possessed him, and he felt no urge to return home. Why? It wasn't the enticements of the land, as much as he was drawn to its beauty and mystery. It was more that here—in this land—he'd found the way to make his life truly meaningful: in the struggle to rescue the Vietnamese from subjugation. His commitment was hardly unique. There was Roosevelt. The president probably never met an Indochinese, and yet he was so strongly impelled to do right by these people. As for what lay ahead in Saigon: He would, as Donovan instructed, work to hold open the door until there was Allied agreement on the future of Indochina. That's all he could do—hold the door open and pray for wisdom in Washington. Jacobson woke and turned to Duncan, who suddenly realized he'd been muttering to himself.

At Tan Son Nhut Airport, Duncan found Lieutenant Conroy, his deputy on the OSS team, waiting for him. "Welcome, sir, to the place that God forgot," drawled the lanky Texan, whose lantern jaw was working on a chew of tobacco.

"So you're Charley, the rustler from the Panhandle," Duncan said, as he returned Conroy's salute. "Hopkins told me about you."

"That's me. And I've rustled a bottle of bourbon, which is waiting for you at the good ole Continental Hotel. And what the hell is this?" Conroy exclaimed as he surveyed the hulking figure of Jacobson, who was stowing Duncan's gear in the back of the lieutenant's jeep.

Jacobson threw an off-hand salute. "Sergeant Jacobson, also a cowboy, Sir, the Flatbush Ranch, Brooklyn."

"I think we're all going to get along very well," Duncan said, feeling more cheerful.

As he drove the jeep out of the airport, past saluting Japanese guards, Conroy said, "We've located forty-two hundred and fifty-nine Allied POWs; two hundred and fourteen of them are Americans who are at two camps outside of Saigon. The rest are British, Australian and Dutch. There are more than three thousand French troops interned by the Japanese in the Saigon Central Prison and at a camp near the city. The Japs say they keep them confined on the insistence of the Committee of the South. They're now waiting for instructions from the British as to what to do with the Frogs. Gracey is due here in four days."

"Well, they'd better stay locked up," Duncan said. "The Vietnamese would blow up the town if they showed up on the streets."

"There may be an immediate problem with the French," Conroy said. "The British Force 136, which is going to evacuate POWs, brought with them agents of the SLFEO—that Gaullist intelligence outfit—the one that worked with the British during the war. I don't know what they're up to."

"That's trouble," Duncan said. "We need to watch them."

At the Continental Hotel, Jacobson, in awe, surveyed the marbled lobby with its potted palms and pronounced: "Like a Hitchcock movie." The top floor of the hotel, to the manager's obvious distress, had been newly commandeered by the Japanese for the British Force 136 and Duncan's Project Embankment Team.

At the desk, Duncan asked if Suzanne was in the hotel. Yes, the clerk told him, but she had gone out. Duncan frowned. He was eager to see her after the fumbling goodbye in Hanoi. He wanted to reassure her, and be reassured, about what they meant to each other.

Duncan deposited his bags in his room and decided to have a quick look around the city while Suzanne was out. He was going out the door when he recalled Hopkins' caution. He went back and pulled his 45. caliber pistol from his bag.

Saigon had the appearance of a city under siege. Shops were shuttered. There were the usual cyclos, horse carts and bicycles on Rue Catinat but few cars. Duncan saw no foreign women on the fashionable shopping street. Vietnamese turned in astonishment to look and remark at the unusual sight of an American in uniform. In Norodom Square, where the shootings had taken place on Independence Day, Japanese soldiers with bayoneted rifles stood beside a tank and two weapons carriers. Feeling the pervasive tension, Duncan cast glances over his shoulder as he strolled the streets.

Impulsively, Duncan decided to visit his old apartment on Boulevard Charner. He walked quickly to the small two-story building just off the Rue Catinat. The building's sidewalk café was dark and the tables stacked. Duncan peered through the door's iron gratings at the bar inside and recalled how drunken Foreign Legionnaires once disturbed his sleep with their singing of German and Russian ditties.

Duncan entered the building and knocked at the door opposite the top of the stairs. After he knocked a second time there was a guttural response in French. Duncan shouted: "This is Colonel Duncan of the United States Army." The door was opened a crack by a man, haggard and unshaven, with frightened eyes. He opened it wider upon seeing Duncan's uniform. Duncan smiled engagingly and said, "I lived in your apartment many years ago. Passing by, I thought of paying a nostalgic visit … but please, don't let me trouble you."

"Come in," the man said. "I'm Doctor Bouchard. You're welcome to look about. But the apartment is not as it would be normally."

The doctor, who was barefoot and dressed in khakis with a pistol stuck in his belt, motioned Duncan into the living room with its bamboo bar, so familiar to Duncan. "I'm alone," the doctor said. "I've sent my wife and child out of the city to the home of a friend at Cité Hérault in the suburbs. Saigon is too dangerous. French women have been raped."

"I'm sorry," Duncan mumbled, not knowing what else he could say. "You're a medical doctor?"

"Yes, at the Saigon Hospital, but I have not been able to go there since the shootings in Norodom Square. The mobs, these Annamites, have gone mad. It's incredible. I've treated so many of them. So many of them have been my friends. But no longer."

"Is it all because of the shootings in the Square?" Duncan asked.

The doctor went to the bar and returned with two shot glasses brimming with cognac. He handed one to Duncan, who was sitting on the wicker couch, and quickly tossed back his shot.

"It's more than that," the doctor said, as he went back to the bar and fetched the cognac bottle. "It's their hatred of the French *colons*. The Annamites hear speeches by those *colons*—those stupid ultras led by Mario Bocquet—about returning to the ways of the old French regime. Many Annamites would rather die than go back to that life. Now, all French people, even people like me who've been sympathetic to the Annamites, have become targets. Every French home is like a fort. We're holding on until the British arrive. The Japanese do little to protect us."

Duncan asked: "Would French troops help?"

The doctor laughed with a hint of hysteria. "That's what Bocquet's *colons* demand—the fools! Saigon would explode if French troops reappeared on the streets. It would be the beginning of civil war."

Duncan left the doctor sitting on the wicker couch clutching the cognac bottle. As he left the building he saw there were no flowers in the stalls of the old market on the boulevard.

At the hotel Duncan telephoned Suzanne's room. His spirits soared when he heard her cry out: "Come at once!"

Suzanne was in a dressing gown when she opened the door. As Duncan embraced her, Suzanne said in confusion: "When did you come? I was just getting ready for dinner."

Duncan laughed happily. "In Hanoi you said we'd meet again, somewhere. Well, here's somewhere."

Suzanne drew him to the leather couch in the alcove under the window. Duncan put his arms about her and tried to kiss her, but she restrained him. "I have a lot to tell you," she said, trembling. "A lot I concealed because I had no choice. Now, I am unsure of everything, everything except that I love you."

Duncan leaned forward again to embrace her, but she gently pushed him away again. "Listen!" she commanded. Folding her hands in her lap, Suzanne told Duncan of Gracey's plan to bring a company of French troops with him and of the message she had conveyed to Cedile. Duncan listened incredulously.

"French troops, that would be catastrophic!" he exclaimed. "I've been here only a few hours, but long enough to know that this town is a tinderbox. It will go up in flames if French troops try to take over the municipal buildings."

Suzanne said: "I know that, Travis. That's why I'm telling you everything without feeling guilty that I'm betraying M.5. Even Cedile agrees that bringing in that colonial company and releasing the interned French troops would provoke a general uprising. But I'm not sure he can dissuade Paris from the plan." She reached out and touched Duncan's hand, looking to him for reassurance. "Travis," she said, looking at her wristwatch. "Cedile is coming here tonight. We're to have dinner. He's to give me a message for Sainteny—his response to the instructions from Paris. I haven't seen Cedile for a week, what with this chaos in the city."

"Can I talk to him?" Duncan asked.

"I don't know," Suzanne said. "I'll ask him." She glanced again at her watch. "He'll be here in about twenty minutes. Wait in your room. If he agrees to see you I'll telephone." She rose from the couch. "I've got to get ready now." At the door, Suzanne put her arms about Duncan. "I'm sorry I couldn't be more open before this," she said.

Duncan nodded, pressed her close, and left.

Just after ten o'clock Suzanne telephoned. "Cedile does not wish to see you publicly. He'll come to your room in a few minutes," she said. "He'll be alone. His two bodyguards will stay outside your door."

Duncan threw open the door for Cedile at the first knock. The Frenchman greeted Duncan in English, shook hands perfunctorily, strode into the room and sank into the couch. "You wanted to see me, Colonel," Cedile said. "We don't have much time."

"*D'accord,*" Duncan said, somewhat ruffled by Cedile's curt manner. "I'll get directly to the point. I represent American interests here. Under the Potsdam Agreement there's no provision for France to resume control of Cochin China at this time. Yet I'm told there's a plan to bring a French company into Saigon with General Gracey on September twelfth—just four days from now. That would be a mistake, a move which could have the most unfortunate con-sequences. I ask you on behalf of my government to do what you can to have the plan dropped."

Cedile stretched out his legs and regarded Duncan coolly. "I must begin by telling you: We French have been in this country for a long time and we don't need to be lectured by Americans. Apart from that, it is the British who have been assigned jurisdiction over Cochin China. However, I do agree with what you say. Marshal Terauchi—who has difficulty hiding his amusement at our problems—has granted me use of his facilities to communicate with Paris. I advised the government to postpone arrival of any French troops. What will the government do? I don't have the slightest idea. There's a total lack of appreciation of the enormous dangers we face here."

Duncan asked: "What do you mean by 'postpone the arrival of French troops'?"

Cedile folded his arms. "Be realistic. Eventually, French troops will have to come in. We can't have the Chinese and British camp in Indochina forever. It's a matter of timing. Frankly, the danger lies in Paris attempting a military takeover before we have some kind of agreement with the Annamites. That would incite civil war."

Duncan said, "I'm not going to dispute with you at this moment the issues relating to the future French role in Indochina. We must deal with the immediate problem. I have letters of introduction from Ho Chi Minh to the Committee of the South. Let me arrange for you to meet with them again. This may be the time for substantive talks on some kind of an understanding that would at least preserve Saigon from further violence."

Cedile shrugged. "I'm quite willing but I'll need clearance from Paris. Some new basis for discussion on the political demands being made by the Committee. My previous meeting with the Committee was without result. I'll ask at once for clearance."

"When would you expect a reply?"

"I don't know. De Gaulle has much higher priorities."

"We don't have much time."

Cedile nodded and stood up. "No need to remind me of that," he said. "One other thing. Not all the French in Saigon accept my advice. There's an owner of a very large rubber plantation—Mario Bocquet—who is very influential with some *colons*. He is violently opposed to negotiations with the Committee of the South or any Annamites. He waits only for the arrival of French troops to put them down totally. He and his fellow extremists aren't averse to eliminating anyone who stands in their way. You notice I go about with bodyguards."

"I've heard of Bocquet."

Cedile inclined his head toward Duncan's pistol, which was lying atop a bureau. "Keep it to hand."

When Cedile left, Duncan went to the window of his room and looked out on Rue Catinat, which was now shuttered and still. A Japanese patrol was marching by. He stood there for a few minutes then went to the telephone and rang Suzanne's room.

"Wait for me, please," he said when Suzanne answered. "I have a report to get out. Yes, he's gone. We'll talk later."

Duncan then asked the hotel telephone operator to connect him with Tran Van Giau, the Vietminh head of the Committee of the South. When the operator called back, there was a Vietnamese secretary on the line. "Tell Monsieur Giau I will be at the palace tomorrow morning at nine o'clock. I have a letter from Ho Chi Minh."

At the desk in a corner of the room he wrote a detailed report to Donovan, went down the hall to the message center of the Embankment Project team, and gave it to the radio operator to be relayed in code. "We are in grave danger of the outbreak of major hostilities if the French land troops," Duncan said in his message to Donovan, and urged him to intervene with Lord Mountbatten, Gracey's superior at Southeast Asia Headquarters in Kandy.

It was after midnight when he went to Suzanne's room. "Cedile ..." Suzanne began, but broke off as Duncan put his fingertips on her lips. "In the morning," he said.

They had made love and Suzanne lay beside Duncan, her leg pressed against his. "Travis, when you were making love to me," she asked softly, "did you pretend it was Mai?"

"I love you, Suzanne," Duncan said. "There's no one else, no one."

# -27-

SHORTLY BEFORE NINE IN THE MORNING, as he drove his jeep up to the palace of the French governor-general, now turned over to the Committee of the South by the Japanese, Duncan recalled his last visit ten years ago. Foreign Legionnaires in their white kepis and red epaulettes were then guarding the gate. Now there were Vietnamese in brown pith helmets and khakis armed with Sten guns standing before the massive iron portal.

A woman guard with a rifle slung over her shoulder led Duncan to a room on the upper floor of the palace and opened a gold ornamented door to admit him. Duncan was not surprised to find Mai and Cong seated at a small conference table with a Vietnamese, evidently Tran Van Giau, the Vietminh head of the Committee of the South. Duncan had assumed the two had already reached Saigon and were at work with the Committee. Giau welcomed Duncan warmly and seated him at the table. Glancing about, Duncan thought: This is the room in which Bollard told me Mai might be sentenced to death for inciting antigovernment violence. But the recurring image of the girl in Saigon was no longer evoked by the hard-faced woman seated opposite him.

Duncan handed Ho's letter to Giau, who examined it quickly, and then said genially, "No introductions are necessary, Colonel Duncan. Mai and Cong have told me of your service to our country."

The pleasantries broke off abruptly when Duncan said, "I have a disturbing report from a very good source. As you know, British troops will arrive at Tan Son Nhut in three days. I've been told that a French colonial company may be with them." Duncan, anticipating the shock his news would impart, went on quickly: "I have asked Washington to intervene, but time is short. If the French troops do land, since it is only a colonial company, it may be possible to restrict its movements." He was not surprised by the outrage registered on the faces around the table.

Fury contorting his features, Cong shouted: "Even one company, only a few French soldiers, would be enough! Our people will believe we've been betrayed, that the French are returning to dominate us again. There'll be rioting!"

"Cong is right," Giau said. "There may be a great uprising."

Mai interjected nervously: "Comrades, do not forget Ho Chi Minh's instructions. He told us to keep order while we negotiate a political agreement—even if we are faced with French troops."

Cong said impatiently: "There'll be no agreement once French troops occupy Saigon. We must …"

Duncan interrupted: "Would you be willing to meet again with Jean Cedile to discuss some kind of an understanding? He's aware of the dangers of bringing in French troops at this time. You may find him more flexible than when you last spoke to him. He has asked Paris to delay the arrival of French troops until he can meet with you once again."

There was silence until Mai spoke, appealing to Giau: "It would do no harm. Ho Chi Minh would approve."

"All right, we'll meet again with Cedile," Giau said in a rasping tone. "You may arrange it. But what if Cedile has been unable to persuade Paris? If that colonial company does come in with the British and is seen on the streets, there may no way we can avert violence."

"I'll be at the airfield when the British arrive," Duncan said reassuringly. "If the French company is with them, I'll have them confined."

Duncan left the Palace with the guilty feeling he was bluffing. He doubted that Cedile would be able to delay the landing of French troops or that De Gaulle would be amenable to offering any acceptable political arrangement for Cochin China. What in the hell would he do if he came face-to-face with those French colonials?

At the hotel Duncan found a message from Suzanne asking him to lunch with her.

Suzanne waited until the waiter had served the demitasses and departed before she said calmly: "Mario Bocquet and two other *colons* called on me this morning."

Duncan, startled, put down his cup.

"They didn't threaten me ... not directly," Suzanne said. "Bocquet said he had friends in the *Sûreté* who told him about me. He knows I'm with M.5. He also knew about my contacts with Father Tricoire, with Cedile and with you. He obviously suspects we're trying to interfere with his plans for a French coup in Saigon."

"What did he ask of you?"

"Nothing. He said he just wanted to get acquainted. We had coffee here and he talked about his family and how for three generations they've worked hard to cultivate their rubber plantation. He said his family would never let go of their land. It was time to put down the Annamites who were agitating to take over. And then he glared at me and said the *colons* wouldn't let anyone get in the way of what had to be done to defend French interests."

Duncan said, "It was obviously a warning to me as well as you, and possibly also to Cedile. They won't hesitate to kill us if we get in their way."

"I don't doubt it."

"Have you been in contact with Cedile?"

"Yes. But he's heard nothing from Paris."

Duncan said: "Contact him again. Tell him the Committee of the South has agreed to meet with him. I'll be there."

Leaving Suzanne on the telephone, Duncan went down the hall to the Embankment Project radio room. There was no response from Donovan to his plea for intervention. He was likely running into trouble with the pro-French clique at the State Department, Duncan speculated. Sending a message to Donovan again, Duncan said he would do whatever he could to sequester the French colonials if they did land. But as he went back to his room he thought ahead to the confrontation at the airport with a growing sense of helplessness.

# -28-

THE FIRST LANCASTER CARGO PLANES landed at Tan Son Nhut precisely at noon on September 12. Duncan was waiting in the airport office of the Japanese commandant. He had just been introduced to Marshal Terauchi and three of his staff officers, who also were awaiting the arrival of the British. The marshal, a short compact man with heavy-lidded eyes and a sardonic expression, was in full dress regalia, samurai sword strapped on, for this first meeting with the forces to whom he was obliged to surrender. Duncan had planned to have Conroy and others of the OSS team accompany him to the airport, but with the exception of Jacobson they were not yet back from the POW camps where final arrangements were being made for the evacuation of the American prisoners.

A few minutes after the first plane was on the ground, a tall British colonel, wearing a Sam Browne belt and carrying a swagger stick, strode into the office and smartly returned salutes of the Japanese.

Duncan was ignored until the colonel fixed a questioning eye on him. "What the devil is an American doing here?" he asked as he shook hands.

"I'm with the OSS, representing American interests," Duncan said.

"What interests?" the colonel asked, with a good-natured laugh. "This is a British show, heaven help us," and he turned back to the marshal.

Duncan stood quietly listening and then intervened. "Colonel, there is a critical matter which I must discuss with you. Do you have a French unit arriving with your troops?"

"Yes, a company of French colonial infantry," the colonel said with a frown. "What of it?"

Duncan said, "We're urging you keep the unit confined. There's great tension in the city among the Vietnamese. If the French uniforms are seen, there may be serious violence."

The colonel snapped irritably: "I don't have any authority to do that. General Gracey is arriving tomorrow. That's a matter for him." He turned to the Japanese marshal: "What's your opinion, Sir?"

Terauchi smiled and said in unaccented English: "You are in charge."

The colonel said: "I've got to get my troops lined up." He saluted the marshal and walked out.

Duncan watched him stride away, thinking that wars are started by little mistakes just like this.

The British transports were now landing in swift succession. A battalion of Gurkhas was disembarking. Duncan learned from the airport commandant that the other two battalions of the regimental force of thirty-eight hundred troops were to arrive from Rangoon the following day with Gracey.

Duncan was standing with Jacobson on the tarmac when the last of the Lancaster transports touched down. As the soldiers disembarked and their equipment unloaded Duncan could see that this was the company of French colonial infantry. Duncan, followed by Jacobson, walked toward the soldiers who were forming up; he had decided to appeal to their commanding officer to stay under cover. Duncan was half way across the tarmac when a dozen foreigners confronted him. At the head of this phalanx was a large, square-faced man with piercing blue eyes, dressed in a white suit and pith helmet. Several of the men behind him, similarly dressed, were carrying machine pistols. Beside them were three men in French uniform, and Duncan could see that that they were wearing the SFLEO shoulder patches of French intelligence.

"Good afternoon, Colonel Duncan," the leader said in French. "I am Mario Bocquet, representative of French planters of Cochin China. We're the hosts—you might say the welcoming committee— for our French soldiers who have just arrived." He gestured at the three men in uniform within his group. "You see here also with us three agents of the *Section de Liaison Francaise en Extreme Orient* who have passes, issued by Marshal Terauchi and approved by the British colonel, authorizing them to escort the French soldiers to their quarters. You can understand," he said, "why—as good French citizens—we wish to offer hospitality to our soldiers."

"Let us by," Duncan said, his jaw clenched. "I don't give a damn who you are. I am the senior officer representing American interests in Saigon. You've no authority to prevent me from speaking to the French officer commanding that company."

"Colonel, please do not do anything foolish," Bocquet said. "The French soldiers do not wish to be disturbed. They've had a tiring journey."

Duncan, frustrated, surveyed the machine pistols now pointing at them, thinking despairingly how useless were the .45s that he and Jacobson were packing on their hips.

A motley collection of civilian trucks had moved across the tarmac to the transport, and the French Colonials were climbing aboard. When the trucks had disappeared, Bocquet waved cheerily to Duncan and walked off with his fellow *colons*.

Duncan was relieved as he drove back into Saigon to see that the streets at the center of the city were still calm. Evidently word had not yet spread widely of the arrival of the French troops. Duncan went to his room and dashed off a message to Donovan, reporting that the French troops were in the city and he could do nothing to restrain them until Gracey arrived. At the hotel desk there was a message from Suzanne saying she had gone to meet with Cedile.

Suzanne did not return to the hotel until evening. She came to Duncan's room visibly shaken. She sat on the wicker settee, took off her khaki cap and vigorously shook out her hair.

"Cedile was not at his villa when I got there," Suzanne said. "I waited for him for hours. He left the villa when he heard French troops had landed at Tan Son Nhut. When he got back he said the troops, waving a French flag, had been driven in a convoy past the Central Prison and through the streets. They are now bivouacked up on the hill near the French villas. Bocquet spoke to them; told them they'll soon have British authority to take over the city. They plan to release the Legionnaires held at the Central Prison. They will then go to the big Eleventh RIC barracks outside of Saigon where most of the French troops are interned and release them. There are about twenty-eight hundred soldiers at the barracks. Bocquet has given maps to the French company commander pinpointing where the arms are stored."

"How does Cedile feel about all this?"

"Cedile says he has spoken to the French company commander, but has no control over what's happening."

"Perhaps not, but everything seems to be moving as De Gaulle planned," Duncan said frowning. "I'm not sure at this stage that Cedile can be trusted. Did he agree to meet with the Committee of the South?"

"Yes. I think he'll do whatever he can to head off any mayhem in the streets."

Duncan sat down beside Suzanne, took her hand and said, "Things are going to get even more wild around here. I can get you out to Kunming on one of our planes."

Suzanne shook her head. "No. I'll stick with you. I'm deep into this mess and I want to see it through."

Duncan said, "All right let's get on the phone. Let's try to get Cedile together with the Committee at the Palace tomorrow before all hell breaks loose."

In the morning Duncan was leaving the hotel for the Palace when the Eurasian desk clerk called to him. "Not a good time to go out, Sir," the Eurasian said with a shy smile.

Duncan went back to the reception desk. "Why?"

The Eurasian said: "There's rioting out there. Mobs have been on the street since early this morning. They're French people. Some are carrying signs welcoming the return of French troops. I heard shooting too."

Duncan went out on Rue Catinat where Jacobson was waiting behind the wheel of a jeep. "Something weird is happening," the sergeant said. "I just saw a bunch of Frenchmen, carrying all kinds of weapons, beat up some Vietnamese. They broke into those two Vietnamese shops across the street."

"I can guess what's going on," Duncan said. "The *colons* have heard that French troops have landed, and they think they're back in control. They're showing the Vietnamese who's boss ... taking revenge for having been pushed around."

At the Palace, Duncan left Jacobson in the jeep in the courtyard and went to the reception room where Giau was seated at the conference table with Mai and Cong as well as another Vietnamese, a scholarly looking man about forty years of age, whom Duncan had not seen before.

"This is Pham Van Bach," Giau said, introducing him. "Dr. Bach holds a Doctorate of Law from the University of Paris. He is an independent and president of the new Executive Committee of all the nationalist parties. He is authorized to negotiate with the French. Monsieur Cedile has not yet arrived."

Duncan said: "I'm sorry but I've heard nothing from Washington. And I was not able to do anything about the French troops coming into the city. There's only one company of Colonials."

Cong said furiously: "That was enough. Their appearance in Saigon was a signal for the *colons*. They now think they're masters of the city again. They're attacking our people. Some Vietnamese have been killed, homes set on fire."

"The situation is critical," Giau said. "The Vietnamese police are too afraid to do anything. The Japanese are doing nothing."

Bach said: "Some of the nationalist parties in my committee feel betrayed. They no longer trust the Vietminh leadership. They're organizing to strike back at the French."

"Dr. Bach will make a radio appeal tonight for calm," Giau said. "But it will be of no use unless we can say we have an agreement with the French—that their troops will be withdrawn, that our independence will be respected."

Duncan looked askance at Mai, who had not spoken.

"Ho Chi Minh can do nothing unless we get some assurances from Cedile," she said.

Bach nodded and was about to speak when Cedile was admitted into the room. The Frenchman, haggard in appearance, shook hands limply.

"I've been around the city," Cedille said. "Conditions are very bad. Some of the French—men and women—have gone mad. They've been frustrated for so long. I deeply regret their attacks on your people. I'll go to General Gracey when he arrives later today with his Gurkhas. They and the Japanese must restore order."

"Will you withdraw your colonial troop from the Saigon area!" Cong shouted.

"I have no control over them. They're obeying Mario Bocquet."

His voice quavering, Bach said: "What can we tell the people about the future? You must have some news from Paris."

Cedile studied each of the Vietnamese faces opposite him as if he was desperately searching for an ally.

"The French troops will not be withdrawn, and as for a political agreement, General De Gaulle is standing by his declaration of March twenty-fourth."

"What does that mean?" Cong asked scornfully.

"The general is prepared to grant democratic liberties, economic autonomy and many other rights to the peoples of Indochina. Cochin China as well as Tonkin and Annam will be admitted as a federation to the new French Union when it is formed next year."

"I'm familiar with the March twenty-fourth declaration," Bach said in a formal tone. "The general makes no promise of eventual full independence. Under his terms, Vietnam will not be a united nation. Cochin China will be a state separate from Tonkin and Annam. That's correct, isn't it?"

"I'm not authorized to provide assurances beyond the March twenty-fourth statement," Cedile said.

"I'll appeal tonight to our people to avoid any kind of violence," Bach said. "But I cannot promise them a better future or respect for their independence. The responsibility for what may happen now rests with you, the French."

Bach stood up, indicating that the meeting had ended.

# -29-

THE STREETS OF SAIGON were strangely desolate as Duncan drove to the headquarters of General Gracey, the newly arrived British commander. In protest against the return of French troops and attacks by *colons* on the Vietnamese, the Committee of the South had declared a general strike. Vietnamese shops and the central market were shut. Police were not at their posts, and there was little street traffic. Many families, both French and Vietnamese, had barricaded their homes against the rampaging mobs. Saigon was without a master. Gracey was suffering the consequences, Duncan thought, of the arbitrary actions he had taken without consideration for Vietnamese sensitivities.

Shortly after his arrival, Gracey had stripped the Committee of the South of the civil authority delegated to it by the Japanese and announced that his troops would maintain order pending return of French forces. The announcement, with its implication of the eventual restoration of French rule, inflamed the Vietnamese further. Now, Gracey apparently had come to understand that his troops were insufficient to keep order and that the Japanese, stubbornly passive, would be of little help.

Furious and frantic, Duncan had waited day-to-day for an opportunity to meet with Gracey, who let it be known he was not disposed to meet with any American. But now, as conditions in the city were becoming increasingly chaotic, Duncan had been summoned urgently to Gracey's headquarters.

When Duncan was escorted into his office, Gracey was at his desk with Cedile and Marshal Terauchi seated before him. The general, a heavyset man with a brush mustache, fresh from combat service in Burma, was wearing a short-sleeved khaki tunic with rows of battle ribbons.

"Good of you to come, Colonel," Gracey said, as Duncan took a chair beside the others. But then he addressed Duncan with a frown: "Frankly, I'm puzzled by what you are about. I find it unacceptable that an American is negotiating in Saigon with the Annamese when Cochin China is a zone of British responsibility." He shook his head impatiently. "I asked you to come here only because Cedile tells me you have influence with those buggers of the Committee of the South who are causing all the trouble. Marshal Terauchi had no right to turn over civilian authority to them. When they came to see me I kicked them out of my office."

The marshal, who was in his field uniform and without his sword, stiffened. "Those were my instructions from Tokyo."

Gracey settled back in his chair with frustration evident across his reddening countenance. "Yes, I understand, Marshal, those were your orders," he said, his chin jutting out. "This whole damn situation is beyond me. I was given no instructions before leaving Rangoon other than to accept your surrender."

Duncan was about to speak when Cedile interrupted. "What we must do at once is restore order in the city. French and Annamese mobs are slaughtering each other. Vietminh guerrillas are taking up positions around the city. They're preparing for a large-scale attack. Colonel Duncan, you're friendly with the Committee leaders. Can't you intervene? Tell the Committee to end this general strike ... call off the guerrillas. We're hurtling toward catastrophe."

Duncan said quietly: "I can try. But what do you have to offer them in return? Politically, you're promising them nothing, nothing that they can hold up before their people in urging calm. They know that more French troops are on the way. What alternative do they have except to fight?"

"I'll consult with Paris again," Cedile said, his eyes averted.

Gracey said impatiently: "I can't wait." Leveling a commanding look at Terauchi, Gracey said: "Marshal, I'm declaring martial law, but I don't have enough troops to enforce it. Until the surrender documents are signed, that's your responsibility. Your troops now have my authority to disarm all Annamese, including the police if necessary, and to open fire on any Annamese who resists. Am I understood?"

"And how will the French mobs be restrained?" Duncan asked, openly dismayed at Gracey's order.

"I'm not soliciting your advice, Colonel", Gracey said, glowering.

Terauchi said: "I'll bring more troops into the city."

Duncan glanced around at the frozen faces. They've put together a prescription for disaster, he thought.

There was scattered gunfire in the city when Jacobson drove Duncan in the evening toward the City Hall where the Committee was now housed. Gracey had ordered the Committee of the South to vacate the governor-general's palace, saying they had no right to be there. As Jacobson turned off on Le Thanh Ton Street, only several blocks from the City Hall, a half dozen Vietnamese in peasant clothes blocked the way and assaulted the jeep, waving machetes and clubs.

"Step on it!" Duncan shouted. Jacobson gunned the motor knocking two of the Vietnamese aside. As one of the attackers reached over and grabbed at the submachine gun on Duncan's lap, he slashed the man's face with his Fairburn knife. The man screamed and let loose of the moving jeep. Jacobson brought the jeep to a screeching halt before the City Hall.

"Things are getting hairy around here," the sergeant said, watching Duncan slip the knife back into its sheath on his leg.

There were Vietnamese guards at the gate, but without guns. The Japanese had disarmed them.

Duncan was not prepared for what he encountered when he entered the City Hall's conference room. It was crowded, not only with the six Vietminh members of the Committee of the South, but as he soon learned, with representatives of other nationalist factions: the Trotskyites, the pro-Japanese Dai Viet, and the religious parties, the Hoa Hao and Cao Dai—all were there except the Binh Xuyen. The Troskyites had been persuaded to join the Committee after the

The Troskyites had been persuaded to join the Committee after the assassination of their recalcitrant chief. Delegates of these factions composed the Executive Committee, which Giau had put together to govern Cochin China.

Flanked by Mai and Cong at the head of the conference table, Giau was inviting delegates to speak. As Duncan listened, he quickly became convinced that his peacemaking mission was hopeless. The delegates in turn, with the Trotskyite being most vociferous, shouted that their people had been betrayed, that the Vietminh policy of negotiations was a failure, and that it was time to battle for Vietnam's independence.

Giau said to Duncan, "You've heard the opinions of the comrades. They see only French flags flying over buildings in Saigon. We cannot live with this."

Silencing the cries in the room, Giau invited Duncan to speak.

Duncan examined the faces of the delegates eagerly awaiting what the American might tell them. Inwardly despairing, Duncan said: "I am still hopeful the United States will persuade France to recognize your independence. I urge you to avoid any action that will bring civil war. The people of Vietnam must not suffer more violence."

Giau rose to his feet, smiling. "Thank you, Colonel Duncan," he said in a gentle manner. "You are a true friend of Vietnam."

They don't believe the United States is going to do a damn thing for them and they are now out for French blood, Duncan thought as he bowed and left the room.

Mai was waiting in the hall. "You've done all you can," she said. "Whatever happens, we'll always be grateful to you."

Duncan smiled sadly. "I've had so little to offer except my love for you and your Vietnam. Goodbye, Mai."

Mai kissed Duncan on the cheek. "I hope that one day our two peoples will be as we are to each other."

As Duncan turned to leave, Mai called after him. "Travis, I must tell you," she said. "The Binh Xuyen have left our Executive Committee. Many of those who've been released by the Japanese from Poulo Condore are out for vengeance. Bay Vien, their leader, is assembling them south of Saigon on the Delta ... perhaps, for an attack. They may kill any white man they come upon. Be careful where you go."

# -30-

A WEEK AFTER DUNCAN HAD BY CHANCE visited him, Doctor Bouchard walked down the stairs of his apartment on Boulevard Charner carrying a small cloth suitcase and a cage containing his children's two Siamese kittens. Fearful of the gangs of vandals who were sacking French homes, he had hidden some valuables about the apartment and double-locked the oak door. Dang, the houseboy, and his wife, the cook, who lived in a room at the back of the apartment with their three children had vanished with their belongings.

At the hospital that morning Bouchard had continued to minister to the scores of Vietnamese savagely wounded by French mobs. Patients told him that Vietnamese women and children were leaving the city. But it was only after reading *Le Soir*, the afternoon newspaper, that Bouchard decided to join his wife, who with their two small children had left the city earlier when conditions began to worsen. The newspaper reported that Giau, the head of the Committee of the South, had ordered a state of siege and threatened to torch Saigon if the French did not withdraw their troops and recognize the independence of Vietnam. Already the central market had been destroyed in a fire and Vietminh guerrillas were blocking the movement of foodstuffs into Saigon.

Before getting into his ancient Citroen sedan, Bouchard went into the café on the ground floor where he deposited the cage with the kittens and profusely thanked the portly proprietor, a *metis* of Italian and Vietnamese blood, for agreeing to look after them.

Bouchard's family was staying at his brother's home in the Cité Hérault, a French-Eurasian district in Tan Dinh, a suburb of Saigon. He drove there full of apprehension, and upon arrival thought himself very lucky that he had not run into a Vietminh barricade. At his brother's home, one of a cluster of small pink villas with neat gardens, he was greeted tearfully by his wife, a small stout woman, who was alarmed by what she read in *Le Soir*. Bouchard reassured her

by saying he had seen British troops on the Saigon streets, which—
*true*—were quite deserted but calm, and as he approached the villa, he
had seen a heavily armed Japanese patrol pass by.

Cité Hérault lay peaceful that night under a full orange moon as
the Bouchards slept, the four of them in a large four-poster bed, the
boy and the girl at their parents' feet. It was toward morning when
there was a hammering on the bedroom door and Pierre, the doctor's
brother, came in, wild-eyed.

"The Annamese are attacking villas in Cité Hérault!" he shouted.
"Two villas are burning. My neighbor telephoned. He's coming over
with his family. It's better if we're together."

Bouchard dressed hurriedly as his wife comforted the two
frightened children. Just as he ran down the stairs, the neighboring
family, in their robes and nightclothes, came in the door. The
neighbor was carrying a hunting rifle and a large kitchen knife.

While the women and children huddled on the upstairs floor, the
men stood guard looking out the windows. Bouchard held a revolver,
given to him by Pierre, who showed him how to reload the weapon
from a clip of bullets.

For nearly an hour there was no sound outside the villa.
Bouchard, peering through the window, clutched the revolver with
both hands. How can this be happening to us, he thought. The
Annamese—living beside them all these years. He'd treated so many
at the hospital, delivered so many of their babies. And his Annamese
friends: the evenings at their apartment, talking about the classic
French writers and painters, showing them the books in his library...
He sympathized with them when they complained of the brutal
exploitation of peasants on the plantations, their stories about *Sûreté*
torture of political prisoners. It was only after the Japanese coup that
he became fearful of some of the Annamese. The Annamese watched
as the Japanese humiliated and beat French soldiers and officials.
Asians doing that to whites. Yes! The Annamese knew then they
could do the same.

Suddenly, there was the sound of a whistle. Bouchard could see
figures crouching on the fringes of the garden and silhouetted in the
moonlight. He heard ghoulish cries all around the house. Pierre,

holding his hunting rifle, came up beside him. "My god, there are so many of them," he whispered. Bouchard gripped the revolver even tighter and tried to hold back his sobs.

In another moment rocks came crashing through the windows and Bouchard retreated before splintering glass. Shooting broke out around the house, mixed with staccato bursts of machine gun fire. Pierre fired through the window, but Bouchard couldn't see anything to aim at. There was an explosion at the rear of the house where the neighbor was guarding the back door and then a scream. Pierre and Bouchard turned as figures in black, holding guns and machetes, with crazed expressions, came charging at them. Bouchard was knocked down, a knife drawn across his throat, and blood spouted from his mouth. The last thing he saw was the women and children being dragged down the stairs.

Japanese and British troops did not reach Cité Hérault until after dawn. In the villas and on the roads, they found more than one hundred and fifty bodies of French and Eurasian men, women and children. Others had been taken hostage. During the day, dozens of the missing staggered into nearby Vietnamese villages crying for help. Many of them had been mutilated. Women had been raped.

The report on Cité Hérault that came to Gracey's desk said that three hundred civilians had been massacred. It had been the gangster Binh Xuyen. But for the French, the perpetrators were simply Annamese and what happened at Cité Hérault would haunt any negotiation.

# -31-

**Saigon**
**September 23**

DUNCAN WOKE TO THE SHRILL RING of the telephone as the first light of morning was seeping into the room. Suzanne lay beside him, breathing gently, her arm thrown across his bare chest. They had indulged in a wild night of love-play; clothing and empty bottles were scattered about the room.

The evening began for them in a mood of anxiety and despair over the runaway events. Vietminh guerrillas summoned from the villages by the Committee of the South had encircled Saigon and were infiltrating Japanese and British positions. Cedile was not offering anything new to the Vietminh that would deter them from a mass attack. The Committee was also calling for a mass demonstration in Central Saigon by the Vietnamese population that was certain to result in bloodshed. Mobs were rampaging through the city. There was no word from Donovan about the possibility of American intervention.

Enveloped in gloom, Duncan and Suzanne sought distraction and comfort in each other with the help of bottles of vermouth. Talk of politics and war exhausted, they engaged in drunken play. Suzanne teased Duncan by shedding her garments as she danced about. They made love on the chaise longue and on the bed. Duncan asked her to marry him and she begged him to repeat the proposal when he was sober.

Duncan had been sleeping well for the first time in days when the phone beside the bed rang. He reached for it, resenting the intrusion. It was Sergeant Jacobson.

"Colonel, something big's going on," Jacobson said. "I'm in my room, looking out the window. Long columns of French troops are going by."

"Get the jeep," Duncan said. "I'll be out front in ten minutes."

Suzanne sat up as he rolled out of bed: "What is it?"

"Jacobson ... he's seeing columns of French troops moving along the Rue Catinat."

Suzanne shouted at Duncan as he scrambled about the room collecting pieces of his uniform: "Travis, the *colons* must have released the troops at the Central Prison and those at the Eleventh RIC Barracks! The British must have told the Japanese to open the gates!"

In front of the hotel Duncan jumped into the waiting jeep with Jacobson at the wheel. The shadows on the streets were shrinking before the encroaching dawn as they sped through the city. Duncan was stunned to see the French Tricolor flying over public buildings, at police stations and at the Central Prison. There had been a French coup.

When they parked in front of the City Hall, Duncan cried out in anguish. The unarmed Vietnamese sentries had been shot down at their posts. Bodies were sprawled at the gates and in the courtyard. Duncan vaulted out of the jeep, ignoring the surprised French Legionnaires who stood about smoking and gossiping, guns dangling from their shoulders, and ran up the steps of the City Hall. Inside, there were bodies strewn in the corridors and in the offices. Frantically, Duncan examined the faces, thankful that he did not see Mai or Cong or members of the Committee of the South among the dead.

Duncan and Jacobson drove quickly to Gracey's headquarters through streets now thronged with French troops, with British and Japanese patrols standing by passively. Sickened by the massacre at City Hall, Duncan struggled to gather himself for a confrontation with the British commander. At the door to Gracey's office, Duncan was blocked by a guard who raised his rifle and then summoned a bleary-eyed colonel in a brown sweater and shorts, holding a swagger stick.

"The general isn't available," the British colonel said, banging the swagger stick on his leg.

Duncan said in a measured tone: "I have a statement to make to General Gracey on behalf of the United States."

"Put it in writing," the colonel said.

"You've no authority under the Potsdam Agreement to turn this city over to the French!" Duncan shouted, his composure cracking. "General Gracey is authorized only to accept the surrender of the Japanese command. You've no right to release the interned French troops. You bear responsibility for their murderous attack on the people at City Hall."

The Briton slapped his leg again with his swagger stick: "Speak to Monsieur Cedile. He's responsible for the French troops and administration of the city. He's at the governor-general's palace."

Duncan tried to brush past the colonel into Gracey's office. The colonel stepped in front of him. "You're out of bounds, Duncan," he barked. "The guard will escort you out."

When the jeep halted before the governor-general's palace, Duncan felt he was reliving the nightmare of ten years ago when he came to the palace to rescue Mai. There, once again, at the gates were the Legionnaires. As he entered the palace, being led by a Senegalese noncom to the reception hall, he could see one very obvious alteration. The walls of the hallway were now bare. During their brief sojourn in the palace the Vietnamese had ripped down the portraits of former French governor-generals.

Duncan was surprised at Cedile's appearance when the Frenchman greeted him with a weak handshake and a wry smile. He was in a rumpled suit, unshaven and obviously exhausted. Duncan had expected to find him jubilant at the success of the French coup. But as Cedile slumped onto the couch before a table stacked with empty coffee cups and an ashtray spilling over with cigarette butts, Duncan thought he had the look of a defeated man.

"You had no right …," Duncan began, but was silenced by Cedile raising a restraining hand.

"I had no choice," Cedile said. "You know very well the city is paralyzed by the general strike. That mass demonstration planned for today … it was sure to end in killings. We have reports that Vietminh guerrillas are gathering to attack the city. What was I to do? My first duty is to protect the twenty thousand French citizens of this city. Gracey agreed to release our interned soldiers because he thinks his troops will need help withstanding a big Vietminh attack. The Japanese are of no use."

Duncan listened, his outrage somewhat abated. As Cedile was lighting a cigarette, Duncan said: "When we met with the Committee you spoke of consulting with Paris on a better offer to the Vietnamese. If you'd come forward with something, there would have been no strike, no demonstration."

"I asked for that something," Cedile said. He drew on his cigarette and inhaled deeply. "Colonel Duncan, in ten days the French ship *Triomphant* will arrive here with one thousand troops of General Leclerc's Fifth RIC. Other troops will follow. That was De Gaulle's reply."

"Then it's all over ... negotiation with the Vietnamese ... finished."

Cedile shrugged. "Oh, there'll be more talk, back and forth. But I'm under no illusions. There's no understanding in Paris of the Annamese: how committed they are to independence, how strong they are. The *colons* won't let go. In the end it will be settled on the battlefield. We'll pay in blood for De Gaulle's obsession with empire."

There was a knock at the door. Cedile stood up. "Forgive me, Colonel. I have a conference." With an ironic smile, he said, "Mario Bocquet is waiting to congratulate me. No matter. There's really nothing more to say." He shook hands with Duncan. "If I were you, Colonel," he said, "I'd get out of here. In fact, all you Americans for your own sakes ought to get out of Indochina before you're caught in the crossfire between the Annamese and us. Goodbye."

Duncan left Cedile gripped with the same frustration that possessed him when he walked out of the palace ten years ago. The French hadn't changed. "Let's get back to the hotel fast," he said to Jacobson. "I've got to get word to Donovan. Our last chance to save this country from a bloody, senseless war is slipping away."

The streets were chaotic as Duncan and Jacobson drove back to the Continental. The mobs of French civilians, many armed with hunting rifles, knives and canes were freely roaming the city assaulting any Vietnamese they spotted. Exultant at the restoration of French dominance over the city, they were now more than ever venting their anger and frustration in reprisal for indignities suffered under the brief Vietnamese rule.

At the hotel, Duncan radioed an urgent report to Donovan appealing even more strongly for immediate American political intervention now that Gracey had grossly exceeded his mandate by turning Saigon over to the French.

# -32-

Washington, D.C.
September 24, 1945

GENERAL WILLIAM DONOVAN, in civilian clothes and carrying a briefcase, entered the lobby of the State Department building, displayed his I.D. at the security desk, and said: "I have an appointment with the Secretary of State."

"Of course, General," the guard said. "That blonde woman in the blue suit beyond the police checkpoint is waiting for you." The woman greeted Donovan with a wide smile. "I'm Joan Watson, Mr. Nelson's assistant."

Donovan frowned: "I have an appointment with the Secretary of State."

"Yes, I know. The deputy secretary will explain."

Nelson was waiting for Donovan at the door. "Bill, great to see you again. It's been ages. You're always chasing around the world. Come in. Sit over there on the couch." Nelson settled into a leather chair beside the couch. "Bill, the Secretary asked me to see you. He's sorry he hasn't been able to meet with you. Hard pressed with everything that's going on in Europe. Hope you don't mind. Indochina isn't exactly high on his list of priorities." Nelson chuckled. "In fact, I have trouble getting him to read any of your cables."

Donovan, sitting erect with the briefcase on his lap, said: "That country is blowing up. Might be a good idea for the Secretary to give it some attention."

Nelson laughed. "Maybe you're right. Oh, by the way, when the secretary turned over your file to me. I got a look at that little shuffle you played on me six months ago when you sent Duncan here. He was on the way to see Roosevelt."

"The president wanted to keep it confidential," Donovan said.

Nelson shrugged. "Roosevelt never talked very much to the State Department about Indochina after Cordell Hull resigned last year as Secretary of State. For some reason he played that one alone, didn't seem to trust anyone, except you of course, and members of his family. We never understood his fixation on Indochina, why he gave it such importance. If you read the minutes on the Yalta Conference and his other meetings with Churchill, Stalin and Chiang, he was absolutely set on not letting the French back in. He'd hold forth at length on how the French exploited the Indochinese people."

"The president felt very strongly about it right to the end," Donovan said.

"But at the end, he was pretty much alone on his proposal for a trusteeship," Nelson said. "Stalin backed off and started to play with De Gaulle for support in Europe. Chiang Kai-shek was more interested in getting back those French concessions in China and ownership of the Hanoi-Nanning railroad. Churchill, of course, opposed him all the way—against any precedent that would turn loose the British colonies."

Donovan nodded: "That's why the president compromised, why he was willing to let France supervise a trusteeship, but only if the Indochinese got a guarantee of eventual full independence. We sent Duncan out to find Indochinese leaders who could live with that kind of trusteeship. The president couldn't trust the French to do it."

"But he got mixed up with that fellow, that Communist … what's his name?"

"Ho Chi Minh," Donovan said. "Duncan checked out Ho at our request. He says Ho is a Communist, true, but that he can be weaned away from loyalty to the Russians. In fact, Moscow isn't backing him right now. Ho tells us he's ready to join the French Union, accept a French president, conclude an economic agreement with us—but only if he gets a promise of independence in five to ten years. De Gaulle won't stand for that."

"You're recalling Duncan?"

"Yes. Gracey has declared him *persona non grata*, says he's challenged his authority. Damn right! On my orders and according to the Potsdam Agreement. We couldn't have had a better man there than Duncan. But it doesn't make much difference," Donovan said with a shrug. "The president has signed an executive order closing down the OSS effective October First. My office is being replaced by what they call the Central Intelligence Agency. By the end of September, all my people will be out of Indochina. I have already resigned to make way for the new agency."

Donovan began opening his briefcase "Did you see Duncan's last report?"

"Yes. I've seen it. There's no question Gracey exceeded his mandate by turning Saigon over to the French. Lord Mountbatten at Southeast Asia Command reprimanded him after he received your protest, but the British Foreign Office overruled the admiral. London's first concern is to keep De Gaulle with us in Europe."

"And what's our policy?" Donovan asked.

"Kind of murky. Truman is standing by Roosevelt's idea of a trusteeship. But only if France consents to it—which of course will never happen. He talks about self-government for Indochina, but doesn't insist on it as a precondition for France taking over again. He hasn't replied to the two messages sent to him by that fellow Ho. We've told the French we continue to recognize their sovereignty. We're providing them with six troopships, from the Allied naval pool to move General Leclerc's divisions to Indochina. We're equipping his French troops with arms, uniforms and vehicles."

"But why get so deeply involved?" Donovan asked.

"Bill, you want a straight answer? Okay. We're not going to quarrel with De Gaulle about independence for that outback when we need his support in the hassle with Stalin. We're buying his support. That's it in plain language."

Donovan closed his briefcase and stood up. "I understand what you're saying, but Duncan is right. We may be missing an opportunity to make friends in Southeast Asia and head off a war. Things would be different if Roosevelt were alive today."

"It's not our show out there," Nelson said.

"It's not our show out there," Nelson said.

# -33-

THE TEAM'S RADIO OPERATOR had brought Duncan two messages. On the writing desk lay crumbled the message from Hopkins. *Gracey has declared you* persona non grata. *Sorry. Donovan informed.* The other message was from Donovan. He read it a second time and then let it drop onto the floor. Donovan had thrown him a personal salute, but the import of the message was devastating. *Return home. You have done all that is possible. We need you here. The policy has shifted to support of the French.*

Duncan hammered his fist on the desk. Support of the French meant there would be no American intervention. Civil war was a certainty now. He propped his feet up on the writing desk, and stared at the old print of the Napoleonic hussar on the wall. He thought of what war would mean for the Vietnamese people and recalled his last meeting with Ho Chi Minh.

"We've been abandoned," Ho had said. He really called it, Duncan thought. Ho was back to where he was in the twenties after his plea for independence had been ignored by President Wilson. It was then he turned to Lenin and found a home in the Comintern. Now, he's been rebuffed by the West again. And for sure he'll turn back to the international Communist movement. It's inevitable. Mao and Stalin are not now positioned to give him much help. But that will change. After Mao's troops push down to the Indochina border the route will be open for delivery of Chinese and later Russian military aid. Vo Nguyen Giap will get the arms he craves, and the payback will be ideological allegiance to Mao and Stalin.

We've lost our chance, Duncan thought. The seeds of hell have been planted. There'll be a harvest of death for the French—and for us if we get into their war. He leaned back in his chair, arms folded and eyes closed. After a few minutes, he picked up the desk pen and wrote a final message to Donovan. He dropped it off with the radio operator and then telephoned the Tan Son Nhut airport where Conroy was putting American POWS on transports for Kunming. Straightening his uniform, and with Donovan's message in hand, Duncan went to Suzanne's room.

"*Bon matin*, my love," Duncan said with a sweeping bow when Suzanne opened the door. She responded with a bow and waved him into the room. Suzanne was in her dressing gown. On the writing desk there was a tray of unfinished breakfast.

"I have a cup of coffee for you," she said, appearing not at all surprised by his early visit.

"Thanks, I can use it," Duncan said. He handed Donovan's message to Suzanne as he accepted the cup. "I'm out of here. Gracey has paid me his greatest compliment. He's declared me *persona non grata.*"

Suzanne read the message and cried out in French: "Brutal! Brutal! But you can't leave. So much depends on you."

Duncan shook his head. "Better I go. There's nothing more I can do here. The Committee of the South is out of reach; they're on the Delta getting the Vietminh guerrillas set for a mass attack. More French troops will soon be landing in Saigon. Washington is staying out of it. I've just messaged Donovan to say I'm flying out today. I also told him Cochin China is going up in flames, that the French surely will be finished here eventually and that all Americans ought to clear out of Indochina."

Taking Suzanne in his arms, Duncan said, "But now it's time to think of you and me. I love you, woman. I'm sober now. Marry me."

"You'll have me," Suzanne said.

Duncan said: "One of our planes is leaving at three o'clock for Kunming. I've booked seats on it for you and me."

"What a beautiful idea," Suzanne said, stroking his cheek. "I love you, Travis, I love you. But no. There's no quick escape. I'm going to stay for a time … see this horror through. I want to tell the world what civil war means for these helpless people. I filed a story last night to the *Observer*. I told them I'd hang on here. I'm sure they'll agree. It's a big story. I'm done with M.5."

Duncan, his face drawn, said, "But what about us?"

"I'll meet you in London. I'm going to use my British passport. You can find me through the *Observer*." She took Duncan's hand. "Go now, Travis. I want to cry. For you, for me, for this sad country."

At the entrance to the hotel, Duncan heaved his duffel into the back seat of the jeep and sat down beside Jacobson with his carbine across his lap. He glanced up as if he were going to get out of the jeep and re-enter the hotel, but then settled back and said, "Let's go."

Jacobson started the engine, but before driving off he looked at Duncan, his mouth twisted. "Conroy just called back from Tan Son Nhut to alert us. The Vietminh have blockaded almost all the roads around the city. There's been a lot of shooting. We might have trouble getting out to the airport."

"Let's go," Duncan said. "I know these people."

Driving out of the city past brilliantly green rice paddies, the sun glistening on narrow canals, Duncan thought: So, farewell Saigon— where it began, where I became wedded to this country. He peered out on peasants working in the fields. In these ten years nothing much has changed for them. Still burdened by poverty and foreign masters. Still fighting for independence without knowing what it will mean for them except the French off their backs. And the Americans? They know as little about this country as when I sat down in the consulate outside the Jardin D'Enfants to write my first report.

The walkie-talkie at Duncan's feet crackled and he lifted it to his ear. It was Conroy at the airport. His voice was barely audible. Jacobson pulled the jeep over to the side of road.

"Colonel, where are you?"

'We're about two miles from Tan Son Nhut."

"Okay. Don't come any closer. The Vietminh and the other guerrilla factions have blocked the roads completely. They've been shooting at any vehicle that tries to come through. All the men of our unit are with me. We've got two weapons carriers. We'll come for you. Wait there for us. We got American flags out of our planes. We're flying them on the trucks. We'll make it through."

Duncan thought angrily: Thank God they've got flags. Gracey, the fool Brit, had forbidden him to fly an American flag on his jeep. This is a British show, he had trumpeted.

"Okay—we'll wait." Duncan said. "We've just passed a Vietnamese village at the Kilometer Four marker. We'll wait for you there. Over and out."

Jacobson turned the jeep around and drove to the village at the kilometer sign. As they parked beside the road, people in the village vanished into their thatched-roof huts. Duncan got out, went to the clearing in the semi-circle of huts and called out in Vietnamese: "We're Americans, your friends."

Faces appeared in the doorways. An elderly man in a pith helmet, wearing shorts and a frayed French army shirt walked out of the largest hut and approached Duncan.

"I am Dinh, the headman," he said in French. "You are welcome."

Duncan bowed and responded with thanks. Peasants emerged from the other huts. Children clustered about. A pretty young woman came forward with a mango and shyly presented it to Duncan, who accepted it with a bow, smiling. She turned away laughing gaily when he offered her a piaster bill.

Duncan called out to Jacobson, who had remained in the jeep, to join him.

"I'll wait here and look out for Conroy," Jacobson said.

Duncan, followed by the children, ambled through the village to the edge of an irrigation ditch bordering a rice field and sat on the embankment. With his knife, he sliced open the mango and ate the ripe golden fruit, while the children observing him giggled. He watched a boy cast a net into the canal and scoop up a small fish.

These beautiful people, Duncan thought. They deserve to live in peace, enjoy this land. It could be so fruitful. But no, there'll be more fighting, bombing and killing. And what then? Colonialism or a Communist straitjacket? When the French are eventually ousted, not the more humane society I'd hoped for—not with Giap's hardliners in the ascendancy.

Duncan looked at the azure, cloudless sky. "If only Roosevelt had lived a little longer," he muttered. He rose to his feet thinking: And so where am I heading? Donovan said he needed me. For what? Better to resign. Speak out against our supporting this French war. And, yes, go to London. Wait for Suzanne. He was cheered by the thought.

Duncan went back to the jeep where Jacobson was trying to contact Conroy on the walkie-talkie but was not getting anything other than static.

At five o'clock, Duncan said impatiently: "Let's go. If we don't get to Tan Son Nhut soon, the planes with those POWs won't be able to take off. There are no lights on that field. The system was knocked out when our navy bombers hit Saigon."

Jacobson looked at Duncan unhappily.

"Jacobson, I know these people and they know me," Duncan said. "We'll get through okay."

They started down the road. Less than a mile from the airport, Jacobson slammed on the brakes. Across the road lay a pile of tree trunks, and behind it were squatting figures dressed in black.

"Vietminh," Jacobson said, falling back in his seat.

"Relax," Duncan said. "I tell you I know these people." He put his carbine aside, got out of the jeep and standing beside it shouted: "Let us by. We're your friends. I'm Colonel Duncan."

There was a shot and then a burst of machine-gun fire. Jacobson cried out and was reaching into the back seat for his gun when he glimpsed Duncan falling. Scrambling out of the jeep, he knelt beside Duncan and saw he had been struck in the head. He was dead. The white jade lay beside his outstretched hand.

Cursing, Jacobson lifted his carbine and fired wildly at the roadblock. He turned about as he heard gunfire behind him. A weapons carrier had come up the road carrying Gurkha soldiers who were shooting at the roadblock.

Suddenly, there was a stillness. The guerrillas had fled. Jacobson stood looking down at Duncan's body. He began to weep.

# Historical Record

ON JULY 16, 1945, OSS agents designated the Deer Team parachuted into Kim Lung, Vietnam, to begin the training and arming of a cadre of Ho Chi Minh's guerrillas.

On September 2, at a mass demonstration in Hanoi, in the presence of OSS observers, Ho Chi Minh proclaimed the independence of Vietnam and announced the establishment of a Provisional Government.

On September 26, 1945, Lieutenant Colonel Peter A. Dewey, leader of the OSS team in Saigon, was killed when Vietminh guerrillas opened fire as his jeep approached their roadblock near the city. In compliance with British restrictions, the vehicle did not display an identifying American flag. Dewey was to leave Saigon that day having been declared persona non grata by Major General Douglas D. Gracey, the British commander in Indochina. In Hanoi Ho Chi Minh sent a personal note of condolence to Lieutenant Colonel Archimedes L.A. Patti, chief of OSS operations in Indochina, to be conveyed to President Truman.

On October 16, 1945, under attack by French, Japanese and British ground and air forces, the Committee of the South and its Vietminh guerrilla forces withdrew from the Saigon area into the countryside.

In February 1946 Ho Chi Minh wrote to President Truman asking for support of Vietnamese independence in accordance with the Philippines example. The letter was his tenth recorded appeal to the Truman Administration since 1945, two of them having been channeled through the OSS. Like the previous appeals it went unanswered. Truman had already approved the restoration of French control of Indochina.

In March 1946, Ho Chi Minh signed an agreement in Hanoi with the French for entry of the Democratic Republic of Vietnam as a free state into the Indochina Federation of the French Union. In June, however, the French, despite violent Vietnamese protests, unilaterally detached Cochin China as a separate state. In September, the Vietnamese leader, visiting Paris, signed a modus vivendi providing for a ceasefire in Cochin China and broad French rights throughout Vietnam. He *received a promise of further negotiations but no assurance of eventual independence. With the end of the British-Chinese occupation, French troops took control of all major Vietnamese cities. In November armed clashes between French and Vietnamese forces erupted at Haiphong and Lang Son. French naval ships shelled Haiphong, killing thousands of Vietnamese civilians. Ho Chi Minh then rejected a French demand that all Vietnamese militia be disarmed, with security functions entrusted to French troops. When negotiations collapsed, Ho Chi Minh fled with his government into the jungle north of Hanoi. Protracted war ensued.*

*Chinese Communist and later Russian military aid began to flow on a major scale to Vo Nguyen Giap's forces after Mao Tse-tung's victorious armies, having ejected Chiang Kai-shek's forces from the China mainland, grouped on the Indochina border in December 1949.*

*French military defeat was sealed with the fall of Dien Bien Phu on May 8, 1954. At the time, the United States was paying about eighty percent of French war costs.*

*Under accords reached in July at an international conference in Geneva, Vietnam was partitioned at the Seventeenth Parallel. Ho Chi Minh established his capital in Hanoi. The French appointed Bao Dai as chief of state of South Vietnam with his capital in Saigon. Later in 1954, South Vietnam withdrew from the French Union and declared its complete sovereignty. When elections for reunification of North and South Vietnam stipulated under the Geneva Accords failed to materialize in 1956, the war resumed.*

*In January 1961 President Kennedy initiated an American counter-insurgency program in support of the government of South Vietnam. Over the next years the commitment evolved into a huge American troop buildup. Ho Chi Minh died on September 3, 1969. The Saigon government, crumbling before a North Vietnamese invasion, surrendered to Hanoi on April 30, 1975. The United States, which had begun a phased troop withdrawal in 1969 under the Nixon Administration, evacuated its remaining forces.*

*In 1979 with heavy casualties on both sides, Vietnam and China fought a brief and inconclusive war that stemmed from disputes over border demarcation and policy in Cambodia.*

*During the French Indochina War (1946–1954), France suffered losses of some 95,000 French, colonial and Foreign Legionnaire soldiers killed. More than two million American military personnel served in the Vietnam during the period of direct military involvement (1961–1975). The United States suffered more than 58,000 killed. South Vietnamese military casualties have been estimated at more than 400,000 dead. The casualties of the North Vietnamese and the Vietcong, their allies in the South, are estimated at more than 900,000 killed. As many as several million Indochinese civilians may have died as a consequence of the war.*

*President Clinton announced normalization of relations with Vietnam on July 11, 1995.*

# Acknowledgments

I AM INDEBTED TO THE VIETNAMESE, American and French men and women who over many years shared with me their recollections and impressions of the events in Indochina and China which took place in the critical year 1945. These include my close friend of early Saigon days, Robert Maisonpierre, who on August 22, 1945, parachuted with other agents onto the Hanoi airfield to safeguard the landing and entry of the first OSS mission into the Japanese-occupied city. The most useful published works in my research were the memoirs of two former OSS agents: Charles Fenn's *Ho Chi Minh* (New York: Charles Scribner's Sons, 1973), and Archimedes L.A. Patti's *Why Vietnam?* (Berkeley: University of California Press, 1980). Other contributing works included: Robert Shaplen's *The Lost Revolution* (New York: Harper and Row, 1962), R. Harris Smith's *OSS* (Berkeley: University of California Press, 1972), Stein Tonnesseon's *The Revolution of 1945* (Newbury, California: Sage Publications, 1991), David G. Marr's *Vietnam 1945* (Berkeley: University of California Press, 1995), and Aileen Palmer's translations of Ho Chi Minh's poetry in his *Prison Diary*.

My profound thanks to Doug Merwin, editor and publisher of EastBridge, and to my agents David Halpern and Sandy Bontemps of The Robbins Office, for bringing the book to realization. As always, my wife, Audrey, a photojournalist, who traveled with me during my reporting of the French Indochina War, provided inspiration and support. I am grateful also to Professor Lawrence R. Sullivan of Adelphi University, to Dr. Judith Economos, who read the manuscript and made useful suggestions and to Michael Buitekant for contributing to my research.

\*\*\*\*\*\*

*Note: The English renderings of Chinese names throughout the book are in the Wade-Giles romanization of the period.*